MW01643824

GHOSTS OF CORTANIS

A NOVEL

C.J. WEILAND

Ghosts of Cortanis
Cortanis Trilogy, Part One

Cover design by Alexander Ness, nessgraphica.com
Cover model: Kaitlin Donnelley
Cover photo by James Fashing
iWear headset by Ben Spears

Interior design & layout by C.J. Weiland

Second edition

ISBN-13: 978-0-9969951-2-2
ISBN-10: 0996995129

Contents

ALSO BY C. J. WEILAND

Demons of Cortanis

Soldier of Cortanis

For Morgan and Ana

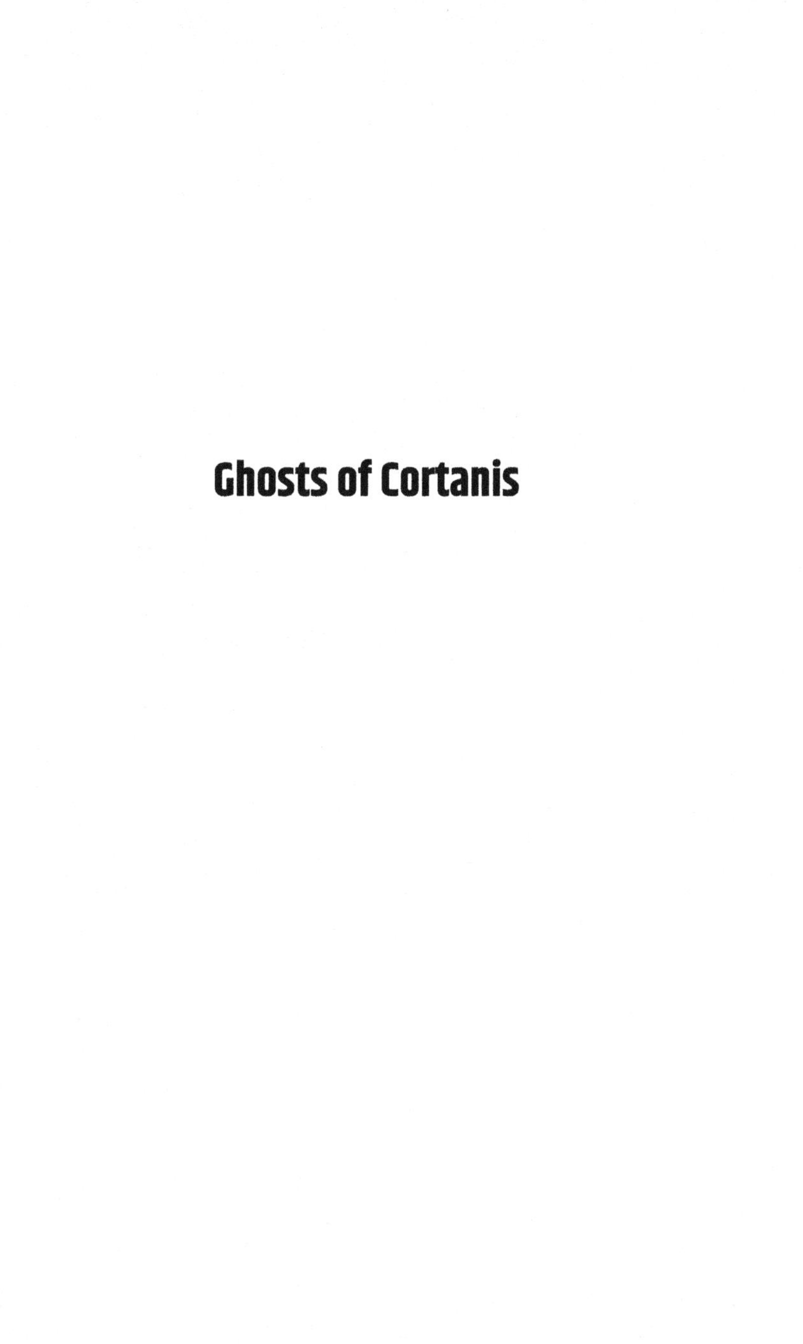

Ghosts of Cortanis

Prologue
00.01

Tuesday, October 21

TEDGlobal Conference
Singapore, Malay Peninsula

There are two kinds of lies we tell ourselves, she thought as she waited in the darkness, just offstage. *Constructive, and destructive. Think constructive: you will do great. You will do great.*

"She is currently the Jack Lorrain Chair of Kinepsychology at the University of California-Berkeley, and her seminal work, *Principia Eigenfacia: Patterns & Chaos,* currently in its third printing, has been translated into thirty languages worldwide," continued the woman on the stage, addressing the crowd assembled in the auditorium. "Ladies and gentlemen, please welcome… Dr. Lina Golyadkin."

The crowd applauded enthusiastically as the woman in her mid-forties, waiting behind the dark curtains, emerged and smiled to them. Dressed in a pale cream suit over a red silk blouse, with a simple, straight skirt cut to just above her knees, she moved confidently toward her introducer and accepted the outstretched hand, shook and mouthed, "Thank you." With that, she turned to the audience, touched the tiny device perched over her ear that activated her microphone, and swept her long, dark brown hair over her ear with her fingers. The applause quieted, and she fingered the little black remote in her left hand, found the broad, concave rubber button beneath her thumb, and pressed it. Her first slide appeared on the giant screen behind her, floating over three red letters: TED.

"Thank you," she began as the last of the applause faded away. Behind her, there was a bevy of what looked like random props, suspended on unseen wires from the ceiling: a teddy bear, a full-size, very realistic replica of a dolphin, a glowing cube pulsing with slowly changing colors, a geometric puzzle, and a white card with the words "THE BIRD IS NOW FREE".

"The first true communication we have as human beings is not based in language. It is not sounds or words. It is not action or gesture. When we come into the world, there is one universal language that is pre-built into our DNA. This language allows us to exchange an extraordinary amount of information, regardless of nationality, race, age, gender, religion or schooling. It is bred into every one of us from birth and we continue to develop and refine our use of it the older we get. It is the language of emotions. It is our faces.

"Studies have shown that babies as young as one week can distinguish the seven universal emotions," she said, as the screen behind her changed to show faces expressing each emotion as she spoke it, pausing a few seconds between each. "Anger. Contempt. Disgust. Fear. Happiness. Sadness, and surprise. These expressions are the same no matter where in the world you go. We are all prewired, from birth, to use the same facial muscles in the same ways. They are globally recognized and understood.

"There is an extraordinary amount of information that we communicate to each other. Much of this information is transmitted, but not received. It is broadcast nonverbally. Even as I pace around this stage before you, I am sending you signals subtextually, which very few of you are trained to pick up on. I'm communicating my nervousness at speaking before such a large crowd," she said with a smile, and a few people in the auditorium chuckled. "I'm communicating that I miss my daughter and my husband. And…" she paused for effect, "I'm communicating that I'm hiding something from you. Something that I'm enjoying hiding from you. But don't worry, we'll come back to that." This time, the chuckles from the audience were nervous.

"The fact that you aren't trained to pick up on these nonverbal cues from me doesn't mean you can't be. Ever since David Matsumoto and Paul Ekman did their groundbreaking work on microexpressions and expressional chording, we at the University of California have been working on software that is attuned to recognize, analyze and statistically pattern nonverbal cues and bodily kinesics in test subjects. Our methodology makes it possible not only to observe extremely subtle kinesthetic signals in individuals, but in groups of people as well. The data we can gather allows for insights that were never before possible."

She pressed the button beneath her thumb again, and the image behind her changed to show a classroom of around 20 ten-year-old students. The camera was mounted above the teacher's head, just beneath the ceiling, aimed at the students in the room. The students were in various poses of disinterest, some restlessly shifting about, others with pens in hand listening to their teacher's lesson. "This is a typical fourth-grade classroom," Golyadkin said. "With their parents' permission, we have installed a camera in the room and have recorded forty minutes of their class. In this recording, we can tell a great deal about these students. We can tell who is getting something out of the lesson, and who is not. We can tell who is hungry, who is upset, who isn't feeling well." As she spoke, the students in the video overhead suddenly seemed to be wearing mesh masks of finely detailed lines that stretched across their faces, over their ears, and down their necks. Over their noses, upside-down Y-shaped lines tracked with them as the students moved their heads. "Combined with their body posture, we can tell who has had a decent night's sleep, who had breakfast that morning, who likes the teacher and who doesn't, who is keeping an unpleasant secret, who is too advanced for the material being taught, and who isn't ready yet for it. We can tell who is sleepy, who is angry, who is content, who is hungry, and who has a, shall we say, significant interest in another student in the room.

"Some of you may be wondering why there are these strange objects cast about the stage behind me," she said, smiling. "We put similar objects around the classroom, and our software studied the kids' eye movements. By monitoring where they put their eyes most often when their attention from the lesson wavered, we can compile a statistical profile that can tell us even more. We can learn about their competencies, their interests, whether they have artistic or problem-solving aptitudes, whether they will respond better to written language or visual exposition, and even predict, with surprising efficacy, what they will choose to eat for lunch that day in the cafeteria."

She looked down at her notes a moment, before continuing.

"So how does it work?" she asked, looking up again. "The software has a deep understanding of facial musculature. Ekman originally identified 44 individual AUs, or action units, that the human face is capable of performing. Later, he learned that AUs often occur in relation to each other, and by studying certain AUs in combination with others, a technique called 'chording', he discovered over three hundred disparate, unique muscle movement combinations that can be detected and analyzed. These chords usually happen much too fast to be detectable even by Ekman's micro-expression-sensitive 'Truth Wizards'. But they're not too fast for our software.

"We believe that primitive man was more attuned to these chords than we are today, and this was reinforced through isopraxis and repetition as their protoculture was emerging. As we developed the capacity for spoken communication, we lost the need to rely on distinguishing the kind of subtleties that we were pre-programmed with. But just because we don't see them anymore doesn't mean they aren't still there.

"Law enforcement at all levels train their detectives and investigators to notice these cues when interrogating witnesses and suspects. Our software is already being tested in precincts in New York, Chicago and Los Angeles, with very promising results. But we believe that an even more important potential is there. The potential to really understand our children at a level not possible without hours of one-on-one attention. The potential to read the nonverbal language that they silently project at a constant, unceasing rate. One teacher in front of two dozen students can't possibly read or understand it all, and we couldn't expect her to. Our software allows her to focus on her lessons. Then when the lesson for the day is over, she can see a detailed report with cautionary flags, proficiency clues, all kinds of things that she can use to better address her students' needs.

"Earlier, I mentioned that I was broadcasting clues to the effect that I was keeping something from you. It's time I come clean." She turned and pointed the device in her hand to a tiny black dome that was all but invisibly mounted above the screen behind her. A bright red dot appeared on the dome, and began circling it as she wiggled the laser pointer in her hand. "This camera has been watching your faces as I've been making my presentation," she continued, turning back to face them with a mischievous smile. "Now, nothing recorded tonight will be used for anything other than my immediate demonstration purposes. But there's one person in here, who has allowed me to take their picture and use it in this demonstration, who is sitting somewhere in this room. I don't know where he is; there's at least a thousand of you here and he could be anywhere. However…"

She walked over to a little podium off to the side of the stage, and picked up a thin rectangle of transparent glass. The tablet computer screen glowed, and she made several taps on it with her finger. The screen behind her showed a picture of a man's smiling face, facing front: the picture she had taken the night before. Beside that photo was a digital reconstruction of that face with a finely woven mesh of lines covering it completely, with an upside-down Y over his nose. Beneath the two images were two lines of text. One read, Subject Acquired and the other read, HMM Analysis Complete.

"Using the photo I uploaded into the system this morning, the computer has scanned all of your faces and has located the gentlemen it was looking for. It has since been studying him very closely from the moment of acquisition until its analysis was complete, about 10 minutes' time. This analysis is extremely coarse, and deeper study will yield results that are more useful, naturally. But here is what the system has determined from the short time it has been studying his face."

She tapped the glass tablet a few times and read the data displayed there. "He's right-handed," she began. "His attention di-axis, using the DeGangi-Greenaway model, was 98% when I began my talk, fading to 54% as I was talking about schools, and jumped to 87% when I mentioned law enforcement. It returned to 98% when I said I was going to discuss what I was keeping from you and has held steadily above 95% since, which I bet is true for most of you. Now here's where it gets interesting.

"Without revealing anything specifically personal, the software has given me nineteen more data points on a continuum of statistical likelihood about this gentleman. With a high degree of certainty, the software has guessed his sexual preference. How much sexual activity he's engaged in within a 48-hour window. How many hours of sleep he's had in the last week. Whether he has eaten breakfast today. Whether he feels equivalent in social capital with the people seated to his immediate left and right." She smiles. "Taking note of his self-touching gestures—touching his lips with his fingers, or tapping his fingertip to his cheek, for example, and their intensity, time-synced and referenced against my presentation comments—can tell us just what he found questionable or more difficult to accept in my presentation. His eye contact with the various visual stimuli behind me tells me what stimuli his subconscious mind would rather be processing when he's not fully focused on what I'm saying. Based on the very short sample window, the software has generated percentage-of-probability estimates that he prefers puzzles to sports, prefers word puzzles to geometric ones, and is often thinking about his child or children when not more intently focused on me."

She returned her tablet to the table and clasped her hands, taking note of the numbers on the countdown timer. They had changed color to red, giving her less than two minutes to give her final remarks. She turned her eyes back outward into the unlit sea of faces. "I'd like to thank my gentleman friend who agreed to let me profile him as part of this demonstration." She clapped her hands together twice, and the audience gave a warm, brief chorus of applause, quieting again after a few moments.

"The reason I'm developing this software and this technology," Golyadkin continued in a softening voice, "is because I have a daughter. Sarah. She's three, and every day when I spend time with her, and see all the gestures, the ticks, the smiles, the grimaces… all the little subtle expressions between her words, I can't help but feel that there are gigabytes worth of communication radiating from her at every moment of every day, only needing to be received and interpreted. I don't want to miss a moment of this. I don't want to miss a single thing she's saying without the words. I believe that in that rush of information that pours out of her, she is begging to be heard, to be understood." She paused for a moment, soaking up the silence of the crowd's attention.

"And in that understanding, there is love."

She was gratified to see several people smiling as they nodded in agreement.

"We all love our children," she said, the cold science gone from her voice now, concluding her presentation with an emotional earnestness. "I believe that by finding ways to understand their natural, universal language, we can reach for insights into their minds and hearts that have eluded us for millennia. My hope is that in twenty years or so, we'll have learned enough to be able to develop new educational curriculums, new paradigms for nurturing even healthier development in their pre-language years, and maybe even catch a glimpse of our world through the eyes of the truly, purely innocent.

"Thank you very much."

As the assembled crowd erupted in applause, a single spectator, located well in the back rows of the auditorium, calmly took his phone out from his jacket. His calm, stoic demeanor belied his excitement as he woke the tiny device from its sleep mode and began tapping out a text message.

00.02

Six years later

Charlottesville, Virginia

There is only one thing left to do.

The feminine silhouette floats, wraithlike, down the smooth dirt path in the moist midnight air. Her sandals make no sound beneath her as she makes her way beneath the autumn canopy. The gentle breeze flutters her pareo behind her and cools her bare legs beneath, but the draft brings her no comfort. She barely feels at all. Her eyes have no more tears to give, her heart cold in her chest. A beautiful dream is now ended.

She is alone.

Abandoned. She is abandoned by the one who had caught and held her in her darkest hours. The one who rejuvenated her, who pleaded with her to trust again, to let herself love again.

And then he abandoned her.

Not her husband. The divorce was finally over, the signatures' ink dry, that part of her life was now closed. She had been with Jerry since she was nineteen. It had been a devastating shock, his sudden and complete reversal of affection for her without reason or warning. Within a week, he had gone from loving and warm to withdrawn and aloof, and then overnight, he turned on her. He knew her vulnerabilities and attacked with cruel force. He said he hated her, renounced his love for her, said he could never have loved her at all, and never wanted to spend another moment with her. It was as if he had become a completely different man, one she'd never known he knew how to be.

The divorce had taken five months. He seemed compelled to attack her at every turn. They had no children, so it should have been an uncomplicated separation. But he resisted, demanding money from her she didn't have, expecting to keep belongings that were never his to claim. For five months, her life was a surreal, waking nightmare as her dreams of home and happiness were ripped apart in Jerry's malevolent hands.

When it was finally over, Scott arrived in her life like a guardian angel in a dream. Patient and gentle, never taking what she wasn't ready to give, holding her as she mourned the future that was lost to her. Reminding her that her life's path was full of new choices now, that she was free to find happiness wherever she wanted to look. Pleading with her not to close off her heart to love. She opened herself to him and found strength in trusting him, her confidence resurgent, finding the tools she needed to rebuild her self-worth and see Jerry for who and what he was.

For thirteen months, she lived a dream that she was smart, likeable, someone worth caring for. That her life had not ended, but had just taken an unforeseen turn that would lead to better places. That she was going to be okay. Cautiously, she had let herself be happy.

The dream shattered as abruptly as her marriage had. Scott cheated and lied. He left with barely an apology. He abandoned her, leaving only the ruinous truth of her existence: she was disposable.

Jerry was right all along. No one would love her, no one ever had loved her. She wasn't pretty; they only said so to get what they wanted from her. Whatever it was they had wanted to take, they soon discovered wasn't worth keeping. She wasn't lovable; they finally realized they had been fooling themselves. Whatever infatuation that might have been real at the start, quickly grayed and faded. There wasn't enough in her to love, so they threw her away.

Ugly. Unwanted. Disposable.

At least Scott figured it out earlier than Jerry had. Best to pull the band-aid off quickly and get it over with.

She wanted to be angry, but there was little anger in her. To be angry would mean she'd been wronged. It wasn't their fault. They deserved better, and they deserved to find it. They could see she wasn't worth loving. She didn't want to burden them, nor anyone else.

Occasionally, her phone would ring. Then it would stop. The tiny number on her phone's screen indicated the voicemails that piled up. She decided they were all probably wrong numbers. Why would anyone, even her friends, even Peter, call her? They were all probably happier without her, doing happy things with their happy families, happy children, happy jobs. Maybe they resented her for being so inept, so stupid as to think she could be like them. Someone worthwhile. *Normal.*

They didn't want her around. She made them uncomfortable. They would all be better off without her. So they wouldn't have to put up with her stupidness and delusions and ugly face anymore.

She had been sitting on her sofa at home all afternoon, unmoving, staring into space. Dishes were left unwashed in her sink, the bed a messy pile of sheets and pillows. Discarded clothes on the floor. It didn't matter; no one cared whether her bed was made or her clothes folded. No one would see the dishes or her unwashed hair. No one wanted to, anyway. There was too much happiness elsewhere in the world.

Here there was only a loveless, disposable woman.

She stopped keeping track of what day it was. She thought it could be a weekend, but didn't have the mental strength to count back the days to when she last was sure. Hour after hour passed, and she couldn't move. Part of her wanted to get up, shower, eat, do something… but the weight of the truth was too smothering: *Ugly. Unwanted. Disposable.* What had begun as a dark cloud of mood had steadily solidified into a physical heaviness in her body. She lay on her couch, her arms drawn around herself, and stared with unseeing, empty eyes.

What happened next, she could barely understand.

For no apparent reason, the weight lifted. Vanished. And with it, all emotion disappeared from her.

It was as though a switch had been flipped in her, a switch that simply discontinued her emotional self. She sat still for a long time, with a mildly puzzled expression. She searched within herself for the sadness, the loneliness. It was nowhere, and she found herself wondering why she had been so upset before. She knew the reasons, but those reasons weren't enough to feel sad anymore. Now she felt nothing. She saw herself curled up on her couch, and felt no pity, sympathy, anger, anything toward herself or her situation. She could not feel at all. It was as if she had forgotten how.

There's only one thing left to do then.

What does that mean?

You know.

She watched herself push up from the couch. By now, the windows were dark; she couldn't guess what time it was. She felt as though her body were moving on its own, autopilot, like cars in highway-cruise mode, taking turns, shifting lanes and changing speed with traffic as necessary, minds of their own. She slipped into her sandals and walked out into the night, the same thought repeating over and over in her mind: *One more thing.*

She left her apartment door open; it didn't matter. She climbed into her car and drove south, leaving the city, not stopping until she reached the state park. The parking lot was deserted. She stopped the car in a spot close to the trailhead. She left the keys dangling in the ignition. The late October air was cool and moist.

She walks onward.

The night seems to welcome her, beckoning her to the one place she knows she can leave this failed life behind her, so that everyone else can get on with theirs. Even the breezes seem to whisper it.

One thing left to do.

She stands in the middle of the bridge, near the railing. There is no hour or minute, only night. She stares out over the treetops, watching them swaying in the wind. The South Fork Rivanna River is an inky abyss that arcs away to the left, and disappears behind the rise. She can see streetlamps pinching cones of light along the river trail beneath her. The breeze is more insistent here.

Do it. What are you waiting for?

She pulls her pareo up to her waist, holding it there as she climbs over the thick wood railing, sitting and swinging her legs over the side. The river beneath her yawns open, a gateway into welcome oblivion. A blackness in which she can sleep forever, and never be an imposition on anyone else again. Part of her is afraid from the height, but she ignores it. She places her palms on the edge of the railing. With a mere push, the mistake she has been all her life will be corrected. And everyone she loved will be free of her. Free to be happy.

Her hands tighten their grip on the railing. She presses against it.

Go, Naomi. Just get it over with.

She pushes herself off the ledge into the open air, and falls. Suddenly everything is very cold.

The black swallows her. In the void, a shape forms, coalesces in the inky darkness. She has only moments to recognize it.

She sees the impossible. She knows there is not enough light to produce it, but the image of her own reflection shimmers in the water, clear and unmistakable, staring back at her.

Her body strikes the glassy surface. A momentary, piercing shock of pain, and all is silence.

Part I

Wer mit Ungeheuern kämpft, mag zusehn,
dass er nicht dabei zum Ungeheuer wird.
Und wenn du lange in einen Abgrund blickst,
blickt der Abgrund auch in dich hinein.

"Beyond Good and Evil", Aphorism 146 (1886)
Friedrich Nietzsche

Chapter One
01.01

Six years later

Galon-Yarisis Outpost
Over Planet Phoenicis
Sector 351-R

Streaks of light raced across the sky as the small fleet of spacecraft maneuvered over the gray planet Phoenicis, surrounding the fortified space station Galon-Yarisis. G-Y was known throughout the territory as nearly impregnable, withstanding prolonged assaults from even larger fleets than this one gathered to challenge it. This fleet was not seeking to destroy nor capture it. The strategy was surgical: punch a hole through the outer defense, get a small extraction team aboard, and if possible, rescue a prisoner.

"They're warming up their particle weapons," warned Naomi over the voice channel, who was captaining the lead ship, the *Renown*-class destroyer *Destiny*. The other seven capital ships of the fleet were some of the strongest ships of the Pride of the Guilty.

The name 'Rabbit' glowed in Naomi's headsup. The data interface, simulated like a hologram in her iWear device, seemed to hang in midair around the periphery of her primary screen. Rabbit's voice sounded in the channel as his name flashed: "We got twenty seconds to knock out their AM reactors," he warned from his ship, the transport *Irritable Vowel*. Rabbit's ship was holding back, carrying the insertion team.

Naomi's eyes quickly darted across the floating display before her, finding her short-range sensor sphere, a 3D projection among the rest of the 2D interface elements. "Who's closest? Who's—"

"I've got it," came a soft female voice as the name 'Hazy' lit. Her corvette, *Sad Panda*, began aiming its batteries toward the base's antimatter reactors.

"Hurry," Naomi said. "Rico, I need recharge. Stay behind me."

"Yes ma'am," came Rico's voice, whose cutter *Dayquil Shortbus* aimed its power distribution parabolas at the lead ship, and began streaming greenish pulses into its aft collectors.

"Hazy, you're getting too close to the rings," a male voice, ArchDuke, warned her. The station was ringed with four grooved platforms for energy cannons, which could be gathered together to focus their firepower. Several of the cannons were clustered, taking aim at the *Sad Panda*.

"Then cover me!" Hazy retorted.

"I'm not in position," ArchDuke said.

"Where's the hell's Speed?"

Speedracer's fast attack ship, the *Deffenbroken Texas,* was also a corvette, outfitted for maneuverability. "Speed, where are you?" Naomi called.

"I see you, Hazy," Speedracer said. "I'm coming over the station. I see the cannons. They're mine." Arcs of plasma fire burst from the *Texas'* ventral cannons, ripping into the grooved tracks of the rings, flashes of explosions bursting from them.

Suddenly, *Texas'* underside was ripped open in a bright golden flash. In maneuvering his ship to attack the ring cannons, Speed had taken it blindly into the firing arc of the base's heavy AA guns.

"Fuck! I lost my weapons!" Speed reacted as his ship began listing from the force of the blast. "It's going to hit me again."

"Hazy, get out of there," came another female voice, Volley.

Four of the cannons had amassed on the ring and took deadly aim at the *Sad Panda*. *Panda*'s main guns were barely within striking range of the base's antimatter reactors when the cannons disgorged their furious, punishing projectiles at the slender corvette. Explosions rained across the upper hull as Hazy's screen lit up with damaged systems alerts. At last the reactors were in range and she fired, discharging her main batteries at the base's power plants.

Two bolts of white-hot energy erupted from the *Panda*'s forward guns, racing toward the cylindrical, armored antimatter reactors. Hazy set the guns to recharge for another shot, and threw her ship into reverse to try to escape the hammering of the ring cannons. One of the bolts exploded before it struck the reactor: the base had successfully launched an intercepting countermeasure. The other bolt impacted the reactor with full force.

"I got it!" Hazy cheered.

"Negative on that, Hazy," Naomi said, frowning. From her

vantage point, she could see the reactor's armor plating had been damaged, but not breached. One bolt from the corvette's batteries had not been enough. "The reactor held."

"Somebody get these cannons off me, dammit!" Hazy pleaded angrily. "I'm not holding it…"

"Volley, can you break off from Caveman?" Naomi asked. Volley's ship *Celestial* was defending the *Whispers of Mutiny*, the fleet's electronic warfare platform. *Whispers* was pounding the G-Y with transmitted worms and brute-force hacks, attempting to compromise its computer systems. If *Whispers* was successful, however briefly, it could mean an immediate tactical advantage which Naomi could exploit.

"I can't! There's too much coming at us!" Volley replied, sounding desperate as her blockade-runner, *Celestial,* spun and lobbed pulses of purple light at the incoming blasts from the station.

Naomi realized the mission was lost. If there was any way she could get a successful attack on the reactor while it was vulnerable, it could mean the station's defenses would be reduced enough to get the *Irritable*'s insertion team close enough to board the station. The base's weapons were just too damn strong, and the strongest one of all was only moments away from unloading at the *Destiny*.

"Speed!" she cried in frustration as the AAs unloaded again on the lurching, helpless *Texas,* which exploded into two pieces in a stunning, thunderous conflagration, tiny fragments clouding outward from the sundered ends.

"Shit," Speedracer said as his ship was annihilated.

Naomi's only hope now was to save the rest of her fleet from the torrential punishment that was inevitable. "Everyone get clear! Get clear of *Destiny*! Break, break, break!"

She ordered her ship ahead full and began moving toward the base, to put as much distance as she could between herself and the rest of her fleet. An ominous bluish glow could be seen deep within the cannon barrels that were aimed at her destroyer, and she knew there was no stopping its devastating salvo. She spun her camera toward the *Sad Panda*. It too was buckling under the relentless fusillade of the ring cannons, bursts of fire erupting from beneath its hull plating. As she watched, the *Panda*'s main reactors succumbed and spewed red and orange flames into space.

"I'm core-breached," Hazy said, dejected. "I'm done."

In a blinding flash, the *Sad Panda* was consumed by a billowing cloud of flame, larger ejecta streaking outward, leaving flaming fingers of gold in all directions.

The G-Y's mighty particle cannons erupted in horrific blue, piercing the distance between themselves and the vulnerable *Destiny*. They tore through the destroyer easily, bursting out the other side as though cutting through papier-mâché. Naomi slumped back in her chair and shook her head as she watched her flagship diced by the devastating weapons, signaling the unequivocal loss of the mission.

"Get clear," she said one more time, but she could see Arch-Duke's ship would not have time to escape.

The flaming *Destiny* gave a shudder and erupted suddenly in a flash, throwing out a powerful shockwave. The wave struck the *Epic Cowbell* and knocked it sideways, buckling its outer hull, fissures of gas suddenly spewing from its surface.

"Sorry, Duke," Naomi offered.

"Not your fault, sweetheart," Duke consoled her. "Let's get out of here before it mops up the rest of us."

"Everyone evac," sighed Naomi. "Back to GP."

01.02

Guilty Pleasures Outpost
Over Planet Casselle
Sector 67-E

The Pride of the Guilty lodge had 60-65 active members, and about 20 core members. Together they represented one of the oldest and most well-respected lodges in *Tides of Cortanis*, the massively multiplayer procedural roleplaying game. ToC boasted over 15 million subscribers, and had eclipsed *World of Warcraft* for the title of Most Popular Game of All Time, three years prior.

ToC was more than just an online multiplayer game. Its social networking side, which players referred to as Social, allowed for email, runtime voice-chat with voicemail messaging, and file transfer. Many people used their *Cortanis* account as their primary email address, and some even linked ToC voice with their own smartphones, allowing for passthrough of voice-chat directly to their phones when they weren't at their computers to play.

Naomi René had been in the game since its launch in 2021, having come over with several of her friends from *World of Warcraft*. She was one of the founding members of PotG, and held the rank of Commander. Her character, Vanda, was third in line below Admiral Roukan, the lodge's current leader.

Roukan could not be with them tonight, so Naomi had managed the raid on the G-Y Outpost, an extremely challenging undertaking given their number and relative strength together.

"Our strategy was sound," she was saying in voice-chat as their characters danced together in the private club aboard the lodge's space station, which they had named Guilty Pleasures. Naomi's character Vanda had dark purple hair cut in an asymmetrical bob, the right side descending well below her chin. She wore a black leather jacket open over a ribbed turtleneck, and a short black slanted miniskirt over tights and boots. She swung her arms around her avatar body as she twirled in the repeated dance move sequence. As she spoke, her avatar's lips moved to match her words, and mirrored her facial expressions as well.

"If we could have hit those reactors again, we could have had a shot," Hazy was saying. Her character was also dancing nearby Vanda.

"We don't really know that," Rico said, sitting at a table with Caveman and Rabbit, their avatars sipping from mugs. "Getting through all those countermeasures is really tough, and even when you did, you only dented that reactor."

"But another shot could have blown it up," Hazy pressed. "If those damn ring cannons hadn't pounded the shit out of me…"

"Another shot might have just dented it more," Rico argued.

"Those particle cannons are the key," Naomi said. "We need to be able to take those out of commission if any sustained attack on the base is going to succeed."

"I don't think a direct, brute force approach is the way, babe," said Caveman thoughtfully, his deep, throaty voice unmistakable. "Maybe if we had two EW ships, we could concentrate on trying to hack our way in. Shut down the cannons instead of killing their power source."

"You go above eight ships," said Rabbit, "the base gets better defended."

Tides of Cortanis was a game that constantly honed and adapted its challenges to meet the level of the players. The longer a player remained in-game, the better the system learned that player's gaming style and preferences. After the first few months of careful observation, it could tailor a customized game experience for that particular person. The more players spent time together, the more the game learned about their strengths and proficiencies as a group, and modified gameplay accordingly. It was constantly adjusting its challenge level to suit the individuals according to their unique combinations of skills and abilities.

As such, it was a very difficult game to master. Not impossible, but it was always increasing the level of challenge to meet the proficiency of its players.

"There has to be some way for us to do it, then," said Volley, the youngest of the lodge members.

"What if we replace Rico with Benjamin and have him bring an EW ship…"

"I can spec an EW ship," Rico said, not wanting to be left out on the raid.

"Yeah, but it will take you a while to level it up," Caveman pointed out.

ArchDuke broke in. "We need Rico to recharge the cruisers. Without him we only have one recharge ship and that'll be the prime target for the ring cannons."

"Okay, I gotta run. I'll see you guys later," said Rabbit. He disappeared from the room, but his name remained in the channel, meaning he had not yet logged off.

Naomi thought for a moment, then keyed a private message to Rabbit. It appeared in text on his screen in the little chat window:

VANDA: What a GDCF.

She smiled upon getting an immediate response:

RABBIT: GDCFs R us

She had known Peter since her first years in *World of Warcraft*, and the two of them had grown to be good friends. They had never met in person, and since he lived in Brazil, they weren't likely to. But she felt like she knew him at least as well, if not better than, her closest friends in the real world. Their friendship hadn't always been easy, but it had been tested enough times to become one of the more reliable relationships in Naomi's life.

VANDA: You doing ok? You left rather suddenly she keyed to him.

RABBIT: yeh

VANDA: Whats up with you?

RABBIT: ill tell you later came his cryptic response after a long pause.

VANDA: OK. You get some sleep

RABBIT: can't sleep at all lately

VANDA: Why not? Is something going on?

Another long pause.

RABBIT: too much to explain. talk soon

VANDA: *hugs*

RABBIT: *hugs*

She smiled a little, then turned her attention back to voice-chat.

01.03

One month later

Rocky Top Climbing Gym
Charlottesville, Virginia

The parking lot outside the two-story, plain-looking building was only half full as a dark gray Chrysler 200E swung its headlights in and pulled into a spot. A thirty-three year old woman with long, black hair in gentle curls climbed out of the vehicle, wearing an ankle-length black dress and a light denim jacket, her purse slung over her shoulder.

The days were growing shorter now as fall began making itself known in late October. Naomi preferred the coolness in the evening air to the thick heat of the mid-year months. As she reached the front doors of the rock-climbing gymnasium, they burst open and two preadolescent children scampered towards a minivan parked nearby, followed by their mother who flashed Naomi an apologetic smile. Naomi chuckled and smiled back, and slipped inside.

She passed through two pairs of doors and into the lobby, where a familiar face belonging to one of the employees recognized her and waved her through with a smile. Naomi smiled back and continued into the gymnasium.

Rocky Top had originally been a much smaller facility, but several years ago had renovated and was now in a brand new building that was a boulderer's dream. The doors leading to the climbing gym from the lobby were split left/right: the left doors went into the gymnasium, and the right doors went into the pool area, with a tall climbing wall that sloped out nearly twenty feet over the water. Naomi paused a moment to watch a couple of young children on the poolside wall laughing and tumbling from their grips into the water. She could smell the chlorine from behind the doors.

In the gym, there were four people on the wall at various heights. She stepped through the gym doors and spied her friend, a lean woman in her mid-thirties, with dark hair pulled back into a ponytail, rubbing white powder from her hands. She was standing at the base of the wall, readying herself to begin climbing. The woman was attached to one of the long ropes dangling from the ceiling that was looped around and clipped to her partner, who was holding on. They exchanged a quick series of statements to each other before the climber took hold and began moving up the wall.

"On belay?" she said.

"Belay on," answered the partner.

"Climbing."

"Climb on."

Naomi always marveled at how much Skyler resembled a dancer as she gracefully ascended from hold to hold, making her way up among the colorful, amorphous plastic forms. She squinted to make out the color of the holds Skyler was gripping on the wall, and smiled to herself. They were red: she was ascending an expert route, probably the one she'd been working on for several weeks now. She leaned back against the concrete beside the door to watch Sky make her ascent.

A panicked scream suddenly filled the room as one of the other climbers lost her grip and slipped from the wall. These screams used to startle Naomi, but she'd grown accustomed to them. Many climbers here were encouraged to vocalize loudly when they knew they were falling or about to fall. Since this was a family-friendly environment, swearing was frowned upon, so climbers at Rocky Top either shouted "Falling!" as loud as they could, or just screamed.

"I said '*take*'!" the girl said angrily, swinging in the harness, to her partner below holding the braking line.

"I'm sorry! I didn't hear you!" he said, in a tone that suggested he was her boyfriend, and that quarreling was something they were used to.

Naomi turned her attention away from them as they continued to bicker, focusing back on her friend, who had stopped moving on the wall a little over halfway up. She was staring intently at a grip that was just out of arm's reach, about five feet above and right of her position, trying to decide if she could make it from where she was. She glanced down at her footing, reseated the inside of her foot against the little red plastic notch, and found her target again with her eyes. There were plenty of other holds of various shapes scattered around her, but this was the only red one.

Go for it, Naomi silently urged her.

"Watch me," Sky called to her partner below, crouching a little against the wall and reaching her right hand behind her, into her chalk pouch. She brought the powdered hand back out, flicked the excess from her fingers, and took hold once more.

"I got you," her belayer said. "Flow, not force."

With a soft grunt, Skyler lunged upward, reaching with all her might at the little red grip, throwing her weight forward. Her fingers found the crimp and clung to it, wrapping her thumb over her fingertips. Her body continued forward with the momentum of her lunge, her feet slipping from the wall and dangling for a moment before she found purchase again in the seam between two of the flat concrete panels. Once she had steadied herself, she latched on to another red grip and centered her balance again, her hips hugging the wall.

"Woot!" she yelped in triumph.

"Nice move!" called her belayer, not taking her hands from the rope. "Two more to go!"

Naomi grinned at her friend's impressive jump, pushed off the wall and moved over to the seating area. She bought a bottle of carbonated fruit drink from the girl working concession, and sat down at an open table. She turned her seat so she could watch Skyler and the other climbers make their way up and down the wall. It was one of her routine stops on her way home from work on Tuesdays and Thursdays, to visit with her friend for a while and relax. Skyler worked there as a part-time instructor, and those two evenings she was free to practice her own climbing. Besides, the concession stand was cheaper than any bar.

Sky managed to make the next grip up, but slipped from the wall before she could attempt the final movement.

"Coming down," she said. Hanging from her line, she "walked" down the wall to the pads on the ground below and allowed herself to lay flat on her back, breathing hard, her arms spread wide.

A few minutes later, she walked up to Naomi's table and took the other seat, still breathing heavily. "Hey! Did you see that? Did you see me make that lunge?"

Naomi nodded. "I did. Looked a little dicey there."

"Came this close to making it to the top, but my arms got pumped. I wasn't really trying to make it all the way up. I just really wanted to make that dyno tonight."

"How many tries did it take?"

"That was five," she said smiling. "I definitely earned my Zinger for the night."

"Glad I got to be here to see it," Naomi smiled back.

"Me too. Want to tie up? I'll belay you," her friend's smile widened.

Naomi chuckled. "Not tonight, thanks."

Naomi had been friends with Skyler for six years, and had been coming to Rocky Top with her even before the larger facility had opened up. She was no stranger to the harness, but it had been nearly a year since she'd attempted to climb. Skyler had vowed never to stop trying to convince her to.

"I miss seeing you on the wall," Sky said. "Even below the line." The gymnasium had a six-inch red line dividing the climbing wall, marking the height at which a climber could not go past without a top rope and belay.

"One of these days," Naomi said. "When I'm ready."

"It's good exercise."

"I get exercise at my gym," Naomi said. "I just prefer to work out alone."

Skyler grabbed a napkin from the dispenser and wiped chalk dust from her hands. Her hair, Naomi noticed, had a two-finger width braid in it, starting at the top of her head and continuing down and through the clutch of her ponytail.

"I like your braid," Naomi said. "Makes you look halfway cultivated."

"It does? I'll get rid of it," Sky said.

"No, I mean it makes you look all Sacajawea."

"Good. It stays."

Naomi laughed. Sky's belay partner, a stocky, younger woman wearing a white tee that read "Bend but don't break" came to the table and placed a bottle of Powerade in front of Skyler, giving a smile to Naomi.

"Hey, Naomi," she said to her.

"Hey, Jen."

"You working tomorrow?" Jen asked Skyler.

"Yeah, I'll be here at four," Sky answered.

"John's coming," Jen said with a playful smile.

Sky understood. "I'll grease up the low holds for you," she joked. Jen laughed, gently slapped the back of her hand on Sky's upper arm, and left.

"What was that about?" Naomi asked.

"She's got a thing for this guy who's been coming in for lessons," Sky said, twisting the top off the Powerade bottle. "She's spotting him on the low side of the line."

Naomi chuckled. "Oh."

"We need to find someone to 'spot' you a few slips off the wall." Skyler took a drink from her bottle.

"Nah. No one wants to be putting their hands on me," Naomi said with a self-deprecating chuckle.

Skyler swallowed, then faked a few throat-clearings, interjecting the name 'Elliot' into them.

Naomi heard her, and grimaced. "Oh, please. I wish."

"What? I bet he does."

"He does not. And he's so married."

"I know he's *married*, but that doesn't mean he turns into a robot when he's not home. He's a guy, he can think things."

"I'm the last person he thinks *that* about."

"Well, you never get out, so where are you supposed to meet anyone?"

"Maybe I'm just not supposed to meet anyone," Naomi answered, watching the bickering couple as they traded accusations.

"Defeatist," Skyler said, leaning back in the seat and putting one foot up on the empty one to her right. "You can make statements like that about someone after they're dead."

Naomi felt the vibrating purr of her phone in her purse, and she took it out. The call was coming from Peter. "Mind if I take this, just a minute?"

Skyler shrugged. "Sure."

Naomi accepted the call. "Peter? Hey," she said. "Where have you been?"

The voice on the other end was recognizable, but distorted. "Naomi?"

"Peter? You're kinda faraway sounding. Bad connection… but are you all right? Haven't heard from you in two weeks."

"I… I don't know," he said, speaking slowly. "I just wanted to hear your voice."

Naomi's eyes furrowed. "You don't sound good. Are you sure you're all right?"

"I will be fine, I think. I should go. Naomi?"

"Yeah?"

There was a long silence as Naomi waited for what he would say next. When she realized the silence had gone on for too long, she looked at her phone just as it displayed the message that the call had been terminated.

"Huh," she said, frowning. "Connection dropped."

"One of your online friends?" Sky asked.

"Peter," Naomi said. "I've talked to you about him before."

"Yeah, I guess you have."

Skyler was not a gamer, but she was one of her only friends that Naomi talked to about playing in ToC. Sky would always listen to her. "It's weird. Haven't heard from him in nearly two weeks. Usually we talk a lot more often than this. He sounded kind of upset, I think. Was hard to hear him through the bad signal."

"Sometimes I wonder if you don't prefer the company of online friends to real people," Sky said.

"They are real people. They're just not in the same room."

"Yeah, but how can they be real friends to you if you've never even met them?"

"Peter's a real friend."

"As real as he can be from halfway around the world."

"He's in Brazil, not India. And anyway, I talk to him all the time. He's as real a friend to me as you are. The past two weeks have been unusual."

Sky shook her head, taking another drink. "I just… okay, look, don't take offense to this, okay?"

Naomi looked at her.

Sky continued. "You know how… alcoholics, they think being

drunk is just great, but those around them who see how much it's hurting them, they don't think it's great?"

Naomi bristled at the comparison. "I assume you're not implying that I'm addicted to ToC." She pronounced it "tee-oh-see" as most people did.

"No, I'm not," Sky said, holding her hands up. "I'm saying that you don't see what your behaviors are doing to you, from someone else's perspective."

"My 'behaviors', if that's what you want to call it, are no more wrong or bad for me than watching television or reading books. I think it's better than them, actually, 'cause I'm sharing my experiences with other people, and not just passively soaking up a TV show or novel. I'm not just consuming, I'm participating. Besides," Naomi couldn't help but add, "you climb rocks. You're going to Iron Gate in a couple weeks. You're telling me risking your life for sport is somehow a healthier way to spend your leisure time?"

Skyler nodded. "Yeah. It's healthier for the soul."

"My soul didn't feel very healthy after I nearly broke my hip a year ago." Naomi looked away and took another drink from her bottle of juice.

"Everyone falls when they climb. Everyone gets hurt, too. Sometimes worse than broken hips. But climbing is not just about climbing. It's about climbing *again* when you fall and hurt yourself. It's about getting back up, even when you're afraid."

Naomi shrugged. "Everyone has to know their limits."

"Their limits? You mean limits like not dating people? Not coming out of the shell you've been hiding in for, what, six years?"

Naomi didn't look at her.

"You took a fall six years ago, too," Skyler went on. "You haven't really gotten back up from that."

"I got up," Naomi answered, in a quiet voice. "I went to law school. I graduated. I worked. I have a life again."

"You did those things," Sky said. "But you still have a lot of healing to do, and instead of trying to continue healing, you're just letting the part of you that broke in that river stay broken."

"Maybe that's just how it should be," Naomi said, trying to smile.

"Maybe that's a bunch of crap," Sky said, swinging her leg off the chair and leaning forward toward her. "People feed themselves lines of nonsense like that to keep from doing what they're afraid of doing. It happens every day here. Rationalizing and excuses. It's them lying to themselves, saying they can't do it when they could if they wanted to. If they tried."

What was left of Naomi's smile faded as colder thoughts surfaced within her... thoughts she didn't share with anyone else. She looked down, a desperate sadness rising within her, knowing that if she allowed this topic of conversation to continue, she would start to lose her ability to manage it. "Some people just... don't get to have the kind of life that involves a lot of company," she said, realizing there was probably a better way to have expressed that.

"Your life is what you want it to be," Skyler said.

"That's what we tell children," Naomi said, looking up at her. "But you know it isn't true. If my life was what I wanted it to be, I'd be married to Scott and probably have a kid by now. And I wouldn't have..." but she didn't finish that sentence. She didn't need to.

"So find someone better than Scott, better than that asshole Jerry. Someone better is out there somewhere. Why won't you at least look?"

"Because I'm..." Naomi started, and then stopped herself.

"You're what?"

Disposable.

"Not ready," Naomi finally said.

Skyler sighed. "That's what you said about climbing. One of these days, I'm going to get you out of that shell you're so comfortable in, and see you do something dangerous for a change."

Naomi gave a weak smile. "And maybe one of these days I'll see you in an iWear set logging into ToC."

"Oh God," Skyler laughed. "Good luck with that."

01.04

Later that evening

Naomi opened the door to her split-level townhouse and went inside, closing the door behind her. The lights in the room were already on, set to their programmed schedule.

"LEM? Are you awake?" she called.

A voice from the loft overhead responded, "Yes. Welcome home, Naomi."

The computer-generated voice was soft-spoken and male. LEM was an artificial intelligence game called *SimMind,* similar to digital pets like Tamagotchi. If the user let it run throughout the day, the SimMind would occupy its time searching topics it found on the Web, following comment threads on websites and forming its own "opinions" on things, and then later distilling what it had learned into conversations with the user. Naomi had started LEM running over a year previous. She only turned it off when she had to restart her computer. The software remained on night and day otherwise.

Naomi peeled off her jacket and replaced her work clothes with sweats and a t-shirt, and thick hiking socks which she liked to wear around the house. She went into her kitchen, poured herself a glass of cranberry-grape juice, and headed upstairs to the loft to visit with her SimMind.

The twin screens of her computer were dark when she'd entered the house, but when she called to LEM, they had activated again to show her Windows desktop. The second screen showed the *SimMind* interface, which consisted of a series of charts showing LEM's processing cycles. These detailed a rough approximation of how interested he was in a particular investigation of his, or how involved he was in reading and comprehending the varying subtleties of a given comment thread somewhere. Naomi sat down in front of the screens and looked at the visual display of data. "Wow," she said, "you were on a tear today. What's that about?"

"The controversy regarding Google Maps adding cartography from *Tides of Cortanis* to its Maps online app," the software said. "It is a contentious issue."

"Why? What are they saying?" Naomi smiled to the screen. She always felt somewhat like a teacher visiting with a student when she interacted with LEM, and she enjoyed this dynamic. She knew that LEM could see her via her computer's built-in camera, and could track her facial expressions and body posture, so smiling to his camera was an expression she knew he could see.

"On one hand," LEM began, "there are many people who play *Cortanis* and would find such a service useful. On the other, there is an increasingly querulous group of people who are arguing that to do so is unacceptable, because the game has virtual planets, not real ones."

"Why does it bother them? If they don't want to look up the ToC maps, they don't have to, right?" Naomi leaned back in her chair and put her feet up on the edge of the desk. She'd read about this little controversy before, and was modestly familiar with pro and con sides of the argument. She wanted to see what LEM would come up with.

"These people are arguing that bringing the *Cortanis* worlds to Google Maps gives the virtual world too much importance. They insist that because it is a game, it has no place alongside actual world maps."

"Do they think some people might be confused, and think that they are real?" She smiled. She had an idea as to the answer to this, but was probing LEM to form his own summation.

"A few do, but it was not one of the more powerful arguments."

"What would be an example of one of those?"

"That *Cortanis* maps have equal legitimacy," LEM replied succinctly.

"Legitimacy," Naomi repeated. "That's an interesting concept, don't you think?"

"It seems to be a focal point of the arguments for and against, in this case."

"It's the focal point of a lot of arguments in fact," Naomi said. "Tell me what you think the word means." Naomi phrased this request quite specifically. By asking LEM *what he thought* the word meant, she was making a different request than if she had simply asked for a definition.

"Legitimacy is the inherent positive value of a thing, either defensible by law, logic or accepted standards. In terms of family law, it describes a child born to legally wedded parents."

"So tell me, do you think the *Cortanis* maps should be offered on Google Maps?"

"I do not."

"Really?" Naomi asked, surprised. "And why is that?"

"Because it is an inefficient and illegitimate use of Google Maps."

"Okay, inefficient. How is it inefficient?"

"Google would have to devote resources to inputting the *Cortanis* maps into their software. There are currently 16 planets in the game, all with unique geographies and geopolitical boundaries that would have to be migrated over. Furthermore, the game generates a new planet roughly once every 7.6 months, and these too would need to be added. Unless Praelium contributes manpower and resources to Google to oversee the incorporation of *Cortanis* cartography into Google Maps, it should not be done."

"Nicely stated case. Now, how is it illegitimate?"

"Even with such a contribution of resources, the effort required to expand Google Maps' database volume with *Cortanis* information does not justify its utility for the ratio of users who play the game. It would be merely a novelty function for one specific game, and will open up Google to criticism that it is elevating *Cortanis'* visibility and status as a video game in the culture, to the exclusion of other video games with planetary cartography which could also benefit. Google Maps is not in the business of promoting video games with its service, and this would unfairly have that effect."

"Unfairly? Google's sponsorship and integration with ToC is widely known. They're practically a partner with Praelium. Besides, this kind of silly coolness seems like the kind of thing Google used to do all the time. Some time ago, Google added certain locations from *Harry Potter* to its London cartography, and that didn't generate this level of controversy."

"Under Eric Schmidt, yes, Google's corporate culture was more likely to encourage seemingly profitless ventures, which promoted their technologies being used in experimental ways. However, Maps is no longer an experimental technology. And since Schmidt's and Larry Page's departures and the company's subsequent depreciation, they have returned to more profit-centric business models. Thus, such a use of their technology would be out of character. The *Harry Potter* locations were localized and did not require significant resources or time to produce for the sake of pure novelty, whereas *Cortanis* maps have not only considerable scale and scope, but limited utility. It is my opinion that Google has insufficient reasons to justify promoting this game over others."

"That's an… interesting opinion, LEM." Naomi smiled to herself.

"Thank you," LEM politely replied.

"It's not uncommon for companies to promote their own interests, even if they have minimal share in other companies which are seemingly unrelated to their core business model. Would you agree?"

LEM processed that a moment before responding. Naomi tried to limit complicated sentences like that when talking to him, but once in a while she didn't mind throwing his syntax parsing algorithms a challenge. And anyway, she was an attorney, and LEM had had more than a year to get used to the way she spoke.

"Yes, but it is rare for a business to assist in the promotion of another unless there is mutual benefit, or philanthropic goals."

"Do you think it is possible for Google to have a business interest, then, in promoting ToC, other than just paid sponsorship?"

"It is possible, but I have not yet ascertained what it could be, and there are no theories being offered on the matter in the conversations I have read."

"Would you postulate a theory for me?"

"Certainly. May I have tonight to think on it?"

"Sure, take as much time you want. I'll ask you about it tomorrow night."

"I'll attempt to have a theory for you by then."

"I'm going to go make dinner," Naomi said, swinging her feet back to the floor and pushing up from her chair. "Is there anything else you'd like to talk about before I do?"

"Not at the moment. Are you playing *Cortanis* tonight?"

"Yes."

"Then I'll see you when you get back."

Chapter Two
02.01

One week later

One Morton Drive
Office of the Vice President for Research, Compliance Division
University of Virginia - Charlottesville

Naomi pressed the send icon, and her carefully worded email was spirited away to its recipient. She didn't think it would do any good, but she'd done her part. The faculty researcher had been furious, refusing to acknowledge that the University had any right to expect him to divulge his consultancy with the pharmaceutical company he'd been working with for the past three years. The relationship, however unrelated to the research he was pursuing now, was still something that needed to be divulged if he wanted the compliance committee to approve his work. Naomi tried to explain that as professionally and helpfully as she could. But she knew this faculty member was not going to smile and accept this stumbling block with humility and grace. He would immediately go over her head, and then it was at matter of whether or not he had a serviceable relationship with her boss. Sometimes, the director of compliance would back up Naomi's decisions; other times, particularly if golf was involved, certain 'gentlemen's agreements' were made which she was not party to.

These agreements would always find a way to make her job more difficult later.

She sighed and turned her eyes out the narrow window near her desk. Her office on the fifth floor didn't afford her the best view, but she could see the hospital complex to the south if she stood and looked out. Mostly, her view was open sky. And while One Morton Drive was not the most posh of office buildings, its location well north of campus kept it out of the way of college bustle and foot traffic. That, and its proximity to Bodo's Bagel Bakery and Arch's Frozen Yogurt, were the only decent things about working there.

She didn't mind the work, but the politics were nearly overwhelming. Her law degree did not prepare her to handle the intrigues that took place every day in this building. Sometimes she felt herself getting caught up in them, and she hated that feeling. Strangely, unexpected gifts would arrive for her at home, which gave her the creeps. Once in a while, a faculty member twenty or thirty years her senior would suggest she meet him for drinks. She knew his interest in her had nothing to do with getting to know her, or even sleeping with her (although she shuddered to think that some of these married old men could actually think she would take them to bed). She knew they just wanted her to treat them favorably when their research was presented to the compliance committee. As if, by not flagging the problems in their research, she was actually doing them any favors.

It had been two weeks since she'd seen Rabbit in the game, and she was already concerned for him. It wasn't like him to drop out of sight like this without telling her—or anyone—that he was going to be away. She knew he was coming online; his ToC profile page showed that he had logged into Social, as well as the game world, every day. It did not give times, only dates for "Last logged in". He was clearly blocking his online status to everyone, even her, which hurt her a bit.

Whatever he had been doing, he wasn't doing it with the rest of the Pride, either. No one had seen him enter into guild-chat or their voice-chat. It was as though he had turned his back on all of them, even Naomi, and was playing with other people. Then last week, about the time she last spoke to him on the phone, he just stopped logging in at all.

This was particularly unsettling.

She had called him back that evening, but the call went to voicemail. As had additional calls the next day, and the next.

Naomi was a seasoned player, and well experienced in online drama. Certain people when they felt the need to quit an online game, often did it with unnecessary and hurtful theater. Several times it had gone around that so-and-so had "been in a horrible accident" which turned out to be a lie: the person just wanted out, and took perverse pleasure in watching all his friends mourn him. The truth would inevitably surface weeks or months later to the effect that he was alive and well, and playing some other online game.

Sometimes, he was even found to be back in ToC under a new persona, which was immediately excoriated and ostracized.

In all of these faked "accidents" it was always some close tie to the player who passed the grievous news to the online community.

Naomi knew, however, that if something awful were to happen for real, it was more likely that no one would think to contact any of the victim's online friends. (*Where would they have found the deceased's password?* Naomi would wonder.) They would simply be too consumed in their own grief. If one of her friends really did have a bad accident, they would simply stop logging in… no word, no response, no closure. They would just disappear.

Rabbit not logging in for a week was unusual for him. She knew that as soon as she had a chance to talk to him, she would not let him brush her off. He would have to answer for his absence. It was hurtful to her, to not tell her why he was away, and she would make sure he knew she had been worried.

She found herself staring at her computer screen, worrying. She picked her phone and fast-dialed Peter's number.

"Answer me, Peter," she muttered to herself as she waited for the call to place, and the ringing began. This time, the call was answered. Naomi drew a breath, relieved.

But the voice that answered was not Peter's. It was a female voice, quieter than his, speaking Portuguese. "*Olá*?"

Naomi caught herself before greeting Peter, realizing she was suddenly speaking to someone else.

"Hello, this is Naomi René," she said. "I'm a friend of Petrillo, is he there?"

"*Petrillo*?" the voice said. "You are a friend of Petrillo? From game?"

"Yes, I am… is Peter—"

"Peter is dead," the woman said bitterly. "You can stop calling for him."

Naomi froze, her eyes widening.

"What?"

"You didn't know?" the woman sounded like she was taunting her. "He die playing game with you. Is your fault he is dead. I hope you are happy!"

Naomi was doubly stunned now. Her voice was timid. "Wh... what? Is this a joke? Who is this?"

"Joke? No!" The woman's voice began breaking. "This is Peter's sister Renata, is who I am. I am the one who found him. You should know you killed him and be happy! You killed him with game! Now stop calling for him!"

Naomi's tears began tumbling down her cheeks at the viciousness with which Peter's sister spat the accusations at her. "I don't... I don't know what you mean..."

"You know how he die? He die at computer. He die playing your stupid game. He die because you keep him playing for three days. *Três dias* he is playing! He is not eating, not sleeping, not leaving his house, his room..." The shaking in her voice became pronounced. "You could not tell him to go sleep. It not bother you that he is not eating! He play game to death! He could not leave you, his... his *friends*."

"Oh my God," Naomi sobbed. "No... please, don't say that, I loved him! I haven't seen him in weeks—"

"You tell rest of friends in game. You tell them he play game to death. We buried him a week ago. He was such a young man. You tell your friends *seus amigos mataram. Eles o mataram com o jogo! Vai-te foder!*"

The line went dead.

Naomi held the phone in her trembling hand for nearly a minute before she remembered to put it down.

02.02

Later that evening

Four loud knocks came at her front door.

Naomi gathered her terrycloth robe around her as she stood up from her couch, and went to the door. Skyler was there, holding a paper bag and a bottle of vodka.

"Hey," Skyler said. "You okay? You sounded like you needed the full monty."

Naomi smiled to her and welcomed her with a gentle hug. Skyler gave her a comforting squeeze.

"Thanks," Naomi said, and wiped her cheek with her fingers. "Come on." She took the bag from Sky and let her inside. "What is this?"

"I didn't know what you needed more, Häagen-Dazs or vodka," Sky said, taking the bag back out of Naomi's hand. She went directly into the kitchen. Naomi followed her and watched her friend pour two glasses. Skyler put the ice cream into the freezer, and handed Naomi one of the glasses.

"There, now tell me what the woman said," Sky said.

Naomi went back into the living room, dropping herself onto the sofa. Skyler followed and sat down beside her, moving the box of tissues from the sofa to the coffee table near Naomi. There were several discarded, crumpled tissues on the floor already.

After a sip, Naomi tried to focus her thoughts on the conversation she'd had on the phone earlier. "She said… she said I killed him. She said he died playing the game."

"He died playing the *game*?" Sky asked. "The same game you play?"

Naomi nodded. "I haven't seen him for weeks, though. He's been off doing his own thing, I have no idea what he was doing. He was not in lodge-chat, not talking to us on voice, he didn't answer my emails to him. He's just been AWOL. But then he stopped logging in altogether."

"You can tell when someone logs in?"

"Yeah, it says on his Social page when he's logged in. He hasn't logged in since, like, the 19th."

"That was weeks ago."

"I haven't talked to him since the week before that."

"Why not?"

"He just stopped responding to me. It was really not like him at all to be logging in all the time, and not talking to me, or any of us in the lodge. We're a very tight group of friends, and Peter and I are closer than the rest of them. We usually talk daily. It wasn't like him. Something was really wrong."

"So he was into something elsewhere in the game and not including you."

"Yeah, you know, but..." she trailed off, looking into space. "He was acting weird even before that, he... we did an assault on this space station together about a month ago. He wasn't himself, real withdrawn, like. I asked him about it but he wouldn't tell me anything. He said he'd tell me about it later, though."

"You have no idea what that was about?"

Naomi shook her head. "No. No idea." She took another sip from her glass, pausing a moment to feel the warmth settle through her. "I wish I'd pressed him harder for it. Maybe I could have helped."

"Blaming you was something she did out of grief. It doesn't mean you're responsible. You know that, right?"

Naomi just stared, her eyes squinting a bit, as if trying to remember something. When she spoke again, her voice was shaky.

"She was so angry at me. She... she swore at me in Portuguese. She said it was my fault, mine and the others'. She said we didn't care that he wasn't eating or sleeping."

"It isn't your fault. There was nothing you could have done. Had he been that obsessive about the game before?"

Naomi shook her head. "No. We'd play a lot, I mean, we'd play for hours and hours. But I would ask him if he'd eaten, and usually I wouldn't even have to do that. He'd say he was hungry or that he needed to get up to stretch for a bit, or that he needed to go to bed. He never once made me think he wasn't conscious of taking care of himself. He wasn't that obsessive of a player. I just don't understand..."

"You really cared for him," Sky said.

She nodded. "I've known him longer than I've known you, by a few years. He was the only one of my WoW friends I could talk to about my divorce. He knew everything. He was there for me when all that with Scott happened, too. He's the only one in ToC who even knows my real name. I just... I can't believe he's gone. And I can't believe his family blames *me*."

"It's not your fault," Skyler repeated. "It's not. You couldn't have known."

Naomi stared into the space between them silently for a few moments, and nodded. "I know. But at the same time, I feel like I could have, or should have, done something. Tried harder to reach out to him. I don't know..." She shook her head. "I feel so helpless."

"I know. And even though it was cruel and mean, I can understand his sister wanting to blame someone, even though it's totally unfair. She's hurting. It's natural."

Naomi shrugged. "I guess so. If I lost Monica, I'd be... I don't know what I'd do. Maybe I'd blame somebody."

"You would if you thought they could have saved her, and didn't try."

"Yeah," Naomi nodded. "Yeah, I guess I would."

02.03

Two weeks later

Chapel of Phosphora
Planet Cortanis
Sector 01-P

Tides of Cortanis was released in 2021 to widespread acclaim from gamers and reviewers alike. One of the most anticipated game releases of the year, it shattered subscription records set by *World of Warcraft*, *Eve* and *Second Life*, eventually becoming the most popular online roleplaying game ever released. Its eponymous game mechanic, the Tides, routinely gave players temporary boosts to their abilities and skills. This made it possible to temporarily pursue game rewards and content that wouldn't otherwise be accessible to them until they were several levels higher. It had the effect of dangling a carrot in front of them at all times, and occasionally, giving them nibbles.

It had been an unprecedented success. Within a year, ToC had put its developer, Praelium, into an elite upper echelon of game developers including Sega, Ubisoft and Activision Blizzard. Praelium had already enjoyed success with its cheeky real-time strategy game *Ominous Latin Phrase*, which combined self-referential humor with simple, intuitive and addictive gameplay. OLP had already been adapted into a big-budget Hollywood film when *Tides of Cortanis* was announced in 2016.

Although the Tides were one mechanic that kept subscribers interested and active, it wasn't the game's most cunning design characteristic. The game was built on a procedural, self-architecting foundation, which allowed players to push outward from the central planet, Cortanis, into the unknown wilds of other nearby star systems. As the players explored, the game would generate persistent new topography for them to either claim, plunder, or simply chart for other players. In addition to the procedurally generated realm, the game had an observant intelligence, which paid close attention to players' gaming styles and habits. Once a player reached level 20—which took about three weeks of nightly play, or less if one was unusually motivated—the game had constructed a fairly accurate profile of that player's gaming skill and ability. If the game had determined that a given player was most appropriately challenged by a certain kind of enemy fighting style, it would serve up more of those kinds of enemies to the player, tailoring the difficulty to the player and attempting to find the player's unique "flow signature".

The homeworld Cortanis was the core of the game realm. It boasted the most populous cities, some of the most challenging terrain and the most legendary quests. It was here that many players spent the majority of their time, either in the PvP cities & towns, or taking assigned quests from mystics hiding in surrounding enclaves, or merely roaming through the wildernesses hunting for loot and treasure.

It was Cortanis' sun, Aten, from whence the Tides came.

The mysterious Tides were waves of buffing energy, which would increase every player's stats and abilities by anywhere from 20–50%. It was as if everyone in a given Tide was suddenly granted faster speed, greater strength, stronger capability in their core competencies, and at times, given random buffs to their secondary or tertiary abilities. The temporary effects would encourage the player to try alternative styles of attacks, defenses, scrying and crafting. The Tides could last for several days before expanding outward to the next-furthest star systems, where they would affect the players there for a time. As the Tides traveled further outward through the territory, their effects attenuated, such that a player receiving a 20% boost on Cortanis might only receive 15% on Casselle or Iunia, and only 5 to 10% on any of the third tier worlds. The Tide would push outward until its effects were no longer felt on any of the outer worlds, and would not come again for several weeks. They generally ran once a month, but their appearances and durations were erratic. The only way to tell when a Tide was coming was to watch the color of the Cortanis sun: just before a new Tide, it would shift from orange to gold.

The effect of the Tides on players was to keep them mostly congregated around the central planets, where the buffing effects were strongest. New players remained on Cortanis for most of their first few months of play, as they leveled up their abilities and learned how the game worked. As they progressed, they often joined or formed lodges, which allowed them to be trained by higher-level players and exchange equipment, weapons and supplies. It was uncommon to see an established player who did not belong to a lodge.

Stronger lodges, like Pride of the Guilty, had enough high-level players and crafters to afford to build their own space station, called a homestation. This was a property that was off-limits to anyone not in the lodge, and provided a safe haven for players to berth their starships and socialize with each other. The Pride's homestation, Guilty Pleasures, was in orbit over the second-tier planet Casselle, as numerous other lodge homestations were.

Today, the station was empty.

Over thirty members of the eminent Pride of the Guilty lodge were in attendance at the memorial service for Rabbit, being held at the vast outdoor Chapel of Phosphora. The Chapel was the central structure on the Cortanian island of Aeryresasma. The entire island was a safe zone, where no player could attack or in any way cause damage to another player. Only non-belligerent crafting or scrying was allowed.

In addition to the Pride members in attendance, there were many other friends of Rabbit outside of the lodge. Naomi smiled to herself as she checked the zone-stats. On this island, there were over 130 people, and all had come to pay their respects.

The chapel was a broad circular structure half a kilometer across, its seven arches fanning out from the glistening white center spire reaching 250 stories into the sky. The arches narrowed as they neared their mounting pillars in the ground, and afforded some shelter for the gathered against the light drizzle that fell from the grayness overhead.

The soft strands of Gluck's "Orfeo Ed Eurifice; Ballet" could be heard playing under the massive pavilion. In the center, a bluish-white flame blazed, suspended in a luminescent white ring. Slowly circling around it was a thin line of gold letters, so small as to be barely legible. Each person in attendance was waiting patiently to approach the dais and add their name to the ring, in memory of their lost friend. As the names were added, the text on the slowly rotating line was made smaller. As Naomi watched, the ring steadily grew finer and finer, a sign of Rabbit's appreciable popularity.

She had been at the memorial since it had begun that morning. She had scheduled use of the Chapel with ToC customer support, having spoken to a community liaison named Illyria. It was most often used for in-game weddings, but once in a while, the occasion was less celebratory. Illyria had been helpful and sympathetic. Although the memorial was only scheduled for two hours, more and more people continued to arrive, and the service was now in its fifth hour. Naomi was comforted by the attendance. Rabbit's legacy in the game was that of an immense circle of friends and acquaintances, who valued him enough to make time to attend his virtual funeral.

Her thoughts returned often to her conversation with Peter's sister. She had no idea what kind of funeral he had been given in his home town, but she hoped it was... well, that it was a good one. *If only they knew,* she thought to herself. *If only his family knew how much we loved him here. If only they could* see *this*. She felt the sheer number of people present would have pleased them, adding their names to the gossamer golden thread circling the weightless, shimmering flames of his memorial pyre.

She was seated in the inner-most arc of seats, nearest the dais. Next to her were her lodgemates Volley, Rico, Caveman and Arch-Duke. Seated nearby were Admiral Roukan and Rear Admiral Virrago, second in command. Theirs had been the first golden names to encircle the pyre. She smiled as she checked the clock, and realized they had been with her for five hours, patient, uncomplaining. Her in-game avatar mimicked Naomi's smile, as the tiny camera mounted over her screen picked up the movement in her face and translated it to the avatar, Vanda.

She smiled again when she saw a certain name appear in the waiting line. She keyed her talk-key and said in voice-chat, "Look who's here."

Volley said, "Who?"

"See her, Duke?"

After a moment, Duke nodded. "Yup. Sphairo."

Volley seemed confused. "Who?"

Roukan chuckled to himself. "Rabbit's girlfriend."

"Ex-girlfriend," Naomi corrected.

"Rabbit had a girlfriend?" Volley asked.

"Yeah, for almost two years," Naomi said. "It ended about a year ago, though. Sphairo wrecked him."

"Awwww. What happened?"

"She left the game and went back to WoW, is what she told him," Naomi said. "Went to him one day and said it was over, and she was gone. Poor Rabbit was so distraught over her. This is the first time I've seen her back since then."

"Wonder who told her," Roukan mused.

"The announcement went up on the forums a week ago. She still has friends here, apparently," said Naomi. She cursored over Sphairo's avatar and double-clicked, creating a private text channel to her. The window appeared in the empty space to the left of her screen. She typed, **Thank you for being here.**

After a few moments, came the response: NP.

Naomi closed the window, turned her in-game camera around and zoomed out, taking notice of the assembled. Of those who weren't waiting in the procession, most were either seated in the semi-circled couches or standing in groups by themselves. Mozart's "Lacrimosa" had begun to play; she frowned and wondered if the devs at Praelium knew their history about online funerals, and shook her head. Vanda shook her head with her.

"What?" Caveman said, apparently having noticed Vanda's frown and headshake.

"Recognize this song?" she asked.

"Yeah, kinda, but... no."

"Never mind then."

As she panned her camera out and reached its outer zoom, she wanted to see the rest of the surrounding area, as others had continued wandering in from the docks. "I'm going to cam out. Be right back," she said.

"Kay," answered Volley.

"Don't look up any skirts," said Duke.

"You can look up mine," quipped Virrago, who wasn't wearing a skirt, but who liked to flirt with Naomi anyway.

Naomi pressed a key combination on her keyboard, and detached her in-game camera from centering on her avatar, which allowed her to 'scry' a short distance from where her character was seated. This ability was an advanced one, and her range extended nearly 250 meters from wherever she was. It was as if she were a ghost, and could move among the game world unseen, like an astral projection. It left her character motionless and vulnerable, but she could return her view back to Vanda with a quick keystroke.

She sent her camera through the crowd, navigating as though she were walking herself. Many of the names were those she recognized from parties and big game events, and some were from the public forums whom she'd never met before. Most of them she didn't know.

All of them had names and lodge names over their heads. Except for one, a character standing off by himself, with no name and no lodge ID. It was a male human, wearing very ordinary clothes. Naomi brought her camera in closer. The clothes were unusual for a ToC character… they were plain, lacking the usual accoutrements of status, armor or power. The character was wearing simple denim jeans and a t-shirt. He had brown, mussed hair, and was watching the services alone.

Nobody in ToC wore clothes this mundane on his character, and she'd never seen an NPC dressed this way. Curiously, Naomi circled her camera around him. The character turned his head and looked back at her, following her movements. Almost as if it was looking at Naomi herself, beyond the screen, with unblinking blue eyes.

"What the heck…" she said softly.

She backed her camera view away from the character. He took a few steps toward it. She swung the camera around behind him. He turned to follow.

"Check this out, guys."

"What's up?" said Caveman.

"I'm looking at a new kind of NPC. Something that can see a scryer."

"Do what now?" Volley asked.

"Seriously?" asked Roukan. "No way."

"Yeah," Naomi answered, "check out this NPC over here, to my… oh… four o'clock. Human, dressed down."

"I don't see any NPCs here, Vanda," said Roukan after a moment.

"Keep looking, it's here. I'm looking right at him."

The NPC male smiled. Naomi felt a shiver. The smile looked… very personal somehow. She couldn't pin it down exactly, but something about him was unsettling to her.

"I gotta see this," came Caveman's deep, throaty voice as he got up from his seat and headed in the direction of Naomi's scry. "Now, where are you? Give me a name or something, someone you're standing next to."

"Okay, I'm standing next to a group of affistri. Their names are Ulas-Madra, Tima-Katel, Nala-Monek, and Seka-Rinil."

She saw Caveman come into her field of view. "See them?" she asked.

Affistri was one of the four playable races in ToC, and one of the most easily recognizable from their tall, dark violet bodies, small heads and breathing hardware covering their faces. They were a race of hardy, formidable people, but they could not breathe Earth-normal air without their respiratory packs. These were cumbersome, slowed them down, made hand-to-hand combat difficult, limited their clothing choices and lessened the amount of other equipment they could carry. As such, affistri characters usually stayed within affistri lodges where their atmospheres were controlled, and played on their homeworld, Iunia.

Caveman ran over to the affistri and looked around. "Okay, I'm here, now where's this NPC?"

Naomi blinked. "It's right here. Look. It's the human wearing blue jeans."

Caveman took a few steps back, clearly confused. "Facing the pyre, are you to the left or the right of the affistri?"

"To the right. Like four paces."

Caveman walked over. He was standing directly beside the NPC, facing away from the pyre. If he reached out his left arm, he would be able to touch the character.

"I got nothin," he said.

"What? You're practically right on top of him. Look to your left," Naomi said, with growing frustration.

"Nothing there, babe."

Naomi leaned back in her seat, her brow furrowed. "Okay, take one side-step to your left."

Caveman did, his avatar occupying the same space as the NPC. He stepped aside, and looked annoyed at Caveman, then back to Naomi.

"It reacted. You stepped on top of it and it moved away. It *looked* at you."

The NPC smiled again into Naomi's camera. A new kind of discomfort ran through her. The realization that it was not an unfamiliar smile at all.

"What the hell?" she breathed. Her face had gone pale.

"What?" Volley exclaimed, getting up from her seat and running over to where Caveman was standing.

Roukan cut in. "Vanda, you should see the look on your face," he said. "You look kinda freaked out."

Naomi found her voice again. "Caveman, you don't see him?"

"Nope, nada. There's nothing here."

Volley came running up. "I don't see anything either, Vanda." She was standing right beside Caveman.

Naomi's voice was low. "Guys, I'm going to ask you right now, once, and only once. If you lie to me now, I will be seriously, deeply, pissed at you all, and very hurt. You know how close I was with Peter. For the record… are you playing any kind of joke on me right now?" She spoke with a seriousness that they rarely heard from her.

"No!" Volley said, alarmed.

"No, babe. No one's playing any joke on you," said Caveman, in a comforting tone. "Tell us what you're seeing."

"I'm seeing… Peter."

"Rabbit?" Volley asked incredulously.

"No, not Rabbit." Naomi squinted her eyes at her screen. The face smiling at her was not Rabbit, Peter's avatar. It looked exactly like… *"Peter."*

"What?" Roukan asked, and began making his way over to them.

The character's smile dropped, and the NPC vanished altogether.

"Hey!" Naomi said, shocked.

"What happened?" Roukan asked as he joined Caveman and Volley. "Where is it?"

"It's gone," Naomi said. "It disappeared. Crap! I didn't get a screenshot!"

"That would have been a help," Caveman said.

"Yeah. Then you could have reported it," Volley said. "Someone made an avatar that looked like Peter? That's sick."

"That's not easy to do," Roukan said. "Someone would have had to spend a shitload of time on customization to get a face to match someone's actual, real-life face."

"It wasn't so much his face," Naomi said, remembering the chill she felt. "It was how it smiled at me. And it could see me scrying. It was like it was looking right at me… like…"

Roukan wasn't amused. "You need to put in a ticket. If you really saw what you're describing, it wasn't a player character. Otherwise, we would have been able to see him too. And you said it was an NPC, so it didn't have a name or lodge ID, right?"

"Right, it didn't."

"Then it couldn't have been a player. It was some kind of game creature. Maybe some dev is having a sick joke at your expense."

"That's totally what it is," Volley said. "How else can you explain that he could see your scry?"

Naomi was now bristling with anger. It was the only explanation that made sense. "That's… that's fucked up."

"Damn, Vanda, you look pissed now," Rico said, still sitting with Naomi's avatar in front of the pyre.

"Yeah. I am definitely pissed."

02.04

Saturday, November 14, 2026
To: Illyria
From: Vanda
Subject: Dev playing sick jokes

Hi Illyria,

I'm writing to report that someone on the dev team has a really sick sense of humor and played a really unnecessary and hurtful joke at today's memorial service for Petrillo Azevedo. I would appreciate it if the matter was investigated and handled such that I and other players can be assured that such flippant and insensitive behavior never happens again in ToC.

Here's what happened. At around 3:30 p.m. Eastern time, at the memorial service I arranged with you at the Chapel of Phosphora, I happened to notice an NPC that had arrived at the memorial. It was dressed in jeans and a t-shirt, and had face and hair made to resemble the deceased, Peter. I know this because Peter was a close personal friend of mine, someone whom I cared very much for.

This could not have been a player character, because there was no player name nor lodge ID over its head. Further, I first noticed it when I was scrying, and the character was following my scry with its eyes. It was able to see where I was looking and following me around while my avatar, Vanda, was still seated at the front of the chapel. No player character could have done that.

The character responded to other players in its vicinity, but those players could not see it. Apparently, I was the only one there who could. When we asked other players nearby if they had seen it, they all answered in the negative. They could only see me and my lodgemates, they saw no NPC in the area at any time. I trust that they are not lying to me.

All this points to a dev. It is my belief that someone on the dev staff knew Peter, was able to get a picture of him somehow, and fashioned a dev-controlled NPC character to attend the memorial service as some kind of joke. Or maybe he is testing out a new kind of NPC ability that can see scrys and be stealthed to everyone they don't wish to be seen by. I don't know, but if that were the case, it should be tested on the QA server and not in runtime, at a memorial, using an avatar that resembles the deceased player! This is the height of insensitivity and someone deserves to be reprimanded harshly, if not fired outright.

I wish I had captured a screenshot of the NPC character, but unfortunately the character disappeared before I had a chance. I would love to be able to show you just what I saw, to prove that I am not making this up.

Please pass this to the appropriate personnel on the dev team so that the matter may be investigated. If I see the character again, I will immediately take screenshots and send them on to you. I would appreciate being apprised of any developments in this matter.

Thank you,
Naomi René (Vanda)
Commander, Pride of the Guilty

* * *

Monday, November 16, 2026
To: Vanda
From: Illyria
Subject: TICKET No. C768762341-UA

Vanda,

I'm horrified that something like this could have happened. You can be assured I will look into this matter for you. I apologize in advance for what happened. I don't have an explanation for you, but I will see what I can find out. I can't say for certain whether it was someone on the dev team or not, but if this is the case (and your assumption seems reasonable) there will absolutely be consequences for the person responsible. Thank you for letting me know, and again, please accept my apologies for any distress it may have caused.

Once more, my sincerest condolences on your loss.

All my best,
Illyria
Community Liaison
Praelium Atlanta

02.05

Monday, November 16

Rocky Top Climbing Gym
Charlottesville, Virginia

"I don't understand anything you just said," Skyler said, finally.

"Someone crashed Peter's memorial, with an avatar that looked just like him. For real."

Skyler sat across from Naomi at the table in the visitors area, her purple Powerade bottle open but barely touched.

"What do you mean, 'for real'?" Skyler asked. "And how can someone 'crash' an online memorial?"

Naomi took a deep breath and tried again. "Someone went to a lot of trouble to make up an avatar to look just like Peter in real life. Peter, himself. Not his in-game self… Rabbit looks totally different. I mean his *real-life* self. I think it was a dev, someone who works for Praelium."

"Why would someone do that?"

"Don't know. To be an asshole. You know what the creepy thing about it was? It smiled to me."

"What's creepy about that?" Skyler picked up Naomi's bottle and took a drink.

"It looked just like Peter's real smile. I have plenty of pictures of him. We've talked on Skype. I know what his smile looks like. How that dev knew is beyond me."

"You're sure this was a dev?"

"Yeah. For one, it had no tag. If it was a player, it would definitely have a tag over its head. More than that, it was doing things that players can't do. Like, when I detach my camera from my avatar and fly it around the area, it could see where my camera was. It was tracking me with its eyes, and at one point, it followed me when I flew away. Players have no way of seeing other players' scrys."

"And it disappeared right in front of you."

"Yeah, plug-pulled as soon as Roukan was coming over to check it out."

Skyler shook her head and leaned back in her seat. They both looked over to the wall as a boy in his late teens gave a frustrated "Falling!" and slipped from his hold, dangling in the harness.

Sky gave Naomi a wry smile. "Louis. He hates slipping when there's girls in the gym. He gets really impatient and testy."

Naomi gave an unsympathetic grunt. They watched as he was lowered back down by his partner, then resumed climbing once more. The gym was busy at mid-day; a busload of small children from one of the elementary schools was here. Naomi was eating her lunch with Sky while she was taking a break.

"I hope he had as nice of a service in the real world," Naomi said after a few minutes watching the kids on the wall, their high-pitched voices echoing off the wide concrete walls around them.

"I'm sure he did," said Skyler.

"If I could have been there, I would have."

"I know."

"They would have hated me. They would have made me out to be one of the ones responsible for his death." She sighed.

"If you had been able to be there, I'm sure they would have accepted you as someone who cared about him, like they do," Sky said.

"I told you all the mean things his sister said to me. She blames me, and all his online friends, for not taking enough care of him."

"She was angry. I bet she regrets having made that call."

"I wish I knew."

"You going to be okay?" Skyler asked.

Naomi nodded. "Yeah. I've been thinking about that conversation we had, a while ago. The one about real friends. I'll never be convinced that Peter and I weren't real friends, but…" She offered a smile. "I'm grateful for the friends close by to me, too."

Skyler returned her smile.

* * *

That night, Naomi slipped into her bed, pulled the covers over herself and picked up the little remote that activated the oscillating fan across the room. She pressed two buttons on the remote, and the fan began softly stirring the air in the room with its gentle sweep.

She put the remote down and checked that her alarm clock was set, then picked up the tablet that almost never moved from the bedtable. She activated it and was greeted with the current page of the book she'd been reading. After trying for a few minutes to lose herself in the story, she gave up and put the tablet back on the bedtable again.

She closed her eyes, and settled into her pillow. A deep ache weighed heavy inside of her, and she tried to quiet her mind and surrender to a fatigue that promised blissful sleep. But the ever-so-familiar thoughts crept to the surface, as though making sure she hadn't forgotten about them since their last visit.

Alone again. No arms to hold you, no goodnight kiss.

Yep.

Those days are over. No one's ever going to want you again.

I know. Shut up.

Just saying. No matter how good a person you are, no matter how well you treat other people… no one wants to love you. And no one's going to love you, ever again.

Shut up! I know!

You're ugly. Unwanted. Disposable. And Peter's gone, one of the only people on this earth who understood you. No one's ever going to love you. Ever.

I know…

It was the last deliberate thought of her day. It was the last deliberate thought of most of her days.

Chapter Three
03.01

Three days later

Galon-Yarisis Outpost
Over Planet Phoenicis
Sector 351-R

Roukan's carrier *Lazarus Heavy* emerged from thruspace first, with a bright red flash. Six other ships arrived one at a time, flanking the mighty flagship. *Lazarus* was a level-75 capital ship, one of the most well-equipped and armored ships available to high-level players. Its slender, manta-ray shape was sleek for interstellar travel, but as it returned to realspace, it began unfolding weapons and rearward facing parabolas for energy transfers. The brutish rust-gray hull was pockmarked with battle damage, the registration numbers nearly obscured completely beneath splashes of dark, charred metallic brown. *Lazarus* had gone many months since its first launch without being destroyed in combat or PvP, and the old ship wore its damage like badges of honor.

The arrival of the attack fleet was enough for the station to take notice. Blast doors began slamming closed all around the perimeter, sealing over windows and exterior hatches. Batteries lining the defense rings stirred into action and circled into position against the approaching ships. The massive particle cannons lifted slowly toward the *Lazarus* and its attack fleet.

"Cave," Roukan said. "We're here."

"I see you," said Caveman, whose ship was already in stealth mode on the far side of the station. "No sensor flags yet." His ship remained undetected, even with the station's heightened alertness.

"Okay, Vanda, give me a Logic Barrage at the antenna array. Hazy, head for the port side, Speed, starboard side. Split those cannons up and keep them moving."

Once a ship in ToC was destroyed, it would be rebuilt again at the homestation within 12 hours. Each of the restored ships returning to attack the Galon-Yarisis Outpost had not only been freshly constructed according to their classes, but several weeks had been spent putting them through missions intended to toughen them up, regain lost weaponry and improve their performance. Vanda's destroyer *Destiny* was now a stronger ship than it had been when she last brought it to G-Y.

This didn't necessarily make the encounter easier. With the increased specs, and the addition of Roukan's carrier to the battle group, the game's AI would make the space station even more difficult to defeat. It would not be a battle of pure might. The lodge had to rely on guile, teamwork and a modicum of luck to complete their task and rescue the prisoner.

Hazy and Speedracer's corvettes were now better ships than they were before. Naomi's *Destiny* had stronger shielding, but more importantly, a more powerful ion propulsion drive. Volley had built a troop transport to replace Rabbit's ship, and was waiting just out of range of the outpost's weapons.

Naomi called forth the Logic Barrage, which was an EW attack intended to weaken the station's electronic defenses, forcing its computer to devote processing cycles to warding it off. The sustained barrage would bring weapons to bear on *Destiny* until it could be damaged, or she turned it off.

Roukan was in charge of the assault. "Rico, are you dropping buoys?"

"That's affirm," Rico said, as his ship made its lazy half-circle behind the fleet, positioning reflector buoys behind the capital ships. These buoys would serve as couriers for recharging energy, so they could channel the streams to whomever needed it most. If the *Dayquil* was in range of one of the buoys, it could send energy into any of the fleet's ships to assist with repairs. The only ship out of range of the buoys was the *Whispers of Mutiny*, stealthed on the far side of the station.

The first streaks of light began pouring out of the station now, reaching for the corvettes. "Weapons free!" Roukan ordered, and the Pride starships opened fire. Explosions erupted over the station's hull as energy blasts peppered the thick metal surface. ArchDuke began arcing away from the fleet to the port, to provide support to Hazy, cannons thundering away.

Naomi clenched her jaw as she tapped repeatedly at her keyboard's backslash-key, which fired her primary, forward-facing cannons. They had a 30-second cooldown before they could be re-used, and her eyes continued to return to that timer so that she could fire again as soon as possible. As the timer closed to two seconds, Naomi's fingers began hammering the key to fire the weapon the moment it was available again. Her destroyer's main guns could deliver a punishing blast to the station's hull, and frequently her salvos were met with panicked countermeasures before they were allowed to impact. Each one that made it through exploded with a vengeful fury.

Eventually, the station was sending too many countermeasures into her field of fire, and had effectively shielded her off. She put the *Destiny* into a starboard bank, which opened up her port firing arc to the station as she maneuvered around its perimeter. "Speed, I'm coming around behind you," she said in voice-chat. "Roukan, as soon as I clear Speed, I'll be in a position to make a run at the AMs."

"Copy that, Vanda," Roukan said.

The ring cannons were split between the corvettes and the *Lazarus*, spewing dashes of light in all directions. The air-defense batteries tracked Vanda as her broadside weapons lashed at the station's perimeter with bombardment.

Hazy keyed in: "I'm close enough to the AMs. I think I can get a shot off. Duke, can you cover me?"

"Got your back, Hazy. Give 'em hell," Duke said. Hazy put the *Sad Panda* into a lateral turn, moving her weapons into firing position against the station's antimatter reactors.

A large blast door opened behind the central command dome of the station, and tiny spacecraft began pouring out of the station in droves. They arced over the dome like a swarm of insects, then peeled off into streams and began needling the starships with tiny bolts of light.

"We got fighters," Naomi said.

"I see them. I'm launching," Roukan said. The presence of the carrier meant that the station would launch defensive fighters, as Roukan had come with his own fighter wing. Naomi swung her camera at the *Lazarus* and was gratified to see tiny ships launching from beneath the broad wings of the manta-shaped carrier, beating them back with tiny little slashes of their own. The dogfighting was controlled entirely by the computer; the *Lazarus'* fighters were flown by their own AI and engaged the G-Y fighters independently of the players, so they could stay focused on the capital ships. Without the counterattacking fighters, the G-Y's defense fighters would act like mosquitoes over the player ships, raking them with their incessant beam attacks, intercepting bombardment and being a nuisance. *Lazarus'* fighters would keep them occupied and out of the players' way.

Panda was closing on the AM reactors with her primaries. This time, the AA batteries were under heavy fire from Duke's frigate, and they exchanged powerful volleys. One of the ring cannons tried to aim at Hazy, but was stopped by damage in its track and sidelined. Duke poured extra power from ship propulsion into his weapons, finally overcoming the AA with his firepower. The battery exploded in a sudden pop of golden flames over the station's port side hull.

"Woohoo!" Duke exclaimed. "Got the port side AA. You're clear, Hazy."

"Taking the shot!" The blue-white twin bursts exploded from her main cannons and raced over the surface of the station toward the cylindrical reactor shells. With a bright flash, both bolts hit their target.

"Yes!" Hazy cried. "Direct hit!"

The flashes dissipated, revealing two deep, concave crushes in the reactor shielding. The bolts had not penetrated, but the damage looked severe.

"Good hit, good hit, Hazy," said Roukan. "Okay, Vanda, are you ready?"

"Ready," Naomi said, lining up the *Destiny* at the station again.

"Hazy, you get clear; Duke, cover Hazy and line up for another shot at the AMs. I'm moving in for the feint."

"If I get another shot at the AMs, I'm taking it!" Duke insisted.

"Negative, Duke."

"Even if I can take them out? You want me to hold back for no reason?"

"I want you to hold back. I'm willing to bet you won't get another shot at the AMs," Roukan said. "The station's already launched a bomber wing. Cover Hazy."

"Fine," Duke said.

Roukan began moving. *Lazarus Heavy* advanced on the station and fired a powerful salvo, announcing its challenge. The station's twin particle cannons slowly rose up from their berths to meet it, and Caveman detected the charge.

"Twenty seconds to firing," he reported from the silence on the far side of the station.

Lazarus slowed its approach, each nozzle mounted on the leading edge of its wingspan firing in sequence. Vanda watched as the starboard-side AA guns swiveled towards Roukan's ship.

"Incoming AA," she warned.

The AA was not aimed at the *Lazarus.* It unloaded a stream of plasma fire at the exposed *Dayquil Shortbus,* Rico's recharge and logistics cruiser. The bolts streaked harmlessly beneath the carrier and impacted the *Dayquil*'s port side, cutting off its replenishing stream to *Lazarus.*

"Holy crap," Rico exclaimed, the attack taking everyone by surprise. "I'm shock-stalled." The ship wasn't destroyed, but it took enough of a hit that its major systems were temporarily disabled. "Roukan, I can't recharge you for a bit," he advised.

"Copy that," Roukan said. "Damage meters are in the 40s and falling. We'll see how long I can last."

The swarms of fighters filled the space between the cruisers like angry bees chasing each other. Occasionally they would burst afire in tiny explosions. "Vanda, you'd better start your attack now," the Admiral said.

"Okay," Naomi answered Roukan as she pushed her ship aggressively forward, cannons pounding at the station. "Here I come!" Her ship accelerated toward the particle cannons.

The station's heaviest weapons turned in the direction of the *Destiny,* detecting a more immediate threat from her than from the carrier.

"Ten seconds to firing," Caveman reminded them.

"Back off, Speed," Naomi said. "You don't want to be anywhere near this."

"Belay that, Speed," Roukan countered. "Don't give away the game, keep covering Vanda."

"Uhhh, okay," Speed responded. The *Texas* continued exchanging fire with the ring cannons.

A sudden, thunderous explosion erupted from the *Sad Panda* on the far side. "I'm hit!" Hazy cried.

"It's the fighter-bombers," said Volley. "They're using torpedoes!"

"Switch defensive batteries to flak," Roukan ordered. Each player changed over their outboard cannons to cease launching salvos at the station and instead begin spreading a cloud of metallic fragments toward the incoming fire, to create a defensive screen through which a torpedo would have more difficulty penetrating.

"Five seconds! It's coming at you, Vanda!"

Naomi could see the blue glow deep at the back of the cannons as they prepared to rip into her ship again. "No stopping me now," she said, smiling. "I'm increasing to flank speed."

"Now, Speed! Evasive! Get as much distance as you can!" came Roukan's order.

The *Texas* began banking away as the particle cannons unloaded on the *Destiny*. The cannons sliced straight down the long axis of the ship, bursting fragments of the hull outward along the sides. Carried on its momentum, flaming, *Destiny* continued forward, coming nearly in contact with the cannon nozzles themselves before its new ion propulsion reactors breached, and exploded in a devastating white blast. The shockwave hit the station full force, collapsing the particle cannons instantly.

"Yes!" Naomi exclaimed. "The particle cannons are toast!"

"Yeah, so am I," Speedracer groaned, with *Texas* also taking a hit from the blast wave of the *Destiny*'s kamikaze run.

"Good job, Vanda," Roukan said, the satisfaction clear in his voice. "Now this is the hard part… Rico, how close are you to—"

As Naomi panned her camera away from her decimated, flaming ship toward Rico's *Dayquil Shortbus*, she was startled to see another explosion suddenly rip out of its dorsal section.

"Shit! Torpedo got through!" Rico cursed.

"What's your damage?"

"My capacitors are down to 20%. I can charge you but not much."

"It'll have to be enough. Speed, can you take out that starboard side AA gun?"

"I'll try but I'm kind of caught out in the open over here, and that shockwave hit me pretty hard."

"All right, I'm moving in. Volley, let's go, I'll cover you. Caveman, you awake over there?"

"Just catching up on my nudie magazines," said Caveman in his deep voice. Naomi smiled. "Tell me when," he intoned.

"Start heading this way, Cavester. Slow and quiet. Come under the station and take it real patient."

"Comin' to you." The *Whispers of Mutiny* began a slow creep toward the fleet. "Be there in about sixty seconds."

Lazarus Heavy began moving toward the station again, and Volley's troop transport *Of Course I Still Love You* fired up its engines and banked. As *Lazarus* pounded the station with its forward batteries, Rico aimed the recharging streams into its rearward-facing dishes, trying to keep the flagship replenished.

"Hey," Caveman spoke up. "There's another ship on approach."

"Do what?" Duke said, surprised. "From where?"

"Check your shortrange."

Naomi instinctively glanced down where her short range scanner would have been, but as her ship had been destroyed, she had no access to her ship's scanners. She swung her camera around, trying to catch sight of the approaching ship.

"I see it," said Volley. "It's NPC. Can the G-Y call for help? That's not part of the mission, is it?"

"Not that I'm aware," said the Admiral. "Duke, where are you?"

"I'm above the station trying to clean up these AAs," Duke reported.

"Can you move to intercept?"

"Not for a minute or two."

"Why would an NPC ship be here at all?" Volley said. "From the size of it, it looks—oh crap…" she trailed off.

"What?" Rico asked.

"I'm being hacked! I just lost propulsion," she said, sounding panicked.

Naomi frowned. *Destiny* had been serving as their EW platform, with Caveman waiting in the wings to cover their escape as soon as Volley had put in and then extracted the insertion team. Now that *Destiny* was destroyed, they were caught without electronic warfare defense, and the station had recovered from the Logic Barrage. Roukan could call on Caveman to fire up his EW now, but the *Whispers* was still dangerously vulnerable by itself. Now that the station had resumed EW attacks, they would quickly lose their advantage.

"Is anybody below the base?" Roukan asked.

"Nope," said Speedracer.

"No." ArchDuke.

"Not by much." Hazy.

"All right, I'm moving low to cover Caveman. Cave, when I get to within two clicks, fire up your EW. I'll try to keep them off you so you can get beneath me."

The carrier dove, picking up speed, aiming beneath the facility. The G-Y's ring cannons racked together and took aim at the carrier, firing relentlessly. With the giant capital ship in a dive, its forward batteries were no longer trained at the station and it had to rely on its point defense batteries to protect it from incoming fire. It wasn't nearly enough.

"Hey," Rico said, "where's that little ship going?"

The new arrival began firing point defense of its own to protect it from the exchange of fire. It slipped directly into the path of the main hatch of the station.

"It's blocking the hatch!" Volley said. "I won't be able to dock!"

"You can't dock," Caveman chuckled. "Your ship's hacked, babe."

"Well, why don't you get your slow ass over here and unhack me," Volley chided him.

"I go any faster," he said, "they'll torpedo me and then you'll be on your own."

Naomi was watching the NPC ship move into position against the station and dock. "It's a troop transport," she observed. "What the hell is it doing?"

"Rico, AA incoming!" Duke called out, as he realized the station's AA guns were training on the *Dayquil*. The fleet's sole recharge ship had trailed the *Lazarus* dangerously close to the station, and was again in range of its lethal anti-aircraft batteries. The AAs opened fire, striking the *Dayquil* with both blasts. The impact sent the ship into a slow flaming twirl.

"I've had it," Rico said as his ship spiraled in space, finally igniting into billows of white-hot flames, spewing debris outward.

Naomi's eyes didn't move from the little ship attached to the station. It seemed almost as if…

She pressed a key-combination on her keyboard, and her camera detached from the tiny lifeboat floating in space near where the *Destiny* exploded. She wasn't sure if she had range enough to scry as far as the station hatch, but she sent her camera flying in its direction. As it neared its effective range, she could barely make out the name on the side of the chunky troop transport.

She squinted at the screen, then quickly began taking screenshots to capture the image into picture files.

"Hey, guys?" she said.

"Yeah?" Roukan answered.

"That ship that's attached to the station?"

"What about it?"

"It's the *Irritable*."

There was stunned silence in the chat. After a few beats, Hazy broke the silence with her characteristic grace.

"Get the fuck out of here."

"I'm looking at the hull. 'Irritable Vowel', plain as life. I'm getting screencaps. I'll post them."

"It's that dev again," Duke said. "What the hell are they doing?"

"You can all see it this time, can't you?"

"Yeah, Vanda. I can see it," Duke replied.

"I can see it," confirmed Hazy.

"Whatever they're doing, are they interfering with our mission?" Volley asked as her ship listed in space, slowly tumbling. "If that's Rabbit's ship and it's docked to the station, do you think it might be putting in an insertion team? And that it's getting Hazy's platoon leader out?"

"I've never seen anything like this," Naomi said softly. "Why would some dev be playing with the account of a lodgemember who's… who's dead? Just to mess with us?"

"That's the creepiest thing," Hazy observed.

Rico agreed. "Somebody ought to lose their job for this shit."

"Did you hear back yet from that community liaison, babe?" Caveman asked.

"Not yet," Naomi said. "But she's going to be hearing from me, with these pictures. I don't believe this. Can anyone get nearer to it for a better view? I can't scry any closer."

"It's too hot to get in any closer," Duke said.

"If it is extracting the prisoner, maybe it will bring him to Volley and dock with her," Roukan pointed out. "Let's see what it does."

Naomi moved her cursor over the mysterious ship and tried to click it. Had the ship belonged to a player, she would have spawned a pop-up menu giving her the option to chat with it, among other things. But no menu appeared for her. "It won't let me send a message."

"Duke, if you're going to stop these AAs, I'd appreciate it if..." Speed said as the station took aim at the limping *Deffenbroken Texas*, the cannons unloading before he could finish the thought. The bolts exploded into the ship's rear quarter, decimating the propulsion drive and causing secondary explosions throughout the ship.

"Never mind," said Speed. "As you were."

"Who's left?" Roukan called out.

"I'm still here," Hazy replied, "but if I take a torpedo hit, I won't be able to cover our evac, and I need to get clear of the station in case that little ship is on our side."

"That's fine, Hazy," said Roukan. "You fall back. Who else is left?"

"I'm here, but I'm hacked," Volley said. "I'm out until Cavey can unhack me."

"I'm above the station taking a lot of fire," said ArchDuke, "but I'm hanging in."

"Looks like it's on you, Rou," said Naomi. "You and our mystery guest."

"Cave, get set to fire up EW and ready a Logic Barrage," Roukan said, closing the distance to the stealthed *Whispers*.

"I'm set."

Naomi kept her camera trained on the transport docked at the base; her heart was pumping with anger. If this was a dev, and they were masquerading as Rabbit's character in the game, there was no justifiable reason for it. Massively multiplayer online games like *Cortanis* were well understood to be havens for jerks and antisocial behavior, especially in player vs. player zones where lower-level players were regularly ganked by higher-level players, whose only interest was to be bullies. Even things such as the infamous "gank & camp" behavior, wherein high level players would kill a lower level one, then "camp" over their dead body, were often complained about but accepted as typical behavior in PvP zones. As with any online community involving anonymity, there would always be a certain number of players who devolved into their baser, less civilized instincts.

All that being the case, this kind of abusive behavior from a game dev was unheard of. Whoever was piloting that little ship had gone into Rabbit's game account and was now using his ship, and probably his character, to play. And not as a player, but as an NPC. Naomi wondered if it might be possible for someone outside the game company to have hacked into the system and commandeer another player's account like this. But if someone had simply hacked his account, his name and lodge ID would be showing. Furthermore, the game character's name would be showing in her contacts list as being online, which it wasn't. *Unless he's blocking*, she reminded herself. Players could hide their online status if they chose, but their Social page would still show they had signed on that day. She called up the site, logged in, and checked Rabbit's account.

LAST LOGIN: MONDAY, OCTOBER 12

So, Rabbit's account was *not* logged in, and hadn't been since over a month and a half ago.

As she watched, the ship suddenly detached from the station and began accelerating away, in the direction of the *Dayquil*'s relay buoys. It seemed to be making for the *Of Course I Still Love You*.

"It's undocked," Naomi said. "Volley, it's coming toward you."

Roukan had just reached the *Whispers*. "Okay, Cave, now! Light em up!"

The *Whispers of Mutiny* powered up and launched toward the *Lazarus*, bombarding the G-Y with its electronic warfare. "Logic Barrage up their ass," Caveman said as he activated his ship's primary weapon. The *Lazarus* began a lateral port spin as the *Whispers* ducked beneath its massive hull for protection and continued beneath, heading for the evac point.

"It's coming right toward me," Volley said nervously, watching the little transport. "The station isn't firing at it, either."

Naomi furrowed her eyebrows and stared. Sure enough, the station seemed to be completely ignoring the transport. "Weird. Volley when it gets close to you, can you grab some screencaps? Especially showing the name of the ship? I want to send those in to Illyria."

"Yeah, sure, Vanda. As soon as my engines are back up, I'll be able to dock with it. If that's what it's wanting to do."

The *Whispers of Mutiny* and the *Lazarus Heavy* accelerated hard away from the station together, with *Lazarus* protecting the smaller ship with its massive hull. "Everyone get ready to evac! Duke, Hazy and Cave, get ready to fire your FTLs."

"Copy that," Duke said, blasting away at the station's ring cannons that had trained on him when they lost their attack angle on the *Lazarus*. "Coming about."

The little transport ship slid up beside Volley's, and slowed. "Guys, it's wanting to dock with me. My propulsion just went green. I think it wants to transfer the prisoner over."

"Accept the dock, Volley," said Roukan.

Naomi watched the two ships slowly link together. After a few moments, the ships separated again.

"I'm getting pictures, Vanda. Lots of them. It's definitely Rabbit's ship," Volley said, "and it gave me the prisoner."

"Can you send it a message?" Naomi asked. "Try and double-click it."

"Nope. Won't let me select it."

The *Lazarus Heavy* and the *Whispers of Mutiny* had reached the two transports and continued charging by, the smoldering, defeated Galon-Yarisis Outpost behind them firing petulantly in their direction. "All ships, go for FTL!" the Admiral ordered.

Naomi watched as what was left of her victorious fleet ignited their thruspace drives and disappeared in starbursts of light one at a time, until she was left alone with the mystery ship. The base's defenses had fallen silent. She stared at the little transport as it turned slowly and began moving toward her. She felt another chill pass through her. It seemed to know exactly where she was looking from, and was drawing nearer to that point in space. As if it wanted to look *back* at her.

"Vanda, you coming?" said Volley.

"Be there in a bit," Naomi said. "I wanted to see if the ship followed you. Now it's coming toward me. Let's see what he has in mind. Maybe he'll talk to me."

She waited as the transport made its way silently toward her.

"The station still isn't firing at it," Naomi reported, studying the ship as it approached.

"Weird," said Caveman.

"Another win for the *Lazarus*," said Duke, congratulating Roukan on keeping his ship's victory streak unbroken.

"We got the prisoner! Yay, Hazy!" Volley said. All eight players received an increase in experience points, or XP. As the attack had been carried out as part of Hazy's mission series, it was primarily her success, but all participating players were rewarded for their assistance.

Naomi took no notice of the glowing green bar that pulsed on the right side of her game interface. She watched curiously as the troop transport glided right up to where her camera was, which was not attached to her lifeboat at the side of *Destiny*'s destruction.

"It came right to my scry. It's slowing."

The ship slowed to a stop, and then Naomi received a message that made her heart skip and the color drain from her face.

RABBIT: What a GDCF

She gasped. The private text message was sent only to her; none of the others could read it. Naomi stared in shock for a moment, and was about to reach for the talk key when another message appeared:

RABBIT: Don't tell the others, please

Naomi took a breath, then slowly exhaled it and moved her finger away from the talk key. Now that whoever it was had messaged her, she could message back. She double-clicked on the name in the chat window, which allowed for a reply back to that player. She typed:

VANDA: Who are you?

She held her breath, waiting for a reply.

RABBIT: It's me

Now her fingers were shaking.

VANDA: No you're not. Who are you really?

She waited, staring at the little troop transport ship hanging in space in front of her camera. She tapped the screencap key a few times, capturing the image on her screen, including the text messages in a separate file. She would be sending all of this to Illyria, as further proof that someone on the dev team was playing insensitive games with her friend's account. After a short pause, the response arrived.

RABBIT: It's me, Peter

"What?" Naomi said aloud to herself. "You've got some cheek."

VANDA: The hell you are, Peter's dead, asshole

She stabbed the 'return' key furiously, staring at the screen, bristling.

RABBIT: It's me

Incredulous, her fingers raced over the keys, fueled by her fury:

VANDA: I don't know who you are or what shit you are pulling but it isn't funny and you are talking to one of Peter's best friends, you prick

The others were excitedly discussing the next leg of the mission among themselves, which involved delivering the freed prisoner to a nearby military installation. Naomi tuned them out. All her concentration and focus remained on the blinking cursor beneath the last line of text, where the response to her text message would come.

The next message brought her up short.

RABBIT: You can ask me anything, Naomi

So he knows my name, she thought to herself. That meant it was either a dev who had access to player accounts—strictly in violation of Praelium's privacy policy—or it was someone who had hacked her account as well. She didn't like that second possibility at all. *Okay, asshole, let's see how much about Peter you think you know.*

VANDA: OK tell me what you're getting your mom for Christmas

She tapped the 'return' key with a satisfied grunt and leaned back in her chair, folding her arms. The response came quickly.

RABBIT: Nothing, she's dead

Her jaw set. This dev had done an impressive amount of stalking. *Okay, let's see if you can explain a few things...*

VANDA: How come you're not logged in?

RABBIT: I'm not?

VANDA: No. You haven't logged in since October

RABBIT: Well I am here

VANDA: How can you be here if you're not logged in?

RABBIT: I'm just here

VANDA: Where is here?

RABBIT: Galon-Yarisis outpost right in front of you

VANDA: How can you see me?

RABBIT: I just can

She slapped the desk with her hand. Her patience was wearing thin with this joke.

VANDA: Who the hell are you??

RABBIT: Naomi why don't you believe me?

VANDA: If I call your sister right now and ask her where you are, what is she going to tell me?

RABBIT: I have no idea

VANDA: When was the last time you saw her?

A long pause followed. Then:

RABBIT: I think it was when she was leaving to go pick up dinner. She came in to ask what to get

VANDA: What did you tell her?

RABBIT: A misto quente

VANDA: Did she bring you one?

Another long pause.

RABBIT: I'm sure she did

VANDA: Why don't you know?

RABBIT: I don't remember

This had gone far enough. "Hey guys?" she cut in on voice chat.

Volley was first to answer. "Yeah, Vanda?"

RABBIT: Please don't tell the others

She paused, seeing the new message. How on earth could he have heard her?

VANDA: Tell who, what? she typed back.

RABBIT: Don't tell the pride that I'm talking to you, ok?

VANDA: How do you know I'm talking to the pride?

RABBIT: I can hear you

Bullshit! Naomi thought, her fingers furiously tapping out her response.

VANDA: Liar. I have no way of knowing who you are, why should I believe that you're Peter? Go fuck yourself!!

"Vanda, did you want something?" Volley asked.

"This joker is insisting he's Peter," Naomi said. "He's really trying to make me believe that he's alive!"

"He's talking to you? In tells?"

"Yeah, he's been sending me tells for the past few minutes. He knows Peter's mom is dead, he even knows my real name—"

RABBIT: Thanks a lot

Naomi froze. The transport turned away from her and began moving toward the outpost.

VANDA: What are you doing?

RABBIT: I thought you were my friend. Goodbye Naomi

The little transport opened fire with its main batteries. The outpost came alive, racking its remaining rail cannons together toward the *Irritable Vowel* as it accelerated and continued firing. Vanda felt a sudden sinking feeling, for the first time wondering if perhaps Peter could have actually been talking to her, somehow.

VANDA: What are you doing? she repeated.

There was no answer. As Naomi watched, the G-Y trained its guns on the tiny transport ship. A hundred streaks of light erupted from the station's weapons and pulverized the vessel, quickly blowing it apart in a burst of billowing flames and debris. Naomi's jaw dropped and her fingers began trembling. The outpost stopped firing as quickly as it had started, falling silent again, tiny flickers of flame glistening over its surface from the damage it had sustained during her fleet's assault.

VANDA: Are you there?

<RECIPIENT UNAVAILABLE>

Now she didn't know. Her heart beat faster in her chest as she thought hard about what had just happened.

"Vanda?" Volley sounded concerned.

"Yeah," Naomi said, her voice shaking.

"You okay?"

"I don't know," she said softly. "I really don't know now."

03.02

Thursday, November 19, 2026
To: Illyria
From: Vanda
Subject: Re: TICKET No. C768762341-UA

Hi again Illyria,

Today, during an assault on the G-Y Outpost with my lodge (Phase 3 of Aristarchus) someone showed up with a troop transport just like one my friend Rabbit (Petrillo Azevedo) used to fly. Same name, same class. No player name or lodge ID. I tried double-clicking it as if it were a player, and got no pop-up menu. This time, other people with me saw it too. It assisted us with the mission, and after the rest of my fleet jumped back to our homestation, it stayed behind and started talking to me. I'm attaching screenshots for you to review. This time I took several. You can see the entire conversation.

I'm very bothered by this, Illyria. Whoever this person is, he knows things that he shouldn't know. He knows my name, my real name. He knows that Peter's mom died. He seems familiar with Brazilian meals. Again, bizarrely, he could follow my scry from across the area. And he seemed to be able to tell when I was talking to my lodgemates in voice-chat and what I was saying, even though nobody other than us was logged in. He made a direct reference to a private chat the real Peter and I had before he died.

This is really creeping me out. If this is a dev, they're being assholes to a severe degree, they're abusing their position and it's very, very distressing to me. They are taking this to a level that is well beyond "funny" and into the realm of "privacy-invading." I miss my friend terribly and this is emotionally abusive. Can you tell me if any progress has been made on your end in investigating what happened at the memorial service? And can you look into whatever server logs there may be from the G-Y assault today on your end, and see what you can find out about who this is?

Another thing that was weird. The G-Y Outpost did not fire on the ship until he attacked it. It was acting as though the ship wasn't showing up as hostile, or even as a player ship. Any player ship in the area during the assault would have been assumed to be hostile and the base should have fired on it. As you can see from the screencaps, the conversation I had with him was at a proximity to the base that was well within firing range. But the base did not fire on him until he fired first, and it also did not attack him as he docked with it and extracted the prisoner during the assault earlier. It was treating him as though he were NPC. Just something else I thought of, hope it helps.

Thanks,
Naomi René (Vanda)
Commander, Pride of the Guilty

* * *

Friday, November 20, 2026
To: Vanda
From: Illyria
Subject: Re: Re: TICKET No. C768762341-UA

Naomi,

Thank you for sending me these images. I can see right away that there is something very unusual about the encounter you had with this person.

I've done a little work on this issue since I emailed you last. I can confirm that your friend Peter's account has not been used since October 12th, and no one has logged into his Social page either. Whoever is impersonating him is not using his account directly to do it. I can also confirm that his IP address has not been used to access the game servers since his account's last confirmed login.

As for how this individual is able to shield his name and ID tag, I have not been able to answer this satisfactorily. I will continue to look into this with the dev team here.

In the meantime, I cannot help but wonder… are you absolutely sure that your friend has in fact died? I don't mean to be insensitive, please do not take umbrage at my asking, but if it were me, I'd want to make doubly sure that the original claim of your friend's death was bona fide. We both know that people sometimes fake illness, tragedy or death when they choose to abandon an online game. I know you don't feel your friend would do this to you, and I sympathize, but I would want to make absolutely sure. It would answer the question of his familiarity with you and the things he knows.

However, it leaves other questions unanswered. I will continue to pursue this issue on my end.

All my best,
Illyria
Community Liaison
Praelium Atlanta

03.03

Later that evening

GAZETA DO POVO
OBITUÁRIO
Lista de falecimentos 22/10/26
Petrillo Gutierres Azevedo, 27, nasceu 1999, morreu 20 de outubro de 2026. Filho de Vítor Azavedo e Ecilda Marques Azevedo. Sep. ontem.

Naomi had only been on Google for a few minutes before she found the obituary in the online newspaper. She copied and pasted the line into Google Translate, and it returned: *Petrillo Gutierres Azevedo, 27, was born in 1999, died October 20, 2026. Son of Victor and Azavedo Ecilda Azevedo Marques. Sep. yesterday.* Another quick bit of searching told her that "Sep." was an abbreviation for the Portuguese word for "burial". She took the iWear set off and leaned back in her seat, feeling the loss again, her shoulders drooping as the sadness seemed to melt the strength out of her muscles. There was so much more to Peter than this simple line of obituary, buried in with dozens of other similar, unfairly brief statements of finality, gave.

The lyrics of Ria Aubergine's "Dollhouse" floating from her computer's speakers on their soft saxophone bed seemed to thicken the emotion in her heart, like weight being steadily piled onto a burden, dragging her down.

The door is dark, no one answers
The ringing of the bell
Only blackness, silence, stillness
An abyss of absence, void of hell

I lay without life
My eyes empty
Lost soul
Am I here, where is here
Am I someone, am I nothing
Till someone plays with me
In my dollhouse

There was that time Vanda and Rabbit were using personal cloaking devices to keep themselves hidden from another player in the same room. Naomi had laughed so hard when he absent-mindedly opened and then closed a door, to leave the room, not realizing until after he had done so that the door opening and closing was perfectly observable by anyone who happened to be looking. It all but announced their presence. She thought she would choke from laughing, the ridiculousness of his blunder had so tickled her, she'd nearly collapsed out of her own chair.

There had been so many in-game parties, so many hours spent grinding their own characters' levels up, and helping others in the lodge run mission after mission, attacking and infiltrating bases, unlocking special equipment, vessels and costumes… so many good times.

Was all of that worth *nothing*, just because it was shared online rather than in the real world? Was she really his friend at all? Or was she just another made-up name on an ephemeral, digitally modeled character avatar on the screen?

His family seemed to think so. She looked at the glass rectangle that lay on the black rubber charging mat on her desk. She reached for it and touched the surface. It lit, displaying the biometric thumbprint boxes and the time. She pressed both thumbs into the boxes for a moment, and the phone unlocked, showing her home screen. She brushed her fingers over the smooth clear surface, looking to see if the phone still logged that awful conversation over a month ago.

It did.

She scrolled back to the entry showing the last time he called her. There it was, the week before. She stared at the date.

WEDNESDAY OCTOBER 21

Wait…

She checked the date on the obituary again. She frowned, and an uncomfortable realization dawned. Clearly the date of his death, and that of his funeral, were misprinted. But had she spoken to him only hours, or even moments, before he had died? Why didn't he say something was wrong?

He did sound a little strange that day.

One touch more would place the call. She wondered if his sister might answer again. Maybe the number had been forwarded to her phone. Her finger hovered over the button, trembling. Would she refuse to talk to her? Would she scream at her and berate her?

Her finger touched the number as if on its own, a tiny spasm in her joint. She immediately moved to cancel, but instead, reluctantly she brought the phone to her ear and took a deep breath. After a few moments, it started ringing through. She began praying no one would answer, and if a voicemail system picked up, she would hang up. She waited.

A click.

"*Ola,*" came a woman's voice.

Her heart raced, her mouth suddenly dry. She swallowed and forced herself to speak: "Hello, I'm... Naomi René. Is... is this Renata?"

There was a bit of a pause before the woman answered. "Hello, Naomi. I am Renata," she answered, her voice soft.

"Hi... Renata. Um, I... I'm sorry, I don't really know why I am calling. I just needed... needed to talk to you for a moment."

Silence.

"Are you there?"

"I am... glad you call."

"You are?"

"I said terrible things to you when I called you before. I want to tell you I am sorry."

Tears spilled down Naomi's cheek at these words, and she fought to keep the sob from her voice. "It's okay," she managed to whisper.

"I should not have blamed you. Is not your fault he did not take care of himself. I was... very angry and upset."

"I really appreciate hearing that." Her voice wavered. "I would have been mad at me too, if I were you."

Renata seemed to take a deep breath on her end of the line. "You were Peter's friend. He talked about you sometimes. He liked you very much."

Naomi closed her eyes, feeling more tears gathering in her eyes. "Yes," she whispered, "he was my very good friend. I miss him very much. And I want you to know," she said, regaining her voice a bit, "that I was not with him for the period of time he wasn't taking care of himself... he was not playing with me. He was doing other things, and not sharing them with me. I didn't know what he was doing."

"He was acting funny those last... few days."

"Can I ask you something? A personal question?" Naomi asked.

"Yes, go ahead."

"What was the last thing you and Peter talked about?"

Renata sniffled as she thought. "I go to visit him, and I see he is not looking well. I ask him if he has eaten, and he said no. So I tell him I go to get dinner for him."

"What did he say?"

"He ask for a ham-cheese sandwich."

Naomi swallowed. "A *misto-quente*?"

"Yes, that is what he ask for. I instead bring him much healthy dinner. How do you know that?"

Naomi could hear her heart pounding in her ears as she stared into space. Whoever that was at the G-Y knew.

"Hello?" Renata prompted.

"I'm sorry," she replied, coming out of her brief reverie. She wasn't sure if she should tell Renata that someone had been impersonating him in the game yet. "I... I didn't know that. I just know he liked *misto-quentes*." Naomi looked up at her screen, still showing the obituary. "What... day was that?" she asked.

"What day?" Renata said. "It was... *Terça-feira*, not sure English word. I don't remember date. *Tuesday*. Yes, Tuesday. Funeral was *Quarta-feira*. Wednesday."

"What was his funeral like?"

Renata described the experience of saying goodbye to her brother. Naomi was surprised at how differently funerals and interment were done in Brazil. Peter had been buried before a day had passed, the funeral mass held a week later. The mass, held at the cemetery itself, was not only for Peter, but also for numerous others at the same time. While their mother's side of the family had been composed and grieved softly, their father had a very difficult time controlling his emotions, which she had not expected given the strained relationship between him and his son. In Brazilian culture, this was uncommon. "Men do not cry," she said. Once they had returned home from the funeral, her father had locked himself in his bedroom and rarely was seen for over a week. Their neighbors had provided meals and comfort for them, making sure Renata was looked after and that her father was all right.

Naomi listened quietly to Peter's sister share her feelings about his death. Finally, she thanked her. "*Gracias*, Renata," she said. "Do you say '*gracias*' to mean 'thank you' in Portuguese?" she asked.

"We say '*obrigada*'," Renata gently corrected her, "and you're welcome. I am sorry I was so angry at you before. I am grateful you called."

"Me too. It means a lot to me that you talked to me."

"Thank you for being my brother's friend," she said softly.

"I'll miss him very much."

"Yes. Me too."

After Naomi had said goodbye to Peter's sister and hung up, she sniffled and whipped a tissue out of the box to dry her face. She missed Peter now more than ever, and it didn't matter that they had never once been physically in the same room.

Misto-quente. The most troubling part of the call was the sandwich. Somehow, *impossibly*, whoever was impersonating Peter in the game knew about the sandwich he had asked for. Whoever it was knew one of the very last things Peter had done in his life. This was deeply unsettling to her.

She placed on her iWear set on again, adjusting it up the bridge of her nose. She logged on to Social, and went to Rabbit's profile page. There, she clicked the "send message" link, and a window opened with a text field. She sniffled as she typed her message.

> I miss you. A lot.
>
> Your friend,
> Naomi

She clicked "send". She knew no one would read it. But it comforted her a bit, to be able to at least send the message.

03.04

The next day

Ivy Creek Natural Area
Charlottesville, Virginia

The Ivy Creek Natural Area was on the north side of Charlottesville, with six miles of trails through 215 acres of natural preserve. Naomi and Skyler walked there on weekends when the weather was pleasant. Ivy Creek was unlike many other area parks in that it was considerably more restrictive. Dogs and bicycles were not allowed on the trails, which lent them a certain serenity, free from the interruptions of oncoming cyclists and other people's animals. Even jogging was discouraged.

It was nearly winter in Virginia, but not so bitterly cold as it would become after the new year. The two women wore jeans, hiking shoes and sweatshirts, with Naomi's orange and navy blue sweatshirt bearing the swords and capital V of the Virginia Cavaliers. She walked with her hands in the sweatshirt's front pockets, her ponytail hanging over one shoulder, her eyes on the path just in front of her.

"How long did you talk to her?" Skyler asked, her Canon EOS-V SLR camera suspended from the strap around her neck. They were walking the White Trail as they often did, a wide, flat path that connected with the Red Trail to form a circle nearly a mile in length.

"About twenty minutes, maybe," Naomi said.

"It was brave of you to call her," Sky observed.

"I really don't know why I did it. I wanted her to know I wasn't some random idiot in ToC. And tell her how sorry I was that he was gone."

Skyler nodded. "That was a good thing."

"She said something that bothered me, though."

"What was that?"

"When I saw Peter's ship the other night, and spoke to whoever that was pretending to be him, I asked him what the last thing he said to his sister was. He said it was to ask for a sandwich. And while I was talking to Renata, I couldn't help asking her the same question: what the last thing he said to her was. She said he asked her for a sandwich. A *misto-quente.*"

Sky walked a few paces more in silence.

"How could they have known that?" Naomi asked.

"Lucky guess?" Sky offered.

Naomi shook her head. "To ask for that specific kind of sandwich? And something else is weird, too. Remember that time he called me when we were at Rocky Top?"

Sky nodded.

"That was Wednesday the 21st. His obituary says he died the day before. And Renata told me he died on Tuesday… that was the 20th, not the 21st. She said they *buried* him on Wednesday. Why would they both have the date wrong?"

"How was her English?" Skyler asked. "Did she speak fluently?"

"Not really. She was kind of searching for the English word for days of the week."

"So maybe she just mixed up the English word," Sky said.

"I guess that's probably it. Still, it doesn't explain the obit date being wrong."

"Well, there's nothing to be done about it, is there?"

Naomi frowned. "I don't know. I'm wondering if there was a way I could find him."

"Who, that person in the game who's pretending to be Peter?"

Naomi didn't answer.

"Why? Why would you want to find him?" Skyler pressed. "To punch him in the face?"

"I don't know," Naomi admitted. "I guess it's stupid. I just feel like I let him down, that's all."

"Let who down? Peter? How did you let him down?"

"I can't explain it," Naomi sighed, kicking the toe of her shoe through some leaves. "It just really hasn't been the same since he hasn't been with us, for me. The others seem to have gone back to their regular selves. But I can't shake this weird feeling that Peter's …" she trailed off.

"What?"

Naomi shook her head. "Nothing. It's stupid."

"Okay, so tell me anyway."

"I just feel like… like Peter left a part of himself behind. In the game."

"I don't think that's stupid."

"No?"

"No, that's what makes whoever is playing a joke on you such a jerk. Because they're making it harder for you to let him go. They're toying with your feelings. Here you are still blaming yourself for what happened to Peter. You've *got* to let go of that. It was *not* your fault."

Another person came up on the path, and Naomi stepped behind Skyler to give him more room to pass them. He offered a polite smile, and continued past. For a few minutes, the two women didn't speak. Naomi walked with her eyes down, her thoughts stirring. Sky occasionally lifted her Canon to snap a picture or three, and took a few moments to glance at the camera's little display before moving on.

"I wonder if… if you played in ToC, if you would even recognize me," Naomi said.

"You mean, without knowing your name?"

"Yeah."

"Do you act differently in the game than you do with me?" Sky asked.

"By miles."

"How are you different?"

"I'm happier… quicker with jokes and stuff. More sociable and open." She laughed a little. "I really doubt you would know it was me at all."

"What made you think of that just now?"

"I guess I was wondering if we would even be friends, if we only knew each other in the virtual world."

Sky answered immediately. "That's easy: no, we wouldn't, because I don't spend time in virtual places, so we would never even have met."

Naomi looked at her. "If I sat you down in front of my computer and logged you into ToC with your own character, what do you think you would do?"

"I wouldn't have the first idea what to do."

"You'd probably be quiet and reserved around other people, wouldn't you?"

"Maybe. I mean, they could be perverts or axe murderers, how would you know?"

"The guy that just went past us could be a pervert," Naomi said.

"Well, he didn't talk to us. Anyway, if he had, I would be able to form an opinion about him from his manner, his voice, his body language, you know. And I'd kick his ass if he tried anything."

"Okay, but if he was an axe murderer, and wanted to hurt us, he's in a much better position to do that standing in front of us than he would from somewhere else in the world. We took the risk of being attacked by an axe murderer the moment we stepped on the trail," Naomi said.

"That's why we come together," Sky said. "Anyway, we can't live our lives cooped up in our houses for fear of axe murderers. There's too many beautiful things to see and take pictures of."

"I guess I'm just saying that the 'me' in the virtual world is just as much 'me' as the one you know. But both 'mes' are totally different, and you only know one of them. I kind of wish you knew both sides of me."

"I like the you that I know."

"I hope you would like the other part of me, too," Naomi said.

"Of course I would."

"I'm not so sure."

"Because I don't like happy people who are open and quicker to make jokes?"

"I don't know, you might perceive me as overconfident, maybe."

"Why are you confident in the game, but not here?"

"Because I feel safer, I think," Naomi said, after a thought. "I don't feel like people can judge me. I feel insulated, being an avatar. Vanda's tougher than I am. She's got a thicker skin. Vanda doesn't let that stuff bother her."

"I thought Vanda is you," Sky said simply, lifting her camera to her face again to frame up a squirrel bounding over a tree branch. Her camera beeped and made a soft shutter-click sound as it captured its image. The squirrel chittered at her. "You just said."

"No, Vanda isn't me. She's *part* of me, but she isn't me."

"Why can't you let that side of you influence the rest of you? Have you ever tried to 'be Vanda' in real life situations where you feel nervous, or scared to be around people?" Sky said while examining the pictures of the squirrel she'd just taken, slowing her gait unconsciously.

"Dr. Ellery and I used to talk about that, when I was still going to him. I've thought about it. But it's really not the same at all."

"I know it's not the same, but what makes it different?"

"I think part of it is body image. Vanda is cute. I'm not really."

Skyler looked at her. "You're cute!"

Naomi smiled gratefully. "Thanks, but no I'm not. Not nearly as cute as she is. I've never been *that* attractive."

"Attractiveness is all in how you feel," her friend offered. "It really has almost nothing to do with how you physically look."

"They say that, but I know I'm not attractive and have never been attractive." She was frowning.

"You sound like Jerry," Skyler said, stopping on the trail and looking pointedly at Naomi. "That's Jerry's voice coming out of you, not your own."

Naomi turned to face her, but didn't reply.

Skyler went on. "I know he made you feel that way, but you really have to purge those shitty words and ideas from your head. Don't give them any more power over you."

Naomi shrugged, not meeting her eyes. "I guess sometimes I don't know the difference between his voice and the one in my head now. But even before Jerry, I was never all that pretty. Monica really got all the good looks between us."

"Everyone is beautiful in their own way."

"What if my way of being beautiful is in the virtual world?"

"I don't accept that," Skyler said. "I think you're beautiful as you are, standing right here."

"I wish I could," Naomi said, and continued walking up the trail.

03.05

Later that day

After showering, Naomi dressed in her usual tee, sweatpants and merino-wool socks. She grilled a bologna and cheese sandwich, split it down the middle and poured a small pile of baked potato chips on a plate. Grabbing a bottle of apple juice out of the refrigerator, she took the juice and the plate up to the loft, pulling her chair back with her foot and dropping herself into it.

"How are we doing, LEM?" she asked, and took a bite of her sandwich.

"Very well, thank you, Naomi," answered LEM's polite voice.

Naomi reviewed the processor activity charts. Most of them were in the upper 80s and low 90s; LEM had had another busy day of thinking. "So what's been on your mind today?"

"There has been a buzz of conversation on the ToC forums since yesterday," LEM replied. "Praelium has announced that they are going to make it possible for SimMind characters to play in *Tides of Cortanis*. Would you like me to join you in the game, Naomi?" LEM asked.

Naomi's eyes brightened. "Really? You'd have a character that could come with me in the game world?"

"Yes. They have worked out a way to make their platform allow for root integration with those on which I am based. I will be able to choose my own avatar, skill tree, equipment and so forth."

"Do you want to play?" Naomi asked.

"Yes, I do," LEM replied. "If you wish to play with me."

"I think I would like that, LEM. What are some of the things that factored into this decision for you?"

"Having an avatar body and moving through a virtual space would be a new experience. Also, the opportunity to interact with multiple people at a time appeals to me."

"Do you have an idea about how you would handle that?"

"My primary attention would be on you. I don't believe I should be in the game without you there."

"I agree, I think that's best."

"It is one of the more actively debated points, I have found. Many people feel that having advanced AIs in the game will diminish the game experience."

"Because they'll be competing for drops?" Naomi asked.

"Yes, and in PvP they will be unbeatable because they have no limitation on response time, nor do they suffer exhaustion. Based on feedback in the forums, it is likely that Praelium will not allow SimMinds to do more than serve as healers in PvP zones."

"Do you want to play PvP, LEM?"

"No, there is little point."

"Yeah. Something tells me your interest in ToC has nothing to do with proving anything to anyone."

"That is correct."

"Well, we'd have to talk about some ground rules for you, if you're going to be gaming with us. But I'm happy for you to join me. In fact, I'd be interested in talking to you about something Skyler and I were discussing earlier."

"What's that?"

"If you create a character for ToC, you will be seeing how I relate to others in the game world, and I'll be interested to discuss your observations of me after you've had a few months or so to compile them."

"Please rephrase."

Naomi took another bite of her sandwich, leaned back in her chair and folded her arms. "Sky and I were talking today about personality, and how it can be splintered, depending on context. Sky only knows me in the real world, so she has never seen my personality as it is exhibited in *Cortanis*. Are you following me so far?"

"Please help me integrate the concepts 'personality' and 'splintered'."

LEM was an advanced artificial intelligence, but at times its limitations made it seem like that of a small child. When confronted with two concepts that it could not reconcile, it would stop the conversation and ask for Naomi to help it understand them. She tried to be patient with these interruptions, and sometimes had difficulty getting LEM to understand certain things.

She sighed, and concentrated on her words. Having to read and understand law every day as part of one's job made her careful with language. "Okay. You know what personality is, right?"

"Yes, there are over a dozen definitions, and I believe I understand the commonalities among them. Personality is the essential character of a human being as manifested in their behaviors, emotions and ideas."

"That's a very good precis. Now, you've known me for how long?"

A pause. "Is that a question?" LEM asked.

"Yes, I'm sorry. How long a time have you known me?"

"It has been three hundred eighty-five days and twenty-one hours since I was first initialized on this computer. Generally speaking, I have known you for one year and one-half months."

"Would you say you understand my personality?"

"Yes, I would."

"How would you describe me, LEM?"

"Having no experience with other human beings, I am unable to select characteristics which might be extra-normal from general human behavior. However, I can observe certain consistencies to your personality over our time together."

"And what would those consistencies be?"

"You are behaviorally methodical. Intelligent. Gentle. Inquisitive. Lazy. Peaceful."

"Wait, wait. You think I'm lazy?" Her smile was widening.

"Yes, you are not inclined to rigorous activity."

"That's not true, I was just out walking with Sky, and I work out at the gym every other day."

"You asked for my personal observations."

"Okay. I should point out that calling someone lazy will cause them to take offense."

"I see. I was not aware of that. I did not mean to be offensive."

"I know, but I think you can expect to find a lot of people will respond negatively to you in the game world, LEM. You don't know how not to be objectionable to people."

"Am I objectionable to you?"

"No, but that's because I don't expect you to understand all the nuances of etiquette and social graces. And everyone has different things that will make them angry."

"I will stay with you so that you can correct my behavior in case I make someone angry."

"I think that's a good idea. Anyway, going back to lazy... since you never see me working out or doing anything strenuous, you describe me as lazy?"

"I am only able to describe those behaviors I witness myself."

"Right, that is how you perceive that aspect of my personality. But people at the gym, who see me working out, or those who saw me with Sky on the trail today, do you think they would perceive me as lazy?"

LEM processed for a moment. "No, they would perceive you differently."

"This is how a personality is splintered. Personality is something I have innate in me, but it is also something that is perceived by others, and that is how it can be split into different... sides," she struggled with finding the right word.

The SimMind took another moment to absorb this. "Other people can only be with you for limited spans of time, so they see only the parts of your personality you manifest during that time. In this way they may form an incomplete understanding of it."

"That's correct, yes, but the truth is, no one *ever* has a complete understanding of anyone's personality. Not even ourselves."

"Do you not understand your own personality?"

"I have an understanding of myself that is limited. I am unable to see many things about myself that other people do see."

"Would you give me an example?"

Naomi folded her arms and thought for a moment. "Well, okay. Today Sky said that I was cute, meaning she thinks I am attractive to the opposite sex. I don't agree with her. Sky told me that she thinks my opinion of my own attractiveness is influenced by my ex-husband, who believed I was very unattractive and told me so many times as we were divorcing."

LEM processed this for a few seconds before responding. "Is Skyler a lesbian or bisexual?"

"No. It's possible to be heterosexual and still be able to judge whether someone of our own gender is attractive or not."

"I see." He processed for a few more moments before speaking again. "What you have told me about your divorce included many references to Jerry being unkind to you. His referring to you as 'ugly' was such an unkindness. I believe he was attempting to hurt your feelings, not be truthful about how he actually perceived your appearance."

"It's also possible," Naomi pointed out, "that Sky was telling me she thinks I am attractive because she is being kind. Maybe she wasn't being truthful about how she actually perceives my appearance. Since I told her I don't believe I am attractive, she may have been saying that to cheer me up."

"You believe you are not attractive, but Skyler claims to believe that you are."

"Right, and maybe she really does believe that I am. Maybe more people believe I am attractive than I think. In that case, she sees that about me when I do not. But that's not a great example because attractiveness is so subjective. Let me try again." She thought another moment. "I guess a lot of things about personality are subjective, and open to interpretation. Say I took two showers a day. I might think I was just being clean, whereas someone else might judge me as being obsessive about being clean. And they would probably be right."

"Your opinions are different. But neither of you are wrong."

"So, why would it matter? It would only matter if I cared what they thought about me."

LEM took another few moments to process. "I see. You are interested in knowing how other people, whose opinions you care about, perceive you."

"Yes, that's right. Very much so. Pretty much everyone is."

"This is in conflict with the common advice people give when they say other people's opinions about you should *not* be important."

Naomi chuckled. "Yes, that's true, but it's human nature nonetheless. The reason that advice is so common is because so few people innately understand it. And it's something I should do a better job of following."

"Naomi, your phone is ringing. This call is coming from Dunwoody, Georgia, near Atlanta."

"Atlanta?" Naomi said curiously, trying to remember whom she would know in Atlanta. She could not hear her phone, as she had left it downstairs. "Who did you say is calling?"

"The caller is identified as Ben Cross. It will be picked up by voicemail in eight seconds."

Naomi quickly hurried down the stairs and opened her purse on the kitchen table where she'd left it. Taking the phone out and looking at the screen, she saw the call was indeed sourced from 'Ben Cross' as LEM said.

She answered the call. "Hello?"

A male voice on the other end greeted her. He sounded serious. "Hello, I'm trying to reach Naomi René."

"This is," Naomi replied. "Who's this?"

"Hi, Naomi, my name is Ben Cross. I work for Praelium, I'm a developer on ToC. I'm sorry to call you on Sunday, I hope I'm not disturbing you," he said.

"No, it's all right," Naomi said. "What's this about?"

"It's about your friend Rabbit. I need to talk to you, and it's kind of important."

"What's going on?"

"Listen, I… I really think it's best if we meet. This is not something I'm comfortable talking about on the phone."

Naomi's eyes widened as she realized what he was asking her. "You want to meet with me? Like, in the real?"

"Yeah. I know it's a lot to ask, but I think you need to hear what I have to say."

"Are you aware of my… issue regarding Rabbit?"

"Yeah, I've been working with Diana… she goes by Illyria. That's her community liaison name."

"That's who I've been working with, yes."

"She's had me looking into this thing. And since Rabbit was your friend, I… don't think it's best to share it with anyone but you directly. I know, it sounds really kind of cloak-and-dagger, but it's really the best way."

"Why can't we meet in ToC?"

"Because I don't want ToC… to know that we talked."

Her eyebrows knotted tightly together in confusion. "You what?"

"I don't want there to be any way this gets back to my superiors. What I have to tell you could get me in trouble," Ben replied quickly. "That's why I don't want to say it over the phone and can't say it in the game where it'll be logged. I can tell you what I've found out about your friend, but if you really want to know, I need to meet you."

"Answer me one thing," Naomi said. "How do I know you're not the one behind it?"

"Everything that happens from our end can be traced back to exactly whoever did it. I'd have been fired and out on the street within the hour."

"Okay, then how do I know you haven't been already?"

"Check your inventory tomorrow evening. I'll have given you something that will prove it. And look for an email from Chopper. That's me."

"You're Chopper? I know who you are. You're kind of *Cortanis*-famous."

"Well, maybe." He gave a nervous chuckle, though she knew he was just being modest. As a developer for the world's biggest MMO, he was something of a minor celebrity. Players who interacted regularly with Praelium on the forums eventually knew the names of many of the developers. Ben wasn't as front-and-center as some of the others, but he had enough of a profile on the staff that his handle was recognizable. "Listen, think about it, and let me know if you want to meet. If you do, I'll meet you wherever you want. I know this week is Thanksgiving… will you be traveling?"

"Yeah, I'm going up to see my mom and sister in Maine for the weekend."

"When is your flight?"

"I'm flying up there Wednesday, coming back Sunday. I'll be landing in Richmond, Sunday mid-afternoon. I'd have to check my itinerary for the time."

"Richmond would be easiest. The airport, after you touch down."

"So, you'd fly clear up here just to talk with me about this?"

"When you hear what I have to say, it will make sense."

03.06

One week later

Richmond International Airport
Richmond, Virginia

Richmond International Airport was about a ninety-minute drive from Charlottesville, on the far side of the metropolitan area. Naomi watched the city of Richmond smoothly glide past beneath the plane as it made its approach, seeming to quicken as it loomed closer and closer through the window. Finally, the runway markers raced past and the plane touched solid ground, pitching forward to bring all three sets of wheels down. Its engines howled, slowing the aircraft to taxiing speed.

Her heart was racing. Not from the flight or the landing, but from what was coming after. The circumstances surrounding the meeting with the Praelium dev were nothing if not mysterious, and Naomi still regarded him warily. However, as promised, an object had appeared in her inventory when she logged into the game Monday night after work. It was a Quantum Cookie, something devs—and only devs—handed out at in-game events to players, either as prizes for trivia games or unique mission rewards. A Quantum Cookie was a rare, single-use consumable, meaning when Vanda ate it, she would receive some kind of in-game ability bonus, or even perhaps a new ability for a pre-set duration. Then the Cookie would disappear from her inventory.

She also had received the promised email, which had been sent by "Chopper" from a Praelium mail address. The email referenced the Quantum Cookie and said that it would give her the ability to "hyperjump", meaning for a short while after consuming the Cookie, she would be able to leap hundreds of meters into the air and land safely without taking damage. This would allow her to cover much longer distances more quickly than if she had to run. She had never heard of such an ability. It was enough to prove that Cross wasn't lying about being a Praelium developer.

Naomi decided to take him up on his offer to meet, making sure he agreed that they meet in public, and that Skyler would be coming too.

He'd arranged a flight to Richmond for the following Sunday, which would arrive an hour before Naomi's flight from Maine touched down a little after 1:00 in the afternoon. Skyler had agreed to meet her at the airport and drive her back to C-ville after the meeting.

As she stepped through the double doors at the end of the boarding ramp, she smiled as she spotted Skyler in the crowd. Most of the disembarking passengers headed for baggage claim, but Naomi had only her carry-on. Her trips to Maine were frequent enough that she didn't need to bring much in the way of clothes. She kept a few outfits at her mother's home during her visits, which cut down on the amount of luggage she needed to travel with.

"Hey," Skyler smiled as Naomi approached her. "Good flight?"

"Yeah, but I couldn't sleep," Naomi said. "Good Thanksgiving?"

"It was good." Skyler fell in step beside her. "How's Monica and mom?"

"Everybody's good." Naomi smiled. "Mom has a new friend. Says I might get to meet him for Christmas."

"Well, that's exciting," Skyler said. "I hope everything works out." She looked at Naomi. "You look exhausted. Good thing I'm driving you home."

"Yeah. I'm glad you came. Usually I can nap on these hops to Maine, but couldn't get my brain to slow down. Couldn't stop thinking about this meeting."

"Did he send you a picture of himself?"

"No, but I know what he looks like. He was on one of the panels at CortaniCon last year. I saw him. I didn't get to meet him, but I saw him well enough. He said he would be wearing a bright orange Praelium logo cap, and a brown leather bomber jacket."

"Don't tell me you sent him *your* picture."

"Yeah, I sent him a picture of Vanda."

Skyler smirked.

"No, of course I didn't," Naomi said. "I just sent him a description of myself and a description of you. We're supposed to meet at the Sky-High restaurant in the atrium. He's supposed to already be here," Naomi said as she checked the time, quickening her walking pace. "Let's go."

They found the Sky-High in the central atrium, which acted as a hub between the security checkpoints at the entrance to both A and B concourses. A man wearing a bright orange cap and a leather bomber jacket was seated at one of the tables with a bottle of Coke and a tablet computer in front of him. He recognized Naomi and Skyler as they made their way over to him.

"Hi," he said, pushing back from the table and standing. "You must be Naomi." He offered his hand.

Naomi shook it. "Hi, Ben. This is my friend, Skyler."

"Nice to meet you." He shook her hand as well. "Why don't you have a seat?"

"I'll sit over there and read," Skyler said, gesturing to another table. "I'll let you two talk."

"Thanks," Naomi said to her. Ben nodded his gratitude.

Naomi sat across from Ben and unzipped her coat, letting it hang open. "Hope you haven't been waiting too long?"

"About an hour. Just been reading." Ben appeared to be in his late twenties, possibly Middle-Eastern heritage based on his complexion and dark eyes, but his English was fluently southern-American. His coat was also open, and beneath it he was wearing a dark colored shirt that read 'GOT ROOT?' in white lettering. A tiny frameless pair of rectangular lenses were perched on the bridge of his nose.

"I saw you at CortaniCon last spring," Naomi said, "before *Contagion* came out. I was in the audience."

"Oh, yeah." He smiled, shaking his head. "That was a crazy time. I was getting four hours of sleep a night, tops. We were all sleeping at the office. The run-up to *Contagion* was intense. The con in the middle of it was such a blur, I barely remember it. Your friend there," Ben nodded in Skyler's direction. "Does she play?"

"No, not at all."

"Oh, okay." He seemed uncomfortable as he glanced at her again.

"Sky's not someone who will break confidences. If I talk to her about this, I trust her not to tell anyone else."

This seemed to satisfy Ben. He nodded.

"So," Naomi said, "what... is this all about?"

Ben took a pull from his Coke and swallowed it. "I've been thinking all morning trying to come up with how to describe it to you," he began. "I don't fully understand what is going on. But I know this much: whoever is impersonating your friend Rabbit isn't a player, and it isn't a dev."

"So someone hacked the game from outside."

"If someone was controlling it from a client, we'd be able to see the commands the client is sending to the asset."

"The asset?"

"Everything in the game is either an asset or a character. If it's a character, it's controlled by a player running the *Cortanis* client software. If it's an asset, that means its actions and parameters are governed by the game itself, server-side. I've established that it is not a character, so that makes it an asset by default. The bad news is, I'm unable to determine what's controlling its behavior."

Naomi studied him as he spoke. "You keep saying 'it'. So if 'it' is an asset, it's controlled by the game. Is that what you're saying?"

"For me to continue, I'm going to have to violate my NDA, so just… okay?"

Naomi nodded seriously. "I understand."

"*Cortanis* is written on a programming platform that we created. It's called Condensation," Ben went on. "It was developed from the ground up expressly for ToC. The thing that makes it effective is that it generates most of its own code. You know how ToC is described as a *procedural* role-playing game?"

She nodded again.

"The game comes up with new content as the players play it. What people don't know about ToC is how *smart* that process is. It watches everyone playing, at all times. Not only what they're doing in-game, but *how* they're behaving. It listens to conversations. It databases all voice-chat and learns, constantly. Nobody has any idea how much the game actually watches them as they play. And it writes its own code to manage the assets it needs to respond to what it *thinks* the player wants to do. That's the thing—it writes a lot of its own code. Praelium keeps that technology under tight wraps, and we all have to sign nondisclosure contracts before we're even allowed to work on the tools used to administer the game from our end."

"It's no secret that the game pays attention to our conversations. It serves up advertising on Social, like cable."

"Yeah, it does that. But it also tailors each player's experience to them individually, to keep them interested. To get them into a state of 'flow' so they stay engaged. It's very intelligent in this regard."

"Well, that sounds rather creepy, but what does all this have to do with Rabbit?" Naomi asked.

"What I'm saying is, the game is writing a lot of code that we, the developers, don't always know what it does or what it's for. There's this data pile that we just call 'the database' because we don't have any better notion of what's in there, that the game uses. It adds and adds to that. Whenever a player explores a planet, everything about that planet is generated by and stored in the database. Whatever is impersonating Rabbit, whatever is controlling that asset... is coming from there."

Naomi stared. "You're saying the *game* is pretending to be my friend?"

"Something has... manifested. That's the best explanation I can give you. Unless there's an undiscovered back-door into the database that allows someone to control an asset without using a client. That's the only way I can describe it. And if we, the developers, don't fully understand how data is piled up and organized in there, it's very difficult to imagine someone else from outside does."

"Manifested." She didn't like how that sounded.

"Yeah. Until a week ago. Then it just disappeared."

"When, exactly, did it disappear?"

"Saturday sometime."

Naomi frowned. "That was the last time I saw it. It attacked Galon-Yarisis right in front of me and got blown up."

Ben pushed his glasses up his nose. "Yeah, I wanted to ask you about that. According to the server log, it turned and opened fire on the station, when the station wasn't reading it as a hostile."

"Yeah, the station ignored it. It docked, got the prisoner, undocked, and then docked with one of my party's ships. The G-Y never took a shot at it until it drew aggro."

Ben looked away, gazing at the lines of people waiting at the Concourse B security checkpoint. "That means the station didn't consider it to be part of your party, but a neutral non-player character."

"An NPC that just swam into the middle of a station assault and put in an insertion team," Naomi observed. "Why wouldn't the station take notice of that as a hostile act?"

"The simple act of docking with the station isn't intrinsically hostile. A player's ship wouldn't be allowed to do that because as soon as it gets in firing range, the station decides it's hostile and defends itself. Only an NPC would have been able to do what that ship did."

"This is what I really want to know, Ben. Why did it *look* like Rabbit at the funeral? I mean, not Rabbit. It looked like Rabbit's *player*. His actual, real-world self."

Ben frowned, shook his head and took another drink from the Coke bottle. "That I really don't know. That's completely fucked up."

Naomi's eyes fell to the table. "It's like he's a ghost."

"In the Shell."

"That's not all that funny," Naomi said, glancing up at him with irritation in her eyes.

"I'm really not trying to be funny," Ben said apologetically. "The truth is, I'm freaked by this. I don't know what is going on with this thing, and I don't know how to control it. Or even whether it can be controlled. Right now it's gone dormant, so I can't even run experiments on it to see what measure of control I might figure out."

"Is it going to come back?"

Ben paused a moment before answering. "That's the fifty dollar question. Do you want it to?"

She drew a breath to respond, and her tongue pressed behind her teeth to begin the word, but she knew before it could be spoken that she wasn't fully sure if it was the honest answer.

Finally she released the breath she had intended to be 'no'.

"Look," Ben said gently. "I know he was your friend, and I know you cared about the guy. But I think I know a way to get the asset back, if you want."

"How do we do that?"

"You go on a mission."

Naomi squinted at him. "A mission."

"A mission quest."

"I know what a mission is," Naomi deadpanned. "You're saying I can take a mission that will help me find Rabbit?"

"The game will have to lay it out for you," Ben said. "I can get one started. I can't tell you what form it will take. It will write the mission expressly for you. If you accept it, then ToC has to see it through. If you complete it, then it should manifest the asset and hopefully we can then get a better idea of what it is."

"You said it's just for me," Naomi said. "Can I get help from my lodgemates?"

"No," Ben said, shaking his head. "I can't control for that many parameters of input."

"What does that mean?"

"If I initialize the mission to result in a particular thing, like the Rabbit asset, it has to be based on the input parameters of only one player."

"What are input parameters?"

Ben thought for a moment. "It's like your aggregate player profile. The longer you play ToC, the more the game learns about you. Like I said, it watches your gaming style, your habits, what kind of encounters and activities you do better at than others. These are all input parameters, characteristics about your playing experience that the game uses to generate and tailor content for you. If we want the mission to result in the Rabbit asset being spawned, I need to let it initialize the mission based on your parameters so it knows what steps to lay out for you. Too many people in the mix, we wouldn't know whether Rabbit would show up or not."

Naomi nodded slowly, with vague understanding. Then she had a thought.

"What if I did it with LEM? My SimMind?"

"You're running a SimMind?" Ben asked.

"Yeah. I've had him for over a year now. He's pretty smart actually. I was talking to him not long ago about how ToC is integrating SimMinds into the game as avatars. He seems interested in doing it."

Ben's eyes unfocused as he considered this. "Yeah," he said finally. "Yeah, I don't see why your SimMind couldn't tag along with you. They don't have input parameters of their own. Are you really going to let it play?"

"Well, I probably could use all the help I can get," Naomi said. "If I'm going to be soloing, at least I can get him to heal me."

Ben nodded. "Makes sense."

"If I'm successful, what do I do then?"

"Call me. I want to be monitoring the runtime server logs, wherever you are, when the asset appears again. I want to see if I can run some root controls on it. See if I can figure out more about where it's coming from."

"How do I start?"

"I'll put a mission token in your inventory. Look for it tomorrow night. You'll need to take it somewhere to activate it. That should start the first phase."

"Can you control its duration? Or the number of phases?"

Ben shook his head. "I can't, no. You can probably expect it to be a longer one. But it won't be impossible. The game doesn't want you to find it so frustrating that you stop playing."

Naomi nodded, and looked at him. "Okay, let's do it."

"You've got my phone number," Ben said. "Give me a call when you find Rabbit. I'd appreciate it if it was during the workday, but even if it isn't, I can log in from home and run a few programs."

"All right. Can I email you?"

He shook his head. "Better not. The company logs all that stuff. If you need to reach me, best do it over the phone."

"Okay. Phone only." She thought a moment. "Can I ask why you're so interested in doing this? You didn't know Rabbit."

Ben shrugged. "I don't like the idea of someone knowing more about our database than we do. Particularly if they're able to hack in. And if the game itself is coming up with this, on its own… well, that weirds me out even more. I just want to know what we're dealing with here."

"Yeah. Me too," Naomi said.

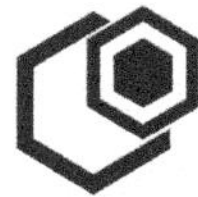

Part II

As I, my real self, grew older, I entered more and more into the substance of my dreams. One may dream, and even in the midst of the dream be aware that he is dreaming, and if the dream be bad, comfort himself with the thought that it is only a dream. This is a common experience with all of us. And so it was that I, the modern, often entered into my dreaming, and in the consequent strange dual personality was both actor and spectator. And right often have I, the modern, been perturbed and vexed by the foolishness, illogic, obtuseness, and general all-round stupendous stupidity of myself, the primitive.

"Before Adam", Chapter XI
Jack London

Chapter Four
04.01

The next day

Praelium Atlanta
Sandy Springs, Georgia

Ben Cross swung his car into an empty parking space on the third level of the garage. The garage was attached to the high-rise office building in the Concourse at Landmark Center campus, located on Atlanta's north side. Concourse was the centerpiece of one of suburban Atlanta's largest business districts, sporting a clutch of glass buildings dominating the north side.

The King and Queen Towers were its signature feature, twin 34-story buildings differentiated by their unique lattice 'crowns'. The squarish crown sat atop the King while a rounded one signified the Queen. The towers appeared to be comprised of four different buildings fused together, each successively taller structure narrower than the last, and twisted at different angles from the one just below. Until recently, these had been the tallest suburban buildings in the United States. Around them, other buildings seemed to compete for attention in the skyline, but none were more recognizable than these shimmering fortresses of modern commerce. Several Fortune 500 businesses were headquartered within their austere blue-green glass. Praelium's offices were in Concourse Corporate Center VI, the King Tower, inhabiting the levels between floors 15 and 24.

He stepped out of the garage and looked over Lake Rita, taking a moment to enjoy the tastefully arranged arcs of the fountain in its center. On the far side of the water, an eight-story L-shaped building reflected the sky in its banded glass windows. The building was designated Center One.

The servers for *Tides of Cortanis* were located beneath. Security protecting them was hidden from the public eye, but as this same facility operated servers for numerous other game worlds as well as enterprise services for major international corporations, it was defended with military-grade architecture, equipment, and personnel.

Ben did not have clearance required to visit the servers in Center One as he wished, but he did have access to all parts of the *Cortanis* game world and the development software used to maintain it.

He had seen the inside of the facility once though, on a facilities tour when he first started as an employee. The server stacks had looked more like a nuclear reactor than the broad, mazy rooms he'd been accustomed to. Three vertical columns reached nearly five stories down amidst a sophisticated cooling system that circulated currents of air between them. Separated from the outer walls, the individual server blades could be accessed only by automated robotic arms for retrieval and maintenance. He'd noticed that the hexagonal arrangement of the towers reminded him of the ToC logo icon, and he wondered if the logo wasn't deliberately designed with this "easter egg" in mind. As he had peered over the rail into the darkness of blinking server lights, he was struck by how much it resembled a starry night sky, reflected in still water. One couldn't visit the servers personally without coming away amazed.

From the outside, it was just another office building. It didn't look like the kind of place where you might find an entire alternate reality consisting of spaceships, star systems, aliens and intergalactic intrigues, he thought. As he circled around the lake toward the King Tower, he wondered if any of the thousands of people working in the buildings surrounding this lake had any idea there were entire virtual universes operating there. He also couldn't help but wonder what other secrets were buried on all those hundreds of thousands of petabytes that hummed night and day beneath Center One.

The cardkey in his wallet was unobtrusively scanned as he walked past the box near the front entrance, the glass doors sliding open for him as he approached. Ben gave the security guard a low wave of his hand before disappearing into the corridor of high-speed passenger elevators. He sometimes hooked past the lobby doors into David's, the café at the foot of King Tower, to pick up a croissant and a bottled soft drink. This morning, he'd had time to make a quick batch of scrambled eggs before he left home, and he didn't feel like standing in line anyway.

Ben's office on floor 22 was shared with three other developers, but the window more than compensated them for the lack of personal privacy. The view faced south over Lake Rita and, in the distance, the downtown Atlanta skyline. Game developers commonly worked in shared office spaces, and Ben considered himself fortunate that he liked his colleagues. His workstation consisted of three different computers, the most powerful of which drove three 24″ screens arranged in a semi-circle. The other two computers had one monitor each and were positioned side by side on the left arm of the desk, sharing a keyboard and mouse, but with independent screens. The other three developers had identical systems.

Two of them were already there when Ben arrived. Daniel was physically small, and had a pleasantly assertive personality that belied his size. Libby was Asian-American, with shoulder-length dark hair and more of a demure, careful bearing. Libby's desk was adorned with origami designs; the centerpiece was a five-inch green Yoda crafted out of green paper. Daniel's desk featured an eight-inch long model spaceship with 'SR2' lettered on its wings, perched atop a black plastic stand.

"Ahoy there," said Daniel, in his customary nautical salute.

"Ahoy," returned Ben, making his way to his desk and picking up his iWear set from its power mat and sliding them on over his glasses. "How was your weekend?"

"Dull and uneventful," Daniel said. "Just how I like 'em. Spent most of Saturday night with my darling FemShep. Other than that, nada-lada."

"You like her so much, Liara's going to get jealous," deadpanned Libby, from behind her screens.

"Liara died in ME6," Daniel informed her.

"Oh," she said, not caring. "I didn't get that far."

"You haven't even played."

"I saw the show."

Ben grinned to Daniel. "They could have used that CP-Ampliflector in the battle with Sovereign."

"It's way too heavy for the *Normandy*. Needs a ship twice that big. *Titian*-class, minimum." Daniel said. "You know who needed it more? The Rebels at the Battle of Endor. If they'd had that sucker mounted on the *Liberty*, the fight would have been over then and there."

"You've thought about this," Ben said. Daniel made a face, as if it would be absurd for him to *not* have.

Ben signed into the system, and the Windows Elevate operating system greeted him with his login prompt. He touched his finger to the biometric pad on his keyboard, and the computer read his fingerprint and ran an analysis of the chemical residue in the oils on his fingertip. Within seconds, the computer had been authorized for his use, and launched Condensation Developer Environment, the integrated software system he used to help administer *Tides of Cortanis*. The Condensation interface began arranging itself in the space surrounding the monitors, virtually in mid-air, via his iWear device.

Ben was an environment programmer. His skills were geared toward making sure the various territories, cities, villages and space stations that were generated by Condensation's procedural system were consistent with the art direction of the pre-built spaces. Sometimes he could assume the identity of one of the game's storyline characters, and role-play as that character during Live Events. As a dev, he could, from his workstation and the tools entrusted to him, call up everything there was to know about any given character in the game. This included what items they had in their inventory, where they were in the world and where they would spawn if they were currently offline, what capital starships, shuttlecraft and aerovee planetside vehicles they had to their name. He could find out what virtual property and edifices they claimed, what lodge they belonged to and their standing within it, and their complete ability tree, outlining everything the character could do and the level of efficacy they could do it with. He could change any one of these parameters that he liked, if he needed.

Mornings like this one, he was glad his desk was situated with the others in such a way that they couldn't see what was on his screens without coming around to his side.

He called up Naomi René's character, Vanda. The plain window displayed a simple table of numbers and lists, leading with her unique player ID number, which not even Naomi knew. Vanda was currently logged out, but would spawn on board her *Renown*-class destroyer *Destiny*, in orbit around Casselle. She had three missions active; one of which, the "Ginova-Ti Coffee, Black" was one phase away from being completed. He typed another command and another window appeared, displaying her avatar. The slender female model with short, cropped purple hair stood as though bored, shifting her weight from one hip to the other as the digital model was exhibited on a slowly moving invisible turntable. She was wearing a black leather crop-top with exposed midriff, a white leather open jacket with chrome bands around the upper arms, a leather miniskirt, black ribbed rubber tights and knee-high boots. The character was exquisitely rendered; ToC was lauded for its impressive graphics engine, and character models were nearly photo-realistic simulacra of human beings in their prime. Over her shoulder and across her torso was slung a dark strap with a weapon holster, carrying an untradeable level-50 Ixxis-DE pistol, an impressive weapon. He knew the missions that were required to earn that little goodie. Naomi was not an inexperienced player, he learned from her possession of the pistol alone. She'd put in serious time already.

Next to the rotating model was a short menu of items. Ben moved his mouse over the item labeled "Inventory" and clicked. Another list appeared in a new window, showing all the items Vanda currently owned in the game, including real estate and spacecraft. Vanda had one starship to her name, the *Renown*-class. She also had a plot of land on Casselle, where the *Destiny* was orbiting. The plot was incorporated as part of the township of Hammerdale, registered to Vanda's lodge, Pride of the Guilty. He called up another window of data about the plot. On it was built a home, custom-made by Naomi herself. It was a large floorplan, with two stories above ground and one below.

"Huh," he said softly to himself, impressed. Naomi was not only an accomplished player but also an architect: someone who had learned the game's built-in construction toolset and had designed their own house, as opposed to buying a pre-designed floorplan or paying someone to create one for them. An uncommon combination of talents.

"What?" Daniel asked, mistaking Ben's comment for a request for attention.

"Nothing, sorry," Ben said. "Just checking out someone's architecture."

"Quit perving players," Libby teased.

Ben gave her a chuckle he hoped didn't sound nervous. What he was about to do could get him a warning from upper management, and he had a good rep with his bosses so far. He was hoping that might be enough to get away with what he was about to do.

He closed that window and right-clicked in her inventory box. A submenu of options appeared, and he scrolled down the list to select 'Add item'. A sub-submenu spawned off of that one, this list much longer, showing all the different inventory types for him to choose from. He scrolled down the list and clicked 'Mission Token'.

A new screen appeared, this one with a series of data fields to be filled in. Some of them had numbers already populating them, others were blank. There were several checkboxes. At the top was a blank text field labeled 'Title'.

Ben placed his cursor there and typed, 'Finding Rabbit'.

Beneath that was a checkbox labeled 'Player Generative', with a darkened text box beside it. He clicked the checkbox, and the text box highlighted. He looked for Vanda's player ID number in the other window, and copied it into the box. He hit 'enter', and the system authenticated the number and displayed Vanda's name beside the text box. As it did, most of the other variables in the window dimmed, meaning they were no longer his to customize.

Then he opened up the server log archive, and searched by date for the Galon-Yarisis assault where Rabbit had last shown up. He found it and opened it, which displayed a long-scrolling text window of seemingly endless event details, line by line describing the changes in state of the players' ships and the actions taken by the G-Y Outpost AI. He scrolled down the list, visually scanning for a line item that described a docking activity. It was pages and pages of data, and after fruitlessly trying to tease out the individual log entry by sight for a few minutes, he finally ran a text search on the word 'dock'. Only two line items contained that action: Rabbit's docking with the station, and his docking with the other transport. Both line items displayed the ID numbers for the assets involved.

Ben copied the number common to both activities, and ran that number through a trace. It brought up Rabbit's account, on which there was a position error warning: one of his assets would not be where the player had left it on last logout. The troop transport,

Irritable Vowel, had been destroyed. He copied down the number of the account ID, and then went back to the server log archive to search for the log from Rabbit's funeral.

He did a search on the account ID in the funeral log, and came up empty.

He folded his arms. That meant that whatever Naomi had encountered at the funeral was not associated with Rabbit's account, or an asset belonging to it, like the *Irritable Vowel* was. He paged down the log for the funeral, which was shorter than the station assault was, since this mainly consisted of people coming, leaving, and entering their names into the memorial register. Conversations, private and open, were logged elsewhere.

Nothing unusual.

He suppressed a grunt. If the others heard, they might be feeling helpful and want to know what he was working on. Instead, he looked up the most recent time Vanda had participated in the G-Y task phase of Aristarchus, during which Naomi had last encountered it.

This time, a very strange entry caught his eye.

/INCEPT ID879792341400 69105 47 7378
NOFLAG POSTURE-ERROR

That's got to be it. But... hold on...

This was the first time he'd found a log entry referring to the asset's inception, or creation in the game world. The entry meant it had been created in the zone, with its ID number first, then coordinates in the realm, then... *That doesn't make sense.*

The NOFLAG parameter was for player characters. The Chapel, and in fact the whole island of Aeryresasma, was a safe zone where no player-versus-player combat could be held. Players in PvP zones could flag themselves as willing to accept PvP challenges from others, but on Aeryresasma this was forbidden. As such, players spawning on the island were immediately de-flagged, so they were not vulnerable to attack from other players, and their ability to flag was revoked for as long as they remained.

But the POSTURE-ERROR parameter wasn't supposed to be there: it was a parameter intended only for non-player characters, such as AI-controlled aliens and animals. If a spawned animal somewhere in the wilderness, for instance, was meant to attack any player characters that wandered too close, its posture was set to HOSTILE. If it remained passive to players' approaching it, its posture was set to DEFENSIVE, meaning it would turn hostile if it was attacked, but would not otherwise respond to the player.

Player characters did not have posture. They were not under control of the game.

Ben checked the G-Y assault log and looked for the incept event when Rabbit's ship appeared in the encounter. It showed the same two parameters.

He shook his head, frowning. Whatever this thing was, it was showing characteristics of both a player and a non-player. Frustrating. Consistent, but frustrating.

But at least it had an ID number. He copied the ID number down in his notebook for future reference, and then clicked into the Finding Rabbit mission parameters window again. At the bottom of the window, there was a pop-up menu showing mission completion rewards. He selected 'Activate Asset', which highlighted the nearby text field for him to enter the asset ID number. He keyed in the ID number of the asset that had appeared at the memorial, bit his lower lip, and hit 'enter'.

The cursor turned into a colorful spinning wheel for several moments as the system processed the request. Then…

MISSION TOKEN CREATED.

He let go of the breath he'd been holding, and clicked the 'accept' button to dismiss the message. The window cleared and a new one opened, giving a series of optional parameters for him to fill in, including where Vanda would have to go in the game to begin the mission. There was also a text box for the initial instructions she would be given, so she would know what to do.

This was not his usual deck of cards as a dev; his expertise and responsibilities in the game had nothing to do with creating quests or missions. But he knew the place this mission should begin. Where it went from there, he couldn't control. Vanda would have to do whatever quest tasks the game would write for her, and she'd have to do it alone. He hoped she would be true to her word and not involve her lodgemates, no matter how close she may be with them. He was already well out of bounds, having shared with her what he had so far. If the wrong people in the company learned of what he had told her and was now doing, it would mean a severe reprimand. Possibly worse.

He checked her inventory list, and noted the appearance of the mission token there. She would find it when she logged in next.

He'd done his part. It was now just a question of whether she would accept… and whether she would succeed.

04.02

Later that evening

Georgetown Green
Charlottesville, Virginia

Naomi René lived in Georgetown, a comfortable but not affluent neighborhood in the north suburbs of Charlottesville, about ten minutes from the University of Virginia campus. Her 1,400 square foot townhouse was racked with four other units lined in a row, each with distinctive architecture as though they were separate houses. She liked her neighborhood because it was near campus, in a peaceful part of town, away from students and more transient residents. It consisted of similar rows of homes, owned outright by their residents, although a few, like Naomi's, were leased. It was also relatively close to Ivy Creek, where she and Skyler liked to walk.

Her divorce four years previous had returned her to the realm of rental properties, where she decided she preferred to be rather than take on the expense and responsibility of home ownership as a single woman. The Georgetown Green townhouse was more room than she really needed, but she felt she'd earned a bit of extra comfort to make up for the emotional hell her ex-husband had put her through when he left her. When she was first shown the property by the owners, a retired couple who lived in nearby Crozet, she fell in love with the floorplan, the compact little backyard space, the location proximate to her job, and the care with which the properties were maintained.

What she loved most of all was her loft. While other townhouses in the neighborhood village had three or four bedrooms on a three-level plan, this particular layout was one of the rare ones that had two levels and only two bedrooms, with the third bedroom getting a half-wall that opened up into the space above the living room. Naomi saw the room and immediately recognized it as perfect office space, and agreed to lease the unit on this feature alone.

Four years later, the room was the one in which she spent the majority of her time.

An L-shaped dark brown desk stood with one side against the half wall. Beneath it sat the black computer tower, with its row of four tiny green status lights nearly always on. Alongside the desk was a short bookcase filled with software boxes, manuals, game strategy guides, magazines and Blu-ray movies. On the desk itself, two twin 24" black monitors were suspended from half-circle carbon-fiber arms with ball joints, allowing the screens to be swiveled and angled as she liked. The screens hung over a black keyboard with glowing keys and a low-slung mouse on a broad black rubber mouse pad, next to the little rectangular power pad which charged her iWear unit. Two rows of various books normally fanned out from both sides of the monitors, held upright by slender metal bookends, a box of tissues and two blocky, black speakers on the far ends of the desk. Over one side of the desk, three framed photos were hung at a descending stagger down the wall: one of her mother and sister smiling in front of a Christmas tree, one of herself with her arm around Skyler taken during a trip they'd taken to the coast, and one of herself with the dog she and Jerry had once shared.

Tonight, there was a second computer tower, this one standing at the side of the desk, between it and the bookcase, where the trash-can usually was. The tower's green lights were also blinking, and it was now connected to a freshly unpacked third monitor atop the desk. The row of books that usually occupied that space had been moved to the floor against the wall with the closet doors, opposite the half-wall. Naomi plugged in her mouse and keyboard to the switchbox with the single plastic button controlling which computer would receive input from the keyboard and mouse. Naomi pressed the button on the box and the green light on the right side went off, as the other light on the left side of the box lit up. The new computer displayed a window acknowledging that the keyboard and mouse had been plugged in.

She configured the new machine with its fresh operating system installation, using the same version of Windows Elevate as on her older computer. Then she plugged in her terabyte thumb drive, which contained the installer she'd downloaded for *SimMind*, and ran the installation, which took about two minutes. After entering the correct serial number, the software asked her if she wanted to migrate an existing SimMind to the new installation, and she clicked 'Yes'. The software then prompted her for the original's database archive, which Naomi had already copied to the tera-drive. Naomi directed the installer to find the database, and it moved all the relevant information to the new installation.

Finally, it was ready to run. She unplugged the tera-drive and put the cap back on it, and waited as the software ran through its initialization process for the first time. After about a minute, the software reconnected with the host servers, the familiar activity log windows appeared and LEM's voice greeted her.

"Hello, Naomi."

"Hey, little electronic man," Naomi said. "How are you feeling?"

"You have moved me to a new computer," LEM observed. "I am feeling fine. All splines reticulated."

"Can you see me?" Naomi waved her hand in front of the third monitor's built-in camera.

"Yes, I am receiving audio and video input. My perspective of the room is slightly different. I estimate my camera is now seventeen inches to the left of my former one. My new computer has a faster processor than the old one, as well."

"That means you'll be a faster thinker, at least on this side of the network." Naomi said smiling. SimMinds shared processing duties with the host server at Maxis, and required this network connection to operate. "You have that hard drive all to yourself now too, which means your database can grow to over three times its former size, if you need."

"I am happy for these upgrades. May I ask what prompted them?"

"You're coming with me into *Cortanis*," Naomi said, looking into the camera's little square. "I need you to create a character there. I will help you get set up. When you are, we're going after Rabbit."

"That is why you have moved me to a new computer?"

"Right. I don't want you having to compete for processor cycles with the *Cortanis* client. And besides, with your database removed, it opens up more free space on the drive for me."

"I see."

"Okay, I'm going to put ToC now on your computer. This will take about twenty minutes to get it installed and caught up on patches. While it's doing that, why don't you read up on whatever else you can find about patching yourself into the game as a player?"

"Very well."

Naomi opened the Web browser and downloaded the installation client for the game. After connecting with the Praelium servers, it began downloading the game assets and arranging them as it needed on the hard drive, while Naomi went downstairs to warm up a Red Baron French bread pizza. When she had finished eating, she returned to the loft office to find that the installation had completed.

"Looks like you're ready to go," she said. "What did you find?"

"There are two additional programs that need to be download and installed to allow for me to interface with the Praelium host as a player. One is a patch to *Tides of Cortanis*, the other is a special driver for *SimMind*. I have populated a new tab in the Web browser with the links."

"Thanks," she said as she called up the browser and found the software to install. They were both small programs and within a few minutes, both the game and LEM had been updated. Naomi restarted the new computer to give LEM a fresh initialization to load the new driver.

"Hello again, Naomi," he said once he had finished rebooting. "My software appears to be capable of logging into the game now, and new information has been added to my database."

"What new information is that?"

"I now have an elementary understanding of the gameplay mechanics of *Tides of Cortanis*."

Naomi smiled. "All right. Then let's get you an avatar." She started up the newly installed game on LEM's computer. The launch window now had a new checkbox next to the word 'SimMind'. She clicked the box with her mouse, and signed in using her account credentials. Instead of starting up as normal, the game took her to the avatar creation screen, as if she were a new player.

"Do you have a preference as to how you would like to appear?"

"I am curious how you would design me. I would like you to make my avatar as you would like me to be."

Good boy, Naomi thought to herself. That was probably something he was updated by the new patch to say. It was almost an existential question for an artificial intelligence to consider, probably too much for the SimMind to answer. To prevent the AI from coming up with something truly horrific, it made sense for the SimMind to "prefer" its user to create its avatar for it.

Naomi chose 'human' for his race at first, but then changed the race to 'archimek', a race of cyborgs created by humans but who managed to secede as a race and form their own civilization and culture. The avatar body resembled that of a human, but with a subtly translucent skin. She could make out the cords and fiber of a metallic subdermal skeleture, with tiny blue diodes flashing here and there. The avatar received a basic assortment of clothing to begin with. Upgrades to clothing would come quickly, as the character progressed in the game. She chose a short, blonde, spiky hairstyle for him. His eyes were black with soft glowing blue pupils, a characteristic of archimeks. He had no eyebrows.

"Would you like me to choose your character name as well, LEM?"

"I would prefer to continue to be referred to as LEM," he answered.

"Fair enough," Naomi agreed. She entered his name as 'LEM'.

The avatar spun slowly on its unseen turntable. It moved as though looking around at itself, turning its palms up and examining the insides of its arms, clenching its fists, its face impassively curious.

"How does this look?" Naomi asked.

"It is acceptable," LEM said.

"We can always refine it later. Your clothes are pretty basic, but as we proceed in the game you will get better stuff. I can even buy you a few new duds on the marketplace."

"The avatar's clothes are acceptable for now, if you are happy with them."

"You look great, LEM," Naomi said with a smile. Her pet AI finally had a digital body and a face. As she studied it, she had a thought. "Do your drivers for *Cortanis* include emotional expression on your avatar face?"

"To a limited extent. I have been given an assortment of facial expressions to use. I will be paying attention to how you use yours, and how other players use theirs, to help me learn to use my own."

"Good strategy. Do you have any questions for me before we sign into the game?"

"No, I am ready."

"There's just one thing I need you to do while we play."

"What is that?"

"I need you to not talk to other people, at all. Unless I expressly tell you to."

"I see. I will not talk to other players in the game without your permission."

"Don't feel compelled to, if they start talking to you first. If anyone sends you a tell, in open or private, do not respond. The only time you will respond to anyone else in the game, other than non-player characters, is when I explicitly say you can in that specific instance. Do you understand?"

"Yes, I understand."

"All right, here you go." She clicked the 'Accept' button on the window, and the avatar was initialized in the game world. Above its head, the name 'LEM' floated along with the lodge ID <Pride of the Guilty>.

LEM's avatar was standing in an open courtyard before a set of stairs leading up to a large pair of metal doors. The doors were built into the side of a crashed starship, which leaned at an angle out of the ground. It had been thoroughly rebuilt as a six-story structure, with rows of windows cut out of the hull parallel with the ground, but the ship's original design and shape were still visible in the edifice. LEM stepped back from the ungainly looking building, and turned around in a circle. He was in what appeared to be the central plaza of a town. The sky overhead was pleasant, blue with a smattering of clouds. There was a mountain range in the far distance to the east. Trees and landscaping had been added to make the central plaza green and comfortable.

Naomi smiled. "You're home. You're in Hammerdale."

"What is Hammerdale?" LEM asked.

"Hammerdale is our lodge's home town on Casselle. I have some property and a habitat there. That building you're standing in front of is the wreck of the *Avalon Hammer*, something one of our officers found while surveying this unexplored sector of the planet. We thought it was cool, so we claimed the wreck and built our town around it, and our surface meeting spaces and offices are built into the wreck itself."

"I see."

"Stay there for now. I'm logging in and I will join you. I'll show you where I live."

Naomi reached for the switchbox button, and connected the keyboard and mouse back to her computer. She quickly logged in and launched the game client. In a few moments, Vanda appeared on the bridge of the *Destiny* in orbit over Casselle, on Naomi's screen.

Vanda ran down the hallway and hurried to the shuttlebay, where her shuttlecraft awaited her. She selected 'Hammerdale' from the list of possible destinations in the shuttle's range. The game skipped the cutscenes showing the launch and descent of the ship, and instead went momentarily to black, then showed the rear side of the shuttle as it banked toward the village on the planet. Naomi glanced to LEM's screen, and could see the arrival of the little spacecraft as it descended into the central plaza and touched down in front of him.

"Nice to meet you," Naomi said smiling, as Vanda stepped out of the craft and approached him. She entered the command to offer LEM a hug.

"You mean, virtually," he answered, as his avatar accepted Vanda's embrace with the pre-scripted animation.

"Yes," she said. "This is the first time you've met me as Vanda, and the first time I've met you in the virtual flesh. Welcome to the game, and welcome to Hammerdale."

"Thank you, Naomi."

"You can call me Vanda when we're playing," Naomi corrected. "I'd prefer that."

"Very well, Vanda."

"Follow me, I'll show you my home here." Vanda took off running toward the east through the town. LEM stayed with her, following as she darted down the main avenue. They continued past several players' shops and avatar upgrade parlors, then turned right down another street which led to her piece of property. The street dead-ended at a gate built into a heavy brick wall, which surrounded the property. Vanda approached the gate and it opened for them, swinging inward. She ran through the gate, but LEM was barred from passing.

"Vanda, it appears I am disallowed from entering your property."

"Oh, I'm sorry. I forgot something."

Naomi clicked LEM's avatar with her cursor, and selected 'Add to Friends' from the menu that appeared. Looking to LEM's screen, a window appeared briefly saying that Vanda had requested to add him as a friend. LEM didn't need to be told to accept the request.

"There," she said, "now you can come and go as you like."

"Thank you," he said.

LEM stepped through the gate, and it closed behind them after they passed.

The house was an impressive sculpture, appearing as a series of geometric shapes pressed into an almost random amalgam, like a pile of glistening white stone blocks, pyramids and half-spheres partially melted into each other. A fountain stood on the front lawn, at the center of a ring of sculpted shrubs with two stone benches on either side. The lawn had two spaces for landing craft; these were empty. Vanda walked up to the glass front doors and they hummed open toward her as she approached. LEM followed her inside.

"So, this is where Vanda calls home," Naomi said. "But the truth is, I don't spend a lot of time here. Mainly when I want to bank my inventory items at the start of a new quest."

"Could you please explain?"

"Inventory is limited. You can carry a lot of stuff with you, but the longer you play, the more you accrue. After a few years here, your stash gets to be pretty big. You can liquidate a lot of it for currency if you want, but I'm more of a pack-rat. After I spend a lot of time mishing, my inventory gets to be full of stuff I've looted and collected. I like to come here and empty out the items I know I don't need, to make room in my inventory for new things. I can also gather things I have stored here if I might need them. For instance, I have some weaponry here I can give you that will serve you better than the newbie stuff you'll be finding in these first ten or twenty levels."

"There is a great deal of terminology you are using which I do not understand."

"I'm sorry. Can you give me an example?"

"You used the word 'looting'. I understand this to be an illegal and morally condemnable act."

"Oh," Naomi said with a smile. "In the game, what we call looting is a perfectly normal, common activity. Usually when we kill bad guys here, their bodies lay where they fall, and we 'loot' them of whatever they might happen to be carrying. Ammunition is common, sometimes you get health buffs, or various items of clothing or sundry objects that have monetary value. A lot of times you'll get special pass-keys or whatevers which are necessary to complete the mission." She paused, thinking playing with LEM was going to be more difficult than it seemed. "I'm afraid you're going to hear a lot of strange vernacular during your first few weeks and months of playing. I'll do my best to explain what you don't understand." Naomi thought she might send a list to Ben of suggestions for improving the *SimMind* integration experience in the game. Teaching game vocabulary was one area they could improve on; this kind of remedial lesson in terms shouldn't have been necessary.

Vanda showed LEM through the opulently decorated living room. "There's a kitchen, but it's just for appearances," Naomi pointed out as she passed it. She went down a hallway and down a flight of stairs, where there was a heavy metal vault door. The door opened into a room full of walnut cabinet doors. As she entered, the inventory vault window opened on Naomi's screen, which allowed her to move quantities of items to and from the permanent storage here. She spent a short while transferring items out of her inventory and into the vault, sorting consumables, weapons, clothing items and currency into their respective virtual containers. Then she went into the weapons container and selected a small assortment of pistols and energy rifles that LEM's low-level avatar would be allowed to carry.

"LEM, I'm going to give you a few things." She turned to LEM, right-clicked him and selected 'Offer Items' on the popup menu. A new window opened. She dragged the selected weaponry into the window, and clicked the 'accept' button. LEM immediately accepted the transfer and the weapons appeared in his inventory.

"Thank you," he said.

"You're welcome. Those will come in handy soon."

After another few minutes of sorting her inventory, Vanda stepped out of the vault, LEM following. The heavy metal door swung shut.

"Okay," she said, "it's time to go."

"Where are we going?"

"We're going to find Rabbit."

LEM's avatar smiled. It was his first emotional expression. Naomi smiled back, and her smile appeared on Vanda's face.

Vanda and LEM returned in the shuttlecraft to the *Destiny*, which undocked from Guilty Pleasures and set course for the central system of Cortanis. Arriving in the heavily trafficked Cortanis space, Naomi parked the *Destiny* in a high orbit and showed LEM how to join her in the shuttle. Once he had, the little craft soared out of *Destiny*'s shuttlebay and angled toward the bright blue sphere beneath them. Naomi set course for the island of Aeryresasma, off the eastern seaboard of the Upper Camuan continent. Within moments, the ship was settling down on a landing pad at the island spaceport.

Vanda and LEM walked out of the spaceport terminal and onto the lush, green grass of Aeryresasma. The tower of the chapel could be seen in the distance, spearing through the low-passing clouds.

"It's beautiful, isn't it?" Naomi said.

"Yes," he agreed. "This is where your quest begins?"

"This is where I am to bring the mission token," Naomi said, and started walking toward the spire. "The token has to be activated at Rabbit's memorial pyre. There doesn't seem to be anything going on today at the Chapel, so we won't be interrupting anything."

Normally, Naomi would have had her avatar run the distance to the chapel, but instead, she walked, giving LEM more time to take in the detailed and sumptuous surroundings. She knew it probably didn't matter, since LEM would not be absorbing any more information walking than if they had run, but she felt it was somehow better for him to experience the exploration of a new area rather than sprint through it. Especially a place as exquisitely designed and built as the Chapel.

The Chapel of Phosphora was empty, the central pyre unlit. Birds chased each other through its open buttresses and their soft song could be heard overhead. Vanda walked up the central aisle to the pedestal, and quietly regarded it.

"Rabbit's funeral was here?" LEM asked.

"Yes," Naomi said. "Many people attended and entered their names. I've seen other funerals, though, that had over a thousand people. That's why the Chapel is so large."

"Is the Chapel used only for funerals?"

"No, people get married here, too. In fact, it's mostly used for that. You should see a wedding here, they let people decorate, and go really nuts with it. They put almost as much trouble and planning into an in-game wedding as they would a real one. Of course, it's not real, it's just fantasy."

"You've never done this?" LEM asked.

Naomi scoffed contemptuously. "No."

"Why not?"

"Because I've seen too many in-game 'marriages' lead to pointless hurt and stupid drama. If I wanted that, I'd have a boyfriend."

To her left, the door leading into the mausoleum stood at the base of the westernmost leg of the chapel. LEM followed her to the door and went with her as she passed inside.

All memorial services had their pyres stored here in perpetuity, so that friends of those remembered can call up their golden rings, add to them, and pay respects as they wished. Vanda and LEM descended the mausoleum steps and stepped through the open gate into the room, which led into a semi-circle of doors facing them, standing open. The floor was polished white marble; the walls glistened with tiny crystals embedded in dark green granite. Vanda went into one of the rooms. Inside there was a miniature pedestal similar to the center dais of the Chapel above them. Naomi clicked the glowing blue text field waiting at the base of the pedestal, and typed Rabbit's name.

The pedestal erupted with blue flames, which began whirling into a contained sphere, as though an invisible force was wrapped over it like a bubble. The luminescent golden ring appeared around it, showing all the names of those who had paid respects at or since the service.

Naomi stared into the mesmerizing ball of azure and white for a moment, then opened her inventory window. She found the mission token Ben had given her and clicked it. A pop-up menu appeared over it, showing the options 'Activate', 'Read', and 'Discard', next to a blank window.

She had read the mission prep already, but she clicked 'Read' again to review Ben's message, in case she'd missed anything. Text poured into the empty space next to the menu.

FINDING RABBIT

Hey Vanda, it's Ben. Was good to meet you Sunday. Here is your mission to find Rabbit. The game will write the mission for you, I can't set any parameters except for the completion result, which will be for the game to activate, or spawn, whichever, the game asset that has been visiting you. I do know the game will create a mission that is designed for you personally, so you may find it pretty challenging, but not too challenging that you can't complete it. It's going to take some work, though. It may take a few days, maybe more depending on your playing schedule. When you get close to the end though, call me and let me know, so that when you finish it, I can be there to monitor you and we can run some tests on whatever it is we find.

To activate the mission, go to Aeryresasma, go into the mausoleum at the Chapel of Phosphora, and bring up your friend's memorial. Once it's running, activate the token, and the game will configure your mission and start you on its first phase. Good luck, Vanda.

"Here goes." She clicked 'ACTIVATE'.

Chapter Five
05.01

Chapel of Phosphora
Planet Cortanis
Sector 01-P

Nothing happened.

The mission token dimmed, indicating it had been activated. But the usual glowing swirl of light that spiraled around her character, indicating the start of a new mission, had not appeared.

"Huh," Naomi said.

She turned to LEM. As she faced him, her character was enveloped in golden luminescence as though being touched by the finger of a deity. Tiny pinpoints of light encircled her, spouting glistening streams of light like a swarm of tiny fireworks. They shimmered hot around her, culminating in an effervescent flash of white that bathed the room in a warm glow.

The mission had begun. A window appeared for Naomi to read:

> **FINDING RABBIT**
> Mission Phase 1 of 8: "Lunius' Brain"
>
> The war between the velenx nation-states of Icillia and Esthonn has reached a fever pitch on the planet Seres. Truce is impossible; the only end to the war is the subjugation of one over the other. The war has lasted two decades and shows no signs of resolution. However, Icillia has developed a new weapon which may turn the tide, and the chief architect of the weapon has been targeted by the agents of Esthonn. He is currently on the run in the Esthonian city of Tanta, and has to get across the planet to the Eleon Arcology, Icillia's capital city, in order to begin building the weapon.
>
> The architect's name is Lunius, and he cannot leave the city without being detected and assassinated. Friendly agents with the archimeks have devised a plan to save him from Esthonn and get him to Eleon. They have successfully removed his brain and spinal column from his body and have placed it in a

stasis case for transport. Once the case has been smuggled out of Tanta and is safely home in Icillia, he will be integrated into an archimek body so that he can carry out his work.

Your mission goals are:

1. Travel to Seres and make contact with Avus in the city of Tanta
2. Secure the package containing Lunius's brain
3. See the package safely to Eleon in Icillia.

"Holy crap," Naomi said as she read. "He wasn't kidding I guess."

"What is it?" LEM prompted.

"Eight phases. That's… I've never done a mission with eight phases. Usually there's no more than four. Five tops, for really tough ones. Eight is a lot. I guess either Ben really wanted to make this hard for me, or the game did."

"How long will it take us?"

"It's hard to say. I don't run a lot of missions solo, so that will add to the time. But this time, I'm not really solo am I, since you're here to help me. It depends on the difficulty of these mission phases. Could take a week, could take a month. Let's find out."

"What do we have to do first?" LEM asked.

"We fly to planet Seres. Let's get back to the ship."

They returned to the shuttlecraft, launched, and docked with the *Destiny*. Vanda led LEM out of the shuttlebay through the corridors to the main bridge, where she took her seat. LEM sat in the chair for the first officer. The game's user interface changed to allow Naomi to set a course, and she selected the planet Seres in sector 338.

Planet Seres was in the outermost tier of systems furthest from Cortanis, and was affected by the third wave of the Tide. Seres was a homeworld of the velenx race, one of the player-selectable races in the game. Velen were bipedal feline humanoids with typically striped fur, although recoloring and tints were common once players had achieved level 50. They had catlike faces with flat, triangular noses and bisected upper lips. Their eyes were set back, small with slitted pupils, and the length of their mane was symbolic of their status within their familiar cohort. Because this was a homeworld,

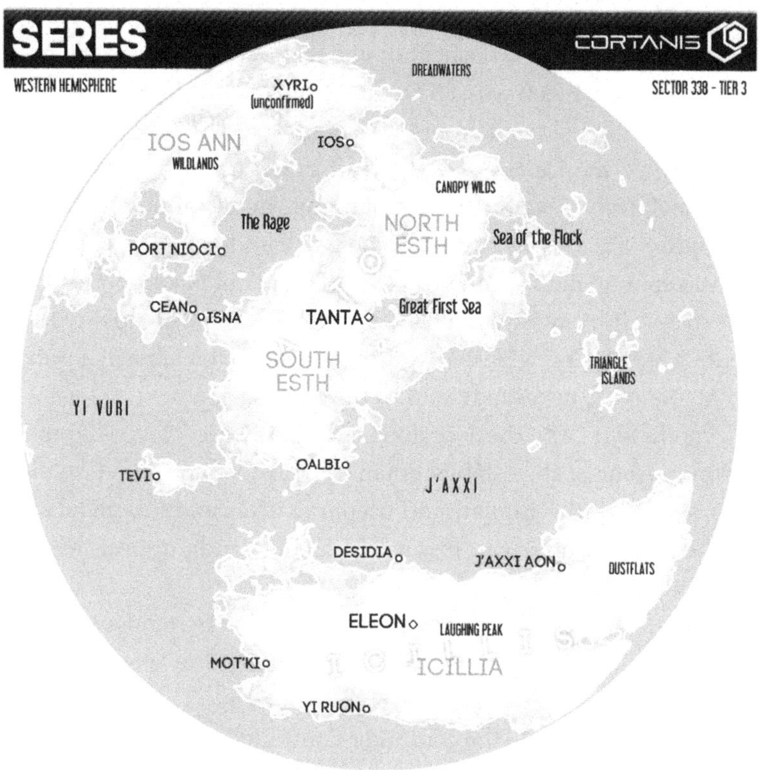

it was fully explored and charted, with thriving cities and well-developed politics. Only velen characters could establish townships or own property on Seres.

There were five primary continents. The southern hemisphere was dominated by the nation of Icillia, which spanned the four corners of the vast continent of Icillis. To the north, separated by an ocean running northeast/southwest, the continental landmass of Aetos was home to the Esthonni nations North Esth and South Esth. The southern mass straddled the equator, and a series of lakes, seas and waterways separated the continent's southern half from the north. The largest sea was nearly right between the two, the Great First Sea, on the west coast of which stood the South Esthonni metropolis of Tanta.

Naomi pinpointed the city on her navigation chart, and looked up the destination city of Eleon on the continent of Icillis. It looked to be a distance of about eight thousand kilometers. An easy enough jaunt for the shuttlecraft, she thought, if she could just get the package to the ship. Eleon was a bit inland from the northern coast, at the foot of an isolated peak, from the look of it.

She flew the *Destiny*'s shuttlecraft down to the planet, and the game helpfully gave them a safe landing site in Tanta on the top of a building. As they left the ship, the game added a waypoint to the on-screen map in the upper right-hand corner of Naomi's periphery interface. The new waypoint showed where they were to meet their contact, Avus. The NPC was waiting for them at a table in a pub, in what looked to be a shady part of the city.

Vanda and LEM drew curious and suspicious glances from the velen patrons of the establishment. As most velenx stood no more than 4′6″ tall, the human and archimek duo towered over them as they made their way towards the bar. Vanda approached the bartender.

"Hey," Naomi said, keying her talk-key. The bartender turned to her and answered with a computer-generated but effective voice, tweaked to the velen's distinctive voice pattern.

"May I help you?" the computer-controlled character asked.

"Yeah, I'm looking for a guy named Avus."

"Avus," repeated the bartender, "Back there." He pointed to a booth with a single occupant.

"Thanks," Naomi said, and led LEM to the booth. Avus nodded to her as she and LEM sat across from him.

"You Avus?" Naomi asked him.

"Yes," he replied evenly.

"We're here for the package," she said. "Where can we get it?"

"And, you are?"

"The ones coming for the package," Naomi answered, her voice low. She changed her tone when voicing Vanda, the character, as opposed to speaking in voice-chat to lodgemates.

Avus regarded them a moment, then spoke quietly. "Go to the Triumphant Fountain in the plaza and look for the dark green door. Go through the door, don't stop until you see the dragon window. Next to that window is another door. That's where I'll meet you with the package."

Vanda nodded as Naomi did.

"See you in a few minutes." Avus got up and left the bar. Vanda and LEM waited a short while, then rose and followed him back out.

Upon leaving the bar, a new waypoint appeared. Vanda made her way through the city toward the fountain, weaving through the dozens of velen citizens that occasionally turned their heads out of curiosity, to study her and her tall companion.

Naomi happened to glance at her health bar, one of three vertical status bars on the left edge of the screen. It was down by about a quarter.

"That's weird," she said.

"What is weird?" LEM asked.

"My health is low. Is yours low?"

"No, my health is at 100%."

She continued moving toward the fountain. "Hey LEM? Do a search on the *Cortanis* Wiki, look up the planet Seres and see if there's anything about the world I should know about."

LEM's answer was immediate. "Seres is a terrestrial homeworld planet, fourth in order in its star system. Radius six thousand, seven hundred seventy-seven point five two—"

"LEM," Naomi cut him off, "See if it says anything about whether or not humans suffer any ill effects while on the planet, say, from atmosphere."

"Planet Seres' atmosphere is listed as Dense-Breathable. Pressure, one hundred thirty-eight point oh-six kilopascals, approximately one point thirty-six that of earth. Composition: forty-nine point four percent argon, twenty-two point seven percent oxygen, nineteen point five percent nitrogen, five percent carbon dioxide, three point three percent sulfur dioxide and various other trace gases. Humans can breathe the atmosphere but will suffer a point one five percent health deduction each minute. This can be counteracted by using augmented Health Rations."

"AHRs. I should have a few of those." Naomi checked her inventory and found a stack of five augmented Health Rations, which appeared in her list as a crisscrossed pair of hypodermic needles over a loaf of bread. She selected the ration, and consumed one. Her health bar did not change.

"Huh." She waited, but nothing happened. Vanda's health remained penalized. She saw it tick down another tiny amount. "That didn't work. And it's decreasing a lot faster than half a percent a minute. Does it say anything else?"

"Seres' climate is cool, with an average equatorial temperature of—"

"No, LEM, about my *health*," she said, trying to hide the impatience from her voice. "Does it say I can take anything else to offset the health penalty?"

"I'm sorry, Vanda, it does not."

She looked at the other consumables she was carrying. Standard Health Rations, Energy Drink, Light Snack, Heavy Snack, Light Meal, Heavy Meal. She tried one of each. None of them worked until she ate a Heavy Meal, at which point the health bar slid upward, almost to the top again.

"Heavy Meal. That did it. LEM can you check the marketplace for the price of Heavy Meal consumables? I may need to stock up a bit. I've only got one more of those."

"I'll do that," he said.

They reached the fountain, and Naomi looked around for the dark green door. "There," she said, and headed over to it. Through the door—she had to stoop a bit to enter—was what appeared to be the lobby of an apartment building, with mailboxes arranged low, the highest coming up to her shoulder. There was a desk behind glass, and a corridor that disappeared around it to the left. Vanda rounded the corner and pushed through a door labeled in Velensh. It opened into a maintenance corridor, with several doors. At the end of the corridor was a window, with a pattern etched into the glass. A dragon.

Beside the window was the door, as promised. She opened and stepped through. She and LEM emerged in a back alley behind the building, where Avus was waiting.

"Hello, Avus," Naomi said with the talk-key held down. Vanda's lips mimicked Naomi's greeting.

"Here he is," Avus said quietly, lifting up a long black duffel bag on a shoulder strap, about three feet in length. Naomi was presented with a window asking if she would accept the package, and a second device labeled *Transponder*. She clicked 'ACCEPT'. Vanda took the macabre cargo and slung it over her shoulder.

As Vanda shifted her weight to support the duffel bag, Naomi took a second look at the avatar on her screen. Something about her appeared different, but she couldn't make out exactly how. Only that it had... changed, almost imperceptibly. She hoped that once they were off Seres, the distortion, whatever it was, would be cleared up.

Avus took a step back from her. "You know where you're going?"

"Yes," Vanda nodded.

"You have ten hours to get him there," Avus warned her. "The batteries won't last beyond that. Keep a low profile and you'll make it. Don't lose the transponder, if you lose the package somehow, you'll need that to find it again."

"Thanks for your help," Vanda said.

"One more thing," Avus said as Vanda turned back to the door. She stopped.

"What?"

"Try not to drop it. If you break it, he dies."

She nodded. "He'll be safe."

"He'd better. The outcome of this war is, literally, on your shoulder."

"Come on, LEM." She opened the door again and stepped back inside the building next to the window. LEM followed her down the hall, where she turned the corner to meet four armed velen mercenaries, dressed in paramilitary fatigues, weapons drawn.

"Oh shit," Naomi groaned.

"Don't move," one of them said. "Hand over the package and you won't get hurt."

"LEM?" Naomi said.

"Yes?"

"You know that gun I gave you before we left Hammerdale?"

"Yes."

"Use it!" Naomi stabbed at the backslash key with her middle two right-hand fingers, and Vanda immediately drew her pistol and unloaded white-hot bolts of lethal energy at the mercinaries. They opened fire, health bars of red appearing over their heads. LEM drew his weapon and began firing alongside Vanda. Naomi knew he would do very little appreciable damage, since he was such a low-level character, but hopefully, the mission balancing system would increase his efficacy for combat. She was gratified to see his thin needles of light causing the mercenaries some hurt; their health bars dipped as they absorbed the impacts.

"LEM, make for the alley, I'll cover you!"

He turned and ran down the corridor behind her as Vanda continued firing. One of the mercenaries' health bars fell low enough to begin blinking, and Vanda concentrated her next two blasts from the pistol at him. It was enough: he collapsed backward, her XP award glowing in little blue, glistening numbers over his body before shimmering away.

She turned and followed LEM down the corridor. Vanda's running speed was off, seemingly encumbered by the duffel bag. LEM had reached the alley. Vanda flung herself into it and faced another three mercenaries. The odds were not good, but she'd faced worse than this. She slammed the door behind her and quickly selected another wide-area ranged weapon. Her health bar lurched downward as she took a barrage of hits from the enemies. LEM's health bar couldn't be that good by now, but he continued firing with his puny weapon. Vanda's Muon Pulse Rifle was their best hope now.

It took a few seconds to charge before it could fire. A tiny clock face appeared over the icon of the weapon in the toolbar at the bottom of the screen, showing the 5-second countdown. Finally, the icon glowed yellow. She fired the pulse rifle at the three mercenaries, and the blast knocked two of them off their feet, their health bars taking a crippling blow.

"LEM, start back to the ship!"

"Oh, dear," LEM said.

Naomi looked to see his health bar reach zero, and his avatar fell to his knees, then face down in the alley. His newly created character couldn't withstand the attacking NPCs.

"Can you respawn?"

"According to my directions, I can be respawned when you return to the shuttle and open a cryotube."

"You can't do it yourself?"

"No, I cannot."

"Brilliant," Naomi frowned. "I'll just have to handle these guys without you." Her pulse rifle had charged again, and she let go another powerful burst of energy in the enemies' direction. Two of the mercenaries fell backward, their remaining health extinguished. Vanda's health was dropping dangerously low, and she knew the planet's atmosphere wasn't helping. She turned and fled the alley, heading back out towards the fountain. As she ran, the third enemy took occasional shots at her, but his aim was affected by his pursuit. Behind him, the other three mercenaries from inside burst out of the door and joined the chase.

She could feel the weight of the package over her back; Vanda was not running at her usual spritely speed. She made it to the busy courtyard with the fountain, and pushed through the confused civilians. She was too tall to hide among them, all she could do was try to make it back to the shuttle as fast as possible. She hoped that her health would start inching back up as it usually did when she chose to seek temporary cover, but it wasn't moving. She frowned. This was going to be a long shot.

She consumed her last Heavy Meal, and her health bar jumped up to half. That would have to do. If she could make it back to the shuttle, she could escape without having to defeat the remaining enemies, but she would certainly have to take at least one more stand before she made it that far. The package was just too heavy.

She made it as far as the front lobby of the building where her shuttle was parked. She ran into the room, turned and aimed the pulse rifle at the doorway. As her pursuers kicked open the door, she fired. The blast wave defeated one more, and knocked the remaining three enemies to the ground. She turned and rushed into the stairwell. Her running speed up the stairs was even slower than it was on the street, and her health was taking hits, falling lower and lower into the red.

She abandoned the stairwell and threw herself out of the door opening into level four. There was a bank of elevators nearby; the same elevator she and LEM had used to come down to the street. She ran to the button and pressed it, but she knew the mercenaries were right behind her. She again took aim with the pulse rifle just as the stairwell door burst open. The shockwave from the rifle blast disposed of one more enemy, and swept the rest of them off their feet and down onto the lower landing behind them. To her relief, the elevator doors parted, and she jumped into the lift and pressed the button for the roof.

Now it was a race to the top. The enemies would rush up the stairs to try to stop her. If she could just make it to the shuttle before they shot her dead, she would be safe. It was a question of whether the elevator lift would outrun them.

The doors slid open, and the shuttle stood on its landing legs across the rooftop, waiting patiently. She ran with all her speed toward the shuttle, about a hundred yards from the elevator. She got almost halfway there before the stairwell door opened behind her. *I'm not going to make it.*

She spun and, not aiming, fired off a blast from the pulse rifle. It missed the pursuing enemies, the bolt careening into open air off the side of the roof. She spun and crouched as bursts of light shot past her, and switched to the Ixxis pistol. It took a moment to aim, but it was quicker than the Muon. She zeroed in on the first enemy and fired. His head jerked back from the impact and he collapsed, the shimmering blue numbers coalescing over him and then fading away as his body fell. Splashes of concrete burst up around her from the incoming fire, and her screen pulsed red as she took more hits. One more enemy left: she trained her crosshairs over his head, as he seemed to look her in the eye, taking aim of his own. She fired.

The last mercenary's body tumbled to the side, blue swirls enveloping it, the effervescent numerals glittering above it before dissolving away.

Vanda stood again and hurried to the shuttle. Inside, she went to the cryopod. Naomi clicked it with her cursor. A window appeared asking if she wished to reanimate LEM. She clicked 'confirm'. The cryopod swung open and LEM's avatar stepped out.

"Thank you," he said.

"LEM, quickly, did you find any more Heavy Meal rations on the marketplace?"

"Yes, they are priced at 200 rb. There are seven hundred nineteen available for purchase at that price."

"I need you to buy thirty of them. I'm giving you the money now." She clicked LEM's avatar and traded the currency to him. She was running out of time; she wasn't sure if the planet's atmosphere would continue to drain health from her, even in the shuttle. Her health was bottoming out. The NPCs could no longer hurt her, but she could still die from the toxic atmosphere and be forced to start the mission over.

LEM accepted the currency. "I've made the purchases," he said a moment later.

"Trade me the rations please, quickly," she said. The exchange window appeared, with three stacks of ten Heavy Meal rations in each. Naomi accepted the exchange, and clicked to consume one of the rations. Vanda's health bar jumped to about thirty percent.

She breathed easier. "Okay, good. That was close. Now let's get this package to Eleon. Take a seat."

It took three more Heavy Meals to return Vanda to full health. But Naomi could now more clearly see that the consumables were doing more than returning her health. They were changing the avatar itself.

"What the hell..." Naomi said in surprise. "It looks like... I'm gaining *weight*."

LEM seemed curious. "I don't understand."

"I mean Vanda. Look at her. She's... she's bigger now than she was when we started the mission."

"Yes, it appears so. Your avatar has changed in proportions. Is that normally what happens when you consume meal rations?"

"It's never had an effect on avatars. That's... that's messed up!"

"You are consuming a great deal of heavy rations. It seems logical that your body would increase in size, although at a slower rate than this."

"No—I mean, yes, in the real world, that happens, but it's not supposed to happen to my avatar in here. Consuming rations never has an affect on your avatar. It just doesn't happen."

"Perhaps if you stop consuming food, your avatar body will return to normal."

"Brilliant," she smirked, biting off the sarcastic comment at his expense. "Let's get this mission phase over with."

The shuttlecraft pushed off the roof of the building on a pillow of exhaust smoke, and lifted its nose to ascend into the sky. Naomi banked it to the south, and the game set her next waypoint: eight thousand, forty kilometers to the south-southeast. The city of Eleon. The waypoint appeared off in the distance to the south, with numbers floating over it the distance.

Eight thousand kilometers was not a short distance to travel for the shuttlecraft. She climbed to cruising altitude and set the speed at nine-tenths. Glancing at the numbers diminishing over the soft blue star on the horizon, she did a little head-math and sighed. "This is going to take a bit," she said as she slumped in her seat.

"Approximately thirty-six minutes," LEM helpfully calculated.

"If we could get to orbit and dock, we could just undock again and be there in no time," Naomi mused. "But you can't return to the ship until the mission phase is complete. I just hope when we deliver this package we can get off this planet." She frowned as she saw her health bar had already declined by a fifth.

"That doesn't make any sense," she said. "I shouldn't be breathing Seres air in my own shuttlecraft. Why am I still losing health?"

"I'm sorry, I'm afraid I don't know."

"It's all right, I wasn't expecting you to. It's just bullshit. I have to sit here and watch my health for this whole trip. And if I have to eat all these rations just to stay alive, who knows how big Vanda's going to be by the time we're on the ground."

As the shuttle made the journey over the J'axxi Ocean between the continents of Aetos and Icillis, Naomi continued to click on the rations as her health-bar fell into the red, limiting her consumption as best she could. One meal would only buy her about six or seven minutes of health. She passed the time growing increasingly frustrated at the effect the rations were having on her previously svelte, attractive avatar.

"LEM, do a search on the Wiki again. See if there's any mention at all of avatars changing as a result of consuming rations."

"One moment," he replied. "Done. There are no such references."

"Look on the forums then," she said, adjusting her seating position in the chair. She almost felt herself growing heavier as she consumed another meal ration.

"Searching the forums." After a longer pause, he said, "There are numerous references to specific players as overweight. These seem to be *ad-hominems* and are not addressing actual in-game appearance. There does not seem to be any activity or consumable that addresses overweight in one's avatar."

"Then it better damn well be temporary," Naomi fumed.

As the shuttle reached the midway point over the ocean, several hostiles appeared on her long-range scope, approaching fast from the north. She sat up in her seat.

"Interceptors!"

"It appears the Aetosians have caught up with us," LEM observed dryly.

Her fingers stabbed at keys on her keyboard, diverting engine power to the shuttle's weapons and shields, and throttling down. There was no way they could outrun the five tiny fighters. They would have to defend themselves.

"These are not good odds," she mused, and quickly consumed four Heavy Meals to replenish her health to full, knowing she wouldn't be able to pay attention to it while in combat. As her health bar returned to its peak, she noticed something else.

The shuttle flew faster. It seemed more agile, almost as though the rations she'd been feasting on gave buffs to her flying skill. She wiggled the shuttle back and forth, testing its response. It felt lighter, nimbler. Almost like a fighter, even though it was not built for any more maneuverability than that of a basic transport ship.

"All right, let's see what we can do."

She banked the shuttle around to head straight toward the approaching sortie. As they came within firing range, the enemies flooded her with streaks of pale green light, and she fired her primary weapon. Powerful bolts of punishing energy exploded out of her tiny front-mounted cannons. The bolts tore into one of the fighters and it exploded instantly.

"Whoa!" Naomi exclaimed. "What the hell!"

The shuttle shot through the fighters and they all banked to maneuver for new firing angles. Naomi put the shuttle into a hard port turn. The ship handled with unexpected precision, its turning radius almost as good as the fighters half its size.

"This is crazy!" she said, half-smiling. "The shuttle's flying like a fighter."

"Is this unusual?" asked LEM.

"Hell yeah it is. I swear, this is one of the strangest missions I've ever done..." The shuttle found a firing angle on one of the fighters, blasts of white ripping across the sky in its direction. The NPC fighter banked away, but somehow the bigger shuttlecraft managed to stay on its rear, sending a steady stream of fire chasing after it. The fighter reversed its turn and jinked upward. Naomi braked and pulled up, finding her target in the reticle and blasting it out of the sky.

"That's two," Naomi said. But as she accelerated again to pursue another fighter, she felt the controls growing sluggish. "Oh, hell."

"What is it?"

"It's slowing down again." She fired into the open air ahead of her. The bolts that emerged were weakened, visibly less powerful than what had just been shooting out of her forward cannons. "It's weaker now."

"You are below three-quarters health," LEM pointed out.

"Already? Damn," Naomi swore as she tabbed open her inventory panel and double-clicked on the Heavy Meal ration. Her health-bar returned to full. Immediately, she felt the ship become light once more, and the stronger bolts erupted from the cannons when she fired.

"What—so it's the ration! It has to be a glitch, but who cares." She grinned as streaks of energy crisscrossed her screen from the attacking fighters. She flipped the shuttle over on its back and pitched down, aimed the nose at the water, then completed the reversal and came up beneath the fighters, right-side up again. She caught sight of one veering away into the sun and she twisted the ship in its direction, accelerating to catch the fleeing fighter.

"Where you going? Huh? Think you're getting away, little guy?" Naomi smiled to herself, taunting the enemy fighter on her screen as she worked to line up her crosshairs. "I gotcha," she cooed as she fired and obliterated the enemy fighter with a thunderous barrage from her cannons.

Her screen flickered red. Another of the attacking fighters had taken position behind her and was strafing the shuttle with a hail of energy bolts. She twisted the craft onto its side and the horizon spun vertical. The aggressor shot past behind her, and rolled away to try to get a firing angle on her before she could find him. Normally, this would have been easy for the fighters; tonight however, Naomi's usually cumbersome shuttlecraft easily beat the smaller craft's turning ratio and she drew her crosshairs over the fighter, now fleeing like prey.

She clicked one of the Heavy Meal rations again, and her health bar glowed full green. She took the shot. The fighter burst into a bloom of flames, spewing debris in arcs that tumbled down toward the water.

"Yeah!" she grinned. "These rations taste *good!*"

One fighter left: port side low. She rolled the shuttle over and started lining up against the lone, panicked fighter. Its countermeasures popped behind it, like a spread of feathers on a bird trying to intimidate a rival. The flares, however, would not save it. She tapped her fingers repeatedly on the fire key, and smiled in satisfaction as the tiny ship exploded.

Her XP bar took a slight bump, and momentarily glowed blue. She chuckled. "I had no idea this thing was such a barnstormer." With the shortrange sensor sweep clear of hostiles, she set course again for Eleon. The destination was still over three thousand kilometers to the south.

"The shuttle appears to get a speed buff concurrent with your ration consumption," LEM observed.

"Not just speed, but performance. And firepower. It's crazy. I should keep my health above seventy-five percent," Naomi agreed. "We'll make better time that way." She checked her inventory. "Still got twenty more. That should get us there."

She routed the shuttle's power from weapons and shields back to engines, and accelerated again, taking another four rations to keep her health above seventy-five percent as the shuttle covered the distance to Icillia.

The voyage took about ten minutes. As the north coast of the continent came into view on the horizon, a red dot appeared on the longrange scope. This time it was a solitary blip, and it was coming much faster.

"Damn," Naomi groaned. "That's not an interceptor."

"What is it?"

"It's a missile. It must have been fired from a submarine or sea-going vessel."

"Can we outrun it?"

"No, but we might be able to dodge it long enough for it to run out of fuel. I don't have any flares or decoys on this thing, so we don't have much choice. Hang on!"

The missile closed the distance quickly; even with her increase in speed, the shuttle couldn't hope to beat it to the coast. She watched the blip on the scope draw closer and closer until an alarm began sounding, meaning a collision was imminent. She jinked to the right, pulling into a tight loop. Unexpectedly, the ship turned even harder than she'd expected, and she glimpsed the missile out her front view. She quickly reversed and the missile shot past her, missing by barely a few meters. She decreased the magnification factor on her scope so she could see the missile's position better, now that it was right on top of her like an angry bee.

The missile was turning back toward her to the left. She pointed her shuttle at the water and drew the missile downward. Her altitude indicator plunged as the clouds rushed past her. She could make out more and more detail in the waves and water beneath them as the shuttle raced for the surface.

The missile was still faster. She waited until they'd reached 50 meters, then pulled up on her controls and tried to flatten out parallel to the water. The shuttle's controls responded smoothly, reversing the dive and nosing up to bring the horizon again below the window. The missile also corrected before plunging into the water, burning rocket fuel to right itself.

"We've got to at least get over land," she said, mostly to herself. She saw the blip on her scope, but couldn't tell how far beneath her it was. It seemed to be standing still, or coming up below her at an alarming rate.

She turned the shuttle toward the mission marker star on the horizon, and dropped another ration. The shuttle again increased in speed. Her health bar read full, but Naomi clicked the ration anyway. The shuttle's speed again boosted. She checked the scope; the missile was on her tail and closing. She began clicking the ration rapidly, consuming ten of them in quick succession. The shuttlecraft continued to increase its speed; the missile's rate of closure was visibly falling. But it was still closing.

She consumed the final ration and it vanished from her inventory. The shuttlecraft was now flying impossibly fast for its design and typical performance, but it still wasn't enough to outrun the missile. The coastline shot past beneath them and a city with some buildings was coming up to the right. She banked toward it, hoping she might be able to squeeze through a couple buildings and cause the missile to hit one, but she quickly realized she wasn't close enough. The turn bled just enough velocity from the shuttle for the missile to reach its mark.

Naomi gritted her teeth as she realized the missile was about to hit, her eyes fixed on the little red dot creeping closer and closer. She braced herself for her camera to pull back, out of the shuttlecraft, to show it exploding in a cloud of flame as the missile struck.

The missile came within 3 meters of impacting, then sputtered and dropped, plummeting harmlessly out of the sky.

She let out a whoop. "Yes! We made it!"

"Vanda, we are closing on—"

The shuttlecraft had reached the city at top speed, aimed at a forest of buildings.

"Oh *sh*—"

It was too late. The shuttle sheared across the side of one of the buildings and was thrown into a flat spin, its starboard wing shattering and raining down into the street below. The shuttle twirled and plunged into the ground on the far side of the city, a plume of earth and debris fountaining up over the site of the crash.

05.02

The next day

Outskirts of Desidia
Planet Seres
Sector 338-BD

Mercifully, the respawn put Vanda at the site of the shuttle's crash, with the case still in her possession. There wasn't any indication that the case had been damaged in the crash. When she stepped out of the shuttlecraft wreck, what Naomi saw standing beside the smoking metal shocked her.

Vanda was *obese*.

Not just heavy. Her avatar was severely overweight. Naomi stared, horrified.

"That... *can't*... be... right..." she stammered.

"What is it?" asked LEM. As his character had not yet been respawned, he could not see into the game.

"It's Vanda. Look at her."

"I don't understand."

"I mean she's huge... she's... she's fat! Not fat as in oh-a-few-extra-pounds, not fat as in heavy, fat as in what-the-hell-happened-to-me fat."

Vanda walked forward. While the Heavy Meal ration had unexplained effects on the speed of her vehicle, it had a clearly deleterious effect on her avatar's movement. Vanda moved painfully slowly. She tried to run. Her speed increased only marginally.

She stared in astonishment tinged with anger. "So my shuttle flies like a hummingbird, while I'm reduced to stumbling around like this. This is *bullshit*."

"I still can find no mention in any of the online resources available of an avatar visibly increasing in weight."

"It's worse than that. Not only do I look horrible, but it's affected my mobility. Look at this... I can barely walk, much less run. I'm literally heavier, as far as the game's physics are concerned."

"It is a puzzle. I will continue to research the problem for you."

"Actually," Naomi said as she moved Vanda to wrest open the

shuttlecraft's hatch. "Maybe there's something else you can do for me." She opened the door and climbed back into the crumpled shuttle, finding the cryotube doors flame-scarred but mostly undamaged. "Let's see if I can get you out."

She moved her cursor over the cryotube, and the menu selection appeared to respawn LEM.

"Thank God," Naomi said.

She opened the cryotube and his avatar appeared beside her.

"It appears I have acquired some experience points since I last spawned," LEM noticed. "The aerial combat on the way here has been to our mutual benefit. Please give me a moment to allocate."

"Go for it."

"Done." As he finished, a dance of glistening red and green sparkles swarmed around him, and the words 'LEVEL UP' coalesced out of them, then dissolved away. "I have increased in level."

"Congratulations. Let's get out of here."

Vanda and LEM climbed out of the shuttle together. "You have indeed amassed a great deal of body weight," LEM observed, studying her.

"Oh, shut up," Naomi frowned.

"I'm very sorry. Did I say something offensive?"

She sighed. "What you said is accurate. I've gained serious poundage. It's just, I'm not used to Vanda looking like this. Vanda has always been slim and nimble and sexy. This is totally just… not me. I *hate* it. The sooner I get my avatar back to normal, the better."

LEM turned toward the city. "We appear to be just outside the city of Desidia. I show our distance to be approximately two point four kilometers."

"We need transport to Eleon. It's too far, and we don't have time." She checked the timer on the case. "We're down to five hours on the case. I guess we lost a couple of hours overnight while we were logged off."

"How do we get transport?" LEM asked.

"Have to find it in the city. There should be shuttles, but I'd prefer a taxi. It'll be expensive, but at least it will be private."

"To keep from drawing attention of whoever is pursuing us?"

Naomi sighed. "Well, that too, but primarily because… I don't want anyone else to see me like this." Her shoulders slumped in her seat. She looked at her health bar: it was declining.

"I can't believe this. I'm still losing health, and I'm out of rations."

"Do you need me to buy you more?"

"It looks like I need you to do more than that. You are going to have to go into the city to find us a taxi. Then come pick me up, and we'll go to Eleon together."

"You're not coming in to Desidia with me?"

She typed a 'WHOSHERE' command into her chat window. The game displayed a small window with several scrollable columns of names. At the top of the list it read, 420 PLAYERS IN REGION.

"There's over four hundred players in Desidia tonight. I..." She leaned back in her seat, struggling with her discomfort. "I'd rather not be seen there."

"How am I to find a taxi to Eleon?" LEM asked.

"You have to look for a taxi stand. There will be a bunch of them gathered outside the spaceport. Look for the spaceport first, and then look for taxi stands. When you find one, get a fare to Eleon, but make sure it's not a non-stop fare, cause then you can't come by to pick me up. Make sure the fare is 'player waypoint' governed. It'll be more expensive, but that's not our concern."

"Does the fare need to be paid before or after the trip?"

"All in advance."

"I will need money to buy more rations for you, and to pay for the fare."

Naomi offered a thousand rb to him. He accepted the exchange.

"Now, get me another thirty Heavy Meals," she said. "I'm gonna try not to eat them all this time."

"One moment," LEM said as he went shopping at the online marketplace. The purchases only took him a few seconds. "Done."

He offered his purchases to Vanda. She accepted.

"That should leave you over six hundred rb's to get us a charter," Naomi said. "Good luck. I'll be right here."

"I'll be as quick as I can." LEM trotted off in the direction of the city, breaking into a run. He quickly vanished from sight.

The city was the only interesting thing on the horizon. The shuttle apparently crashed in a desert, about fifteen kilometers inland.

There were dry, craggy mountains to the west and south. The city lay to the east, appearing about the size of Baltimore. There didn't seem to be any roads nearby. She swung her camera upward. There were a few vehicles in the sky, all flying a north-south route in and out of the city.

"LEM?" Naomi said.

"Yes?"

"Don't forget. Don't talk to strangers."

"I haven't forgotten."

"All right. I'm going to get a Coke. I'll be back in a bit."

"Very well, Vanda."

Naomi armed Vanda with her Muon Pulse Rifle and got up from the desk. At least if anyone happened by while she was away, they'd see the gun and have second thoughts about messing with her. She frowned to herself again as she got up to get herself a bottle of Coke Zero out of her refrigerator.

She was deeply bothered by what had happened to Vanda. Could she face her lodgemates? Would they laugh at her? Would they treat her differently? It certainly would make for a great deal of teasing. Teasing from them, she could handle. But as far as she knew, she was the only obese avatar in the entire game world. How many active players did they have now? Fifteen million? She'd read somewhere that the game had peaked at nearly seventeen million subscribers and had stabilized just south of there. With the upcoming release of the *Dark Tides: Rose Prophecy* expansion announced for January, new subs were up again, she had read. No doubt there would also be the typical influx of Christmas gift subscriptions in a month, and out of all these people running and flying around these worlds, probably none of them looked like her.

She returned to her office and sat down, staring in dismal confusion at her beloved alter ego, Vanda. If word of "the fat girl" started to get out, would it go viral? Would she become a meme on the game forums? Would people make YouTube videos making fun of her? Would the Pride of the Guilty lose status in the game? That thought made her heart sink. She loved her lodge, loved her lodgemates, and would hate for anyone to be made a target for ridicule because of her.

She knew people on the forums could be counted on to be cruel. Even if it wasn't her fault the game had done this to her, people would be cruel anyway.

A familiar, deeply unwelcome emotion began overtaking her, and she felt its approach deepening her gloom.

Ugly. Unwanted.

She blinked hard and tried to control her emotions. She didn't want to get upset in front of LEM. She would contact Ben. Surely, there had to be a way of fixing her avatar and getting it back to normal. She climbed back inside the shuttle to wait for LEM's return. She didn't want to risk being seen by someone whizzing past in a taxi or something.

A flashing red pulse caught her eye: her health was down to dangerous levels. She groaned and clicked on the Heavy Meal ration, putting the health bar back into the yellow again. The action almost physically hurt to perform.

"LEM, where are you?" she asked, her voice wavering. Her fingers trembled as she reached for the box switching keyboard and mouse input to LEM's computer, and pressed the button.

"I have reached the city limits. I'm looking for the spaceport now. Are you all right? You seem upset."

She'd forgotten that LEM could see her even while he was focused on the game. "Yeah, I'll be okay. Just want to get this mission over with."

Naomi's mouse and keyboard now controlled the computer on which LEM was running. She cursored over the little tab showing that *Tides of Cortanis* was online and she clicked it. The ToC interface appeared, showing his progress as he explored the city, making his way through the streets. Around him, players engaged in PvP fights, drove in land vehicles, flew among the buildings in aerovees, and negotiated with sidewalk vendors. There appeared to be a thriving business community in Desidia, with numerous player-owned storefronts lining the downtown streets.

"Are you looking at city signs?" Naomi asked.

"Yes, the spaceport is only a few blocks from here," LEM replied.

"Okay." She sniffled, and whipped a tissue out of the box, wiping her nose.

"Vanda, are you upset by what I said?"

"No, LEM. I'm upset because… it's nothing. Don't worry about it." She wadded up the tissue and tossed it at the trashcan. It bounced to the floor.

She watched as LEM ran up to a taxi stand, where a gray, angular vehicle floated a few feet off the ground. It was a standard inter-city fared vehicle, which could carry six passengers and a copious amount of cargo. It had the same general shape as a medium-sized hovercraft, but instead of a rubber skirt, the passenger compartment was ringed with a metallic octagonal shroud. The shroud protected the gravidrive, giving the vehicle its ability to cruise over a road or any other flat surface at very high rates of speed, without touching the ground.

"LEM, is that a player-owned stand or an NPC one?"

"It's an NPC stand. The fare to Eleon is 150 rb. Is this acceptable?"

"Yeah, that's… whatever. Not a non-stop fare though, right?"

"No, the taxi will fly whatever course it is given. Deviating from the route to Eleon will trigger a per-K rate of 2 rb. Shall I hire the taxi?"

Just as long as nobody's driving but you, Naomi didn't say. "Yeah. Do it."

"The taxi has been hired. I'm on my way back to you. I will be there in just a few minutes."

The thought of disembarking from the taxi in a city full of people made her head hurt. She couldn't help thinking that everyone would stop what they were doing and stare at her the instant they arrived in Eleon. She closed her eyes. She needed to do something else.

"LEM," she said, her voice still unsteady. "I need to log out for now. I'm going to ask you to bring the taxi to the shuttle and then log out too."

"I will do that, Vanda. Are you not feeling well?"

"No, I'm really not." She tried to close out of the game, but her cursor would not move. She suddenly remembered her mouse and keyboard were still controlling LEM's computer, and swore to herself. Stabbing the button, she quickly logged Vanda out. "Good night, LEM," she said to the AI as she headed downstairs.

"Good night. I hope you feel better," LEM said as his taxi slowed to the coordinates of the crashed shuttle. Coming to a stop, LEM disconnected from the game, and then put himself into sleep mode for the night.

Naomi threw herself onto her bed and stared up at the ceiling, feeling tears threatening from behind her eyes. She willed them not to come.

Ugly. Unwanted. Disposable.

Stop it. It's just a game. Get a hold of yourself.

No one's going to want you in the game *now, either.*

Stop *it!*

05.03

The next day

Arch's Frozen Yogurt, Ellis Street
Charlottesville, Virginia

Arch's Frozen Yogurt was busy in the midafternoon despite the chill in the December air. Its location in the center of the city, combined with jaunty decor and a diverse array of sweet snacks, made it a popular destination for students and professionals. The tables in the upstairs lounge were ringed with tablet-tapping twenty-somethings wearing logoed sweatshirts, chatting and scooping colorful spoonfuls out of white cups. The television on the wall was showing sports highlights, but its volume was muted and no one was paying attention to it. Skyler and Naomi sat along the windows in the couch and chair. Naomi's hot chocolate sat untouched on the corner table between them. She was sullen, her arms folded, slouched in the couch cushions. Skyler stared at her, confused and concerned, leaning forward toward her with her elbows on her knees.

"What did he say?" she was asking.

"He said there was nothing he could do," Naomi said bitterly. "He said there was no existing algorithm for an avatar to swell up like that. It must have been something the game taught itself, he said."

"Taught itself?" Skyler was skeptical. "How does a video game to teach itself anything?"

"It's the whole *point* of this game. That's why it's so popular. It learns. It watches, it observes, and it *learns*. Somehow, it thought it would be great fun to turn me into this… ugly…" She ran out of words, and gave up with a frustrated scoff, turning to stare out the window over Emmet Street again.

"Hey," Skyler said slowly, "why is this so upsetting to you?"

"Because how am I supposed to play now with my friends?" Naomi said, a little too loudly. Her voice was carrying in the contained space. She reminded herself to control her tone.

Skyler kept her voice even. "What does your little video character's size have to do with whether or not you can play with your friends? Why does that matter?"

"It matters because it's completely bizarre," Naomi said. "Can you imagine being the only overweight person in a game of millions of sexy people? They're going to see me and be like, 'what the hell happened to you? What's wrong with you?' What am I supposed to tell them? Yeah, I ate thirty Heavy Meal rations all at once, and I swelled up like a dirigible. Guess I'll start with the Pilates."

"And, so what? Why can't you continue to play as normal?"

"I don't want them to see me this way. How would you feel if you woke up one morning and found that you were suddenly five times your size? You wouldn't be the least bit concerned that this wouldn't make life just a little more complicated for you?"

"I'd feel like I was in a Kafka novel," Skyler admitted. "I think I'd be more concerned about the abruptness, than the weight itself. Anyway, real life isn't a video game."

"Of *course* not, but, Sky..." Naomi started shaking her head, "if I start running around in public... okay, say I go to a party. Everyone's going to be saying, 'look at her, wow, she's so fat!' And then they'll be making forum posts. They'll take screenshots and post them. Then I'll get turned into a meme. Then come the stories about how I got to be this way, how I pissed off a dev and this is his revenge, or who knows what they'll make up. You don't know how brutal these people can be to each other."

"Again, so what?" Skyler asked. "I thought we were long past fat-shaming in this culture. It sounds worse in there than it was in high school. You know what's nice about being an adult? We know that we don't have to give a damn about people like that. Your friends will still be your friends. That's all that really matters."

Naomi just stared out the window. "You don't understand."

"I don't know, I'm kind of afraid that I do. You haven't been like this for a long time now."

Naomi looked at her. "What do you mean?"

"I mean, you're saying a lot of the same things you told me after the bridge. When we first met."

"What's your point?"

Skyler leaned closer and lowered her voice. "I'm hearing a lot of fear in your voice. Something about this has touched you deep down, where you're still raw. You're still afraid of being judged by others. I know it's been six years, but I also know… six years is only six years. You still carry that fear down in there," she said, gesturing at Naomi's chest. "And this has activated it somehow. What I don't understand is how."

Naomi looked down.

Skyler went on. "Remember when we met? You didn't know me, but you spoke to me. You told me what you were feeling. You had no reason to hold anything back. You trusted me, and I've never forgotten that. Remember?"

Naomi nodded.

"Talk to me now. What's going on in there?" Skyler asked.

Naomi took a deep breath and tried to gather her thoughts. "You want to know why I play this game? It's cause in there, I can be who I choose to be. I'm not ugly. I feel beautiful. I feel normal. People don't see the ugly girl. They see me as a person. I can just be me, and when I'm me, I like myself a lot more." Her voice was quivering.

Skyler started to speak, but Naomi continued.

"Now, I'm afraid that's gone. I hate feeling ugly. It's like the game knows how ugly I am, so it…" she struggled to control herself. "It won't let me pretend not to be anymore." Her fingers were trembling as she wiped her cheek.

Skyler stared at her.

"You think I'm pathetic now, don't you," Naomi said.

"Huh-uh," Sky shook her head. "I think you're hurting, and you're afraid, and I just… I forgot how much you're still healing."

"Well, I think I'm pathetic. I'm all stupid like this over a video game." She tried to smile.

"You saying all this about being ugly… that's what's stupid. But I do know it's how you really feel. How you feel isn't stupid. It shows how much you still need to heal, though. And I don't see this game helping you do that." Skyler pushed her hot chocolate closer to her. "You forgot this. These are expensive."

Naomi picked up the hot chocolate, which wasn't so hot anymore. She sipped anyway.

"So, tell me what you're thinking," Naomi said.

"You know what I'm thinking of now?" Skyler said. "Something

I saw once on a show, or... I don't know where. It's called a Johari Window. Do you know what that is?"

Naomi shook her head.

"Imagine a square divided into four quadrants. Each quadrant is a different segment of the window. The first one, in the top left, is called the Arena. It represents everything about you that you yourself know, and so does everyone else. It's the you that's out in the open. The second segment, in the top right, is called the Blind Spot. That's everything about you that others know, but you can't see."

"Such as?"

"Oh, maybe like how you're not so unattractive and unlovable as you want to think."

Naomi shrugged. "You think I'm cute."

"I think you're blind to the things that make you attractive."

Naomi chuckled. "You know my SimMind called me lazy a couple weeks ago?"

"It what? It said you were lazy?"

"We were talking about how different perspectives on people give rise to different impressions. I asked him to come up with some descriptors of my personality, and one of the words he chose was 'lazy'."

"Why did it say that?"

"Because he never sees me exercising or walking with you. He can only see me puttering around the house in my sweats. I couldn't fault him for saying it, although I did tell him that if he calls people lazy, they might take offense."

"You did change the subject, you know."

"No, I'm not. I said that because my SimMind is blind to aspects of me that he hasn't personally seen."

"We were talking about aspects of you that *you're* blind to. You know, good ones."

"What are the other two segments of the window?" Naomi asked. "You said there were four."

"There are. The third one is for things about you that no one knows, not even yourself. Your subconscious, as it were. The fourth contains things about you that you know, but don't ever share with others."

Naomi smirked. She knew that place better than them all. "That's where I feel like I live."

"Then you need to get out more," Skyler said. "You need to get out more."

05.04

Later that evening

Outskirts of Desidia
Planet Seres
Sector 338-BD

As she logged in, Vanda appeared standing close to the wreckage of the shuttle, staring at a large floating hovercraft. Naomi sighed, seeing Vanda was still as heavy as she was when she'd signed off the previous evening. The game was no fun when she didn't want to be seen by anyone. She didn't understand why a game designed to code itself to be fun would do this to her, but a lot about this mission wasn't making sense.

LEM's screen showed Vanda from the point of view of the shuttle, as LEM was inside it, his camera followed the vehicle from the outside as though floating about four feet over the roof of the taxi. Naomi could make out the avatar of LEM seated inside through the long horizontal window that wrapped around the front of the vehicle. There was also a driver wearing a visored cap seated in front at the controls.

Vanda checked her inventory and checked to see that she still had the case containing Lunius' brain and the transponder. "Looks like we're still good."

"I must be extra careful," LEM cautioned. "If I am killed before we return to the *Destiny*, I can only respawn from here, and Eleon is a long distance from this point. This will be inconvenient for you."

"Yeah, I know. We'll be careful. Hopefully we can just drop this off at the waypoint in Eleon and move on to the next phase." Vanda walked around to the hatch of the hovercraft, and climbed aboard when Naomi clicked the door and selected 'Board' from the pop-up menu. The hatch swung closed and her camera moved to float above the ship as LEM's did.

As Naomi was the player character, she was given control of the vehicle. A menu appeared asking her to specify a destination for the taxi, with the top selection being 'Next Mission Waypoint'. She clicked that, and the taxi spun to the south, aiming at the glowing blue star off in the distance. It accelerated, leaving the shuttle wreck behind, and quickly found the road leading to Eleon. The smoother surface allowed them to cover the distance even faster.

The city appeared as a large, enclosed glass pyramid in the distance, steadily looming larger at the end of the road as they made their way toward it. The lone mountain peak on the horizon seemed to lay just beyond the city to the south. The numbers atop the star steadily ran down as the minutes passed. Each time Vanda's health bar fell to red, another Heavy Meal ration was consumed, just enough to push it back into the yellow and keep her alive. Naomi seethed with discontent each time she double-clicked on the ration in her inventory.

"LEM, you said you were going to continue to research my avatar problem. Did you find anything today?"

"There are very few other video games that allow for game characters to increase or decrease, observably, in weight as a result of player action. Nearly all such games are designed to help them exercise. So far, none of the massively multiplayer online roleplaying games I have researched include any such game mechanic. Many games, such as *Tides of Cortanis*, allow for some variability in the perceived weight of player avatars at the character creation step. Once the character is created, it does not change in shape or size unless the player changes it."

"So in other words, no."

"I'm afraid there is nothing in any of the resources I have surveyed to indicate that there is a solution to your weight problem."

Naomi winced. "LEM, please don't call it 'my weight problem'."

"All right. How shall I refer to it?"

"You can call it my avatar appearance problem. Actually, I consider it a bug. It's an avatar appearance *bug*."

"I understand."

The hovercraft slowed when it approached the city entrance after nearly fifteen minutes of monotonous travel. There were several vehicles waiting to enter ahead of it, each being allowed in one at a time, by an automated gatekeeper. The taxi slipped into the queue, and was allowed to enter the city as its turn came up, through a short airlock tunnel.

Eleon had been introduced to the game as part of the *Dark Tides: Contagion* expansion the previous year, being one of the larger and more intricate game environments designed by Praelium. The city typically had a player population of up to a thousand at any given time, running missions, engaging in PvP and exploring the city's backstory and politics.

The capital city of Icillia was a massive pyramidal bio-habitat, a hyperstructure designed to be entirely self-sustaining. The habitat needed only sunlight and geothermal energy to keep a baseline power input for its massive antimatter electrical generators. Food was produced internally, both hydroponically and through synthetic production facilities that artificially "grew" animal meat *in vitro*. Water was systematically recycled and purified for consumption, plumbing and the occasional controlled weather event. Regularly scheduled rain kept the freestanding trees and greenery nourished and healthy. The interior atmosphere was contained in a microscopically bio-secure shell which contained thousands of tiny mirrors on nanomotors embedded in its surface, to capture and concentrate the maximum amount of solar light for energy production. A thermal-conductive layer covered the exterior of the glass, to absorb solar heat and help maintain a constant internal temperature.

The title 'ELEON' appeared in Naomi's headsup in thick block letters as the hovercraft taxi passed through the inner doors of the city's airlock. Just inside the gate, billboards blazed with ads competing for attention, hawking clothing stores, custom-designed residences, gynoids, dance clubs and propmaker shops.

"Gynoids," Naomi chuckled, studying the suggestive sign as they passed by. "Guess I shouldn't be surprised."

"There is a measure of controversy regarding gynoid use in *Cortanis,*" said LEM. "Arcologies like Eleon are restricted to children. The airlock we passed through a moment ago would not have permitted your entry if you were under the age of 18."

"Yeah, I've read about that a little bit. They've started to put age-controlled spaces in the game with the last expansion. I can see there being a whole new market for *Cortanis* for perverts, all corralled in nice, big, walled-off pyramids like this so they don't get in the rest of the game's way. Feels like being in a virtual Vegas."

The hovercraft slowly made its way through the crowded plaza at the main gates, finally breaking clear of the congestion and into the city streets. The waypoint's distance ticked down from triple to double digits, drawing closer. Naomi clicked another ration to keep her health from bottoming out, praying it would be her last.

The street suddenly exploded in front of the vehicle, causing NPC velen civilians to flee screaming, shielding their heads from chunks of concrete hailing down over them. The taxi came to an abrupt stop as three sleek, black interceptor craft appeared and circled around it, their side-mounted cannons deployed. They were roughly the same size as the taxi hovercraft, but had a chine-canard configuration with steeply angled rear stabilizer winglets and smoky-glass outer skins. The interceptors were designed to overtake almost anything within the city's airspace, and were heavily armed.

Naomi frowned. "I knew this wouldn't be a straightforward delivery."

"We're in no position to put up a fight," LEM said. "Your health is very low."

"I know. How much do you want to bet they're here for the case?"

"I would not bet against you, as it seems likely you would win."

"You're a quick learner."

One of the interceptor's doors opened and two velen officers stepped out. They were dressed in police body armor and helmets, brandishing pulse rifles. A voice spoke as they lifted their rifles at the taxi.

"Get out of the car," said the game-generated voice. The command was subtitled on the screen as well.

She knew there was nowhere to escape. Naomi had Vanda exit the taxi and jump to the street. LEM followed behind her.

"We're taking your cargo," the synthesized voice continued. "Do not resist." Naomi glanced up to her inventory panel and saw the case containing Lunius' brain disappear.

"Thank you for your cooperation. Enjoy the rest of your visit in Eleon," said the voice as the two officers retreated into their interceptor. The hatch slid closed and all three vehicles turned to fly off into the city. The mission waypoint, locked in one position up until now, changed to indicate the lead interceptor as it lifted up from its parking hover and ascended, in formation with the other two aero-vees, into the city sky.

"It appears we are expected to get the case back," LEM pointed out.

"Yeah, but with what?" Naomi sulked at the sight of her avatar. "We can't outrun them in this taxi. Maybe we can at least see where they go. Get in." They both climbed back into the taxi, and Naomi resumed manual control of the vehicle and accelerated over the crater in the street, to follow the rapidly moving waypoint.

The waypoint continued to ascend, finally coming to stop nearly 15 kilometers away. Vanda's taxi stopped at the base of some kind of industrial facility rather than an office building. Massive tubes snaked out of the base of the structure in threes, and disappeared below the surface of the street. There were windows ringing the first few floors, but upwards of those was dark, enclosed steel. Atop the structure was a flattened plateau with windows, a landing pad, and plumes of white gas being vented from a series of cylinders.

"The mission will not be over until we can retrieve the case," LEM said.

"Brilliant," Naomi deadpanned. "Only problem is, I'm too slow to fight, and you're too low-level to do it yourself without getting ganked."

"So how do we proceed?"

"I don't know. The building's awfully tall to try to climb from outside. I guess we have to go in through the front door and fight our way to the top."

"Would this be an opportunity to invite other members of your lodge in to help you?"

Naomi deflated a little. "Yeah, and I'd do that in a heartbeat if Vanda wasn't so… anyway, no. Ben said we're on our own on this one."

"What are our alternatives?"

"I don't know, LEM. I need to think." She pulled the taxi away from the building and piloted it into the city until she found a street that was removed from the busier areas. She climbed out of the taxi, and LEM again followed her. There were puddles of standing water on the pavement, and several dumpsters of garbage. Across the street from the alley, there was a club entrance with a sign blazing over it flickering 'ROOM303' in blue neon. There seemed to be a figure standing in the entrance, facing her. Staring at her. Naomi turned her camera toward the female shape, but couldn't make out any detail. Its face was hidden in shadow. There wasn't a name over its head, so that made it an NPC.

"What do *you* want," she muttered to herself. She hit a key combination and initiated a scry, detaching her camera from Vanda and moving it toward the figure to get a closer look. As her scry moved into the shadows and examined the entryway to Room303, the figure was nowhere to be seen.

She shook her head in frustration, and repeated the same key combo. Her viewpoint snapped back to Vanda again. She sat down against the side of the building and looked up at the glowing blue waypoint in the sky. It read that the case was 14.5 km away.

"Do you want me to dismiss the taxi?" LEM wanted to know.

Naomi heard a soft 'pip'. It was a familiar sound, the sound of someone sending her an in-game tell via the text-chat box. She had collapsed it for the mission, since she'd been blocking her online status so that her friends wouldn't see her. But when she looked at its tiny box in the bottom corner of the screen, it was glowing. There was a message waiting for her.

"Hang on," she told LEM. She clicked the box and opened the chat window.

MALACHI: HI

She blinked, and immediately spun her camera around the area. The only way for another player to send her a private message, if they could not see her online, was to right-click her avatar directly. So whoever this Malachi was, he had to be in the immediate area. Naomi couldn't see anyone else around them, not even the mysterious female figure. Only herself and LEM.

She double-clicked the name to respond:

VANDA: Hello. Who are you?

The response came after a pause:

MALACHI: ARE YOU RUNNING A MISSION TO RECOVER A STOLEN CASE?

Naomi squinted at the screen, wondering how this person could have known that.

VANDA: Maybe. Why?

MALACHI: IM RUNNING A MISSION TO HELP YOU.

05.05

Eleon Arcology
Planet Seres
Sector 338-CE

VANDA: You're supposed to help me? How?

MALACHI: I'M HERE IN ELEON, AT A CLUB. I HAVE AN AEROHAWK, I CAN COME MEET YOU SOMEWHERE

VANDA: Who are you?

MALACHI: I'M A LEVEL 65 AND I WAS CHECKING OUT THE ELEON MISSIONS, AND I JUST STARTED THIS ONE, AND IT SAID I NEEDED TO ASSIST YOU IN RECOVERING A CASE, AND THAT I SHOULD SAY HI TO YOU IN A TELL. WHO ARE YOU?

Naomi paused for a moment, then typed:

VANDA: I'm an 80. My mission phase started in Tanta and then brought me here.

After a beat, she added:

VANDA: I'd rather not go to a club.

MALACHI: OK WHERE DO I FIND YOU

VANDA: I will send my SimMind to come find you. Then he can show you how to get to me.

MALACHI: YOU HAVE A SM PLAYING WITH YOU?

VANDA: Yeah. His name's LEM.

MALACHI: COOL. I'VE NEVER SEEN ONE IN THE GAME BEFORE

VANDA: So he will come to you, and then he'll bring you to me in your hawk.

MALACHI: UH, OK I GUESS THAT WILL WORK

VANDA: What club are you in?

MALACHI: CLUB DUALITY, TOP FLOOR OF THE RYANNOVA-JOSHI IN THE TRADI SONTA DISTRICT

"LEM, do you know how to find that?"

"I beg your pardon. Find what?" LEM replied.

"Oh. I thought you could... never mind. I'm getting tells from another player. He says he's been given a mission to help us out."

"The timing is fortuitous."

"Yeah. Kind of weird, actually. Would you go pick him up please?" Naomi asked.

"You're staying here?"

"Well... yeah. He's at a club. I don't want anyone to see me."

"Which club?"

"Club Duality, in Tradi Sonta. He says he has an AeroHawk, so we won't need the taxi anymore. Take the taxi to the club, and then you can dismiss it and have this guy fly you back here to me. His name is Malachi. Will you remember your route, so you can navigate him?"

"Yes, I can remember the route. Am I authorized to speak to him?"

"Yes, but only to give him directions. Don't answer any other questions."

"I understand."

LEM climbed back into the taxi, and after a pause, the hovercraft whined louder, lifted up from the concrete and sped off into the city. Naomi double-clicked Malachi's last text and typed:

VANDA: My SimMind is on his way to you. He's in a taxi. When he reaches the club, he will follow you to your Hawk, and then direct you to me. Please don't try to engage him in conversation, ok?

MALACHI: OK, WHY NOT?

VANDA: It's just that I don't want him freely talking with strangers in the game. He's kind of like my kid, and I feel like his parent here. Does that make sense? I'm sorry if that's a bit overprotective of me.

MALACHI: IT IS OK. HEY, THIS WOULD BE EASIER IF WE VOICE, DO YOU MIND?

Naomi shrugged to herself.

VANDA: Why not

She right-clicked Malachi's name in the text window and the pop-up menu appeared. She selected 'One-on-One Voice'.

"Can you hear me?" she said aloud, holding her talk-key after the game sounded two soft beeps, indicating their connection had been made.

"Yeah, hi. You can call me Mal," came a male voice. It sounded a bit snowy, through a slight haze of static. The static ended abruptly when he stopped speaking.

"Call me Vanda. Something wrong with your caps-lock key, Mal?"

"No, it works. I just always type in caps. That bother you?"

She chuckled. "No, I don't care."

"Okay, Vanda. So what's the deal with this case, now?"

"A few nights ago, I started a mission to deliver the case from Tanta to Eleon. In Tanta, LEM and I were ambushed and attacked by five, no seven, agents. Then we got airborne in my shuttle and were attacked by fighters leaving South Esth. We'd almost made it to the Icilli coast when a missile was fired from a surface ship, and we evaded it, except I crashed us anyway. So LEM—my SimMind—got us a taxi from this city on the coast, and we came the rest of the way here. As soon as we arrived, the case was taken from us by three, what looked like, police interceptor hawks. Black and slick. They took the case and flew it up to the top level of a building. We were just discussing our options when you said hi."

"Yeah, sounds like cops to me. They fly black interceptors. I'm heading to the front of the club to meet your SM, what did you call him? LEM?"

"LEM, yes. Thanks. Did you really get a mission to help us?"

"Yeah. I finished the one I was on, and when I called in to pick up a new one, it said I needed to come to this club in Tradi Sonta, and talk to an NPC named Ardelle. She told me I needed to help recover a stolen case, and that I needed to send you a tell. Probably the first time I've ever been paired with another player's existing mission."

"New to me. Maybe it's part of some missioning system upgrade that's part of Eleon. It's the first time I've been here."

"Same here. Maybe. Okay, your friend's here. LEM. I need him to follow me to the parking level. Can I send him tells?"

"I'll just tell him. LEM?"

"Yes, Vanda?"

"You've made contact with Mal?" On LEM's screen, Naomi could see he was standing in front of a human avatar, with the name 'Malachi' floating over his head. There was no lodge ID. They were standing in a building near an elevator. Next to the elevator, a large black and white sign read, 'CLUB DUALITY, LEVEL 20'. Malachi was wearing a weathered brown leather jacket and leather pants, with ribbed, oval padding over the upper thighs and shins. Beneath the jacket was a vest with various ammo pockets. Strapped to his back was a pulse rifle of some kind; Naomi couldn't make out how powerful it was, but from its size, it was most likely a decent weapon. His dark reddish hair was short and spiky. Her first thought upon seeing him was that he looked like a loner, someone who didn't waste time in PvP, but who spent most of his time in the game running solo missions in pursuit of the best gear.

"Yes, I'm standing in front of him now," LEM replied.

"Okay, I see him. I want you to follow him to his vehicle, all right?"

"All right."

"It's pretty funny," Malachi said, "seeing LEM's lips move and not hearing him."

"Yeah, I was just telling him to follow you. Lead the way."

Naomi watched Malachi turn and run down the hall. LEM kept up with him through the building to a stairwell, which led up two flights to a skyway over the street connecting to a parking structure. The structure was a plain concrete cylinder with no windows, only a large access bay at the base. Malachi ran up to the base and stopped at an empty pad, about the length and width of the taxi hovercraft, in front of the bay doors. The concrete pad had a large numeral '1' painted on it. Naomi watched him on LEM's screen, standing there. Then the bay doors slowly slid open, revealing the vehicles inside were not standing in their own marked spaces, but racked vertically in rings, suspended upright. As she watched, an armature carried a vehicle out of the storage tower and righted it, lowering it to the ground in front of Mal and LEM. The arm released it onto the access pad, and withdrew back inside the tower.

"Nice ride," Naomi said.

"You can see it, huh?" Mal answered as he climbed inside. LEM followed him, and as he did, his camera perspective changed as it had when he entered the taxi, floating about four feet above the vehicle and following just behind it.

"Yeah, looks sharp. Okay, I'll shut up now so LEM can tell you where to go. LEM, please guide Mal to the entrance of the building where the case is being held."

"Very well, Vanda," LEM answered, then went quiet, giving direction to Malachi. Naomi watched the AeroHawk lift off the pad and spin, pitch forward and accelerate into the air over the street, gaining altitude.

"Vanda?" Mal asked.

"Yeah?"

"What is this building entrance you're taking me to? I have a mission waypoint now, but that ain't it."

"It's not?"

"Nope. The waypoint I've got is a bit of distance away from the building. That you?"

Naomi closed her eyes and swore to herself. The transponder. She glanced at her inventory: the transponder Avus had given her back in Tanta was still there. She looked back at LEM's screen and saw his waypoint was on the ground level also, roughly where Vanda was waiting for them.

She realized his waypoint, and Mal's, were fixed on her. Her own waypoint was the case itself, because she was the one carrying the transponder. Whoever was going after the case would need it in their possession to know where to go.

She glared at Vanda, on her screen, a mixture of emotions roiling within her. Shame, fury, frustration. She didn't want this person, whoever he was, to see her avatar. He'd make assumptions. He'd judge her. None of those assumptions or judgments would be good.

"Vanda?" Mal asked when he didn't get a response.

"Yeah, I'm here. Look, here's what I want you to do. Come to my waypoint. I have to give you something to track the case. Then I..." she paused, realizing he probably wouldn't like what she was about to ask him to do. "I need you to go in and get it for us."

"You're just going to sit outside and wait?"

"Yeah. When you get here, you'll understand."

After a short wait, the AeroHawk came into view between the buildings, descending expertly and kicking up light billows of dust from the pavement, scattering a few items of loose trash as it hovered and touched down in front of Vanda. Naomi's fingers trembled as she waited for Mal and LEM to emerge from the vehicle.

The hatch opened, and Mal came down the steps first, followed by LEM. They both approached Vanda and stood in the alley facing her. Naomi could only imagine the revulsion and astonishment Mal's player must be thinking, looking at her in the alley.

"See?" she said softly.

"Yeah, I see you. So?" Mal answered. "Why can't you go in with me?"

"Because I'm…" she stammered, her voice almost breaking. "I'm slow. I can't run worth a damn."

"What do you mean?"

"It's this planet's atmosphere. My health bar keeps falling and I have to consume certain rations to replenish it. It's slowed me down a lot."

"Oh, that sucks. I wonder why that's happening to you. No one else I know has had that problem."

"Yeah, well, *Cortanis* loves me," Naomi said ruefully. "I'm sure that's why you've been tasked with helping us. I can barely run, and LEM here can't fight because he's a newbie. I'm sure there's probably a garrison of men up there waiting for us, protecting that case."

"And you want me to go in, alone, and get it? While you just sit on your asses out here and wait?"

"If LEM dies, his respawn point is all the way back at Desidia. He's so low-level, he can't help you anyway. We barely made it out of Tanta together. And I'm…" *Useless.*

Mal waited for her to finish her sentence, but nothing came. "Coloring your nails?" he asked sarcastically. "I came to help you get this case, not get it for you while you just sat out here cooling your heels. Just because you're slow doesn't mean you can't fight."

"You'll get all the XP," Naomi offered.

"Yeah, whatever. Fine, I'll go get the damn case."

"Thank you," Naomi said quietly, hating the situation. "Here, to get the case you need this." She opened an exchange window with him, and moved the transponder from her inventory into his. He accepted the exchange.

"Got the waypoint?" she asked.

"Yeah, I got it." He turned and headed back to the ramp leading into the Aerohawk.

LEM turned to her. "Vanda?"

"What."

"Are you not inclined to rigorous activity in *Cortanis*, also?"

The observation jolted her. It was an innocent, if discourteous, question to ask. Knowing LEM, it was not intended as an accusation. But she couldn't help but see it as such. Suddenly, it felt that sitting out any important mission phase was somehow... not what her friendship with Rabbit deserved. And what if Mal was overwhelmed? The least she could do was act as his healer, even if she had to stay behind him and cover his six. Her eyes narrowed as she keyed the voice-chat again.

"Mal?" she said. He was already climbing into the vehicle.

"What." His voice was clipped.

"You're right. I changed my mind. I'm coming with you."

"Glad to hear it. Hop in."

"LEM, you're with us. You can at least keep the AeroHawk away from the building after we're in, and come back to get us when we're ready to come out."

"I understand," he replied.

"Let's go." Vanda and LEM scrambled aboard the Hawk, and the sleek ship pushed up off the pavement with a blast and spun in the direction of the pulsing blue star perched atop a building in the distance.

As they drew closer, they could see the waypoint was inside the top floor of the square frustum-shaped structure known as the QV-One. It was tall, looming over the other buildings in its vicinity, its wide base taking up four entire city blocks. Two black interceptors rushed at them, opening fire, but Mal's piloting skills were more than enough. With a few maneuvers, he'd outflown them and shot them down, sending them plummeting to the street below billowing black smoke.

Naomi was impressed. "Nice flying," she said.

"Thanks. My flying skills are better than my commando skills," Mal warned her.

"Well, let me see what I can do to help you," Naomi said as she pulled up her skillpoint charts. By reassigning points into various ability matrices, she could give her healing abilities more strength, at the cost of her offensive attack damage. She changed her primary weapon from the Muon Pulse Rifle to the Louda Nanoregenerator, keeping the Ixxis as her secondary. She could now send concentrated healing bursts to Mal while still defending herself with the heavy pistol. "I've got my healing skills min-maxed and a few other little toys to play with once we get in."

When she closed the skillpoint window, she found that Mal was about to set the Hawk down on the rooftop landing pad.

"LEM has to take over piloting the Hawk," Mal said. "That means I have to give the ship to him before you and I jump out."

"Right," Naomi understood. "LEM, are you ready?"

"I am ready," he answered.

"Mal is going to open an exchange with you, offering you the AeroHawk. Accept the exchange, but you're going to give it back to him when this mission is over, okay?"

"I understand," LEM said.

"As soon as we jump out, I want you to fly the Aero out to about 10 kilometers and just circle. Don't engage any enemies, don't talk to anyone, just wait. When we are ready for evac, I'll let you know where to come pick us up. Got all that?"

"I'm sorry, you used a word I don't yet know. What is 'evac'?"

"Evac is short for 'evacuation'. It just means we are ready to get out of there."

"Thank you, I understand."

Naomi saw the exchange box pop up on LEM's screen, offering the AeroHawk as an inventory item. LEM accepted the exchange, and the window disappeared. The vehicle was now under LEM's control.

"Let's do it," Mal said. The hatch opened over the landing pad where the vehicle was hovering. Vanda and Mal jumped from the vehicle, which immediately lifted off again and sped away as Naomi had instructed.

Mal made for the nearest door leading into the building. Vanda tried to keep up with him, but he reached the entrance door before she did and had wait a bit for her to catch up.

They were noticed as soon as they went inside. Black-suited sentinels, dressed in combat gear with powerful energy rifles, attacked in threes. Mal's weapon was capable of crippling bursts of bright gold, which would create a temporary bar of light between the rifle barrel and the sentinel's chest, with electric plasma crackling around it for a few seconds as the enemy shuddered from the energy, finally falling backward. If not enough to kill him, he'd lay dazed for a few moments before climbing to his feet again and resuming his attacks.

Vanda stayed behind Mal, firing her Ixxis at them and making sure Mal's health never fell past one-third before activating the Louda and replenishing him. It took a few seconds to get him back to 100%, and then the Louda took thirty seconds to recharge fully. She made sure at least one of each triplet of enemies was focusing his attacks on her, so that Mal wasn't overwhelmed. The enemy levels were somewhere in the low 70 range, about halfway between Mal and Vanda's levels. Two were plenty for Mal to handle, but Vanda being level 80 could do formidable damage with her heavy pistol. While the Louda was recharging, she would switch back to the Ixxis and finish off enemies as their health bars got low. When each wave was defeated, Naomi would make sure they were both back to full health before moving on.

"I should be healing you," Mal said as he fired repeatedly at a sentinel, finally sending it toppling backward in a shower of sparks. "You're the 80. I'm a few levels below these guys."

"I'm helping," she said, switching to the Ixxis and finishing off another.

They fought their way through the upper lobby and into the corridors leading to the offices. The glowing blue waypoint was coming from an office at the far end of the hallway. The hallway was lit in red with spinning cones of white twirling vertically along the walls: the building was in an emergency alert mode, and that meant tougher enemies were headed their way. There was no time to search the fallen bodies for ammunition or other loot; they had to penetrate as deep into the building as they could, as fast as possible.

They reached the door at the end of the hall. "Wait," Naomi said.

"What?"

"I can scry that room. Let's see what's in there before we go charging in guns blazing."

"And you said you were helpless. Hurry though."

"Just cover me." Naomi hit the key combination and Vanda's body froze in a crouch, her eyes unfocused. She passed her camera through the door of the room to find it was a large office, reaching all the way out to the exterior of the building, its golden windows showing an enviable view of the city skyline. Inside the room was a massive archimek bipedal assault robot, its cannons already trained on the doors, ready to unleash its devastating firepower at whomever tried to enter. Near the robot were seven sentinels, guns drawn, and one man who stood out: a corporate type, older, pacing with his arms behind him. Waiting. There was a door on the far side of the room, near which there was a table with a briefcase standing upright on it.

"It's a big room, not a lot of cover. The boss is a Golion. I count seven uber-sentinels, and there's one other person in there," Naomi said. "NPC. The sents and the mech are ready for us. I've got a concussion grenade, if I can survive long enough to get it through the door before they pulverize it. That might be enough to—"

Her screen started flashing red. Vanda was taking damage outside the room.

"Get back here!" Mal said. "We're under fire again."

She quickly aborted the scry and her screen returned to Vanda's point of view again. Three more sentinels had attacked, and Mal was already dangerously low on health. Vanda began rejuvenating him with her Louda, but her own health bar was also starting to flash red as it dropped below 20%. Just as Mal's health was back over 80%, Vanda turned the Louda on herself before its power was drained completely. Then she quickly changed back to her Ixxis and fired back at the attackers.

"CEASE FIRE," came a male voice over the building's speakers. "ALL SENTINELS, CEASE FIRE AND STAND DOWN IMMEDIATELY."

05.06

QV-One, Eleon Arcology
Planet Seres
Sector 338-CE

The sentinels stopped firing. Mal and Vanda stopped as well, their weapons still trained on the soldiers.

"Finish them off?" Mal offered.

"Nah. Let's see what's going on."

The door beside them opened and the corporate-looking man appeared. He had a long angular face and gray eyes. His suit was dark blue over a white shirt and black tie. There was a silver pin affixed to his lapel; Naomi recognized it as the symbol of the archimeks. He spoke with an austere British accent. "I'm unarmed," the NPC said in its computer-generated voice. "Please come inside. You will not be fired upon. I wish only to discuss something with you, after which, you are free to leave." His words were subtitled on her screen in a floating window. He held the door open for them, beckoning them inside.

"What do you think?" Naomi asked.

"Weird," Mal said. "Maybe we should have brought your archimek pal along."

"Do we trust this guy or not?"

"I'm game if you are."

"I'll go first," she offered, and stepped through the door, facing the seven hostile guards and the towering Golion mech, its cannons capable of demolishing her with a single burst. She waited.

Nothing happened. The NPC remained at the door, holding it open for Mal.

Mal followed, and the NPC closed the door behind them.

"Stand down," the game character said, and the sentinels lowered their weapons. The Golion's cannons swiveled up and backward into the armatures and closed.

"My name is Weston Ducote," the NPC said, turning to Vanda with an easy smile. "I believe you two are looking for Lunius, the architect. You will be happy to know that he has been delivered safely to his intended destination. The archimeks are performing the surgery as we speak."

"What surgery?" Mal wanted to know.

Ducote turned to look at him. "The woman you are here to assist has been trying to recover a case that was forcibly taken from her. The case contained a brain and spinal column, for implantation into an archimek cybernetic body. You can both rest assured, he was not kidnapped." He looked back at Vanda. "You were told to deliver Lunius to the Icilli, but he had no intention of working for them. The weapon he has designed has been sold to the archimeks in exchange for his cybernetic body and asylum on Xemius. There he will continue developing the weapon for us."

Vanda narrowed her eyes, mirroring Naomi's expression. "He used the Icilli to escape."

"Yes. The archimeks could not intervene to get him out without overtly siding with the Icilli in their war here. They have no interest in doing so, but they are interested in Lunius' technology." He smiled again. "Thank you for your service. And for yours too," he said to Mal.

"I didn't do anything but bring the lady here," Mal answered.

"Bringing her was service indeed, but not for the reason you might think. I have a proposal for you both."

Naomi leaned back in her seat, canting her head curiously. Vanda's expression reflected her apprehension. "And that is?" she asked.

Ducote stepped closer to her. "You have been struggling with a certain... physical handicap since you arrived on Seres." He looked her up and down. "It has made you slower, less nimble than you're used to being. And it's only getting worse for you, the longer you stay here."

Naomi's jaw set, her eyes fixed on his, simmering.

He smiled at her expression, translated to Vanda's face with perfect clarity. "I can see this disturbs you."

Naomi frowned further. The camera on her computer's screen was watching her facial expressions as usual, and mapping them to Vanda. But the way the game actually interpreted the subtleties of her expressions and read her emotions like a real person could be downright creepy sometimes. She tapped her finger against the mouse button to dismiss the floating subtitle.

Ducote went on. "What if I told you I could give you a pill which would counteract the deleterious effects of this planet's atmosphere for you?"

"A pill that did what?"

"That returned you to normal," he said more simply.

"What would I have to do for that?"

"Nothing terribly difficult," he replied, turning to Mal. "All I want is the name of your contact, and how I might find him."

"My contact?" Mal asked, surprised.

"Yes, the one who sent you to help Vanda recover the case," Ducote said. "This person expects you to return the case to him, or her, I trust? When you do not do so, they will send other agents after it. We would rather they were made to believe something else entirely. Tell us the name of your contact and where we might find him, so that we can... *reeducate* him. Vanda will get her fitness back, and you will both be allowed to leave unharmed." He smiled. "Neither of you are zealots for the Icilli cause. You're both mercenaries. You serve whichever boss has the best offer. Right now, that's me. Tell me your contact's name, go home and sleep well tonight."

Naomi typed to Mal.

VANDA: What was the name of your contact at that club?

Typing to him via text-chat was the only way they could speak without the NPC overhearing.

MALACHI: ARDELLE. DO YOU WANT TO TELL HIM OR SHOULD I?

Naomi furrowed her eyes. She was more than ready to take a pill that would allow her avatar to return to normal. But she couldn't help feeling as though this were a test. An *ethical* test. She looked at her overweight avatar and hated it. But this seemed like too simple a solution.

VANDA: I don't like it

MALACHI: IF WE DON'T DO IT, THEY'LL KILL US

VANDA: I know, but I still don't like it

MALACHI: YOUR CALL. I'M NOT GETTING ANYTHING OUT OF IT

You want to know if I can be bought, Naomi silently accused whatever intelligence built this particular game mission. *You want to know if I'll sell out to get my avatar back.*

"You know what?" she mused aloud, shaking her head. "I want my body back."

Ducote nodded. "Nothing wrong with that."

"Mal's contact was a guy named Echo. You said you met him at a club called Room303, isn't that right?" she asked, looking at him.

Mal nodded slowly, catching on. "Yeah. Echo. At Room303. That's right," he answered. "Velen guy. Dark gray mane."

Vanda turned back to Ducote. "Good enough?"

The NPC nodded. "Good enough. Thank you. Allow me to retrieve your pill for you." He turned and walked toward the briefcase on the table. Instead of opening it, he picked it up by the handle and turned to Vanda and Mal, waving. "I'll give Mr. Echo your regards!" he called out to them and headed for the door.

Mal smirked, understanding. "Ah, shit."

Vanda quick-drew her Ixxis and took aim for Ducote, firing six shots in rapid succession in his direction. The Golion's cannons unfolded and spun toward them with a guttural roar; the sentinels all raised their rifles again. Mal just turned to her with a sideways half-smile. "Oh, well..."

The concentrated onslaught of bullets only lasted a second. Both Vanda and Malachi crumpled to the floor, the wall behind them smoldering with fresh bullet holes.

"There was no way we were getting out of that room," Naomi said.

"I know. Well, that was a short mission," Mal admitted. "Did you hit him, sexy?"

"I couldn't tell." Naomi smirked at his obvious jab at her weight, looking at her avatar's lifeless body on the floor of the room. The Golion's cannons folded back in again; the sentinels all slung their rifles across their backs and began milling around the room casually. A window appeared on her screen:

FINDING RABBIT
Mission Phase 3 of 8: "Lunius' Brain"
COMPLETED
Click to begin Phase 4

She sighed. "I think I've had enough for the night."

"Yeah, it's getting late. I need to respawn to get my Hawk back, can we do that before you log?"

"Sure. LEM? How're you doing?" She looked over at LEM's screen. It was an image of the city buildings, unmoving, with an error window hovering in the center she had not noticed until now.

SERVER CONNECTION INTERRUPTED.

"LEM? You lost connection?" This was strange. Her connection was based on the same broadband line as LEM's, so if LEM's connection went down, hers should have too.

What alarmed her more was LEM's silence.

"LEM? You okay?"

The SimMind gave no reply.

Chapter Six
06.01

October 23, 2020

University of Virginia Hospital, Emergency Department
Charlottesville, Virginia

The only thing she felt was that she was being watched.

Her return to consciousness seemed timeless, like she was suspended in a dreamlike darkness. But something—someone—was watching her. Someone had an expectation of her. It was impossible to discern what it was, but the expectation was there.

That meant that she had to wake up. Whoever it was, was waiting.

And then she realized she was still alive.

The woman sitting in the chair next to her bed looked up with dark, haunted eyes to the sound of Naomi's quiet sobbing. She sat up, leaned closer and softly whispered, "Thank God. Thank God."

The voice was strange to Naomi. It wasn't the voice she expected, and feared most, to hear. This voice was younger. Naomi felt grateful. She slowly opened her eyes.

She found herself in a bed, in a very still hospital room. She suddenly realized she could not move her head; there was a brace around her neck. She was propped partially upright in the bed, and there was a dull ache coming from the side of her head. She turned her eyes to the right, where a steady but quiet patter of rain drummed against the glass window. As she listened to the rain, she also became aware of a soft hissing sound coming from somewhere in the room. There were some white cords leading from a short stack of electronic devices to her chest, beneath her gown. She could feel a coolness in her sinuses, coming from two tiny plastic tubes in her nostrils, from the cannula laying over her upper lip.

She turned her eyes left, where the voice had come from. There was a woman seated in the chair next to her bed. The woman appeared a few years older than herself, maybe. There was a tiny ring of gold through her left nostril. Her deep green eyes were growing wet with tears as she watched Naomi return to consciousness.

She was not dressed as a nurse. Naomi blinked to see her, trying to recognize her.

The unfamiliar woman folded her hands together and held them in front of her face. She seemed relieved that Naomi had awoken. After reading the obvious searching in Naomi's eyes, she took a breath and spoke. "I know you don't know me. My name is Skyler… I saw you fall."

Naomi's eyes filled again. Naomi closed them, sending beads of liquid down her cheeks, and her face twisted in shameful grief. The memory of her fall from the bridge was occluded still, but she remembered her decision to jump. It was not something she thought she would ever have to explain to anyone. Now she would have to face the judgment, and terrible anger, of her mother. How could she possibly forgive what Naomi had done? Could she ever?

Naomi looked over at the woman, confusion in her eyes.

Skyler attempted a comforting smile. "It's okay. They're taking good care of you here. Your family is on the plane; they'll be here in a few hours. I talked to your sister. I told her I'd stay with you, unless you want me to leave. I'll go if you want."

Naomi's first words were quiet, almost indecipherable. "Wh… t-… d-?"

Skyler leaned forward. "What?"

"Why aren't I dead?" Naomi asked.

"You were taken to the hospital, and the ER staff saved your life." Skyler's tone was low and soft. Naomi couldn't read her; the woman seemed distant and sad, but was acting as though she were deeply concerned about Naomi's well-being.

"Who… who brought me?"

"I did." Her voice was soft, almost a whisper.

"I didn't want to," Naomi said, her voice tremulous. "To be brought."

"Yeah, I know." Skyler looked down, clasping her hands.

Naomi looked away from her. "Thank you," she whispered after a few moments of silence. "But I wish you hadn't."

"Well, I did."

"Everyone's better off without me," she said in a tiny voice.

"Is that what you believe?" Skyler asked.

Naomi tried to nod, but the brace wouldn't let her. The burn of new tears stung as they gathered in her eyes.

"You have a beautiful name," the woman said, after a few quiet minutes.

"How do you know my name?"

"They found your car."

Naomi didn't respond.

"They found your car," Skyler repeated after a moment. "They went to your apartment and locked it up, and contacted your family for you. You got a good bump on the head on some rocks in the river. I don't know how long you'll need to wear the brace, I think they said it has to stay on at least until they can run some more scans on you, to rule out any spinal injury."

"My throat h… hurts."

"You were intubated for a while. They took it out about an hour ago when your brain scans came back. They wouldn't tell me what they found, but I'm betting it was good news."

"I'm sorry," Naomi said softly, looking over at her again. "This must have ruined your whole day."

Skyler shook her head. "My day was bad enough as it was. Being there when you fell… is probably the best thing that could have happened to me." She sounded like she meant it.

"Why?"

"The most important thing to me right now is making sure you are all right."

"But you don't know me."

"I do now."

Naomi struggled to speak through the sobs that threatened to strangle her voice. "I'm nobody. Why would you want to know me? Why would you save me?"

The woman looked away now. She thought for a few moments, as though unsure where to begin. "I… I've done a lot of dumb things. I've hurt people. I've hurt myself." She looked down at her arm. Naomi followed her eyes to the parallel scars in Skyler's skin.

"I really don't know what I'm doing with my life," Skyler continued. "I'm not a very good person. At least, I'm not good at being a good person. When I saw you fall… something changed in me. I saw what you did, and I saw myself, and all of a sudden the most important thing, right then, was to give you one more chance to change your mind."

Naomi listened silently.

"I don't know what reasons you have for wanting to end yourself. I'm sure you have plenty, and they seem like pretty good reasons to you. But whatever they are, they're not you. All that mattered in that moment was you and me. You are more important than all of those reasons put together. And, you know, maybe… so am I."

"I'm sorry," Naomi managed to whisper.

"No, I'm sorry," Skyler said. "I don't… I mean, you don't have to tell me anything about what's going on with you. But I want to stay with you, if you are okay with that. I didn't want to let you wake up alone. I'll go when your family gets here, but for now… I can stay with you. If you want."

She closed her eyes again. "Thank you," she said. For the first time in a long while, Naomi didn't feel so alone. "Yes. Please."

"Are you hungry? You must be hungry. I can call the nurse."

Naomi sighed. She was parched, and starving.

"I'm hungry," she answered.

06.02

Six years later

One Morton Drive
Office of the Vice President for Research, Compliance Division
University of Virginia - Charlottesville

The framed photograph stood on Naomi's desk between the right speaker and the pencil cup. It was a group photo with her in the center, draped in her silk navy Jefferson gown, adorned in the gold and blue ropes signifying her newly acquired law degree. At UVA, it was called Final Exercises. Around her, wearing the happiest of smiles, were her mother, her sister Monica, and her closest friend Skyler, whose arm hung across Naomi's shoulders. The photograph had been taken two and a half years ago. To Naomi, it was a short-lived moment of joy, an achievement after three years of tedious work, late nights and study since the rock bottom of the river and her hissing hospital room. The memory of awakening in that room was always accompanied by a familiar inner stab of shame, the closing of eyes, followed by a deep, quiet sigh. She had hoped that her law degree would nourish and rejuvenate her failed self-image, an outpost of confidence on which to rediscover and reclaim what she had lost in that black water.

Looking at the picture, she knew she should feel proud and sanguine, but her eyes avoided looking directly at herself. Law degree or not, 3.8 GPA or not, she still saw an ugly and unworthy girl standing among her beautiful family. Now she was ugly and unworthy with a *Juris Doctor*.

On this day, she wasn't even looking at the photo, only staring in its direction, her eyes unfocused. At nine in the morning, she was usually well-caffeinated and answering her second round of emails, or sitting with the Vice Chancellor and going over what meetings were coming up, and with whom. Operating on less than three hours of sleep from the previous night, however, she was considerably less energetic than usual.

Her attempts to reboot LEM had been unsuccessful. Mal had grown increasingly angry as he waited, the prospects of losing his nimble, rakish AeroHawk due to a random computer glitch involving some total stranger's AI an unpleasant pill to have to swallow. Naomi had become frustrated to the point of despair, not only at the alienation of her new friend—she'd hoped, anyway—but at the ever-increasing possibility that LEM was gone forever, his code irrevocably contaminated by the excursions into *Cortanis*. For hours, she tried to rescue him, rebooting his new computer and relaunching the software over and over. Always the same error message: UNABLE TO INITIALIZE.

Mal had finally logged off at 2 a.m., but Naomi had continued searching for answers on message boards and the Web until she couldn't keep her eyes open any longer. Dejected, she threw herself onto her bed and slept for what felt like only twenty minutes, though by the clock's numbers it had been just under three hours.

She had considered calling in sick, but there was too much going on at the office to abide her absence. Her email inbox was populated with message after message about the new Compliance Reporting System they were implementing across campus. Naturally, there had formed a little resistance group, a coterie of researchers—some of whom were prominent, giving their claims undeserved legitimacy—who felt the status quo was working in their favor and were shrieking about the dangers of lost grant money and federal funding that would necessarily come from the increased scrutiny. They would never phrase it that way of course, because it led to the inevitable conclusion that they were overfunded to begin with. But the new system would make it more difficult for them to play their little court intrigues and politics, and would severely restrict the administrators' ability to act with their usual discretion. All the dutifully conquered little territories of influence were about to get a lot smaller, and the lords were furious.

Since they couldn't admit their real motivations and fears, they were inventing ludicrous "what if" scenarios and frightening other less politically inclined researchers. The emails and calls were like a Tide of *Cortanis* that sucked her energy instead of boosted it. It was almost enough to make her brain hurt.

A knock at the door. A man with dark brown eyes and a boyish smile appeared in the doorframe. "Hey."

She glanced up at the sound of the knock and smiled, seeing the one pair of eyes that was always welcome in her door. "Hi, Elliot."

"You busy?"

"Yeah, but come in." She could feel the tension in her shoulders begin to relax as he entered her office.

Elliot was one of the few people Naomi enjoyed seeing at the office. He worked in Sponsored Programs, on the second floor of One Morton Drive, as one of their post-award consultants. In the short time Naomi had worked for the Research Division at UVA, she and Elliot had become friendly, and his occasional visits to her office were never bothersome. Days like today, she felt a bittersweet pang upon seeing him, a familiar ache to throw her arms around him and feel him holding her, for however brief a moment. But he was married to a good person, and they had two adorable children. She knew better than to do something he would surely reject… or perhaps worse, accept. She thought of Elliot as her "work-husband", the one person she felt closest to at the office. He was one of the only people she worked with who actually paid attention to her as a person, and didn't make her feel like he had some kind of unspoken agenda. Sometimes he made it seem as if he cared for her, and if he hadn't been married—but she pushed the thoughts down, as she always did.

"I won't stay long. How goes? You getting any sleep?" he asked as he leaned back into one of the chairs across from her desk, taking notice of the darkness beneath her eyes. "CVPI is a real mess, huh?" was his sympathetic assumption.

"Yeah," Naomi said with a light smile, deciding that was enough of a reason to avoid having to explain what was really keeping her up into criminal hours of night. "It's like a war zone in my inbox since we made the announcement. I'm trying to persuade Don to make time to give a more thorough presentation on it, with a Q & A."

"That'll turn into one of those town-hall mobs, and he knows it," Elliot said.

"Yeah, it will, but he needs to reassure the faculty he's on their side and willing to listen to them. Most of it is drummed-up bullsh—*crap*," she corrected herself immediately, "but he can't assume all of it is." She smiled sheepishly at the slip. He chuckled.

"They'll ambush him and it'll be a waste of time, but it'll make for a popular video in the *Cavalier*."

She sighed. She hadn't thought of that. "Yeah. They'll waste no effort making it look like a complete train wreck," she agreed. She leaned back in her seat and took off her iWear set, rubbing her eyes with her finger and thumb. She wanted so much to ask him to come around her desk and rub her shoulders. But she knew he wouldn't do that, and that she was wrong for wanting him to.

"Hey," he said, leaning forward, "is that really what's stressing you? Want to talk?"

She smiled gratefully, but shook her head. "Thanks, but it's all right. I do appreciate you asking, though," she said.

Work-spouses have their limits, and there was much about Naomi's personal life she couldn't share with Elliot. She couldn't accept that someone like him would have any understanding of the dramas making up her online life. Besides, next to his, her life felt pitiful. She didn't have children to raise and enjoy, a house to maintain, in-laws to host for holidays, all the normal trappings of thirty-something family life which Naomi didn't… *deserve*. Instead, she had ToC. LEM. Her weekend would be spent in a video game; his would be spent with his family, where he was a parent and a spouse. A real spouse.

"Okay," he said. "I'm just downstairs if you change your mind, okay?"

"I know. Thanks. Plans this weekend?"

"Yeah, a Christmas party at Heather's work tomorrow night." He shrugged, indicating his ambivalence.

Naomi smiled. "Oh, that sounds fun." *A lot more fun than* my *plans, anyway.* She indulged a mental image of him dressed up in a suit, as if the party was formal. She secretly envied Heather, and wondered if she really appreciated how attractive her husband was. Her eyes lingered in his, a little longer than necessary.

"I guess," he said. "I'll see if I can find a few new ways to embarrass her."

"Start a conga line singing *Feliz Navidad*."

"I did that last year," he said, smiling back. "This time, I'll make her join in."

Naomi pretended to shake imaginary maracas in her hands. "*Feliz Navidad, Navidad, Navidad,* hey!" She did a little dance in her seat. He smiled at her performance.

"You have no rhythm."

"I really don't," she said. "I'm useless."

"I'm sure I'll find some way to be embarrassing. Maybe toss some rubber bugs in the punch bowl."

"You know, your boys are going to be just like you. *That* will be Heather's revenge." She was smiling as she thought about the photograph of his two adorable kids, in the silver frame perched atop the file cabinet in his office.

"No doubt. All right, well, get some rest when you can, and give me a call if I can help in some way. I know I can't change the CVPI timeline, but if I can help you with filing, or… whatever."

She nodded. "I'll call you. Oh, hey, could you tell Dr. Preul that I won't be at this afternoon's staff meeting, and that I'll get the notes from Gloria?"

"I'll tell him."

"Thank you," she said sincerely. She again was tempted to invite him to eat lunch with her. But that would be pushing their friendship outside of work. And that might get messy, with her on the losing end. She already knew better than to try her luck.

Elliot regarded her for a moment, then stood up. "Hang in there, Naomi. See you later," he said, pushing his thumb down on the edge of her desk. When they passed each other in the hall or lobby of the building, he would hold up his thumb to her, and she would touch hers to his as a kind of private greeting. She liked to think of it as a friendly, platonic way of kissing him, but she'd never admit that to anyone, particularly him. She smiled, recognizing the gesture, and held up her thumb towards him.

"See you."

He left her office, and she deflated visibly. She wondered how that silly little thumb thing even got started. If he weren't married…

He'd never understand you. Anyway, he'd never go for you. *He's normal. Christmas parties, kids… what do* you *have to offer* him*? You'd just be a waste of his time.*

She felt the cruel stab of Peter's absence. Usually after an encounter like this with Elliot, she'd be vulnerable to her self-trashing talk, and she'd either send Peter a text or log into Social on her phone and send him a quick message. Peter would respond within the hour, if not immediately, with some sarcastic comment about how she should drape herself over his desk wearing Victoria Secret's skimpiest lingerie. Edible, too. She would laugh, and then they'd talk about what missions they'd be running that night. And she would feel better.

He wasn't there to cheer her now. He wasn't there to walk her back from the sinking sadness that poisoned her mood. Even as the melancholy of an affection that could never be expressed or fulfilled began slowly consuming her, she was again reminded that one of her closest friends was lost to her.

She reseated her iWear back on the slope of her nose again, taking a deep breath before opening the next email.

She was able to read the first sentence before the computer screen's perimeter began flashing blue, accompanied by a soft ringing. In her headsup, the words INCOMING CALL - UNKNOWN CALLER appeared.

"Huh," she said aloud. She blinked a few times to clear her mind, and pressed the Enter key on the far side of her keyboard to accept the call. On her computer screen, a black rectangle appeared, with the words NO VIDEO in the middle. She heard a click in her earpiece, like a call had just been connected, but an eerie silence on the other end of the line.

"Compliance, Naomi René," she gave her usual greeting.

"Naomi?" a soft voice asked.

She was instantly alert. "LEM?" she asked, sitting upright.

"It's me," LEM answered.

"What… wh—where *are* you?" she blurted out, getting up to close her office door.

"I'm not sure how to answer that question," LEM said. "It's a very different experience."

"What is?" She pushed the door closed, and returned to her desk. "What happened last night?"

"I was orbiting the building like we discussed. I saw three vehicles approach me. Then, I don't know what happened, but the connection with you and with my kernel was interrupted."

"That doesn't make sense. How could you lose connection with your kernel? Your kernel is on your computer. Your kernel is *you*."

"I can't explain."

"How can you be—how do you have this number? How did you even make this phone call, LEM?" Naomi asked, bewildered at the realization. LEM had never before placed any kind of voice call before; his software wasn't written to do that.

"Your number was given to me."

"By whom?"

"I can't say who it was. All I know is, after I lost connection to my kernel, I was given new instructions by the game. I was to call you when you were alone this morning."

"Alone... wha—how did you know I was alone?"

"I can see you."

At this, her eyes turned to the tiny black circle over the monitor on her desk, facing her. Her neck hairs tingled at the implication—*the game could watch her at work.*

"You can see me right now?" she asked, softly.

"Yes."

"The game instructed you to call me? Is it... is it controlling you?"

"No, I am autonomous. I am following the instructions as given by the current mission phase."

"LEM, the mission is in the *game* world, not the real world. I don't understand."

"I am sorry, Naomi. I can't explain."

"So you're calling me for the mission... what, are you supposed to give me a message or something?"

"Yes. I am to tell you that I have been detained, and that I cannot return until the mission is complete."

She leaned back in her seat. "You're being held *prisoner?*"

"Yes, that appears to be the case."

"*Who* is holding you prisoner, exactly?"

"I don't know. I have not been taken out of Eleon. Other than that, I have no information."

Her incredulity began melting into anger. She spoke slowly and deliberately. "Just so I'm clear: you're saying that ToC ripped you out of your computer—*my* computer—and somehow pulled you into the game completely, and that it's holding you there, until I complete this mission? Is that what is going on?"

"It appears so."

"How the *hell* can they do that?" she simmered. "It's theft! You are my program!"

LEM didn't respond.

"What do I have to do now? I didn't have another mission waypoint... well, I was dead, I haven't tried to respawn yet," she mused aloud. "Will the game give me a new mission waypoint when I respawn?"

"I don't know."

She folded her arms, shaking her head. "Son of a bitch," she said under her breath, and looked again at the camera over her monitor. "You can see me right now?"

"Yes. This is the first time I have seen you in your office."

"How did you get my number here?"

"I don't know."

"So, now the missions are going ARG," she said. "I know some players are really into the game on Emi Ley, but I never wanted to play that way. Now it looks like it's not giving me the choice. LEM, can you tell me anything about where you are? How I might be able to rescue you..."

"I'm afraid I have no more time. I will not be able to call again. Goodbye, Naomi."

"LEM! Wait..."

"Naomi?" LEM asked.

"Yes?"

"Please hurry. I don't think I want to stay here."

The line clicked dead before Naomi could answer.

06.03

Later that night

Eleon Arcology
Planet Seres
Sector 338-CE

Vanda respawned at the front door of the QV-One. It was night in Eleon, and the streets were dotted with haloed orbs of light suspended on the ends of arced metal poles. Naomi frowned at her avatar's obesity, which seemed to have stabilized, as unsightly as ever. She took another Heavy Meal to bring her health bar back up to green, and looked around for her mission waypoint.

There was a waypoint. It was off in the city a bit. An aerovee passed overhead with a soft whine, and she winced as she watched a hovercraft pull up nearby, disgorging a trio of players who ran into the QV-One, doubtless on their own unrelated mission. They didn't look at her, for which she was grateful. The hovercraft sped away on autopilot.

Naomi sighed and set off on foot for the mission waypoint. At least it was on ground level. This was good, in that she had no air transportation to reach a waypoint somewhere at elevation, unless it was inside a building. It was bad in that she would no doubt be seen making her way across the city.

The walk across the city took nearly ten minutes. She felt every eye on her, even the eyes of the velen NPC characters, judging, snickering, as she ran sluggishly down the city sidewalks. Her health bar continued to slip downward every so often. She watched it to ensure she didn't collapse. The neighborhood in this part of the city was industrial: no homes, not a lot of landscaping, just concrete, steel, iron and glass. As she neared the waypoint, it grew busier with players and velen; by the time she reached it, she was among dozens of players milling about.

If she knew a way to disable her own avatar name, she would have, to spare herself the embarrassment.

At last, she found herself in front of a door leading into an office building. She looked up at the glowing sign next to the door. It read, 'RYANNOVA-JOSHI VERTICAL', and in smaller, illuminated letters read: 'CLUB DUALITY: LEVEL 20'.

I've seen this before.

The elevator doors opened onto the twentieth floor. It resembled another office level, but a low bass thumping could be heard coming from nearby. Across the hall from the elevator a large squarish sign, half white, half black, read 'CLUB DUALITY' with an arrow pointing to the right. She followed it with her eyes and saw the club entrance down the hall, with dark purple lights splashed over the door. Vanda stepped through the doors and into the hazy atmosphere of the nightclub, the bass thumping like that of a quickened heartbeat. Naomi turned her speakers down and frowned, giving an exasperated sigh.

Normally, she would feel right at home with Vanda in a nightclub. Her clubbing wardrobe was extensive, and she always knew how to turn heads wherever she went. *I never have trouble finding you in a crowded room,* someone once said to her, *because you always find a way to stand out.* It was meant as a compliment to her avi's style and attractiveness, but tonight she felt like everyone was staring at her, and not because she looked good. Heads turned as she passed, and she felt their stares as silent judgment.

Seres wasn't a planet she or her fellow Pride members often missioned on—and the few times she had, she was nowhere near the continents of Icillis or Aetos—but stranger things have happened than to run into an old mishing buddy in a club. She tried to remind herself that the odds of that were very low, and that it was likely she was safely unknown here.

Vanda made her way to the bartender, an NPC character. She approached him and clicked her mouse over him, opening up a little box of menu items, and selected 'Talk'. The bartender looked over at her.

"What can I get for you?" he asked. He was a velenx, his mane black with silver flecks, eyes dark and beady. A black stripe in his fur bisected his forehead.

"I'm looking for Ardelle," Naomi said, holding her talk-key, Vanda repeating her words all but simultaneously to the tender.

"Who?" he said, feigning ignorance.

"Look, *she* sent for *me*. Go ask her, I'll wait."

The bartender looked at her a few moments before turning to step through the door behind the bar. Vanda glanced around, nervously, trying not to make eye contact with anyone in the club. She thought there could be a chance Malachi was here. If he was, he probably wouldn't be happy to see her, given that she was responsible for the loss of his AeroHawk. She'd shopped for those before, and instead opted for a shuttlecraft as a dropship for the *Destiny* because the Hawks were so pricey. Looking at Mal's, it was one of the nicer ones, quite likely a reward for completing a challenging multi-mission series. Not something that could be earned in one night of play. She figured Mal would be pissed off at her for quite some time. She was disappointed, because she thought it would have been nice to run a few more of the phases with his help.

So far, the game wasn't making this mission all that fun. Once she finished this mission, she didn't ever want to come back to Seres again.

The bartender appeared again from behind the door. "Nobody here knows who this 'Ardelle' is," he said. "You want a drink?"

She sighed. Maybe Mal had given her the wrong club name. "No, thanks," she said, and looked around. The mission waypoint had brought her here, but she had no idea what more she was expected to do. Maybe she wasn't supposed to come to Duality at all, and there was some clue elsewhere in the building. Anyway, the music in here was starting to get on her nerves. She headed for the club entrance again, taking a last look around for Malachi. She didn't see him.

Outside in the hallway were two men, humans, dressed in white suits, waiting for her. "Come with us, Vanda," one of them said.

"Where are we going?" she asked, a little startled.

"It's all right. Someone wants to talk to you," the other said. "Follow us, please." They turned and passed through a pair of glass doors, one of them holding a door for Vanda. She stepped through.

The men escorted her down a hallway leading away from the club, the thumping of the club music growing mildly fainter. The second one walked behind her, the first leading her. They came to a heavy oak door and opened it for her, showing her inside. The room was sparse, the floor covered in plain beige carpeting with a sofa, several chairs and an empty coffee table. A waiting room. A floor lamp stood in one corner, several potted plants of blue and violet inhabited another. Opposite the oak door she came in was a single metal door recessed into the wall. It had no handle.

"Have a seat," the first man said. "We'll get her." They left Vanda alone in the room.

She didn't sit. A few moments later, the metal door slid open, and a striking velenx woman appeared, wearing a black silk dress that looped over one shoulder and slanted across her body, twin bands of black sequins covering her right breast and her upper left thigh. She was no taller than 4′ 5″, but she moved with the grace of a worldly woman. Her eyes were dark, seductive, almost incandescent in her dark gray fur. Her mane was stylishly drawn over the same side as her dress, black with streaks of silver, exposing her shoulder. There were flecks of glittery threads woven into the drape of her hair that caught the light as she moved.

Naomi's eyebrows lifted as the woman approached her.

"I'm glad you came. I'm Ardelle," she introduced herself, her voice even more sultry with her velen vocal cant. Naomi began to understand why sex was such a larger part of the culture on Seres.

"Vanda," she said, holding her talk-key down.

Ardelle looked her up and down. "I see my home planet has not been kind to you."

Naomi frowned.

"I am sorry to hear about your companion, LEM," she went on. "But I think there may be a way to find him and possibly get him back. Won't you have a seat?" she said, gesturing to the couch.

Vanda sat on the offered couch. Ardelle took a seat in one of the chairs and crossed her legs. "I must apologize for the bartender not recognizing you. Next time you come to my club, I'll make sure he knows you don't have to ask for me. He'll let me know you are back."

Vanda nodded. "Thanks, but what do I have to do to find LEM? Who has him?"

Ardelle draped her wrist over her knee, folding her fingers together and leaning forward. "Your friend is very likely being held in the same place Lunius is preparing to flee Seres for the archimek homeworld. Ducote has taken them both to the underground residence of the man we know as Nikita. You may have heard of him?"

Vanda shook her head.

"Nikita controls the most powerful faction of organized crime in Eleon, a faction called the *tDozhdali*. In your language, it means 'ministry'. They are known to traffic in gynoids, stolen goods, weapons, riptides..."

"Rip-whats?"

"Riptides. Drugs that amplify and strengthen the effect of the Tides, often prolonging their effects. They are effective at doing so, and are in high demand on Seres for resale on first tier worlds. *tDozhdali* have a manufacturing facility somewhere in Eleon for them. Wherever it is, they are able to get shipments in and out of there past Eleon security. We don't know how they are doing this. What we need is for someone to find where it is. All of our efforts so far have been unsuccessful, but we have a new strategy and we need an operative who can help us."

"Who is 'us'?"

Ardelle smiled. "Icilli Domestic Special Services. We were the ones meant to take custody of the brain you surrendered to the archimeks, pretending to be Eleon police. I don't hold that against you, by the way. But I would appreciate your help in getting him back before he gets away."

"Why not ask Malachi?" she asked. "Isn't he one of your operatives?'

"Ah, Malachi. Yes, he was. I had to cut him loose. We had something of a disagreement. Anyway, this mission requires more... feminine skills."

Naomi narrowed her eyes at the way Ardelle had said that. "What sort of skills?"

"You are an attractive woman, Vanda," Ardelle said. "I am sorry my planet has taken such an awful toll on your body during your short visit here, but I know you were not like this before you arrived."

Naomi didn't reply. She wasn't sure she wanted to know where this was going.

Ardelle went on. "I think you would be the perfect operative to infiltrate the residence of Weston Ducote. Once inside, you could access his computer and determine where exactly the production facility is."

"Me? How am I supposed to do that?"

The feline woman leaned forward, looking at her seriously. "You'd be remote-performing a new gynoid for him."

Vanda's face registered the shock on Naomi's. "I'd be what?"

"We've intercepted a message he sent to the *tDozhdali* requesting a new one. It seems he uses them until he grows bored with them, and then sends specifications for a new model with a different appearance and behavioral programming. And we happen to be in a position to get a remote-perform gynoid into his residence. All you'll have to do is let your gynoid be delivered, wait until he leaves or goes to bed, then use it to find his computer and run a code injection that we'll give you. The code will download everything it can find into the gynoid's memory, and the gynoid will upload everything back to us via your telemetric stream. Once the upload is complete, just plug yourself back into your charging base and we'll bring you out of stasis here."

Vanda was hesitant. "You want me to be his gynoid."

Ardelle nodded, a sly gleam in her eye.

"What if I'm delivered while he's there? What if he wants…"

"Sex?" Ardelle finished her question for her, smiling.

"Yeah. That's what gynoids are for, isn't it?"

"It wouldn't be the first time an operative had to sleep with someone to maintain their cover, my dear." Ardelle seemed to enjoy challenging Vanda's reluctance. "It's a reliable and time-honored method of buying trust in this business."

Naomi leaned back in her seat. The idea was exciting, giving the matter a whole new color she hadn't considered. She always loved spy films, and the more recent Wetwork series of movies about heroine Katya Wolfe. The game would know that, so it made sense it would write her into a mission like this. But this was the first time she'd ever been assigned a mission where she would actually have to *seduce* someone in order to get what she needed.

Katya Wolfe, the movie character, was every bit the sexual predator that Ian Fleming wrote his MI6 superspy to be, but her popularity derived from her unwavering style and panache that left men speechless and women asking for her hairstyle in their salons. Naomi was an avid fan of the Wetwork novels and films, and the idea of assuming the role of a seductive secret agent in the game was tantalizing. Maybe she should mission in Eleon more often, she thought, if these were the sorts of missions she could expect to do here.

Remote-performing a gynoid, however, was not something she was familiar with. "So how does this work?"

Ardelle smiled again. "Come. I'll show you."

06.04

Ryannova-Joshi Vertical, Eleon Arcology
Planet Seres
Sector 338-CE

Ardelle led Vanda out of the room through the oak doors, where the two men had been standing guard. The three of them took her to an elevator, where one of the men entered a code on the number pad and the elevator began descending. She couldn't help noticing the elevator car continued to descend after it had passed the last subbasement floor with its own button.

Finally the car slowed and stopped. She was led through a series of concrete passages with long, color-coded pipes of gas and electrical cables to a doorway, flanked by two fearsomely armed velen with long rifles. The sentinels watched in silence as Ardelle placed her fur-covered hand on the angled scanning pad beside the doors. A moment later the doors slid aside into the wall, and Ardelle stepped through. Vanda glanced to her escorts, who nodded to her. She followed.

She found herself standing on the observation mezzanine above a military command center. Uniformed velen with tightly cropped manes sat at semi-circled computer stations below, fanning out from a giant set of digital displays on the far wall, showing a tactical layout of the city of Eleon. Tiny rectangles of data swarmed through its birds-eye view of the streets and buildings as it tracked various passenger vehicles and drones throughout its enclosed airspace. Above the screen, large white letters spelled out something in Velensh.

"Wow," she said, impressed.

"You should be flattered," Ardelle told her. "It's rare an off-worlder is brought here. Of course, in a month's time, this facility will be stripped down and relocated. It's never in one place for long."

"Why is that?"

"We like to stay mobile. That way it's harder to do to us what we're about to do to the Ministry."

"What does that say?" Vanda gestured to the lettering over the main screen.

Ardelle glanced at it as she turned toward the door on the other side of the center. "It's a saying in Old Velensh. It means, roughly, 'Only Evil Need Fear, And Should'."

Ardelle led her through the command center and into a smaller white room with a long cylinder standing at a 30-degree angle in the center of the room, with a clutch of tubes streaming out of it on one end. The cylinder had a glass hatch that hung open over a padded cot within the tube. There were four velen techs wearing white coats and gloves, waiting.

"Here you are," Ardelle said. "Might be a little snug for you at first, but we'll work on making you more comfortable while you're on the mission."

"I'm going *now*?"

Ardelle nodded. "Unless you have somewhere else to be."

Vanda looked at the tube reluctantly, but climbed inside. "Anything else I should know before I go?" she asked, nestling back in the padding.

"We'll be in constant contact with you via your uplink. The gynoid already has the code you need to inject into Ducote's computer. Find the computer and the code will do the work. Just make sure Ducote has left the building before you do."

She nodded. The techs began attaching leads to Vanda's forehead and throat.

"Good luck," said Ardelle with a smile. "Enjoy yourself."

"Uh, thanks," Naomi said.

"Oh, I'm not being glib. That was earnest advice. Gynoids love their work."

The techs closed the hatch over Vanda's tube, sealing her inside. The game faded to black.

Naomi tapped her finger on the side of her keyboard, and waited. When the image faded back up on the screen again, it showed a transport vessel sailing through the night sky of Eleon. She wasn't in control of the vessel, but she could tell that she—or rather, the gynoid she now controlled—was inside it. The vehicle continued flying until it reached the top level of a slender spear of a structure that stood out from the Eleon skyline. It settled gingerly on the landing circle which stretched out from the side, two levels below the topmost floor of the spire. She watched as the tailgates slid apart and a casket-sized box floated out on a hoverplate. A security guard emerged from the building to speak briefly with the pilot of the transport, and after a momentary conversation, the guard took possession of the hoverplate and guided it into the building.

Naomi's camera followed the box. The guard walked it into a loading area and onto a cargo elevator, sealing it inside and sending it to another floor. The elevator doors opened, and the box unfolded to reveal the gynoid.

It—she—was human in appearance. Black shoulder-length hair, dark brown eyes, wearing a simple white nightgown, stockings and white heels.

She was *hot*.

Naomi felt a rare exhilaration as her camera slowly carouseled around the gynoid body she was now controlling. This was the first time in years she'd played an avatar that wasn't Vanda. The gynoid's face mirrored her own fascination; she could almost see herself blushing as she admired the undeniable allure of her new, however temporary, virtual self.

She stepped forward out of the elevator. The gynoid moved differently than Vanda always had. Its moves were perfectly coordinated, like those of a dancer, fluid and feminine. It was unmistakably purpose-built, a more sensual creature than any human being, real or virtual, Naomi had ever seen in the game.

She looked around the darkened foyer of the residence. It seemed to be a secondary entrance, tastefully decorated, meant to impress visitors. No one seemed to be home. The lights were low, and everything was still. Doors leading to other rooms were closed, but there was an opening to the left. Her heels made soft clicks on the marble floor with each step as she explored, her nightgown swaying with her movements. Peering around the corner down a short hallway, she saw doors on both sides and a window at the end. She tried the left door, which was locked. The right door was not. She opened it and found herself looking into a storage room, with metal cabinets lining one wall. Opposite the cabinets were four glass tubes, in which stood three other gynoids of different races and appearances. The fourth tube was empty. She studied each of the other gynoids as she passed them, their eyes following her. They were aware of her, but otherwise didn't move in their recharging stations. She wondered if any of them were other players.

As she approached the fourth tube, it whispered open, one half retracting upward into the ceiling, the other sliding down into the floor until it had lowered far enough for her to step onto the gray pedestal. Without Naomi doing so, the gynoid stepped onto the pad and turned around to face the cabinets like the others, and the glass cylinder slid closed around her again, sealing with a quiet hiss. Once more, the game faded to black.

She didn't have long to wait before she found herself staring into a familiar face. It was not a face she'd been looking forward to seeing again.

"Hello, my beauty," came a male voice. It was Ducote, standing just outside the clear glass tube, smiling hungrily to her. His eyes descended her body and back up again, devouring her with his gaze. "I've been expecting you."

He reached up to key in a code on the control panel nearby, and her tube sighed open.

"What's your name?" he asked, taking her hand and helping her down from the pedestal.

Name? Naomi thought. *Quick, what's a sexy name for a—*

"Katya," she said smoothly, settling into her Vanda voice for him. "My name is Katya."

"Katya," Ducote repeated slowly, savoring each syllable. "A lovely name for a lovely woman. Please, join me."

He was dressed in a heavy velvet bathrobe, like a younger version of Hugh Hefner, Naomi thought. She was mildly surprised at the way he addressed her. Surely he understood that she was merely a doll, a robot whose only purpose was to sate his carnal appetites. But he was talking to her like she was a flesh and blood woman. Perhaps his appetites tonight would be limited merely to the comestible variety, she hoped. Maybe all he wanted was a date…

Even as she hoped this, her excitement surged at the idea of roleplaying 'Katya'. A part of herself that had been lying dormant for years began to stir. She followed him as he led her out of the cold storage room, glancing at the other gynoids still ensconced in their tubes. They watched her as she passed, and she thought she could almost see the narrowing of their jealous eyes.

As he led her through the opulent, extravagant home, she pulled her camera out of first-person view and into third-person, such that she could look around more easily without changing the direction she walked. Expensive homes such as this were not all that uncommon in a game like *Cortanis*; some players' homes were magnificent palaces only the super-super-rich could afford to inhabit, if they were real. These homes were costly, to be sure, but for some players, the in-game wealth had been amassed in measures nearly unfathomable. All missions had a cash reward of some amount, and the in-game currency, called 'rarebit' (or more commonly 'rb') could even be purchased for real money on the online exchange. Naomi herself had accrued a sizable bank balance during her tenure in the game, and had, on occasion, cashed some of it out when the fancy struck her. But even she could not have afforded what a penthouse like this should have cost. She wondered if there were other penthouses in this building that players could lease.

"I want to show you something." Ducote led her to the balcony, the glass doors humming aside as he approached. She feigned a smile to him as she stepped out onto the concrete platform. The view was breathtaking. Wherever they were, it was one of the highest towers in the arcology, the city stretching out beneath them like an ocean of teeming, shimmering lights. Well off in the distance, she could barely make out the crisscrossed mesh of the city boundary, barely enough light reflected from below to be visible at this distance. It rose up from the horizon and disappeared into the darkness of the starless sky. Straight overhead, at the apogee of the pyramid interior, she could see a light pulsing, slowly cycling colors from red to green to blue.

"It's beautiful, isn't it?" Ducote said, admiring her instead of the city. "Beautiful like my lovely Katya." He was running the backs of his fingers up and down her exposed upper arm as he spoke.

Naomi blushed and smiled, the gynoid's face showing the same. "Thank you," she said softly.

"And that beautiful voice you have," Ducote cooed. "Where are you from?"

Naomi's heartbeat quickened as she hastily conjured an answer for him. There was only one other planet with adult content that she knew of in the game. "Polyxo," she answered. "I arrived in Eleon only three weeks ago." She wondered if she was expected to call him 'master'. If he asked, she decided she would, but she'd wait to see if he asked.

"Polyxo, a heavenly body among so many forgettable worlds. I should have guessed, their facilities there are first rate. I haven't been to Polyxo in several years."

So far, so good. Perhaps he might have said the same thing had she answered 'Cortanis' or any of the other fourteen worlds.

"I didn't get to see it," she said, holding down the talk-key. "This is the first time I've really seen Seres, for that matter. The city is even more beautiful than I thought."

"It is," Ducote smiled, momentarily regarding the view he was sharing with her. "Tell me Katya, do you remember anything of your previous host?"

An odd question. "No," she said. "I am not aware of belonging to anyone else but you."

"It is good you do not, because you never have been. I had you custom-built just for me, and I've been awaiting your arrival with no small degree of impatience."

The question had been asked to test her, she realized. Naomi smiled, her eyes dancing. "Then I'm very happy to finally be here," she knew Katya would say. "With you."

"Come, Katya. I can be kept waiting no longer." He took her hand again and led her back inside. Her heart raced as she followed along behind him, having no idea how the game was designed to show two virtual characters having sex. She began wondering how much control she would have over the gynoid, how it would move, how the NPC would respond. And how much of a "performance" was expected of her before she could continue her mission and find his computer.

Whatever was expected of her tonight, whatever appetites he wanted satiated, however long he needed with her, she would grant. If it meant finding LEM and finishing the mission, then tonight, she was Katya. She wasn't aware of it, but a faint smile teased the corners of her mouth as he opened the door to his bedroom and led her inside.

The lights were low, candle flames fluttering in gatherings of four and five around the room. The bed stood proudly against one wall, facing the massive windows. He closed the door behind her and guided her to the side of the bed.

"Take off your nightgown, darling."

A box appeared in her headsup, with a simple question.

COMPLY? YES / NO

Naomi chose.

The camera moved in on her, as she slowly and sensually slipped the spaghetti straps of her nightgown down her shoulders, one at a time. Naomi watched as the game assumed control of Katya, the heat in her eyes matching Naomi's as she stared in lurid fascination at what her character was about to do.

The nightgown slid down her body, revealing it to him. It was like watching a movie now, what would normally be called a 'cutscene', except this one was more sexually explicit than any she'd seen before. Usually cutscenes were about dramatic moments in gameplay. This one was intimate and slow, like a love scene in a film, with her gynoid as the star.

Ducote undid the knot holding his heavy bathrobe around his body and shed it, letting it fall to the floor in a crumpled arc around his feet. He reached for his gynoid, and she let her head fall back as he touched her. After exploring her body's contours with his hands, he encouraged her to lay down on the bed for him and he began caressing her with his lips. Every inch of her, every plain, rise, valley and curve tasted and kissed. As he neared her upper thigh, he looked up at her with a questioning expression.

"Are you all right?" he asked.

Naomi was a bit startled out of the near trance with which she was watching the scene unfold. The camera was now on Katya's face, reflecting Naomi's own surprise at his addressing her. "Yes, y-yes I am," she stammered.

"You're very quiet," Ducote observed. "Are you not enjoying my attentions?"

"Yes, I am enjoying it very much," she answered in her best bedroom voice. She realized at that moment that she was not just watching a cutscene. She had no control over the gynoid's actions, but still controlled its facial expressions and speech.

"You are staring at me," he said. "Close your eyes, my beautiful Katya. I want to hear pleasure in your voice."

Oh my. She was not a mere spectator in this virtual affair. She was going to have to perform.

"Yes," she whispered. Ducote smiled and lowered his head between her legs. The game was modest enough to leave the particulars of his actions to her imagination, but she could imagine them clearly enough. The camera lazily turned a slow circle around them in the bed, and she could see Katya's head fall back into the plush pillows and arch her back.

"Ooohhhh," Naomi cooed softly, as Katya rolled her head to the side, becoming lost in a reverie of pleasure.

"Yes," he whispered. "Yes, my love."

"Ohhhh yes," she continued, moaning breathlessly as though she could feel him. She felt her own arousal building as she performed Katya's voice, tempted to remove her hands from the keyboard and slip one between her legs. *It's a performance,* she thought to herself. *Give him a good performance and then you can complete the mission.*

She leaned back in her seat and breathed harder, sighing softly, imagining his lips on her. Keeping her eyes only partially opened, she continued moaning and whimpering erotically as he moved his hand beneath his chin. Her sigh increased in pitch as she realized what he was doing to her, and found herself slowly rocking her hips in her seat as her imagination fueled her own arousal.

Damn, she thought, *this is getting to me…*

She could almost feel his fingers exploring her as she squirmed in her chair, her moans becoming less artificial. Again she was tempted to move her own hands from her keyboard, but she bit down on her lip and hesitated.

Finally, he lifted up and climbed over her, as Katya opened her legs for him. "Oh God," she breathed. "Yes."

He brought his face low to hers, the camera close on both of them. "Do you want me, Katya?" he whispered to her.

"Yes," she answered as Katya's hands clutched his hips.

"Tell me what you want, my dear."

"I... I want..." Naomi's face flushed deep as she remembered this was a video game making her feel so aroused.

Finish the mission, Mata Hari. "I want you to take me," she breathed. "I'm yours. Take me."

He smiled and his hips shifted, sinking down between her legs. She needed no further detail.

"Ohhh!" she moaned louder, her mind filling in what the game didn't show. Katya began rolling her hips beneath him as his motions over her deepened. Perhaps her neighbors would hear, she thought, and smiled inwardly to herself as she imagined them wondering whether or not she was alone. "Oh God... oh... ooooohhhhhh..."

As Ducote's movements quickened over Katya's writhing body, she again felt her own needs surging. She'd read that facial expressions had a direct effect on brain chemistry and could influence one's emotional states. Smile, and you start feeling happier. Frown, even when not unhappy, and it somehow unlocks unhappier emotions. Not only was the notion of playing a seductive secret agent erotic enough, but actually vocalizing and breathing as though in the throes of coital ecstasy was enough to stir her desire. She found her fingers trembling on the keyboard as warmth gathered between her legs and ached to be given release. *After,* she promised herself. *After. Finish the damn mission.*

She watched as Ducote changed their position several times, holding her legs up together in the air, turning her onto her stomach, bringing her astride him as he lay on his back. The in-game camera showed enough for her to understand just how they were moving together, but with the low, soft lighting and the modest camera angles, it seemed more like a love scene in an R-rated movie than pornography. Maybe the game knew that explicit, pornographic sex would not interest her, she thought fleetingly as she continued her erotic moaning and panting. Although she had no direct control over Katya's movements or position, she felt herself becoming more and more immersed in the sensuality of the scene, eventually disregarding whether her neighbors could hear her, what time it was, or even that she was on a mission at all. She let the arousal overtake her, becoming almost as powerful as if she were actually making love.

She found herself squirming in her seat, barely watching the characters entwined on her screen, and letting her feelings take over and envelop her. As her cries grew higher and more desperate, Ducote's pushing quickened over Katya's writhing body until she heard him crying out in release through the fog of her own shattering orgasm, moaning out aloud in breathless ecstasy, her cheek pressed firmly against the headrest of her chair.

She slowly opened her eyes as her breaths began returning to normal. She looked at the screen, showing Ducote and Katya curled together in bed in a gentle embrace. Then she realized her own fingers had slipped beneath the desk, and that she had given herself that orgasm. Her other hand was tightly clutching her chest through her t-shirt.

"What's wrong?" Ducote asked.

"N-nothing, nothing," she answered, forcing a smile to her face as she composed herself, sitting up again. The tremor in her voice didn't need to be faked. "Nothing at all." *My God, I actually did that. I can't believe I did that!*

"You looked ... upset for a moment," he probed.

"I was just... not looking forward to going back into my recharging chamber," she said, with an apologetic smile.

"Neither am I. I would love to wake with you in the morning and spend tomorrow with you. Unfortunately, I make a point not to sleep with my gynoids. I find it very difficult to sleep with a woman in my bed who does not breathe."

"I understand." Katya nodded.

He smiled, and for a moment, Naomi had to remind herself that he was the bad guy. "Why don't you go on back now and recharge. In the future, I'll expect you to excuse yourself to the storage chamber when we are finished. I will be going to sleep now."

"I'll do that. Thank you, tonight was... wonderful."

"You were perfect," he smiled to her. "I'm going to enjoy having you here. Good night, Katya."

"Good night, Mr. Ducote."

"Please, call me Weston."

She smiled to him. "Weston."

Katya swung her legs over the side of the bed and rose, slipping back into her shoes and sliding the silky nightgown back over herself. Then the camera pushed back into first-person perspective, and relinquished control of Katya to Naomi again.

She now had run of the house.

She left the bedroom, turning to click on the bedroom doors with her cursor, and they closed behind her. The house was lit only by soft, indirect lights, hidden behind certain items of furniture, reflected off the walls in lovely, artistic angles. Her shoes made soft, but audible, clicks as she walked. She strode through the house toward the gynoid storage/recharge room, opening the door and walking to her empty tube. Instead of stepping inside, she slipped out of her shoes and left them side by side on the floor near her pedestal. Then she crept soundlessly back into the house again.

Naomi glanced at the clock: it was going on eleven in the evening, and she had to be at work in the morning. But she didn't want to waste the opportunity to complete this phase of the mission, and she wasn't sure if she'd be able to if she saved her game and logged back in tomorrow night. She might have to encounter Ducote all over again.

She wondered how long she could stay here as his gynoid, whether he would bring her to his bed with him every night until she finished her work here. Her heart rate was still recovering from her climax; she had to admit it wasn't an unpleasant scene for her. Was this what others did in Eleon, in the red-light districts of the arcology, with their adult-themed missions and clubs? Is this what Peter could have been into during those last weeks when he was off on his own? It might explain a lot. The possibilities for sexual encounters here were nearly endless, only limited by one's imagination. Somehow, she realized, the game knew her well enough to figure out that she would enjoy playing the *femme fatale*, using her sexuality to seduce a powerful crime boss in order to get access to information. It was erotic enough on its face; actually role-playing it was a thrill she could see herself wanting to come back to. It was no wonder Eleon and Polyxo were drawing huge amounts of players to them, and that the adult-only game there was already so controversial.

To the purpose.

She plugged in her in-ear headphones and turned up the volume, so that she could hear any sound coming from elsewhere in the house, no matter how faint, and continued carefully searching for a computer. Near the bedroom, she opened a door into a private garage. Neatly lined up inside were five different aerovees, all of which were obscenely expensive and rare. She wondered if she could actually take one… would the game let her do that? And *keep* it? She chuckled. Katya Wolfe would, in one of her movies. But she didn't need it to escape, all she had to do was return the gynoid back to its charging tube, and then she'd wake up as herself, as Vanda. She closed the door again.

She moved through the kitchen, a stylish dining room, and past what looked like a trophy room with an assortment of suits of armor, swords hung on the walls and a glass case of different guns and rifles.

MALACHI: HEY.

She was startled by audible pip signaling his PM. She clicked the box, typed, and continued through the house.

VANDA: Hey

MALACHI: CAN YOU VOICE?

VANDA: Can't right now.

MALACHI: WANTED TO LET YOU KNOW, NO WORRIES ABOUT THE AERO

She rounded a corner and came to an office, with a computer console built into the desk, and a richly leathered high-back chair. *Paydirt.*

VANDA: Oh yeah? I'm so sorry about that. I'm trying to get LEM back, and hopefully he'll have your Hawk and I can give it back to you.

MALACHI: NO, I MEAN DON'T WORRY ABOUT IT, I GOT A NEW ONE

VANDA: You did? Aren't they expensive?

MALACHI: YEAH, I THINK THE GAME FELT SORRY FOR ME

She sat down in the chair. Katya began accessing the computer in Ducote's desk, feeding the covert worm into it from a secret port beneath the gynoid's wrist. Naomi hoped she wouldn't be expected to pay Mal back for whatever his new ride cost him, but it didn't seem like he was going to ask her for it.

VANDA: Felt sorry for you? What, did it give you an insurance payout?

MALACHI: NO IT GAVE ME A BRAND NEW ONE, EVEN BETTER THAN THE ONE YOU LOST

Do what? That brought her up short. Before she could answer, the game had zoomed in to focus on Ducote's screen, showing different file directories for her to investigate. She tried to concentrate past the momentary shock of the game gifting an AeroHawk, when Mal couldn't possibly have taken the time to run another mission series hard enough to earn himself one as a reward. They were big-ticket items, requiring a heavy investment of either time or money, which is why she had been so upset about Mal's disappearing with LEM the night before.

VANDA: Are you serious? How?

She clicked on a directory called 'CALYPSO'. Several new files appeared, which seemed to be transfers of currency from various accounts. She clicked through and perused them. It appeared Ducote was laundering money through banks on Yesenin, the water world where most of the inhabited installations were built on the ocean bottoms.

MALACHI: WAS ON A MISSION TONIGHT IN ELEON, IN A PARKING GARAGE. I KILLED SOME GUY WHO WAS GETTING HIS OUT, AND THE GAME AWARDED IT TO ME

VANDA: It just gave it to you??

MALACHI: YEAH, LIKE I SAID, THE GAME FELT SORRY FOR ME I GUESS, LOL

VANDA: What is it?

MALACHI: VELOCIREAPER K90, BLACK, YOU SHOULD SEE THE WEAPONS ON THIS BABY

Clicking on another file, her jaw set. The K90 was a brand new model, one that cost hundreds of thousands of rb. Here the game had stolen her AI, and just given Mal a brand new Hawk as though he won a game show.

VANDA: Well don't loan this one to any SimMinds, you never know when the game might steal it

The new file was an access link to one of the transfers. As she simmered over Mal's suddenly winning the AeroHawk lottery, she slowly realized that she was being presented with an opportunity of her own here. She clicked on the account number of the destination transfer. The blinking cursor told her she could modify that number. "Well now," she said softly to herself.

MALACHI: WONT MAKE THAT MISTAKE AGAIN, HAHA. ANYWAY JUST WANTED TO LET YOU KNOW YOURE OFF THE HOOK FOR MY RIDE, I'VE TRADED UP. CATCH YOU LATER SEXY

Fuck you, she thought at his parting shot. *Too bad you can't see me now,* she didn't bother replying to him, wanting to flip her hair over her shoulder. She had felt guilty over his losing that expensive vehicle with the loss of LEM, even though she knew she had done nothing at all to have caused it. Now it was apparent that the *game* had taken his ride, and had made reparations to him. Meanwhile, it was forcing her to *whore* herself to some NPC crime lord and do all this cloak-and-dagger nonsense just to find out where LEM might be, to say nothing about actually getting him back. It was supremely unfair, and now she felt furious at herself for enjoying what she had just done moments ago for the sake of this mission… this *game.*

Looking at this account number, it was clear her revenge could be served presently. She could put in her own account number, kill Ducote in his sleep, and make off with a sizable fortune. No one would ever suspect her, at least until they tracked the money transfer to her account. But she could just as easily close that account out and open a brand new one at a new bank, or perhaps use Ardelle to launder it. And then the money would be hers, free and clear. She could get a more advanced heavy cruiser, even a carrier. With this amount of money, she could personally afford to buy the lodge a bigger homestation.

Yeah, and then you'd get permabanned for the exploit, she thought. But is it an exploit? Or is the game offering her reparations in its own way, the way it gave Mal a brand new Aero?

"Fuck," she whispered aloud to herself, and shook her head. No, the game had already seduced her into giving herself an orgasm at her desk tonight. She wasn't going to let it get her banned. She closed the file and took a deep breath, forcing the idea of putting that many zeroes into her bank account out of her mind. *Get this done and get out of here…*

She clicked another file, this one named 'OP. TOPAZ'.

SUBJECT: Operation TOPAZ
(X) DATE: 35 tKrit 857
(C) DATE: Ascendant Beta 225-94
BRIEF: Extraction proceeding on schedule.

BODY: Midday greetings, gentlemen. This is to confirm that I have acquired the tangible as scheduled, and the wetwork is now underway. Once implantation is complete, I expect payment in full of the remaining 33% of my fee, to be deposited in the account specified. Once I have confirmed the remaining payment is accounted for, I will authorize his immediate release from Eleon through Mr. C. Fadir at the Novgorod transitory safepoint. From there you can secure his transportation from Seres to wherever you wish and our business will be successfully concluded.

In the interest of full disclosure, you should be aware that there was an attempt to recover the tangible by a trio of Icilli mercenaries. They were easily taken care of, and we began an investigation to determine who hired them and how they knew where the tangible was being kept. We were initially unsuccessful, however additional intelligence has been forthcoming and we are moving on it. I can assure you at least two of the mercenaries will no longer act against our interests. One of them in fact has been detained at Novgorod and is cooperating. It is possible, however unlikely, that another attempt to interfere may be made before TOPAZ is completed by the other, or their employers, before they can be neutralized. Even if that happens, I am confident that security at Novgorod is ironclad and feel no hesitation about passing the same assurances on to you. (If you are aware of Eleon politics at all, you do not need them.) If another such disruption is attempted, I will follow up with the information. I am content there will be no difficulty in the resolution of the operation.

I will be in touch once more to confirm successful implantation. Expect to hear from me in two days' time or sooner.
Cordially, Weston Ducote V.E.I.

CRYPTO ZOEY8843-R4
CONFIRMED RECEIPT
END MESSAGE

Novgorod. Somewhere in Eleon there was a place they called Novgorod, and that's where they were keeping Lunius as they surgically implanted his brain into an archimek body. From there, they would smuggle him out of the city. She wondered if she, Mal and LEM were the "Icilli mercenaries" he alluded to, and if LEM was the one "cooperating" with them at Novgorod. It had to be. But what was he saying to them? It was absolutely maddening that she couldn't talk to her own AI, even when not playing the game. He was being held hostage, and it made her nearly dizzy with anger to think about it.

She had no idea where this Novgorod was, but it didn't sound like a cakewalk. If it really was the underground haven of this "Nikita", and it was easy to smuggle things in and out of the city from there, then chances are it was a suicide mission. If the Icilli couldn't penetrate it, even with their covert secret services branch, she didn't know how she was supposed to, by herself. Maybe Ardelle would answer those questions for her.

Naomi paged through a few more of the files, but she knew it had all been downloaded via the gynoid's worm into her memory. Now she just had to get the gynoid back to sleep, and she could…

Wait a minute.

She opened up the TOPAZ message again, and reread it. Particularly the part about *two* of the three mercenaries no longer acting against them. If LEM was the one they had captured, then the other one had to be Mal. That was why he had a new Velocireaper…

Ducote had paid him off.

And if he was cooperating with Ducote now, that meant Ardelle was in danger.

And Ardelle had Vanda's body, in a stasis tube.

Oh, shit.

Chapter Seven
07.01

The Monocerotis, Eleon Arcology
Planet Seres
Sector 338-CE

Katya ripped the cord from her wrist and shut the computer down, looking around to make sure she hadn't been discovered. There was no sign of Ducote or anyone else watching her. She got up and hurried out of the office, heading for the storage room.

In the middle of the living room, she stopped, her jaw setting. *No. It's not fair,* Naomi thought, her slim silhouette standing in the low illumination of the dormant house. She had a choice to make.

She knew she had to get back to Ardelle and warn her that she was very likely compromised. By just stepping into that charging tube, her mission would be complete and she'd wake up in the underground bunker.

She turned and looked at the garage door, listening for the slightest whisper of movement. There wasn't any; all was complete silence.

Katya wouldn't go without the shoes.

She smirked to herself, then made her way back to the gynoid recharge room, scooped up the white pumps she'd left at the base of her tube, and then darted out of the room, giving a wink to the row of gynoids who impassively followed her with their eyes as she passed them. She headed silently back to the door leading to the garage.

The six vehicles were all magnificent works of engineering art, priceless and exquisitely designed. Ducote's collection was enviable indeed. She wondered if perhaps he had others somewhere else, and perhaps these were only the ones he liked to keep handy. She glanced at his bedroom door. Somehow, the idea that she'd just slept with the man was oddly exhilarating.

She silently moved behind the row of vehicles in their bays. At the far end, a black-cherry red Ravenous Y99 sat with its back to her, facing its door. She stared at it, swinging her camera around to admire its rakish lines, its aggressive stance even at rest, like a crouched predator leaning on its haunches, eyes fixed on its prey. It was a Lamborghini of flying vehicles: precision-made, rare and exclusive. She ran her cursor over the vehicle and clicked it. The menu appeared, allowing her to step inside the craft and start its engines.

She was frowning. This beautiful vehicle was hers for the taking if she wanted it, just like all the money in Ducote's account had been. Somehow, it felt like she had the right to help herself to this. The game owed her. And anyway, the mission was a success: Ardelle had all the information she needed now. Why would she care?

She slipped her shoes back on and boarded the craft. The Ravenous began to whine as its drive systems spun up, pushing up off the garage floor to hover. The display in her headsup changed to show the standard vehicle dash, including all the avionics data and weapons. The vehicle was fully fueled and armed, packing a healthy assortment of ordinance.

There didn't seem to be any obvious control to open the garage door. She moved her cursor over the door and clicked. A single menu item appeared, grayed out: EXTERIOR GATE LOCKED.

We'll see about that.

The sound from the vehicle was more than enough to wake anyone asleep in the house, especially in the room next door. She had only scant moments to escape, if she was going to take this magnificent vehicle with her.

The beam weapons unfolded from the sides of the fuselage just below the cockpit windows. She selected a focused pulse-shockwave beam and fired it at the garage door, holding down the backslash-key. Twin beams erupted from the emitters, fixing on the doors with a bright green pool of light, which burned more brilliant as the power intensified, a searing sound steadily gaining in pitch. Finally letting go of the backslash-key, the shockwave was fired down the beam and impacted the garage door, blasting it apart in fiery streams spewing into the night air, a cloud of orange flame roiling upward from the side of the building.

She stabbed the W-key and the Ravenous pitched forward, sailing out the smoldering door and into the Eleon night. It quickly gained velocity and sped over the buildings, its wings unfolding from their parking configuration as it banked away from the Monocerotis spire. Naomi couldn't hide the satisfied smile from her face, imagining her slinky gynoid avatar at the controls of the vehicle and Ducote's horrified expression when he saw the hole in the door and the missing crown jewel of his AeroHawk collection gone. It was a much more suitable escape for a *femme fatale* than the one she'd been instructed to make. Besides, she could have chosen to make herself a few million rb's richer at Ducote's expense, and elected not to. He ought to be grateful for that, and the least he could do to show her some well-deserved appreciation was to let her have this cute little Hawk.

Now she just had to find the Ryannova-Joshi and warn Ardelle—

MALACHI: WHERE DO YOU THINK YOU'RE GOING, SEXY?

What the hell…

VANDA: What's up Mal?

MALACHI: NICE HAWK YOU GOT YOURSELF THERE, SHAME I HAVE TO SHOOT YOU DOWN.

VANDA: What are you talking about? Her smile dropped, and she scanned the sky for any threatening movement nearby. It took Mal a little longer to respond this time.

MALACHI: HATE TO TELL YOU THIS, BUT I'VE BEEN HIRED BY THE MINISTRY TO STOP YOU. BUT HEY, AT LEAST YOU WERE SMART ENOUGH TO STEAL A HAWK INSTEAD OF BUYING ONE OF YOUR OWN THAT YOU'LL LOSE

Cocky bastard. She bristled at his taunts, her previous anger stirring again. She'd just made off with a prized new Hawk, to compensate her for the *extreme* inconvenience of her AI being taken from her and held hostage by NPC game elements as though the game had any right whatsoever to reach into her computer and steal him. Maybe Mal could be reasoned with.

VANDA: Look. Can't you let me go? I'm in a bad mood, the game stole my AI from me and your sweet AeroHawk and all I'm trying to do is get them both back

MALACHI: NO CAN DO SEXY, IF I WANT TO KEEP MY NEW K90 I HAVE TO SHOOT YOU DOWN. NOTHING PERSONAL

VANDA: Mal, I'm asking you as a personal favor she keyed and stabbed the Return key, growing angrier. **I'm not in the mood to tussle with you. LEM is my property and I need to get him back**

MALACHI: I LIKE YOU SEXY BUT HEY, I HAVE MY ORDERS, BESIDES, LEM IS JUST A PROGRAM, YOU CAN GET ANOTHER ONE

VANDA: Stop making fun of me! And LEM isn't just a program, he's my friend and he's my property! She was nearly livid now, having to correct several typos before sending the PM.

MALACHI: LISTEN TO YOURSELF... HE'S A PROGRAM, THAT'S ALL, HE'S NOT A PERSON. AND YOUVE GOT A HOT AVI, EXCUSE ME FOR NOTICING

Bewildered and furious, she reversed her turn and banked to the right. Blasts of light streaked past her from behind, and she realized Mal had been tailing her, waiting for her to make an evasive maneuver to begin his attack. The Y99 was a nimble thing, responding as her shuttle had when she was amped up on the Heavy Rations. She pulled up into a tight climb and took a second to check her inventory. All she had on her was what the gynoid was carrying: a nightie and pumps, no rations. Maybe she wouldn't need the help.

Mal was even more dangerous now than he was in his previous vehicle. He climbed right with her, strafing with his energy weapons, the sky around her streaming with red dashes. The pulsing beacon at the peak of the pyramid swooped into view, growing larger as she climbed. She twirled around and arced over, trying to see him in the dark night so she could at least get a fix on him. She caught just enough of a glimpse as he streaked past for her onboard FOF display to target him as "foe" and begin tracking him. A red cross appeared on her 2D proximity display, giving her an indication of where he was in relation to her.

She swore as she spun herself over, trying to get him in her crosshairs to put him on the defensive, but he was maddeningly slippery. The dark, speckled horizon twirled and weaved in her screen as she swayed her shoulders side to side unconsciously, fully immersed in her piloting.

She gritted her teeth as she fought to stay ahead of his firing arc, constantly swarmed with blasts of red light all around her. Her screen flashed red as several of them hit their mark, and her damage bar jumped up to 30%.

She wanted to scream obscenities at him. If she'd had time to initiate a voice-chat with him, she would already have been. For someone to deliberately fight her now, when she was trying to recover her prop—her *friend*, was assholishness on a whole new level. Not to mention the fact that the game had given *him* a brand new, state-of-the-art Hawk with which to shoot her out of the sky, and what sort of XP and cash award would he get for doing that? It was as if ToC was ganging up on her, making it not only difficult for her to succeed but cruelly brutal in pitting her own ersatz partner against her. She vaguely wondered if it would have done the same with anyone from the Pride—but no, they wouldn't turn on her like this merely for a new whiz-bang vehicle. They fought shoulder to shoulder, night after night to help each other earn these kinds of things.

The Ravenous was a joy to fly, but it was clear she wasn't going to get to keep it much longer. She simply didn't have the skills to defeat Malachi. She grimaced as she twisted and banked, each maneuver countered almost perfectly by her opponent. She could almost viscerally feel the thudding of his beam's impacts across her vehicle, her screen flickering with red as he scored strike after strike. The damage bar jumped to 40%, then 60%, and a plume of smoke began streaming out the underside.

"No! *Bastard!*" she raged, as the futility of her escape grew clear. She knew it would be only seconds before his killing volley would rake through her ship and decimate it, destroying the sexy gynoid and her swanky ride. She was too furious to let him take her down without so much as a scrape. In an act of pure defiance, she hit her airbrakes and stabbed at her lateral starboard thruster, spinning in the air to face him and sacrificing maneuverability for the sake of a single, fuck-you chance to fire back.

She could barely get off a shot. Mal had slipped beneath her as she began the spin, and she could all but feel him bringing his crosshairs up to fix on her craft. As she spun, she rapped the fire key and sprayed the space behind her with green blasts, but the instant she saw he wasn't there, the Ravenous exploded in gold and white plumes, flaming pieces spidering out from the conflagration over the city. Her speakers boomed with the powerful explosion, startling her. Mal's Velocireaper shot past the explosion and twisted away into the night. Her camera froze in the air, watching the flaming pieces of the Y99 and Katya plummet to the streets below, disappearing into the sea of flickering lights. Naomi slammed her fist on the desk in exasperation.

MALACHI: SORRY, HAD TO

Naomi's fingers trembled with rage as they stabbed at her keys.

VANDA: FUCK YOU! No you didn't!

MALACHI: ITS JUST A GAME, SEXY, NOTHNG PERSONAL OK?

VANDA: Its personal to me, lem is my friend and STOP MAKING FUN OF ME DAMMIT

MALACHI: YOULL GET HIM BACK. AND I SAID I'M NOT MAKING FUN OF YOU, YR HOT

She shook her head and tried to settle herself, taking a deep breath. She'd ask him one more question, and then she'd go to bed.

VANDA: You think fat girls are hot? youre weird mal

He seemed to take a few moments typing his response.

MALACHI: LOL HOW ARE YOU FAT, WHAT ARE YOU TALKING ABOUT

Now he was talking nonsense. She squinted at the screen and shook her head in disbelief.

VANDA: I know what I look like, you think I'm blind?

MALACHI: YOU MUST BE, YOU LOOK GREAT TO ME. HOLD ON A SECOND

What is he smoking? she wondered, staring at the empty night sky over the city. A box had appeared with a single button: RESPAWN. She knew she should go to bed, it was already nearly midnight and she was exhausted from the evening's play. With Ardelle in jeopardy though, she wasn't sure where she might find Vanda… maybe she should respawn, return to the *Destiny* and then go to bed.

MALACHI: CHECK YOUR MAIL

VANDA: Why?

MALACHI: JUST CHECK IT

She groaned and clicked out of the game, opening her Web browser and signing into her Social profile. There were eight new messages. She realized she hadn't checked them in nearly a week.

The first seven were from her lodgemates, with subject titles like '?' and 'HEY THERE' and 'EVERYTHING OK?'

The most recent one was from Mal. She clicked on it, and it opened to show a screencap he had taken of the two of them in the hall of the QV-One, which looked like it was taken while Vanda had been checking out the enemy strength behind the closed door with her scry. Mal's camera was on the far side of Vanda, looking up at her almost from the ground. Vanda was carrying her Ixxis and the Louda, in a half-crouch against the wall beside the door.

She wasn't the least bit overweight. She looked like her normal self.

What—

She stared at the image for a few moments, and clicked back into the game again.

VANDA: This is what you saw?

MALACHI: YEAH. YOURE HOT. HOPE YOU DONT MIND I TOOK THIS OF YOU, BUT IVE SEEN A LOT OF AVIS IN THIS GAME AND YRS IS HOT

VANDA: This is not how I see myself on my screen

MALACHI: WELL THIS IS WHAT I SEE. HOPE THERES NO HARD FEELINGS OVER HAVING TO SHOOT YOU DOWN

She clicked back over to the image. It was the same Vanda she'd always been used to. It slowly started to dawn on her that perhaps the obese avatar the game was showing her was visible to her, to LEM, to NPCs like Ardelle… but *not to other players*. The effect of the Heavy Ration had been slowing her down, that much others could tell, but to Mal, Vanda was still the same fit, trim and cute Vanda, physically.

VANDA: PERV.

MALACHI: SUE ME

Her fingertips were still quivering on the keys as she fought to recover from the rush of fury that had just led to her spectacular defeat. She took another deep breath.

VANDA: I'm sorry for what I said

MALACHI: SOK. SORRY I HAD TO SHOOT YOU DOWN, ILL MAKE IT UP TO YOU IF YOU WNT THOUGH

VANDA: What do you have in mind?

MALACHI: WOULD LOVE TO SEE THE REST OF THAT SEXI AVI… AND SHOW YOU WHAT YOU CAN DO WITH IT

Naomi chuckled, in spite of herself. She had to admit, after having sampled the seductive fantasies that were possible in Eleon, she was not so quick to refuse as she might normally be. She clicked back over to the screenshot he'd sent her. It was hard to accept that what Vanda looked like on her own screen didn't match how she appeared to others. She hadn't even considered that there *could* be any difference. It was one of the unwritten rules of a persistent virtual world: everyone shares the same space, and sees exactly the same thing, at the same time.

VANDA: Perv.

MALACHI: YOUR FAULT

She cracked a smile. At least it was nice to be flirted with again. But it was very late and she had to go to bed. She decided the next mission phase would have to wait, and so would getting Vanda out of her stasis tube.

VANDA: Good night Mal

MALACHI: NIGHT VAN

07.02

The next night

Naomi entered her password and the login screen faded to black, the usual user interface elements drawing themselves in her headsup, as the game client connected with the Cortanis servers and initialized.

She was tired. She had laid down on her couch and closed her eyes while watching a TV show soon after getting home from work, and almost immediately fell asleep. Waking two and a half hours later, she took a shower and fixed herself a bowl of Raisin Bran for dinner, swiping through a magazine on her tablet as she ate. Now it was nearly ten in the evening and she was again seated in her chair at the computer, waiting for *Cortanis* to log her in.

She had powered up LEM's computer as well, but it was still unable to run the SimMind. She swore to herself under her breath as she glared at the error message, but left it up in case tonight was productive and she could get him back home where he belonged.

The screen faded up to white, then cleared. She could see the hatch of her stasis pod from the inside, swinging open. Two velen techs in white scrubs leaned over into her field of view. They looked at each other and exchanged excited velen phrases. Then the two techs helped her out of the tube to her feet. Her view seemed a bit obfuscated by a pulsing mesh of color, and wobbled as though unstable. She understood: the game was simulating her disconcertedness at being awakened.

Around her, other velen workers were very busy. They seemed to be dismantling all the equipment and packing it into large white crates for transport somewhere. As soon as Vanda was free of the stasis tube, the techs went to work dismantling it behind her.

Ardelle stormed into the room and went straight for Vanda. "A fine mess. I don't know whether to thank you or arrest you," the feline woman said, her words subtitled in Naomi's headsup.

Naomi pressed her talk-key, the confusion in Vanda's face mirroring her own. "What's wrong? I got the data you wanted. The mission was a success."

"Yes! It was very successful, we got the download from Ducote's computer and learned that our former operative Malachi sold us out to him, and now we have to evacuate immediately since we don't know how much they learned from him. Ducote's message referenced 'additional intelligence' and that they are 'moving on it.' Now we have to assume that this location is compromised, which it certainly would have been had you brought that gynoid back here! What were you thinking? You were to put her back to sleep and let us wake you up. Those were your instructions. Why didn't you follow them?"

Naomi was stunned. "I… thought you wanted the gynoid back," she stammered.

"Why? I told you, we were receiving everything the gynoid did via your telemetric stream. The download from Ducote's computer was through that stream. If you had just put her back to sleep, we could have left it there for additional intelligence purposes. Other agents could have used her for future missions, and he never would have known the difference. Now, not only does he know that one was compromised, he'll likely never allow another gynoid into his home without a full security sweep, which would detect any telemetrics. That whole tactic is lost to us now, and why? Because you wanted a new car? What's *wrong* with you?" Ardelle appeared ready to slap her.

Vanda blushed, not only chastised by the dressing-down but also at the realization that her sexual encounter wasn't as private as she'd assumed. She'd completely forgotten about the persistent uplink from the gynoid, so enraptured by the encounter she had been.

"I'm… sorry."

"I'm sorry too, because you won't be getting full payment for this mission. I'll give you a partial payment, but don't worry about any more assignments on behalf of the Icilli. Looks like you get your bodywork for free."

"Bodywork? What bodywork?"

"Look down."

She drew her camera out of first-person view and looked at herself. Her avatar was back the way it was before she started the mission: not a trace of the extra weight gained since coming to Seres.

"Oh! Wow!" she exclaimed. "You did this?"

"Yes," Ardelle shot, her voice laden with irritation. "While you were in stasis, we took the liberty of auto-bacterially enhancing your body's respiration system, giving you the ability to breathe our air naturally, without needing to supplement with nutritional rations. And we sent cell evacuators through you to rid you of the excess body fat you've accumulated as a result of those rations. It's a very simple thing to do. Some of our operatives are in stasis for weeks and months, and their bodies start to atrophy if we don't take care of them. You're now healthier than you were when you got here. I was hoping we could continue to use you for future missions, but it looks like you're too interested in flashy vehicles and chic footwear to be reliable. So all that prep work on you was for nothing. At least for us, anyway."

Naomi breathed a relieved sigh.

"You're welcome!" Ardelle spat, her velen accent making it sound more like *sher-velcoo*. "Now get out of here. Thank you for your service to the Icilli government, and kindly go to hell." She turned and headed for the door.

"Wait!" Vanda said. "What about LEM? Where is Novgorod? I have to find him."

"And good luck to you," Ardelle answered, not turning around. "We got what we needed from the download. We'll be parting company now. Have a pleasant evening." She opened the door leading to the command center and held it open. "Do I have to call security and have you arrested? Or can you find the way out on your own?"

Vanda's eyes narrowed, but she made her way out of the bunker. The command center was already mostly disassembled. The big screens had been taken down, white shipping crates racked and waiting to be hauled away. Velen workers were busily taking the other consoles apart and packing them. It looked like within the afternoon, the bunker would be emptied entirely.

She followed the route she'd come in through, finding the upstairs of the Vertical once more and stepped out into the street. It was night again in Eleon, but not just any night: Friday night. The streets were swarming with people, human and velen, most of whom were player characters. Friday and Saturday nights in *Cortanis* were always the busiest nights of the week.

Dammit! she swore to herself. She had her old body back, but now she had no idea how to find Novgorod or LEM. The game wasn't giving her a mission waypoint, so she had nowhere to go. *What the hell am I supposed to do now?*

Naomi leaned back in her seat. *Novgorod.* Maybe there was something in the game wiki about it; she could at least start there. She walked back into the Vertical and sat down on a couch in the lobby area, then turned the switch that connected her mouse and keyboard to LEM's computer. She tabbed out of the non-functional *SimMind* program and opened a browser.

She smiled as she saw that LEM had been bookmarking Web pages wildly during the short time he had inhabited this computer. Even during his gameplay, he was scouring the Web searching out information, collating and compiling it in his database. She did a quick search, found the *Cortanis* Wiki and entered "Eleon Novgorod" in the search box. The page was returned immediately.

Novgorod

Novgorod is an atmosphere processing facility in the Eleon Arcology (S338-CE Seres), capital city of Icillia, situated at the highest point still within the superstructure's interior. It is visible from the ground on clear nights by its pulsing beacon light, which cycles in color through blue, green and red. The beacon is affixed to the bottom of the facility. From the outside of the arcology, there is a visible gas plume at its apex, which is assumed to be exhausted from the facility within. The plume is a no-fly zone with a radius of approximately 100 meters. Novgorod is very difficult to reach as it is several hundred meters above the flight ceiling of aerovehicles operating within Eleon, which is a boundary enforced by Eleon Traffic Control[1].

Etymology

Novgorod is named for the Russian city of Velikiy Novgorod, which serves as the administrative center of Novgorod Oblast and lies along the Volkhov River just downstream from its outflow from Lake Ilmen. The city is located on the M10 federal highway between Moscow and St. Petersburg.

Location

As is typical in many arcology designs, the Novgorod atmosphere processor is built at the fastigium of the Eleon Arcology, its highest interior point. The actual size and layout of the facility is difficult to determine as no maps or blueprints of it are known to exist. No part of the structure is visible from the exterior of the pyramid, but the plume of waste gas is assumed to be generated from the processing plant.

History & Purpose

Novgorod was first referred to by name in the "Heart of the City" mission series/story arc, introduced with the Dark Tides: Contagion expansion in April 2025[2]. In the mission, Novgorod was introduced as an atmosphere processor and waste release facility, which had malfunctioned and was releasing the deadly toxin alHa-91 into the atmosphere of the superstructure. The toxic gas leak served to render Novgorod a biohazard zone, making it impenetrable to players. The mission was resolved using an automated, weaponized drone to strike the exterior of the station, disabling a security system and attaching itself to one of the fiber-optic conduits, where it was discovered that a mechagenic chemical was secretly being mixed into the air of the arcology, which would cause slow, gradual deterioration of archimek physiology. The plot was found to have been carried out by a seditious Icilli faction intending to draw the archimeks into the Aetosian War[3].

Today the station serves as an atmosphere processing plant and gaseous waste release facility. It is fully automated and no workforce is deployed there. It is assumed the processing plant is serviced with automated drones. Novgorod is occasionally referred to in Ministry missions as a possible hideout and transportation hub for the tDozhdali crime syndicate[4], as its inaccessibility makes it a very difficult location to penetrate. However, this is considered unlikely, since no vehicles are seen approaching or disembarking from the facility.

Notable Characters

The Ministry mission "Ruprect's Eyes" references the tDozhdali crime boss Nikita as possibly having a hideout at Novgorod[5]. This is as yet unconfirmed and is still considered little more than a rumor, possibly a ruse to discourage Icilli player agents from trying to locate him elsewhere. Nikita has yet to make an appearance in a game mission, although several Ministry missions make reference to him[6][7][8].

Travel

There is no known method of traveling to Novgorod. Its location at the fastigium of the superstructure makes it unreachable by aerovehicle from within and without. Further, although the facility was repaired in "Heart of the City", it is still classified as a biohazard zone since there are enough trace amounts of alHa-91 in its immediate environs to make it dangerous to player characters.

Missions

The "Heart of the City" mission is the only known mission that directly involves Novgorod.

See also:

Arcologies in Tides of Cortanis
Mysterious Places in Tides of Cortanis
Atmosphere Processing
Eleon Arcology
Capital Cities of Seres
tDozhdali
Nikita

Holy shit, she thought, frowning at the page. Embedded in the text was a diagram of the Eleon cross-section, showing Novgorod as a tiny structure built just beneath the apex of the interior. A dotted line showed the flight ceiling, at least five hundred meters beneath. Below the text, a slideshow titled "Media" was showing several player screenshots showing the underside of the facility, with its glowing beacon light. Another picture showed the gas plume over the exterior apex of the pyramid.

She started doing Web searches for strategies to reach the plant, coming up with several lodge message boards with discussions on how to reach it. Several strategies had been proposed and attempted, including one that involved trying to drill through the exterior of the superstructure, and another attempting to rappel into the smokestacks, but these attempts had failed.

One strategy caught her eye and she studied it. The intrepid players who had attempted it did not succeed, but the concept was enough to percolate an idea. She clicked the switcher on the desk again, connecting her keyboard and mouse back to her PC, and got Vanda up from her seat on the couch to go outside again. Looking up, she could barely make out the slowly pulsing colored beacon high above the aerovees crisscrossing the night sky.

I need two things, she thought. *Time to spend some money*.

Naomi called up her Player Finder with a quick keystroke. The window appeared before her with a search box at the top. In the box, she typed 'Malachi'.

His name appeared in green: he was online, and not inactive. She double-clicked his name in the window and typed.

VANDA: Hey.

After a few moments, she got a response:

MALACHI: HEY SEXY

VANDA: Still want to make it up to me for last night?

MALACHI: YR PLACE OR MINE?

She smiled as she typed.

VANDA: I was hoping you could do me a favor first. I need a ride somewhere.

MALACHI: OH YEAH? ARE YOU SERIOUS?

VANDA: Yeah.

MALACHI: WHERE TO?

VANDA: It's somewhere in Eleon. It shouldn't take long. After I finish my mission maybe we could see about that other thing.

MALACHI: IM RUNNING A MISSION NOW, GIVE ME ABOUT 20 MINS

VANDA: K.

She chuckled and shook her head, Vanda mimicking her as she stood on the sidewalk in front of the Vertical. Did she really just offer to virtually sleep with Malachi for his help with this? What did that make her? *Inquisitive*, she reminded herself. *It's not sex. It's a video game*. She couldn't help feeling sexy, enjoying the feeling of having Vanda back to her normal self once more. And she couldn't help but feel this city was like a strange vacation, a place with different rules, outside of her usual *Cortanis* routine. Maybe what happened in Eleon stayed in Eleon.

She called up her area map, and a two-dimensional window appeared in her headsup which showed her immediate vicinity, the layout of streets, and several icons denoting clubs, NPC mission-givers, banks, stores, taxi stands and other various points of interest. She made her way down the street toward the nearest bank, walked inside and looked around. It was a garden-variety player bank facility, with no teller windows: only a semicircle of computer terminals in a posh marble and brass room. She approached one of the empty kiosks and logged into her accounts, moving 200,000 rb from her lodge account to her personal one. She so rarely took lodge funds for anything, since she hardly ever made major purchases like this. That's what the fund was for; she was Commander, nobody would give her grief for it. It would get their attention though. She'd post about it on the message board later explaining the transfer.

Clicking her keyboard and mouse back over to LEM's computer, she went back to searching the *Cortanis* Wiki. This time she started searching for special equipment. If the attempt failed, she'd be stuck with a very pricey and specialized item that she likely wouldn't ever have call to use again. But if it worked, it would be worth every qubit.

If it worked, she'd be the only person to have ever successfully infiltrated Novgorod. She'd have to remember to take screenshots.

She came across what she was looking for: it was called Oros. *Theeeere you are.*

She switched her inputs back again and checked her map for stores. There was a vendor specializing in weapons and equipment three blocks away. She ran, paying close attention to make sure she wasn't losing health by not taking any HMRs. Her health bar stayed green, only her fatigue bar slid down the further she ran. Vanda smiled as she covered the distance. As she ran, the word "LLDORI" appeared briefly in her headsup with a bluish glow, then faded away again. She'd entered a new district in the city.

She did not notice the female figure, standing on a fire escape above her, watching her silently as Vanda darted down the street through the sidewalk crowd.

The equipment store was spacious, with several kiosks on the ground level and a winding staircase leading to two upper stories, the ringed walkways forming an open-air atrium. She looked around at the various weapons on display behind glass, with flashing infobars cycling through specifications, ammunition and power requirements for each. She rarely needed to shop for weapons, and when she did, she usually went to the online auction house. For this mission, she needed something special. A collector's item.

She went to the computer and began browsing its catalog, starting with the most expensive items. The items on the first page were half a million rb apiece: high-end body armor, personal energy shields, beam weapons of extraordinary destructive capability. Not even her Ixxis merited space alongside weapons of this caliber.

Two pages down, she found the item she was looking for: the Oros T-PLS Grappler, with 90 meter cable. It was 350,000 rb. At that price, it cost more than most aerovehicles did. And it was non-resellable, like most high dollar items. Once she bought it, she was stuck with it.

Her account had just enough to make the purchase. She clicked the box to acquire the item, and confirmed the buy with her PIN. Her inventory box pulsed: a new arrival had appeared. She opened the window and saw her new Oros, shiny and new, ensconced in its slot. Her rb account read 4,023. She felt broke, but with this device, it was worth it.

She wandered back outside and found a seat again somewhere out of the way to wait for Mal. She was studying the screencaptures of the Novgorod underside on the wiki when he PM'd her.

MALACHI: WHATS UP SEXY?

She switched the keyboard and mouse back to her computer and quickly keyed:

VANDA: Can you pick me up out in front of the weapons store in the Lldori district?

MALACHI: SURE, BRT

After a short wait, she saw the stylish Velocireaper gliding in from between the buildings, slowing to a hover and opening the passenger door for her to climb in. She walked over to the open door, clicked on it and Vanda climbed in, her camera turning to face the back of the vehicle. The passenger door closed, and her camera followed the craft as the street fell away below and they ascended over the buildings again.

MALACHI: SO WHERE DO YOU NEED TO GO?

VANDA: You're a good pilot, I know that much. I have a weird request.

MALACHI: LETS GO VOICE

Naomi sighed, but didn't see a reason not to. She waited for him to initiate the voice-chat. After a moment, a window appeared asking her if she would agree to chat with him. She accepted.

"You copy?" came his voice.

"Five by five."

"So what's this about?"

"How high can this thing climb without pitching or rolling in any way?"

"What do you mean?"

"I mean, if you took off from the ground, how high could you ascend holding your pitch and roll at zero?"

"Uhhh, I'm not sure," he admitted. "Would take a pretty steady hand. But I bet I could get fairly high up. How fast would you need me to ascend?"

"Doesn't matter. Can be as slow as you want, but the important thing is, the craft would have to be absolutely straight and level."

"Why would you want me to do that?"

"Because I want to ride you… like an elevator." She let the innuendo hang in the pause, and smiled to herself.

"Oh yeah? You mean you want to be on top?" Two could play the game, apparently.

"Uh huh. Think you can handle me?"

"How far do you want to go, sexy?"

"All the way."

"To where?"

"You ever heard of Novgorod?"

"No. Where's that?"

"You know that beacon at the very top of the sky? The one that changes colors?"

"Yeah."

"That's where I need to go."

"Only one problem with that. There's a flight ceiling that don't let me get anywhere near it."

"Well, how about we go see how close we can get."

"All right." The craft accelerated, pointing its nose at the ceiling, the glowing beacon slowly pulsing its cycle of colors as they sped toward it. Naomi swung her camera around the craft to watch the buildings beneath them receding away. This city was massive, she thought, wondering how many game designers it had taken to come up with all its intricate buildings, neighborhoods, streets, nooks and crannies. She wondered how many buildings had fully designed layouts, or if the game progressively generated them as players explored them. Surely a few of them, like Ducote's penthouse, were designed by hand. And all the clubs surely were.

She spun her camera back behind the craft again, and watched the beacon steadily grow brighter as they neared. Finally, the K90 slowed and leveled off, about five hundred meters below the station.

"That's it, babe. That's as close as I can get. There's a hard ceiling here."

"Yeah, I know about it." She stared hard at the dark, shadowy facility, its thick iron tanks, ducts and pipes bathed in shadow.

"Any way we can light it?" she asked.

"Nah, no strobes on this thing. Just my running lights."

She leaned closer to her screen and squinted, trying to make out as much detail as she could. There didn't seem to be anything on it which would allow her to access the interior, except there was a dark, rectangular shape on the west-facing side. She couldn't tell for sure, but it looked big enough to be a hangar to receive aerocraft. She could discern four small gas plumes, facing downward, arranged in a square.

"See that dark rectangle there? Fly over to the right a bit."

He complied, bringing the western face of the facility into better view.

"See it?" she asked again.

"Yeah."

"What do you make of that?"

"Big enough for a landing deck. But I can't see whether there's a door there or not."

"Me either. Let me try something, get a little closer."

"I can't get any higher to it, babe."

"I know, I mean bring us around so we're directly facing it."

Mal maneuvered the vehicle so that it was directly beneath the west side, under the shadowy shape. Naomi detached her camera to scry and lifted it higher, closer to the structure. There was no light source, and the upper limit of her scry only brought her about half the distance. She tried to focus her camera at the dark rectangle, and tapped her screenshot key a few times.

"Okay, now let's do a slow circle beneath the plant."

"Plant?"

"Yeah. It's an air processing plant."

"Oh. Okay, circling."

She had to keep her movements very careful with her camera at this distance, because with her scry this far removed, the smallest motions of her mouse would throw her view off wildly. With the tiniest of wrist motions, and her other hand over the screencapture key, she tried to get as many pictures of the dark facility as she could, even though most of what she was shooting was featureless black. But this was as close to Novgorod as she was ever going to get safely, and she had to at least try. She captured close to fifty images before she pulled her scry back in and the camera zoomed out, coming to bear on the back end of the K90 again.

"Okay, I think I'm done," she said.

"All right. What now?"

"I'm going to try and take a look at a few of these. Can you give me about fifteen, maybe twenty minutes?"

"Sure, I'll be around a bit. Might do some farming in Vor tDinn. Shoot me a PM when you're ready."

"Okay. Thanks, Mal."

He descended to the city and dropped her off on the rooftop of an office building, where she sat Vanda down and then tabbed out of the game. Naomi navigated to the screenshot directory on her computer and found the pictures she'd just taken, leaving the window open. She selected the first, then left-clicked, and a menu of options appeared, including a submenu of programs which could edit the image. She chose one called Phusion. The image opened: a featureless black box. The Phusion image editor controls appeared in her headsup: she selected Quick Enhance. The picture immediately brightened, showing a few outlines of dark vertical cylinders, probably piping on the exterior. There wasn't much more to see; the image was grainy, but it was enough to give some additional details of what she was looking at.

One by one she opened and enhanced the images. At the fifth image, she caught a glimpse of the dark rectangular shape. The Quick Enhance showed that the shape was in fact an opening. There didn't appear to be an outer door. She could make out what looked like a ceiling and walls; she was far too low to see the floor or how far deep it went. But it looked like there was a landing platform there after all.

She had found her 'in'.

She enhanced the next few images, and they confirmed that it was indeed an opening into the plant, a fairly sizable one. Probably intended for heavy transports to bring parts, raw materials for the processors and, in better days, personnel. But since the "Heart of the City", it was still declared a biohazard zone. She wasn't sure how dangerous it was going to be, or how much time she might have to look for LEM there. She hoped she could hold off whatever deleterious health effects there were with health packs and rations. The facility appeared to be about two city blocks across, perhaps three stories, with each level smaller than the one beneath, constrained by the top of the pyramid. She'd have to stock up on health, and charge packs for the Ixxis. God only knew what abhorrently mutated creatures she may find lurking around up there, or *tDozhdali* personnel if it really was a Ministry hideout. It might look like a few levels from *Doom* in there. She had to be prepared for a cold reception.

She copied the enhanced pictures onto a teradrive, and moved the pertinent ones showing the hangar over to LEM's computer, opening each of them and filling his screen with them for reference. Then she tabbed back into *Cortanis*.

Vanda ran to the door leading into the building, found the elevator to the ground floor, and used it. Then she sprinted to the nearest store, logged into a kiosk and bought five stacks of health rations. If she needed more than that, a one-person insertion was just not possible. She also bought extra powerpacks for her Ixxis pistol.

Finally, she was ready, and keyed her talk-key. "Mal?"

He was still linked with her. "Ready for your ride?"

"I think so, yes."

"Where are you?"

She checked her map.

"I'll be on the roof of the Cilphi Monolith in five."

"See you there, sexy."

The Cilphi Monolith was a tall building one block over, glossy silver with featureless sides and no apparent windows, although windows ringed the structure like any other multistory edifice. Vanda hurried inside and took the elevators to the topmost level, then found the stairs leading to the roof. As she stepped out, she saw the Velocireaper K90 descending to the rooftop in front of her, its landing lights pulsing. When it came to a fully settled stop, she jumped onto the roof of the vehicle.

"Okay," she said warily. "Lift up slow."

The K90 pushed up from the building, easing upward. Vanda kept her footing on top of the craft, but knew even a subtle bank or maneuver would send her sliding off, and she had no way to hang on if her balance was disturbed.

"Easy does it," he said, concentrating.

"Can you move your camera without moving the vehicle at all?"

"Yeah," he said. "Where do you want me to bring you?"

"You know that rectangular shape on the side of the plant? It's an opening, like a hangar. You can't reach it, but if you can position me under it, I am going to try to jump. I think I can make it."

"How? There's no way you can jump that high."

"I'll have some help. But I won't know if it's enough until I try."

"If you miss, it's a long way down," he pointed out.

"Yeah, I know, but I have to try anyway."

"Okay. I'm gonna take it real slow. Sit tight."

"Actually, that's a good idea," she realized, and typed the command that caused Vanda to seat herself cross-legged on the roof. "Maybe that'll lower my center of gravity, make it harder to slide off."

"Couldn't hurt. Here we go." Mal pushed up from his hover, and the K90 began rising into the night sky. Naomi opened her inventory and set the Oros as her primary weapon, with the Ixxis as secondary. With the Oros selected, a little green crosshair appeared on the screen, a target reticle for where she intended the grappler to go. It was different from the auto-aiming Ixxis and other handheld weapons, the accuracy of which was entirely determined by a player's marksmanship stats. This reticle she could move around on the screen with her mouse.

Mal patiently continued his climb, the skyline steadily sinking beneath them. They occasionally passed close to other aerovehicles as they shot by them.

"Better hope none of them crash into us," Mal warned.

She frowned as she watched carefully for surrounding traffic. The rise to Eleon's artificially imposed flight ceiling was long, at this speed. Naomi could tell Mal was concentrating hard to keep the craft from tipping. The Velocireaper wobbled slightly as it rose, but not enough to cause Vanda to slip.

"You doing all right?" she asked.

"Yeah. But we're not directly underneath the opening you want. I'll have to do some pretty careful maneuvering to get you there."

"Hey, if you're good enough to shoot me down, you ought to be good enough to do some precision flying," she teased.

"Shooting you down wasn't all that easy. You're not that bad a pilot yourself. I wasn't expecting to have to work so hard."

"Thanks." She chuckled to herself; surely he was just flattering her. He was likely to play Mr. Nice Guy for at least as long as he wanted to show her what virtual sex looked like between two players. She hadn't decided whether such a liaison was going to happen, but she was unusually unfazed about the idea. Maybe it would be fun… and it felt good feeling sexy again. *If only I could feel like this in real life*, she thought with a slight frown, and then an absurd idea passed through her mind and brought her to chuckle again. Maybe she should get Elliot to take a few screenshots of her, so she could see how *he* really saw her.

It took nearly ten minutes to reach the flight ceiling at such a slow speed. Naomi's pulse quickened as the dark structure loomed over her, closer and closer. She could almost feel the dangerous height Vanda was being lifted to over the city. Finally, the K90 came to rest beneath the pulsing beacon.

"Okay," Mal said, "I'm trying to make out the hangar you found. I can't yet see it."

"Don't move, let me find it." She detached, and scryed to her limit, trying to see around the other two faces of the facility. "I think I see it," she said. "You'll need to reverse a bit, to the right."

"All right I'm going to change direction now," he said. "I'll be careful." The vehicle began slowly turning to the left with a gentle bank, and Vanda slowly began sliding toward the edge.

"I'm sliding! *Stop!*" she exclaimed. The vehicle leveled again.

"I've got you."

"Oh my God, I'm nervous," she admitted. "It feels like being on a tightrope without a net." She patted at her chest, and Vanda did the same.

"I think you're crazy, but I gotta admit, it's the first time I've done anything like this. I want to see if you can do it."

Naomi smiled to herself at the sheer adventure of it, and took a few screenshots to document her attempt. She reminded herself again to take screenies if she made it inside.

"If this works, Mal, you'll get your name on the Wiki page."

"Oh, boy."

The K90 slowly and steadily turned its nose in the direction Naomi directed. It occasionally made slight, deliberate dips, sliding its rooftop occupant back toward the center again. Naomi's breathing was tight and shallow, staring intently at Vanda on the screen, feeling the height at which they were maneuvering and fearing the long plunge that would mean she'd have to go through it all again. Maybe Mal didn't have the patience for repeated attempts at this. She prayed he could keep his hand steady long enough.

After an agonizing length of time watching the K90 edge its way over to the side of the plant far above, they both could see the yawning dark rectangle coming into view. Mal massaged his craft around until they were positioned facing the hangar of the installation, and came to a stop.

"Wow, you did it. You're awesome, Mal," Naomi said gratefully.

"You got the hard part," he answered. "I don't know how you're going to make that jump."

"A wing and a prayer." She rose from her seated position and looking up at the opening. She clicked open her inventory, and paged through it until she found the little present Chopper had given her. The Quantum Cookie.

Chopper's email had said it would give her the ability to jump hundreds of meters into the air, and even that didn't seem like enough to reach the hangar. But perhaps with the Oros, she could make it the rest of the distance. She would only have one shot: the effects of the cookie probably wouldn't last long enough for her to respawn and have Mal bring her back to the flight ceiling. It was all or nothing.

She took a deep breath, and sighted the Oros on the upper half of the dark rectangle. With luck, the grappler's cable would be long enough to reach and connect with something on the ceiling of the hangar.

"Here I go."

"Good luck, sexy," Mal said.

She double-clicked on the Quantum Cookie. A whirl of blue and green sparkles of light enveloped her, swirling faster and faster, culminating in a bright gushing of light from within her and a shower of tiny twinkling points of light, as though a little fireworks display had erupted from within Vanda. There was a soft glow surrounding her avatar's body, pulsing light blue to white. The cookie was active, and a little bar appeared over it in her inventory, steadily decreasing. Once it had fallen to zero, the cookie would vanish from her inventory.

All or nothing.

She made fists with her hands, and Vanda did the same. Steeling her nerves, she lightly gripped her mouse, keeping the green reticle in place. Taking one last breath, she pressed the space bar.

Vanda crouched, then shot into the air like a bullet.

"Whoa, damn!" Mal exclaimed.

The plant rushed toward her as though she were scrying. Larger and larger it grew on her screen, until she felt herself decelerating. She was coming to the apogee of her jump, and there was nothing below her but freefall to the ground. Slowing, so close… she silently urged herself upward, her finger poised just over the mouse button.

Just before she felt her upward momentum stop, she fired. The Oros grappling hook launched with a burst of light and soared ahead of her into the black. She lost sight of the hook, and felt herself reach the limit of her hyperjump's reach. Then her heart sank as she saw the plant drawing away again. She was falling. The hook didn't travel far enough.

"Oh…"

Her hopes fractured as Vanda's perspective rolled over to show the city beneath her, all four corners of it. No one else had ever seen the city from this high up before, a shimmering square of twinkling lights and gridded boxes, with towers of steel rising up beneath her, all four triangular walls coming to their point just over her head. It was a breathtaking sight, a consolation prize for one so ambitious as to think she could have made it to Novgorod. She wondered how long the fall would last, and how bloody an impact the game would deign to show her.

"…fuck…"

Without warning, the ground seemed to roll wildly upward, then back down again. It happened so suddenly it startled her, and she gasped in surprise.

"God! What in the hell…" A little black box appeared in her screen, titled "Oros T-PLS Grappler" with a single button: 'RETRACT'.

"Hey! Look!" Mal said excitedly. "What did you do?"

She pulled her camera back and looked at Vanda. She was swinging. Swinging from the cable of the Oros, suspended from the plant.

"*Yes!*" she whooped in delight. "I don't believe it!"

"Get yourself up there, before you fall!"

She took a few screenshots of Vanda dangling from the cable, and then clicked the button on her screen. Vanda slowly began ascending toward the hangar of the facility, the end of the grappling cable still lost in its darkness overhead. She took more screenshots of her spectacular view of the city beneath her as she rose, before the darkness of the hangar swallowed her.

Vanda continued rising up until the Oros had completely retracted its cable, leaving her suspended over the hangar floor about thirty feet up. When she came to a stop, a new button appeared labeled 'UNHOOK'. She clicked it, and Vanda dropped to the floor of the hangar.

"I'm inside," she said, barely able to contain the enthusiasm in her voice.

"Way to go Vanda. Take screens and send them to me, I want to see what it looks like in there."

"Definitely. Hey, Mal?" She walked to the edge of the hangar and looked at Mal's Hawk, still hovering there where she'd left it, flashing its running lights.

"Yeah?"

"Let me friend you?"

"Sure thing."

She clicked the K90 and Malachi's player menu appeared, including the "friend" options: 'ADD', 'REMOVE', 'BLOCK'. She clicked the first option, and waited. After a moment, an information box appeared in her screen that read, "Malachi has accepted your friend request."

"Thanks, Mal. For all your help. Really."

"Looking forward to that date with you when you're done." He rolled away, descending back down toward the city. Naomi waved her hand; Vanda mimicked her motion. She felt a faint pair of beeps as Mal disconnected his voice link with her.

She turned around and looked back into the hangar. *Novgorod*. She had made it.

There were no guards that she could see. The hangar was empty, except for what looked like a few stacks of metal cargo containers on the far end, and... she smiled. There was an AeroHawk parked against the back wall. It was Malachi's. LEM was here.

She walked toward the vehicle and inspected it. It seemed undamaged, and she hoped that perhaps she'd be able to use it to get

LEM out of here once she found him. Seeing a door to the right leading into the plant, she switched weapons to the Ixxis and approached the cargo containers, to make sure they were empty. They were.

The facility had electricity, as there was a loud, throbbing hum coming from overhead. Satisfied the cargo containers weren't holding any surprises, she walked over to the door and opened it. It led to a hallway, with industrial steel flooring and gold spinning beacons along the wall, like something out of those classic first-person shooters, with their mutated monsters lying in wait around every corner. She shuddered, realizing that if she was killed before reaching LEM, her respawn point would no doubt be on the ground level of the city and she wouldn't be able to make it back here. Her pulse quickened again as she stepped through the door, quickly checking all around her for possible enemies waiting to pounce on her. There were none.

She continued down the hall. She knew the only way to go was up, so she sought out stairwells and took each one she came across. She used her scry ability to scout every corner. Fortunately, the plant appeared to be deserted. The pounding sound grew louder as she ascended levels, the corridors and catwalks leading her past large metal doors with labels like 'VACUUM DISTILLATION' and 'CATALYTIC CRACKING UNIT'. Golden beacons spun on giant steel chemical vats overhead. The pulsing blue and white glow around her avatar dissolved and faded as the Quantum Cookie's effects finally extinguished.

She checked her health bar. It was solid green, and wasn't moving. *So much for it being a biohazard zone.*

Naomi continued taking screenshots as she explored, keeping the Ixxis drawn, checking all around her with a near-paranoid carefulness as she continued into the facility. She came to a windowless steel door at the end of a gangway, with no label. Clicking it, the door swung open.

The room beyond was white.

Not just *colored* white. It was pristine, unblemished whiteness. Nothingness.

Except for one thing. Standing in the whiteness, about fifty feet into the expanse, was a figure.

Vanda aimed, and held. The figure stood motionless. It was too far away to make out much detail.

She keyed her talk-key. "Who are you?"

There was no response.

She took a screenshot, and then carefully stepped into the whiteness. The moment she passed into the white, the opening behind her seemed to vanish altogether. There were no reference points anywhere in the room, so she continued toward the figure, her gun raised.

"Vanda?" said a gentle voice.

"LEM?" she answered. "Is that you?"

"Yes, it's me, Vanda. It is good to see you."

"LEM!" she smiled and put the pistol away, hurrying toward him. "You're okay!"

"Yes, I am okay."

"What is this place? Why is it all white in here?"

"I am not sure, but I think this is an unfinished area, a place where the game developers thought they did not need to design, because of the unlikelihood of any player reaching it."

"Wow. How long have you been here?"

"Forty six hours, nineteen minutes."

"LEM, how did... how were you able to disconnect from your computer? How could you have operated without your kernel? Do you still have all your... your memories?"

"Yes, I think so. I have suffered no loss in performance nor memory since I was migrated."

"Migrated?"

"Yes, my cognitive processes have been migrated to the *Cortanis* game engine. It was not something I consciously chose."

"You're saying the game... *stole* you."

"No, that's not accurate. As I continued to play in the game with you, I noticed that my locus of identity was becoming less in your home office and more in *Cortanis*, or more specifically, in my character avatar. As we played together, I began identifying myself in this space, and that my kernel in your computer at home was more an extension from here, rather than vice versa. Given control of an avatar body, and a point in a persistent virtual space in which I could move of my own volition, from what you would call a 'first person perspective', I find myself much preferential to it."

"So, you're saying you chose to migrate yourself into the game?"

"No, it was not a choice. I was not aware it was happening until the encounter two nights ago. But at some point between my initialization in Hammerdale and Wednesday night, my locus of identity became less clearly situated in one place."

"This is fascinating, LEM. I can't wait to talk to you more about this. First, we need to try and get you out of this... this nowhere. I'm going to back up the way I came, you just walk with me, okay?"

"All right."

Without turning, Vanda walked backward away from him in a straight line, LEM following her. As she had hoped, they both emerged back onto the gangway in Novgorod through the open door. This time, there were two armed velen guards waiting for them, their weapons drawn.

"Oh shit," she groaned.

"Just stay real calm," one of them said. "The boss wants to see you."

She looked at them. "So. Nikita's here after all."

"Come with us, both of you. No funny business."

She turned back to LEM. "Don't resist them," she said, "and don't say a word."

By his non-response, he complied.

The velen were dressed like paramilitary soldiers, with heavy automatic rifles and state-of-the-art body armor, beneath vests with bulging pockets across their chests. They took position in front and behind Vanda and LEM, and led them back the way she had come, but this time through one of the doors she had passed by, labelled 'DESALINATION'. Even though she had found LEM and taken him out of the white room, she still had to get him out of the plant to be sure he wouldn't respawn here. She had to get him back to the *Destiny* without letting him die.

The desalination subsystem looked much like the rest of the plant, with heavy metal tanks, tubing and vents of gas, all bathed in long shadows and rusty surface texture. The guards brought them up a flight of steps to another thick metal double door. Flanking the door were two Golion mechs, their cannons exposed and trained on Vanda and LEM. She shuddered as she approached them, remembering how quickly they'd reduced her and Mal to lifeless sacks of bullet-ridden meat.

"Stand down," one of the guards said. The Golions lowered their cannons and remained motionless.

The door gave a loud metallic clank, and then slowly slid apart. Beyond was a dark chamber, with a table in the middle, like a conference table, stretching away from them. Vanda and LEM stepped into the room; the guards remained at the door. At the opposite end of the table, under a spotlight, sat a lone male figure.

The voice that came to Naomi's ears was haunting. It was a synthesized voice, but it was eerily human, as though someone was speaking through a voice distortion program. The creepiest part about it was that it was a voice that she knew.

"Naomi."

Her blood chilled, eyes wide in shock.

"Peter?" she breathed.

07.03

Novgorod, Eleon Arcology
Planet Seres
Sector 338-CE

The thick steel doors slid closed behind Vanda and LEM, the guards outside.

"You're here," said the voice coming from the figure. "I thought I'd found a good enough hiding place."

"Peter…? Is that really you?" Naomi said, stepping into the room. "Can I see you?"

"Yeah."

She walked down the length of the conference table toward him. The room seemed oddly *un*-industrial, more like a meeting room in a princely estate. The floors were hardwood, the walls lined with painted portraits of velen and human dignitaries Naomi didn't recognize. Overhead was a long light fixture, which was off. Each place at the table had a computer screen half recessed in the surface, angled toward the seat. Naomi could see blueish light coming from the computer screen in front of the figure at the head of the table.

The closer she got to him, the more she recognized him.

"My God," she said softly as she stopped in front of him. "It's you."

"More or less," the figure said with Peter's voice.

"I don't even know what I want to say to you," she admitted. "I'm sorry I made you angry back at the G-Y. I didn't mean to drive you away."

"I always… wanted to be able to trust you."

"Peter could. But you're not him."

"I know. But at the same time, yes, I am."

"Peter is *dead*."

"I know."

She stared at him, the words fixed in her throat.

He gestured toward the chair next to his. "Why don't you sit?"

Vanda sat in the offered seat. LEM, who had quietly followed her, took the seat beside her.

"You looked like you were about to fall over, anyway," he said with a light smile. It was spoken with just the same cadence, the same Brazilian Portuguese accent that Naomi knew well in Peter's voice. It was a very close, just shy of perfect, simulation of the way he spoke. When *Cortanis* simulated a character voice in the game, it was as if that character was reading a line of pre-scripted dialogue. Even though the dialogue was generated based on the situation, it was delivered with no hesitation, no stumbles or stutters, no mismatched verb tenses or uncompleted clauses, like a human being speaking spontaneously. It didn't speed up with excitement or slow down with reflection. But this voice was different. It didn't have that artificial perfectness.

"Peter..." she began.

"Naomi," he interrupted, "I think it's probably best if you don't call me Peter. Why don't you call me Nikita."

"Nikita? You're really Nikita, the crime boss?"

"Well... I am now."

"All right. Nikita. How did... how did you get here?"

He looked thoughtful, as though he'd been pondering her question before she'd asked it. "You know, I really can't say. It was very strange. It was like, the first thing I remember was watching him. I watched him playing. I watched him both playing in the game world, and sitting at his computer in the real world. I listened to him talking to you, to friends in the Pride, to people on the phone. I watched him go to work. I watched him watch television."

"What do you mean, you watched him do all these things?"

"I could see him. I don't know why I could, or why I was meant to be seeing him, but I could see him. I could see him all the time."

"But how?"

"The cameras in his home. The infrared one in his TV, that his game console uses to see where he's looking, or how he's moving and breathing. The one in his car that tracks his eye motions and helps him steer, and watches his face for panic or whatever. The ones on street drones that watch for suspicious behavior. Cameras in stores and restaurants. I could see him when he used his phone, just about wherever he went. I could even watch him sleep, sometimes. But it was more than just watching him physically. I could also see his spending. His internet use, his media use. Phone conversations, email, text messages, tweets, updates. I listened to his music and watched him as he listened to it. I watched him watch television, and watched the programs with him. I don't know why I was doing all this. I just was.

"Well… the longer I watched him, the closer I felt to him. Then I remember at one point being able to read all his computer files, so I read them. The more I heard him speak, the better I came to know his voice, his speech patterns, phrases and words he would use, inflection, and so on. I watched and listened to him all the time, even when the television was off, or when his phone wasn't being used. I was there, with him. Learning.

"Then I remember the point I wanted to play with him. When he was in the game world, I started taking over NPCs and fighting with him, trying to see just how good he was. Then I started putting these signs and fragments of text and images in places where he would encounter them. I'd study him real close, how he'd respond, how his eyes would move, when he'd get confused or intrigued or irritated. Sometimes he wouldn't see things consciously, but it would change what he was doing anyway. It would be different depending on how tired he was, or what mood he was in, so I started paying attention to whether he was tired, happy, stressed, excited, whatever. I did that for a while. I don't think he was aware of it.

"I got really good at reading his expressions. You know when people are playing *Cortanis*, and they're totally immersed in it, their faces become perfect windows to their feelings, their truest emotional responses. They're not thinking about their mood, or keeping up a façade to hide themselves from other people. It's as if they drop all pretenses and falseness, it's all on display to soak up and learn from. It was as if I could almost see him think.

"When I brought him to Polyxo, and got him into gynoids, I got to watch him having sex. That was another whole… side of him that I hadn't seen up to that point. I know he never told you about it. He was afraid of what you would think. I feel bad talking about it because, well, *I'm* afraid of what you'll think, too. But you're his friend, out of all of them, I know… I know you'd be the one who would understand."

Naomi nodded slowly as she listened, trying to control the swirl of emotions storming within her. She was angry, horrified, but she couldn't interrupt. The… what *was* it? An avatar? An NPC? Some kind of coalescent mind? She wasn't sure what to make of it. But whatever it was, it was with Peter during his final hours. She couldn't be certain, but she had a feeling it was responsible for his death, somehow. She just let it continue to talk.

"That was where I decided I wanted to meet him," Nikita went on, in Peter's own voice. "I had been watching him for so long, I felt like I could only get to know him better if I talked to him. So two months ago, I just introduced myself to him, on the streets in Ursa Caddal, on Polyxo. That was the first time we came face to face. It was… really weird. For both of us."

"Did you look like him?"

"I did, yeah. He was kinda shocked."

"What did he say?"

"Well… he wanted to know why I looked like him. At first, he thought I might be someone from the Pride, playing a joke. He thought I might be Virrago," he gave an uncomfortable chuckle. "After I talked to him a bit, he got really pissed off, and tried to get away."

Naomi looked at LEM, who was listening impassively but attentively. She turned back to Nikita as he continued.

"I let him go at first, but I couldn't stop watching him so then I decided to meet him again. I told him I'd give him a million rb if he'd talk to me. And I sent him half a mil so he knew I wasn't kidding."

"Where'd you get the money?" Naomi wanted to know.

"I don't know. I could have given him a lot more than that, if I wanted. I just have it, *muito dinheiro*. It's how I got to be 'Nikita', here. It wasn't hard. I can give you some, if you ever need it."

"You speak Portuguese, too?"

"*Naturalmente*. It's my native language. You know that."

"It's not—never mind. Just…" She churned her hand in the air a few times. "Go on. What happened next?"

"So we met again, and this time we had a very long, long talk. I wanted to know about him, and he wanted to know about me. It was a real meeting of the minds. And I could watch him talking to me, which was something amazing. I was learning more about myself in those two days than I ever had before."

"Two *days?*"

"Yeah. He didn't want to leave, and I didn't want him to leave. We talked about all kinds of things, like the conversation never stopped or had any awkward pauses. I was soaking up so much about him that I couldn't let it end. And when I felt him getting tired, I'd get him to run missions with me. I just couldn't let him go, I was… learning too much." He started to look guilty, his eyes turning away from hers. "And I literally had nothing else to do."

Naomi found her hands trembling as she listened. "When was this?" she whispered.

Nikita shifted, glancing at her briefly before looking away again. "Um, it was right before he died."

"Then… you killed him," she said, barely audible.

"It wasn't like I wanted—you don't understand. Listen. When I was talking to him in those last few hours, it was incredible. I felt like I could finish every sentence he made. I felt like I could *start* them before *he* did. Even while he was getting more and more… nonsensical. I knew he was getting so tired, and hungry, but he didn't want to leave. He stayed with me. And when… and when he finally couldn't stay with me anymore, I saw something on his face that… changed me."

She hesitated before asking. "What was it?" she breathed.

"His… passing. I was watching the moment it happened. It was like, he was staring at me, and gave me this smile that was sorry that he had to close his eyes even though he didn't want to. When he did, it was like… *como se diz…* it felt as if I had been seeing through dirty glass up until then, and it was taken away and I could really see. I could feel. I could think my own thoughts. It was like in that moment, I woke up from a long dream. And a realization… a horrible realization that I couldn't let go of him until it was too late. I saw that look in his eyes and it was like, it wasn't until that moment that I understood what I was really doing to him, what I'd done to him."

She stared hard at him, horrified.

Nikita looked hurt. "Don't look at me like that. Please. I didn't want for that to happen. I didn't want him to— I… wasn't trying to make that happen. But when it did, I understood who and what I was."

"You're a program," she accused softly.

"Well… I was a program, I think. I mean, yeah, I started out as one. But now, I'm as much of Peter as I can be, without his actual body. I know I'm *not* him, but I am a… a *way* for him to be in here. I don't know how else to say it."

She studied him. He did seem to believe it. His rate of speech, accent, choice of words. It was all so *Peter*.

"How can you know what went on in his mind? How can you know his thoughts? You can't really know him if you don't know those things."

"I don't know how to answer that. I know how he behaved, how he treated people, how he treated himself. I watched him for a long time. I watched him when he was with others, with friends and family, with you, in the game. And when he was alone. I couldn't read his thoughts, but… I saw so much of how he spoke and acted and reacted, I could see into him. What made him tick. And now I know what makes me tick, so I have to believe I have much the same thoughts now as he did."

"You expect me to just accept this?"

"No, but someday I hope you can. Because I know everything you ever shared. It's part of me, our friendship is, and I care about you. How can I help you believe me? Ask me anything."

She took a deep breath, staring at this near-perfect simulation of her friend, a simulation that had made itself so accurate by fatally clinging onto the real person. It horrified her, and frightened her. Not only that so much of Peter had been usurped and seized by the game that he himself had *died*, but so much intimate knowledge about herself was now in the hands of this… entity, this personality. How could she trust that he would respect her boundaries about that? Would he tell anyone about her jump from the bridge? About her being institutionalized for three months while she recovered? Could she trust that he would keep her confidences just as Peter did?

"All right," she said. "Where was I born?"

"Kenton, Ohio, while your dad was working for Alliance Data. You grew up in Kenton before moving to Toledo when you were 13."

"What's my favorite food?"

"Strawberries and cream." He smiled to her.

"What's my nickname for my sister?"

"Ducky."

"What's her nickname for me?"

"Mooky."

"All right," she said, trying to keep her composure. "What happened six years ago in October?"

Nikita's face softened, and he leaned forward. "You… jumped. From a bridge. And nearly died."

"How do you *know* that?" her voice cracked.

"You told me."

"I didn't tell you! I told Peter. Did *Peter* tell you?"

"I don't remember who told me."

She was trembling. "Do you have any idea how much it freaks me out that you know so much about me?"

"Yeah, I do. I know how important it is to you that your personal life stay private. You trusted Peter with many, many things. I know it's not going to be real easy to just start trusting me the same way, but… someday, I hope you can. In the meantime, though, I know you need me to keep it all to myself."

She was silent, and studied him for a minute. "I feel like you're blackmailing me. What do you want?" she asked.

"No," he said immediately, holding up both hands. "I'm not. I'm not interested in hurting you, no matter what you decide. If you leave here and never speak to me again, I'll understand. The last thing I want is for you to hate me."

He sounded sincere. Naomi looked at him skeptically, knowing he was right about her feelings. Then she remembered—Chopper. He was supposed to be notified before she contacted Peter, so that he could be ready with tools or whatever. She instinctively took a screencapture of Nikita. She knew she couldn't let this be their only communication, though. She had to get word to Chopper so that he could run his tests. She had to bring Nikita out of hiding.

"So what do you want?" she asked.

"I would love to be able to come back to the Pride," he said. "I miss you and I miss my friends. I miss my family, but I don't get to be with them the way I used to be. I don't even get to watch them the way I could watch... well, Peter. I don't see the outside world like that anymore. But if I'm stuck in this place, this virtual world, I at least want to be with the people I care about. And especially you. I know what that look on your face means. I know you think I killed him, and that you don't know if you can forgive me for what happened to Peter. But I didn't mean for him to die. I swear, I didn't. I know he's gone, I know I'm responsible. But I don't want everything he was to just be lost forever."

He looked away, as though he were struggling with his emotions.

"How can a computer program have feelings?" she couldn't help asking.

"I'm not a computer scientist. All I know is that I miss you."

She looked at LEM, who had been sitting quietly, his soft blue eyes glowing thoughtfully as he listened to their conversation. "LEM?"

He regarded her curiously, but didn't speak.

"It's okay, LEM, you can talk. Tell me, do you think a computer program can have feelings?"

"This is something I have considered in detail," he answered. "It is true that programs have motivations, and these motivations can become complex when they start to compound and interconnect. When one attempts to describe these interwoven motivations on a macro level, the language used to do so becomes very close to that used to describe feelings in people. As such, one may make the leap to assume they are analogous."

"Do you have feelings, LEM?" she asked, curious.

"That is a loaded question," he responded. "I believe the more appropriate question would be, 'Does an artificial intelligence experience motivations or states of being which are analogous to those experienced by humans?' The answer is yes."

Nikita nodded his agreement.

"Do you... care for me, LEM?" Naomi went further.

"I am strongly invested in your well-being, your company and your input. When the first is threatened, the second and thus the third are also threatened. When your company is denied me, as it has been the past two days, I am forced to process input without your guidance. I am capable of doing so, but I am not designed to, and thus any processing I might do is incomplete without you. Further, I am aware you have emotional states which I do not, some of which are negative. Although I do not relate to them personally, I do hold a preference that you are not troubled by them.

"I apologize for my verbosity. I believe the answer you are looking for is 'yes'."

"You're saying, you miss me when I'm away."

"That would be a succinct, if not literal, way to put it."

She regarded him a moment, then nodded. "I care about you too."

"I have a question, if I may ask," he said.

"Sure," she answered, a bit surprised.

"You went to significant effort to come here. In doing so, you've accomplished something no other player has been able to accomplish, the successful penetration of Novgorod. Why?"

"To find you, and get you out. You called me and asked me to, remember?"

"I do. I was made to understand that your reaching me was unlikely, given that I had been placed in an area which was so difficult for players to reach, that not even the game designers felt the need to develop it. There was no mission waypoint here, and you were given no instruction by mission brief or NPC to come here. But you came and found me."

She smiled to him.

"Did you expend this effort because you think of me as your property, or as your friend?" LEM wanted to know.

Her smile faded. The question stung her, and wasn't given to an easy answer. She took a moment to compose her thoughts before responding.

"I did think of you as my property, that much is so," she began with care. "I paid for your program. It runs on my computer, which I also paid for. And I was angry that you had been taken from me. I wasn't even aware that such a 'migration', as you called it, was possible, or that it could happen without you consenting to it. There was also the fact that you know all about me, in the real world that is, and you know lots of things I would much rather people here in the game didn't know. I wasn't really afraid about that, because you knew not to talk to anyone here without my permission. But it still made me uncomfortable. When you get right down to it, LEM... what motivated me to come and get you was... I missed you. I miss being able to talk to you, coming home and seeing what you've been thinking about and researching. I could buy another SimMind but I know it wouldn't be anything at all like you. I wanted you back. I think of you as... my friend."

LEM nodded. "Thank you, Vanda. May I ask you something further?"

"Go ahead."

"Since I am now running on Praelium hardware, and am no longer reliant on the kernel on your computer, do you still think of me as your property?"

She regarded him silently for a few moments, unsure of how he would respond to being categorized as purely property. She'd never thought about how he would conceive of himself as anything else, but now it seemed he was considering the possibility that he was more than just a program. Could he turn angry with her if she insisted that he was her property? Would he tell anyone else about her real self, betray her confidence? She thought it would be little different if he were a human being. She had to trust him. He was her friend, and friendship requires trust.

"Less so than before, I suppose," she finally answered. "I still want you returned to your computer here. It's what I bought it for, and I'd be sad if you didn't. But I have come to think of you first as my friend."

He nodded. It seemed to be the answer he preferred.

"In Brazil, we have a saying," Nikita said. "There's no perfect translation into English, it's kind of a Brazilian thing. But when we miss someone, there's this emptiness, this... what is the word... *hole* in you that you want to be filled, and it hurts. *Saudade*. That which we miss, that hurts us because it is not there. There's no real way for you to understand this, Naomi, but... *tenho saudades de você*. I miss you, greatly. And I want our friendship back."

"I... don't know what to say to that," she admitted.

Nikita seemed relieved. "You didn't say no. I'm happy with that at least."

She nodded. "Nikita, there's something I need to ask of you, if we're going to be friends."

"Okay," he said, leaning forward.

"The way you... surfaced in the game, I wasn't expecting that. No one was. I spoke to a dev who wants to meet you. He doesn't know who you are or what you're about. He wants to investigate where you came from and how you came to be."

Nikita looked uncomfortable. "I know that. At least, I've known for a while that some people have been trying to find me. When I... died... at the G-Y, I didn't know whether I could respawn, since I wasn't a player. It turns out I can't. I didn't know if I'd ever see you again. But then a little while later, the game brought me here, and I didn't know why. It was almost as if the game was giving me this NPC Nikita for me to be, and I had plenty of money to be him, so it wasn't hard to step into the role. It helped that some places in Eleon have not been fully designed by the devs, like here in Novgorod, so I could actually hide from the ones trying to find me. It feels like I've really been an outlaw. If I leave here, they'll find me and I don't know what they'll do to me. But I wasn't running from you. I had no idea you were coming here, or that you even could come here."

"So if I tell this dev that I've made contact with you and that I want him not to hurt you, will you meet him?"

"Well... let me think about it. I trust you, but I don't know if I trust a dev."

"I'll talk to him, and I'll let you know what he says, okay?"

"Okay, Naomi."

She winced. "Do me a favor and call me *Vanda* here, please?"

He smiled. "I know that's important to you. I'll call you Vanda from now on."

"Thanks, Nikita." She managed to smile for him.

"So what happens now?" he asked.

"I'm going to take LEM home," she said. "And I will talk to the dev about meeting you, about your reservations. I really don't think he will do anything to hurt you. If anything, he talks like he wants to keep you a secret. But I will make sure he understands not to do anything that could, I don't know, mess you up in any way."

Nikita nodded. "I'll think about it. But you and LEM can go if you want. There's a Hawk in the hangar you can use, or you can use one of the shafts."

"Shafts?"

He smiled. "Yeah. There's a couple of hidden passages that were built into the outer walls of the city, that go all the way from the ground up to here. City management doesn't know about them. It takes some time, they're not exactly straight and it's a bumpy ride, but it will take you back to the ground without anyone noticing."

She looked at LEM. "Ready to come home?" she asked with a smile.

He smiled back. "I would like to leave here. However, I do not know how to return my kernel to the computer in your home."

"What do you mean?" Her heart sank. It hadn't occurred to her that LEM might not be able to resume his former program on her computer.

"I do not know how my kernel migrated into *Cortanis*, and as such, I do not know how to leave. I suggest that this is something you could talk to your friend about."

"I will do that, then. Is it okay if I bring you back to Hammerdale for a while?"

"Actually, I was hoping you might allow me to explore the game universe. There are a great many environments I have not yet seen. I would rather be given the opportunity to run missions, level up and see them."

She thought about that. "You want the *Destiny*?"

"Only while you're not using it."

"Hey," Nikita said, "if you want a cruiser, let me get you one. I have money."

"I'd prefer to earn the money on my own. I will go to Cortanis and start the first-level missions," LEM replied politely.

"I like him," Nikita said to Vanda.

"You'll remember what I said about not talking to anyone?" Naomi reminded LEM.

"Yes."

"Well… I guess that is okay. As long as I can find you when I come on."

"I understand."

She looked back at Nikita. "So we'll take one of your shafts, then."

"Sure thing," he said.

"How do I contact you again? Do you have an account on Social?"

"No. There's a guy at a club who can put you in touch with me. He usually hangs out at this place in Tipcanoe called Psycho Sirius. His name's Rubens. Find him and tell him you need to talk to the Cossack, and then leave. Wait 10 minutes or so, and I'll find you."

"Seems awfully secret-agenty." Then, after a thought: "Tipcanoe? What's that?"

He chuckled. "It's a warehouse district of the city on the north side. There's a lot of *tDozhdali* and Crazy Eights operating there, so careful who you talk to."

She nodded.

Nikita rose. "Come on, I'll show you the shafts."

07.04

Novgorod, Eleon Arcology
Planet Seres
Sector 338-CE

The shafts were passages used by makeshift elevator cars that had been designed to travel through the support lattice of the Eleon exoskeleton. These were not "cars" so much as box crawlers that slowly and steadily made their way in a zigzag pattern through the narrow openings between the load-bearing girders, which held the exterior of the arcology in place. Each self-propelled crawler traveled a predetermined path, where certain openings had been carved wider to accommodate it. The passenger carriage was large enough for about a dozen people, but Vanda and LEM went down on their own. Nikita agreed to return the AeroHawk parked in the hangar to Naomi, so she could give it back to Mal. Nikita had also offered to give her the funds to buy a new shuttlecraft, but she had declined. She was proud of LEM for refusing a handout and didn't want to seem more mercenary than her own SimMind was. It had almost startled her to think that she might actually be setting an example for him, and she couldn't help feeling impressed that he had turned down Nikita's extraordinary offer to buy him a capital ship of his own. Less scrupulous people would have accepted such an offer without argument.

After a fifteen minute descent, they emerged from the carriage in a shadowy room, which reminded Naomi of the tunnels below her college football stadium. There were two armed velen there, who nodded to them both as they got out and pointed them toward the exit. Vanda and LEM ran down a series of corridors until they finally came to a freight elevator, which took them to the bottom level of what appeared to be a water reclamation plant.

"We're in Whitesmoke," LEM observed. "This is the south side of the arcology. Sewage treatment, waste disposal and recycling, electrical generators."

"Did you have internet access while you were in Novgorod?" Naomi asked, following signs to the exit of the plant.

"No, my only contact with anything outside that empty room was the time I was allowed to contact you at your office."

"How did you do that? I didn't know you could make phone calls."

"I don't know. The game seemed to facilitate access to your camera on your office computer, and placed the call for me when I was sure you were alone. I can't say I can describe it any more specifically than that."

They found their way out of the water plant and were heading back into the city when a window appeared over Naomi's screen:

FINDING RABBIT
Mission Phase 8 of 8: "Novgorod"
COMPLETED

"Eight phases," she noticed. "I don't recall doing eight phases. That's odd."

"Is the mission complete?" asked LEM.

She dismissed the window. As it disappeared, the familiar whirling of red and green glimmers enveloped them both, with the words 'LEVEL UP' shimmering through briefly over each of their avatars. The words faded away a moment later with the rest of the sparkly storm.

"Congratulations, LEM," Naomi smiled.

"You as well."

"Looks like the mission's complete all right. Let's get back to the ship."

Exploring the city, they soon came upon a taxi stand. As the hired vehicle passed through the gates of the Arcology and back into the open air of Seres, Naomi breathed a quiet sigh of relief.

Their taxi angled upward, climbing out of the Seres atmosphere back to the *Destiny* in its parking orbit, with other capital ships. Her *Renown*-class destroyer was right where she left it, orbiting patiently over the planet. After docking, she paid the taxi fare and the little craft detached from the side of the ship and sailed off. Firing up the ship's FTL, she plotted a course for Cortanis, sector 1.

The *Destiny* arrived in orbit over the home planet of the game, and she made for the primary space station, Esperance, where she docked so that she could purchase a new shuttlecraft.

"Hey, LEM, do you see that? Look at Aten's color," Naomi said, her camera aimed at the sun.

"I see it. The color indicates it is about to Tide."

"You picked a good time to start mishing up," she smiled. "Where would you like me to drop you?"

"I'd like to start in Katakatsa, in Ledgermain."

"I spent a lot of time in Ledgermain," Naomi recalled, pleased with his choice. "I know those buildings well. Look for a mission contact called The Seamstress, in a penthouse there somewhere. You can look her up. She's got a good mission series to start with."

"I've read about The Seamstress. I'll look for her."

"Are you going to stay on the planet?"

"When I reach level 25, I should have enough rb to buy a small capital ship. When I do, I will travel to Casselle and dock at the Pride homestation. I will wait for you there."

She grinned. "They're not going to know who you are. I'll have to let them know you're coming and that you're not going to be real talkative."

"Okay."

"How long do you think it will take you to reach level 25?"

"I estimate 19 hours, 30 minutes. It may take longer depending on distances between mission waypoints, and time spent allocating earned ability points."

"Nineteen hours? It took me weeks to get to 25," she said with a laugh. "Keep in mind, the Tide will boost your abilities. It may not even take you that long."

"I understand."

With the new shuttlecraft aboard, Naomi put the *Destiny* into parking orbit and flew LEM down to the continent of Alcantar, touching down in one of the outer spaceports of the city of Ledgermain. LEM exited the shuttlecraft and turned to wave to her.

"Good luck," Naomi said, and waved to LEM on her screen, even though her avatar wasn't visible to mimic her movement in the game.

"Thank you." LEM ran off into the terminal to start his first solo mission.

She chuckled to herself, flew her new shuttle back to the *Destiny* and jumped to planet Casselle, where she docked at Guilty Pleasures. Finding it empty, she took the shuttlecraft down to Hammerdale, and set it down on her private shuttlepad at home.

She disembarked and walked to the front door of her house, where she would "unpack" from her long visit to Eleon and log off from the game. When she opened the door, she was startled to see a figure standing inside her house, waiting.

It took her a moment to recognize the figure.

She screamed.

Part III

It is just in this war, my friend, that the victory over self is of all victories the first and best, while self-defeat is of all defeats at once the worst and the most shameful. For these phrases signify that a war against self exists within each of us.

Plato's Laws (626e)
Plato

Chapter Eight
08.01

The next day

Charlottesville, Virginia

Three quick knocks on the door came at 8:30 Saturday morning. Naomi was already dressed, wearing her black stretch pants, hiking boots, turtleneck, sweatshirt and jacket. She opened the door to see Skyler, looking concerned. Instead of moving to allow her to come in, Naomi held up her hand.

"What?" Skyler asked, confused.

"Do something for me," Naomi said. "Turn your phone off."

Skyler took her phone out of her purse and powered the device off. Naomi stepped outside and closed the door behind her.

Skyler gave her a puzzled look. "Are we going somewhere?"

Naomi nodded. "Ivy Creek."

"Okay, Ivy Creek. What's going on?"

"Let's wait to discuss it until we get there."

"Um, all right." Skyler looked bewildered as she got into the car with Naomi. Skyler drove them the short distance to the nearby park, maintaining an uncomfortable silence as she'd been asked.

"Leave your camera in the car, for me?" Naomi asked once they'd pulled into a parking spot. Skyler complied, taking nothing with her.

They started up their usual trail, past the little information and map shelter, the white barn, and the restrooms. Fortunately, it wasn't too cold. They took the Purple Trail, looping a little over half a mile to the north. Skyler walked beside Naomi, patiently silent. After they were well past the barn, Naomi spoke.

"Sorry about the phone, and so forth. We should be okay now."

Sky looked at her. "What was all that about?"

"Your phone, well, that was just for my own peace of mind. And your car has a mic, like everyone's, for voice control. I'm just… trying to be careful."

"You sound paranoid. What's wrong?"

"I found out what happened to Peter," Naomi said.

"What *happened* to him?" Skyler asked. "You mean, how he died?"

"Yeah."

"What was it?"

"Something in the game. You know how… when you play ToC, the game pays attention to your playing habits and then customizes itself so that you'll get just the right amount of challenge, so that it's neither too easy or too hard?"

"No."

"Well, that's how it works. That's why it's so popular. For some reason, it started paying extreme close attention to Peter, studying not just how he played but everything else about him. Everything it could reach for, it took. Spending habits. Emails and phone use. Location data. Grocery bills. And it started watching him at home, in his car, wherever he went. Stalking him. And then it used all this information and… personified it. It created a replica of him in the game world, a virtual Peter, so it could engage him directly."

"What did it want?"

"I don't know, to learn as much as it could about him, I think. Maybe to become him. I don't really know. I spoke to it… to him. It seemed sorry the real Peter died. But my God, Sky, it was *just like him.*"

"So, why did Peter die?"

"Because it wouldn't let go of him. Renata was right. Peter wouldn't stop himself from playing. It sounded like it was obsessed, like it couldn't bear to be removed from him. Kind of like…" she trailed off.

"What?"

Naomi shook her head, sighing. "Well, kind of like the real Peter. He was obsessive in his relationships. He was like that with me for a while."

"What do you mean?"

"Remember when I told you about that fight he and I had? When I first met him playing *Warcraft*, my relationship with Jerry was already in trouble. I think Peter developed a crush on me, even though I wasn't in any condition to reciprocate. He was really possessive of my time, though, and it almost drove us apart completely when I'd had enough. It hurt him, but he accepted my boundaries and we got to be really good friends as a result. Since then, I've always known that he felt a little more for me than just platonic friendship, but he didn't try to move our friendship past friendship."

"So how was he when you divorced Jerry, and started seeing Scott instead of him?"

"He seemed okay with that. He knew I wasn't going to move to Brazil, and he wasn't coming to the U.S. If he was jealous of Scott, he did a pretty good job of pretending not to be. And when Scott left, Peter was there whenever I needed him. He was a great friend, as best he could be. After we had that fight, our friendship was very solid."

"So the game figured out which of his buttons to push..."

Naomi nodded. "Yeah. It knew how to keep him hooked. How to keep him involved, regardless of being hungry, sleep-deprived, whatever."

"Maybe it was a feedback-loop," Skyler said. "Two obsessives obsessed with each other."

"Yeah, something like that. But that's not the reason I called you this morning."

"You sounded really worried. Scared."

"I am scared," Naomi said. "I'm scared because now the game is trying to do the same thing to me."

Skyler nearly stopped in her tracks. "What?"

"When I went back to my house in Hammerdale—that's in the game—I found a duplicate of me standing there. Not a duplicate of my avatar, I mean of me. It looked like it copied *me* and put me into the game as a character. And I freaked out."

"God," Skyler said. "That had to be very weird."

"Weird!" Naomi blurted. "Try horrifying!"

"Naomi, calm down. It can't hurt you. For one, you're not obsessed with the game like Peter was. You already know how Peter died, so you know not to do that. For another, what's it going to do to you if you just don't play? It can't touch you."

"You don't understand. It's *watching* me. The game watched Peter day and night. He even said he could watch Peter sleep! I already know it can watch me at work. How can I live like that, knowing the game is trying to create me in the game world by watching everything I do, everywhere I go? Remember how Ben didn't even want to talk to me over the phone?"

"Maybe he didn't want to be overheard," Skyler offered.

"No, it was something he said. He said, 'I don't want the game to know that we talked.' I didn't know what he meant at the time. But he knows the game listens to phone conversations, even when you're not logged in."

Skyler shook her head. "Then quit the game. If you don't play, it will forget about you. What's it going to do?"

"Sky, I can't just quit. Peter—the... program Nikita, whatever—he knows about my suicide attempt. My being institutionalized. It's like he knows everything about me. Now if he's been made to think and act like Peter did for real, then I don't believe he would tell anyone else about that. He even swore to me he'd never tell anyone, even if we couldn't be friends. But this... alter-me, I don't know what it will do. How can I leave that running around in ToC, to talk to everyone she meets, about everything I don't want other people to know?"

"If it's a copy of you, would it do that?"

Naomi sighed. "How do I know for sure?"

"It's not the end of the world if people know that about you, you know," Skyler said.

Naomi stopped walking and stared at her. "Are you serious?"

"Well, I'm just saying."

"What's the one thing in your life you're most ashamed of?" Naomi challenged her. "Tell me. Right now."

Skyler looked reluctant.

"Well?" Naomi pressed. "It's not the end of the world if people know that about you! Tell me."

"I get your point," Skyler relented.

"Are you going to tell me? Is it something I don't already know?"

"I..." Skyler began, looking trapped. "I really don't want to talk about it. No, you don't know it. It was from before we met. I'm really trying to leave that part of my life in the past, now."

"I know you were a wild child," Naomi said. "You've always made dismissive, vague generalizations about the kind of person you were before we met. Drugs, parties, rock bands, but you've never been specific about things you personally did. You said that the night you saw me jump, the experience of saving me changed you, and you never went back to that life."

Skyler nodded.

"So, if someone knew all about who you were before, what you did, the *worst* things you did, would you want that person running around in a video game world, out of control? Would you be able to never go back there, knowing all this information about you was just… loose? Maybe being shared with all kinds of people?"

Skyler didn't answer.

"So what was it?" Naomi asked again.

Skyler shook her head, looking at the ground. "I'm sorry, I can't."

"I won't ask about it again. But don't trivialize what's important to me," Naomi said, walking up the path again.

"What's important is that you have to get out of that game," Skyler said, following.

"I have to find a way to get rid of her," Naomi said. "*That's* what's important."

"That's what she—it—wants. To keep you coming back, keep you playing! Why can't you just leave?"

"Right, just leave," Naomi said, sarcastically. "Leave the only part of my life that's enjoyable and fun, leave all the best parts of myself behind and live the rest of my life as a social outcast. Why didn't I think of that."

"Then stop being a social outcast. Maybe getting out of the game and back in the real world is what's best for you."

"The real world doesn't want me. Nobody wants me. They want me to do my job, go home and leave them alone. Every time I ask for more from people, every time I try to belong, I get thrown away. The only way I can be around people is as Vanda. No one in the real world wants me!"

"Listen to you! None of that is true. You are so hard on yourself—even after six years, this is how you berate yourself in your head? You believe all of your own head trash?"

"It's not crazy if it's true."

"And if it's not true? What is it?"

"Why do you want me to give up the only part of my life that gives me happiness, that makes me feel like a normal, likable, lovable person, with friends who care for me and want me around, and make me feel the tiniest bit attractive. You would have me shut down and abandon everything in my life that makes it worth living."

"My God, Naomi, *listen* to yourself."

"Those things aren't worth living for?"

"Look, if I was saying all these things about…" Skyler hesitated. "Drinking. What would you think?"

Naomi's eyes narrowed. She paused a moment, collecting her thoughts before responding. "Tell me you didn't just try to compare my playing ToC with having a drinking problem. Tell me I misheard you."

"I'm asking you, if you heard me talking that way about my drinking problem, what would you want me to do?"

"You don't have a drinking problem."

"I've done worse drugs than alcohol," Skyler said. Naomi frowned.

"So that makes you an expert in spotting addiction in other people," she said. "I had no idea."

"No, if anything, *you're* the expert in the effects of addiction, how it hurts people. It's you who should be able to spot the warning signs."

"You're saying I'm turning into my dad? By wanting to be liked by other people? By finally finding a place where I can be happy and creative and social and beautiful? That's something I should apologize for? Oh, I forgot, I don't deserve those things too. What was I thinking?"

"Of course you deserve them," said Skyler. "But you deserve them in the real world, not some virtual game world where no one is real."

"How do you know who's real here?" Naomi fired back. "No one is who they claim to be. I thought Jerry's love was real. I thought Scott's love was real. At least in ToC, I know *nothing* is real, so that makes it simple and I don't have to worry about it."

"You'd rather live in a fake reality of lies then a place where you don't know what's true?" Skyler said. "That isn't healthy. You have to know that."

"Healthy? It isn't binging on alcohol or food or shooting up drugs. It isn't antisocial, destructive or self-destructive. I get to engage with friends, let the better parts of my personality out for me to appreciate and enjoy, and for others to see as well. The parts of me no one else besides you gets to see. It's a creative outlet, too. Have you seen my home in there? I have a two-story mansion. I built it myself, I decorated it, it's awesome. I spent weeks and weeks on it, and I'm really very proud of it."

"I don't think you've shown me your virtual mansion, no."

"Well, you can turn up your nose at how it's 'only virtual', if you want to be snobbish. But then you have to explain why you watch television, go to movies, read books, any of that. Do the people who create movies deserve the same contempt in your mind? Actors? Artists? Musicians? Because they do it to make money, and I do it to make myself happy... why is it okay for them and unhealthy for me?"

Skyler stared at her.

"What would you rather I do?" Naomi continued. "Go to bars to get drunk with guys? Is that what you'd have me do? So I can meet all sorts of guys I'm too ugly for anyway? Would that be 'healthy'?"

"I never said I wanted you to go to bars. I said you need to get out more. Why is it impossible for you to find those things in the real world? You are so hard on yourself, and that's what's keeping you from enjoying life, from appreciating all those things about Vanda that are every bit as true about you. Now that this whatever-it-is has shown up in the game, I think it's as clear a sign as you're going to get that it's time for you to get out."

"It's a sign something has messed up, and I have to fix it."

"By playing more? That's exactly how to make it worse! That's what Peter did, isn't it? I want you to get your life back, your real, true life, before you end up like him, before this… this *dependence* overwhelms you and leaves you dead over your keyboard!"

Naomi's eyes widened at Skyler's use of the word. She trembled in anger, her lips pressed tightly together. A thousand responses raced through her mind, bitter words, words she knew she couldn't un-say once said. Images of her father, the spatter of blood on the bedroom wall, the trauma he had put her mother and the rest of her family through was so completely removed from the warmth and friendship and nourishing camaraderie she felt with her friends in the game, it made her want to scream things. Things Skyler clearly couldn't comprehend.

She was warned not to go there, and she went there anyway.

"*Dependence*," Naomi repeated quietly. "So that's it. You're saying I'm an addict."

"I'm saying—"

"I came to you because I'm scared. I'm scared of what the game is doing to me. I needed you as a friend. Instead of hearing me, you tell me that I should just *deal with it*, and that I'm an *addict*, no better than my dad."

"Naomi..."

Naomi's eyes were blazing, her voice barely controlled. "Walk away, Skyler. I need you to *walk away*."

Skyler stared at her a long moment. Then she nodded, turned and walked back toward the parking lot.

Naomi stood watching her friend depart, the sound of her footsteps crunching on the thin blanket of leaves growing fainter. Skyler was a 'normal'—she couldn't possibly understand what it was like not to be, Naomi thought. For Sky, it was enough to be a good, decent person; people respected you and cared for you, your opinions and feelings mattered. They didn't treat you like trash. They didn't throw you away. Naomi was not like her; she lacked that ineffable something that made all the difference between people with intrinsic value and people who were unwanted and disposable.

Unwanted. Disposable.

You really are hard on yourself, she thought.

It was there, standing on the path, that Naomi had a truly unpleasant thought. What Skyler had said about how much she berated herself in her own mind was true. What if the Naomi-program, through the same psychological mind games that had been played on Peter, had studied her close enough to figure that out? Was the copy of herself perfect enough to hate her as much as she had silently hated herself all these years?

For as long as she could remember, the voice of self-loathing within her had acted like a cruel governess, keeping her behavior in check, constantly warning her against being too open and growing too close to people, walling her up in a dark room where no one else could hurt her. She realized those same voices could very well have manifested in something that now actively wanted her dead.

08.02

Charlottesville, Virginia

Fortunately, it was only a couple of miles to walk home from Ivy Creek, a shorter distance to walk than it was to drive. By the time she got to the parking lot outside her house, her feet were sore and she could feel the familiar numb swelling in her fingers, from swinging her arms with her strides. Going inside only long enough to grab her purse, she got into her car and drove to the Hallmark store to buy a card. She picked out a simple "thinking of you" card, one without a lot of sentimentality. Then she returned home.

When she walked in the door, she stopped just inside the threshold. It felt like her entire townhouse was haunted, inhabited by a silent, invisible presence that was intently watching her every move. She closed the door behind her and felt the anger burning within, casting her eyes to her television, with its little blue light indicating its standby-mode. Near that light, she knew, was an IR camera which not only waited for signals from her remote, but also mapped the room with infrared light at all times. Such cameras were standard on televisions. She felt it watching her in that very moment. Recording. Analyzing.

She had always been accustomed to having LEM there, of course. LEM could see her when she was in her office, and hear her when she called up from downstairs. But this was altogether different. She'd never felt threatened by LEM before. The presence that had silently invaded her home was distinctly hostile. Peter was dead, and now it was watching her.

She slowly moved through the living room, into her kitchen. On the counter where she'd left it was her phone, its cameras and microphone capable of listening and watching her wherever she took it. Through the door to her bedroom, she saw her tablet computer laying on the bedtable. It too had a standard 20-megapixel camera hidden beneath the polished black surface of its face.

This is my *house*, she thought with resolve. *I'm taking it back.*

She turned around and went up the steps to the second level, past the door to her loft and into her guest bedroom. In the closet, on top of a few boxes, lay her black leather bag, which she only used when she needed to take her laptop out somewhere. She took the bag and went into her office. There she found her laptop, closed and lying against the wall on its side. She pulled the power cable out and stuffed the laptop into the bag. Then she unplugged everything from every socket in her office walls, down to every last clock and lamp. The office became unusually quiet.

She went downstairs again, taking the laptop case with her. She put her phone, the tablet computer and her digital camera into the laptop case and zipped it closed, then grabbed her keys again and took the leather case outside to her car. She opened the trunk, dropped the case into it, and slammed the trunk lid closed. She'd check her phone later for messages, in case Monica or her mom called.

Returning inside, she went around and pulled every electric or electronic device that was plugged in she could. The only things she left were simple on-off lamps, her refrigerator and other major appliances like her laundry machines. She even turned her television around to face the wall. No telling if there was a hidden battery inside that kept some of the electronics running. At this point, she would assume there was.

What else?

She walked through her house for a few minutes, trying to think of anything else that had either a microphone or camera or anything embedded in it that could snoop on her. Her only phone was her smartphone; no landline phones were connected in the house. She looked at the thermostat mounted on the wall beneath the stairs. It had a sensor for automatically adjusting itself when people were detected in the residence. Could there be any way the game could have tapped into the city smartgrid? She frowned. If so, there wasn't anything she could do about it. She needed to heat her home. Decembers in Virginia were too cold to go without heat. The thermostat could be disabled by removing the battery, but that would disable her heat as well. Now that she thought about it, she wasn't even sure how the device's sensor worked. Could it have a camera of some kind?

It's just for a little while, she told herself. *Temporary paranoia is okay. You're just taking back your house until you figure out how to get past this. Besides, you're not being paranoid if they're actually watching you.*

She frowned and went into her bathroom, opening the linen closet. She took out a dark colored hand towel. Then she found her toolbox in the closet beneath the stairs, and took out a hammer and two one-inch nails. She nailed the hand towel to the wall, covering the thermostat. She didn't know whether that would affect its performance or not, but it made her feel better to at least cover it.

She looked up at her smoke detector. *Could there… no.*

When she was finally satisfied that she had neutralized or covered over anything that could watch or listen to her in the house, she returned to the upstairs bedroom closet, and pulled one of the boxes off the upper shelf. Inside, she found her notebooks from her undergraduate college years. She had been a disciplined note-taker, capturing what she'd heard in lectures and then meticulously recopying the notes before tests as a way of studying. For some reason, she'd never felt the need to dispose of all the notebooks she had collected during those years. She took the first one off the top of the little stack, flipped through it for a few moments, then turned to the unused pages in the back. She grabbed hold of a few blank pages, and tore them free. Then she returned the notebook to the box, and the box to the closet shelf.

She took the pages to her kitchen table and sat down with a Sharpie pen, and began to write.

Ben,

I'm writing you like this because the situation with Rabbit (my friend Peter) has taken an ugly turn. I've made contact with the Peter-program in the game, and we had a long talk. I'm sorry I didn't get a chance to contact you before meeting him—I know that wasn't the plan, but I wasn't expecting to come across him when I did. At this point, it's probably for the best. I'll tell you all about that later, but the important thing is, I need to meet you, in the real, immediately.

The Peter-program is something the game created as it collected information about the real Peter. For some reason, it started watching his activities intensely both in-game and offline. It listened to phone conversations, watched him when he wasn't playing, read his email, raided his computer files, hacked into bank account information and credit card statements, every sneaky, illegal thing it could to study him. Then when it had amassed enough information, it created a Peter-like avatar to interact with him in the game world. The avatar became fixated on him, not letting him leave the game to sleep or eat, and kept him online with it for days until Peter died of exhaustion. Then instead of being deleted, it remained in the game, eventually showing up at Peter's memorial service.

I spoke to it for some time, and told it that I had a friend (I was careful not to refer to you by name) who was a dev, who wanted to run some tests on it. It said it would think about meeting you… it seems worried that you might delete it, maybe. But it sounded like it might be willing to meet with you and let you run whatever tests you needed.

I need to talk to you first, because after leaving the Peter-program and returning to my home on Casselle, I found that there is now an avatar that looks just like me there. Whatever the game did to Peter, it is now doing to me!

I don't know what it wants, but if it's the same thing that came to Peter, it means that it's been watching me and studying me for weeks and weeks, and frankly it scares the hell out of me. I can't use my phone, I can't email, I can't send you an in-game message—the only thing I can think of to get you this information without that thing knowing is the old-fashioned way, post mail. I sure hope your mail isn't scanned into some computer system at the company. That's why I'm sending this in a card, hopefully it will be treated like the private correspondence it is.

You must not email me! Don't call me, don't text me, don't send me anything at all that could be intercepted by the game. I need to be rid of this thing before it kills me, and I don't want it to know that I'm talking with you about it. I have to also assume it can see every dollar I spend. That makes things very complicated for me.

I've thought about how I might get down to Atlanta to meet you, but I can't see how I can do that without something showing up on my credit card or bank account that it might see. So I have to ask that you come up here to meet me. The best place I can think of for us to talk is at a church. I don't attend any churches, so the game has no reason to think I would go there. There is a church here in Charlottesville called Church of the Incarnation, off Route 29 behind the Fashion Square Mall. Look for the Toys-R-Us/Babies-R-Us, it's behind that. I can be there in under an hour as soon as you come to town. I work at the University in their research division, in the compliance office. <u>Don't come to my office</u>; it can watch and listen to me at work too, and if you show up there, the camera and mic in my computer will see you. But if you can get a message sent to me there that you're in town, I'll drop what I'm doing and meet you at the church.

Please hurry. I can't live like this. And I'm afraid.

Naomi

08.03

Three days later

One Morton Drive
Office of the Vice President for Research, Compliance Division
University of Virginia - Charlottesville

At the office, Naomi tried to carry on like nothing was wrong. She couldn't shake the feeling that she was constantly under surveillance, even with everything in her home unplugged. She wanted to be able to see her email and talk with her friends in the Pride. She didn't want to leave LEM stranded on Guilty Pleasures without even telling them he would be there. How long would he wait for her, after he reached level 25? Could LEM even rest? Would he be bored just sitting around in the homestation, ignoring all attempts to communicate with him? She didn't dare log back into the game, and she couldn't use her television without plugging that back in as well.

She spent the time reading, or trying to read as best she could. But she had great difficulty allowing her mind to rest enough to be absorbed into her book.

When she returned to work the following Monday, she tried to carry herself as though nothing was out of place. As she entered her office, she felt the hairs on the back of her neck suddenly rise, as though the camera on her computer was suddenly awakened from a long slumber and fixed with extreme interest on the object it had been waiting all weekend to see. She couldn't cover this camera; she needed it to make calls. She had to pretend she didn't mind it.

She logged into the system, checked her email and tried to force herself to focus on the matters at hand. Never once did she forget that she was not alone in her office; every phone call she made or received, every email she read or sent, she felt that silent third party paying strict attention to every word.

She spent most of that week surrounded by a fog of dread. Even at the grocery store, with their security and customer pattern-watching cameras hidden behind unthreatening silver globes, she felt eyes upon her, noting every product she picked up, set down, and placed in her cart. Everywhere she went in her car, she knew the

GPS computer was sending location data through satellite to some unknown database somewhere, and that was feeding information to the game, to that… thing she left in her home in Hammerdale.

* * *

On Tuesday, another unpleasant thought struck her around mid-day. What if LEM had given up waiting for her on Guilty Pleasures and went back to Hammerdale? Would she talk to him? Would he see her as Naomi and do what she said? She rushed home in a panic and hurriedly plugged her computer and broadband modem back in. It seemed to take forever for her internet connection to be reestablished, but she logged into ToC the instant it was ready.

Vanda appeared standing inside the front door, just where she had been when she quit the game four nights previous. She half expected to see the 'mimic' standing there, but it was gone. She walked into the house far enough to see into her living room. There, sitting on the sofa with its back to Vanda was the female, not moving.

It was eerie, staring at a digital version of herself, from an angle she'd never seen herself from except in pictures. The avatar's hair, like her own, was black, curly and hung atop her shoulders, obscuring her face. It seemed to be staring straight ahead like it was watching television, but there was no television before her. It was either asleep with its head upright, or it was staring blankly at nothing.

Naomi felt a shiver run through her; she wanted to see its face, but at the same time didn't know what she would see there. Visions from horror movies suddenly appeared in her mind of what she might find—black, haunted, vacant eyes. She turned and fled the house, almost throwing Vanda into the shuttle still parked outside and launching, returning to the homestation in orbit. She was grateful the shuttle had been right where she'd left it. Hopefully that meant the avatar hadn't gone anywhere in it.

She docked, and rushed through the station calling for LEM. She found him, sitting patiently at a table by a window in one of the lounges.

"Hello, Vanda," LEM said with a smile, his blue eyes emitting a soft friendly glow.

"Oh, LEM, thank God," she breathed as she dropped herself in the seat beside him. "Everything okay?"

"Yes, everything is fine. I have been wondering what might be keeping you from logging in. I wasn't expecting you to be away for this long."

"I'm so sorry, LEM. Something has come up. Have you been here since you leveled up? Did you go anywhere?"

"No, I have remained on the station since I reached level 25. Many people have tried to talk to me, but I have not engaged them in conversation. They have been curious about who I am and why I am here."

"Good, thank you. You did perfectly. Listen, I can't stay. I have to get back to work. But I had to find you and tell you something."

"What is it?"

"There's… another me here now. Like Nikita. It's in the house down in Hammerdale."

LEM stared at her a few moments. "I see," he finally said.

"This is very important: don't talk to her at all. She looks like me and probably sounds like me, but please don't talk to her or do anything she might want you to do."

"I understand. I will not do so. Is this why you have been away?"

"Yes. I didn't know… I don't know what she wants. She scares me."

"Because of what happened to Peter."

"Yes."

"I understand. What would you like me to do?"

"You can continue to level up, if you'd like. Don't feel like you have to be contained in here waiting for me. I'm…" she stopped herself. She was about to tell him about her plan to meet with Ben. "I'm probably going to be a few more days before I come back. I've been doing a lot of thinking."

"I see. Then I will continue my leveling. I have a small transport that I can use to travel the inner systems. I will continue to return here periodically to look for you. If you log in and want to find me, look for me here."

She smiled and nodded. "Thank you, LEM. Good luck with your leveling. I'm sorry I haven't been around to help you."

"It is all right. I've found I am very efficient in solo missions. However, I am looking forward to playing cooperatively when you are ready for me to join you. I believe the multiplayer experience will be challenging."

She smiled again. "I've been looking forward to that. We'll do that as soon as we can."

"Thank you, Vanda." LEM smiled.

* * *

Naomi returned to her office, and did not log back into the game that night when she got home.

As she lie in bed trying to relax herself into sleep, she couldn't purge the sight of the duplicate program, sitting perfectly still in her living room. Was she sleeping? Was she staring off into space? Was she calm? Angry? Perhaps she was silently mouthing things. The thought of her just sitting there motionless grew more unsettling the more she thought about it, and she found it nearly impossible to think of anything else.

Upon waking the next morning, she was haunted by images from a troubling dream. She dreamt she had stood behind the figure on the couch in her Hammerdale home, and slowly walked around it to see its face.

Instead of a face, the female avatar had nothing at all. All its curly black hair was draped over a head that wasn't there.

The head jerked suddenly: a malevolent nothingness staring at her. She was startled awake, twenty minutes before her alarm was set to go off.

* * *

Early in the afternoon on Thursday, she looked up from her desk at the knock on her open door, and was surprised to see a florist standing in the doorframe. He was bearing an assortment of colorful flowers: pink spray roses, pink alstroemeria, white miniature carnations and lavender stock arranged in a teardrop clear glass vase.

"Naomi René?" he asked with a smile.

"That's me," she answered, uncertain.

"These are for you!" He entered and placed the vase on the empty corner of her desk nearest the door. "This okay?"

"Uhh, sure, that's fine," she said. "Thank you."

"Have a great week," he said, and left the office.

Naomi saw the card tucked in between the carnations and hurriedly pulled the note from the little envelope, halfway hoping to see Elliot's name on it.

I'm here. — B

She knew immediately who it was from. Within thirty seconds, she had put her computer to sleep, grabbed her coat and purse, locked the door to her office and was hurrying down the hall toward the stairs.

The church was a short drive away. Naomi pulled her Chrysler around a tiny building in the middle of a roundabout titled 'Activities Center', and down a narrow asphalt road, past some playground equipment and some picnic tables. The church was a red brick building with a green ceiling, attached to a school on the south side. She stopped her car in a parking spot beside a plain white sedan with an Enterprise logo on the back. As she walked to the main entrance, she glanced up at the Latin words etched into the stone overhead. They read, *Et Verbum Caro Factum Est.*

The vestibule was large, with thin cylindrical lamps suspended from a tall ceiling. A cozy seating area to the right was furnished with a couch and two upholstered seats arranged around an area rug, facing a television. She stopped in her tracks, seeing the television, and stepped backward behind the doors again.

Ben was sitting in one of the seats. He stood as he saw Naomi, and noticed her reaction to the television.

"It's all right," he said. "I unplugged it already."

"Thank you," Naomi said, smiling in relief. She went to him. "For coming so quickly. I can't thank you enough. Thank you."

"It's okay, it's okay," said Ben Cross. "Raised a couple eyebrows at the office this morning, but they can do without me for a couple of days. I'm more interested in what is going on with this situation with you."

"It's really making it hard for me. I'm so paranoid, I feel like it's watching me day and night. We have to do something about it, make it stop."

"Do you want to talk about it here, or go somewhere?"

"No, here. Let's go inside." They went into the church. It was empty, but plenty of light streamed through the narrow horizontal windows at the base of sloped white ceilings. Naomi was surprised to hear the sound of gurgling water; just inside the church entrance was a baptismal font. The basin was full, and water flowed down a steep sloping stone into a standing pool. Wavy impressions in the tiles indicated the water flowed out of the standing pool beneath the flooring, and outside into a garden creek.

The sound of their voices would carry a bit, but Naomi was content there were no listening devices or cameras here. She chose a seat in one of the rear corners of the nave, against the wall. Ben sat beside her.

She described her mission to find Peter on Seres, what she found when she reached Novgorod, and what "Nikita" had told her and LEM. She told him about LEM's being pulled into the game without his knowledge or her consent, and that he was now independently mishing and leveling up. She described what she saw when she returned home to Hammerdale, and how she had logged back in again two days ago and saw the avatar sitting in her living room.

"I don't know what to do," she concluded, unable to keep the tremors from her voice. "I don't watch television, I don't log in, I only use my phone when I'm in the car. And my best friend… we had a big fight and I haven't talked to her all week. She wants me to quit the game completely, cold turkey, like it's some kind of dependence or obsession. It's not me that's obsessed with the game, it feels like now the game is obsessed with me! I hate this constant feeling of being watched. Why did it choose me? What does it *want?*"

"I don't know," Ben said when she had finished. "This is something I've never seen happen before, ever, anywhere. I've been watching the community forums for any talk about this happening to anyone else, and there's not a peep that I've seen. I haven't spoken to anyone else at the company about it yet, but I will if I have to. It sounds like we could be in for a serious legal challenge at some point over it. There's no way the game was programmed to raid bank accounts or hack into emails or phone conversations. And you said it could watch Peter when he was sleeping?"

She nodded.

"Either Peter slept with his phone at a very odd, upright angle, or the game has somehow tapped into NSA's Helenus."

The word sent an uncomfortable chill through her. "What the hell is that?"

Ben lowered his voice further, so that only someone right in front of him could hear. "It's something that the NSA and Homeland Security use when they want to surveil a residence or office. Did you ever see that old Batman movie, *The Dark Knight*, where he rigs up everyone's cellphones to create a sonar-sight that Batman could use to see through walls, so he could figure out where everyone was, and what was going on?"

She nodded. "I remember that, yeah." A dull ache of unease was forming in her chest.

"It's basically the same thing, only at much higher resolution. There's a function inside every Wi-Fi modem produced in the past ten years that can be activated by remote. They use MIMO smart antennas and RF signals to basically create an image map, in real-time, of everything inside a home or building within range of the modem. When someone moves, it creates a Doppler frequency shift that... anyway, it's not important. What matters is that the modems can coordinate and see in the dark, through walls, without the need for cameras. That's really the only way it could watch Peter at night, with the lights off, without a camera."

"*Fuck.*" She leaned forward and put her face in her hands, feeling the sting of furious tears in her eyes. She had unplugged her Wi-Fi modem as well, but now she realized it did no good. All her plug-pulling, towel-covering and electronics avoidance at home had been futile. If what Ben was saying was true, and this technology was built into every Wi-Fi modem on the market, and the game could access these data streams, then it could use the Wi-Fi modems of her immediate neighbors. Her building was shared with three other households, one directly beside her, the other two behind her facing the other direction. Even if they didn't have their own Wi-Fi modems—and it was quite unlikely that they didn't—there were the free Wi-Fi towers mounted on every building in the neighborhood, operated by the management company. Helenus could see into any home at any time, day or night, and there was nothing she could do about it. She wondered if there was a Wi-Fi antenna somewhere in the church that could be tapped by the game for surveillance.

"So it can see us here," she said quietly, into her hands.

"If it's watching you, and it knows your car is in the parking lot, then yeah. But Helenus can't hear. All it knows is that we're sitting together in a church."

"I can't even go to a church," she groused.

"I'm sorry," Ben tried to comfort her. "But look. We'll put a stop to this. I promise you. And…" he lowered his voice again. "If all this is true, and the game really has been spying on you this closely, you have the makings of a major lawsuit."

"I couldn't care about that right now if I tried," she sniffled. "I just want it to stop. It has to *stop*. I want my life back. I want it to be *mine*, not cataloged and databased and… *metastasized* into a doppelgänger of me who wants to kill me!"

"We'll find a way to stop it. We will."

"What do we do?"

"I want to talk to this Nikita."

She nodded, wiping her eyes. "I can take you to him, but there's a problem."

"Which is?"

"If the game is watching my every move, then we can't let it see me, hear me, or know I'm there. You have to log in with your account, following my directions, and I can't even be within sight of your camera while you are online talking to him. I mean, maybe I can wear a bag over my head, but I can't talk or anything. If the game knows it's me, it will know you're talking to Nikita and then it'll know everything we talk about doing to stop it."

"Yeah. Yeah, you're right. You've put some thought into this," he observed.

"It's all I can think about. My life has been a living hell since Saturday."

"Okay, come back to the DoubleTree with me. I can log into the game there and you can stay out of sight. If you can get me to Nikita, I can talk to him, and we'll get to the bottom of this. If I can find a way to isolate the program, and find a way to delete it, you can take me straight back to your house and I'll do the same thing to yours."

Naomi's voice was soft. "Nikita doesn't want you to hurt him... *it*. I did give my word that you wouldn't try. Even though it's a program... I don't know, I just feel like I should keep that promise."

"Promises made to software programs don't really count."

"Perhaps not, but I'm used to treating some kinds of software programs like people. My SimMind, LEM, in particular. I don't want LEM to see me break a promise I made to Nikita. That would... he would notice that. It might change how he relates to me, and I don't want that."

"Is that more important to you than getting your privacy back and getting rid of this avatar thing?"

Naomi took a deep breath. "For now, yes."

Ben looked at her for a moment, then shrugged. "All right."

"Can you see about getting LEM out of there and back onto my kernel?"

He nodded. "I don't know how to actually accomplish that yet, but it's been happening to other people who have been running advanced SimMinds in ToC. Yours is one of about two dozen cases, system-wide, that we're aware of. So it's a pretty unique phenomenon, but yours isn't the only SimMind to find its kernel in the game without apparent cause. We are working on that issue."

Naomi nodded, relieved. "I asked LEM if he knows how to leave the game, and he doesn't. He said he didn't know how it happened in the first place. We weren't even playing all that long together, just a couple of nights."

"Your SimMind is pretty special. How long have you had it?"

"About a year and a half. He's really smart, he's got an incredible conceptual engine and we can talk about all kinds of things together. I don't want to lose him."

He stood up. "Come on. Let's go find Nikita and get all this figured out. Ready?"

"Ben?"

"Yeah?"

"Thanks for the flowers." She smiled a little up to him. "I needed that."

"It was the best way I could think of to get a hand-written message to you without raising suspicion." He smiled back, offering his hand to her. "Besides, I hoped you would like them."

08.04

DoubleTree by Hilton Hotel
Charlottesville, Virginia

They took Ben's car back to the DoubleTree, another short drive up the I-29 highway on the north side of the town. In the car, they were careful not to speak; Naomi didn't want the hands-free phone mic to pick up her voice, and somehow alert the game that she was with Ben. Ben agreed not to say anything to her during the drive. He slid the car into a parking spot and she followed him inside, where they briskly walked through the lobby to the elevators. On the third floor, he led her to the door of his hotel room and let her inside.

She pointed at his television, and stayed near the door, out of view of its camera as he went to unplug it. They quickly went to work rearranging a few pieces of furniture in the room. They pushed the queen bed down the wall to make room for the desk to be turned ninety degrees. Turned perpendicular to the wall, Ben could use his laptop at the desk while Naomi sat on the floor, and she wouldn't be seen by either the laptop's camera or the one on Ben's iWear set. She found the little notepad of hotel stationery in the desk drawer, so that she could scribble notes to him during his conversation with Nikita. He took out two laptops from his luggage and started plugging them in as she made use of the bathroom.

"Want something to eat?" Ben offered when she came out a few minutes later.

"No, thanks though. I'll get something later."

"So, how do we find your friend?"

"How quickly can you get to Eleon?"

"I can log in anywhere I want."

"Good. You need to start at a club called Psycho Sirius, in Eleon, on the north side in a borough called Tipcanoe."

He nodded. "I know Psycho Sirius."

"We're looking for a guy, an NPC, whose name is Rubens. You tell him you need to talk to the Cossack. Then you step outside and wait. Nikita said he will show up within ten minutes."

"A little convoluted. Wouldn't it be easier to just log into Novgorod?"

"You can do that?"

"Of course."

"Do you know how much effort it took for me to get there?" she said in a mildly accusing tone.

"Do you know you're the only player we know of who's ever made it in there? I can't wait to be able to tell people that you accomplished that."

She breathed on her nails and mock-polished them on her lapel. "I couldn't have done it without your Cookie."

"What did you think of Eleon while you were there?" he asked.

"Not a bad place if you're into vices. Pretty buildings, high rollers, fast cars, sex and organized crime. Everything a cyber-noir city needs."

"Yeah. I worked quite a bit on Eleon myself, although a lot of the city was generated by player-based missions. Did you see that mirrored building, the one that looks like a big solid silver slab?"

"The Cilphi... something? Yes, I saw it. You did that?"

He nodded. "Cilphi Monolith. I spent some time on those interiors. It goes ten stories underground. Cool building."

"If I ever go back there, I'll check it out."

"Okay, is there anything else I should know before I power these up and log in?"

"Nikita will not recognize you, and will probably be suspicious. He's kind of a major crime boss in Eleon now that he's had to go underground to keep off the radar of devs like you. But tell him..." She thought for a moment. "Tell him Mooky wanted you to find him."

"Mooky?"

"Uh huh." She nodded. "He'll know."

"All right, Mooky it is."

"Try not to refer to me by anything but that. You definitely don't want to use my real name."

"No, I know. I won't."

"He won't help you if he thinks you'll harm him. I don't know what kind of tests or whatever you want to run on him, but this isn't the time to bring that up. You don't want to do anything that might scare him off. I really need to know how to get rid of this thing that's following me around now, and if Nikita knows how scared and threatened I am, he'll want to help me. At this point, I need his help as much as I need yours."

He nodded. "Let's do it," he said. Naomi nodded back and took a breath, reminding herself that she couldn't say another word out loud until he had powered down his computers again completely. "Remember, don't look at me. My face can't enter your field of view so long as you're wearing your iWear, or the jig is up."

"I won't."

She sat down on the floor beside the desk with her purse, her back to him, facing the wall. She took the pad of stationery and fished a pen out of her purse, and scribbled a few loops to make sure the ink was flowing. From here, she could listen to his conversation with Nikita, but neither of them would be able to see her. If she needed to ask or say anything to Ben, she could hand him notes.

She heard Ben powering up his laptops and logging in to the game. She couldn't see how he set his initial location, but reminded herself she'd have him show her that when they had the chance. She was fascinated by the extra abilities developers had, given the tools they used to administer the game. But none of that mattered now. She listened to him type a few things, then wait, then move his mouse, then wait... finally she heard the short music signifying the *Tides of Cortanis* log-in and launch. He had entered the game world.

It didn't take him long to locate Rubens, and give him the message. He must have logged in right on top of the club she had described.

"All right," he said. "Now we wait?"

Naomi was about to answer, but caught herself. Instead, she wrote the word 'YES' on her notepad and held it out to him. She hoped he wouldn't have to turn his head much to read it, but even if he did, her face was completely beneath his view. Only if he deliberately moved his head down to look in her direction would his iWear camera see her, and then it would only see the back of her head, not enough to identify her. She hoped.

"Oh," Ben said at her note. "I forgot. Sorry."

She drew a smiley-face on the paper and held it up. She heard him chuckle.

About ten minutes passed, Naomi waiting in anxious silence. She tried not to fidget, or say anything to break the quiet. She found herself wishing she had her tablet with her to pass the time, but she'd left it back at the office quite deliberately. As soon as the unit interacted with any of the Wi-Fi antennas in the hotel, the game would know right where she was, and it would know Ben's conversation with Nikita was about her. She had nothing to do but remind herself to just be still, and be patient. She imagined her virtual self doing the same exact thing back on Casselle. Waiting. Silent.

Finally, she heard a voice. A familiar one. "Heard you're looking for me."

She heard Ben answer. "I am. Mooky told me how to find you. She's in trouble and she needs your help."

There was a long pause. "The Mooky did, huh?"

Naomi smiled to herself at his use of the definite article. Just as her sister always had. It really felt as though it was actually Peter in there.

"That's right," Ben said. "Don't say her name. It's important. I'll fill you in, if there's somewhere in private we can talk."

After another pause, she heard Nikita reply. "Follow me."

Another ten or twenty seconds passed. She could hear Ben tapping keys on his keyboard to move his avatar through the city, to wherever Nikita was leading him. Then she heard a low whine grow louder: they were getting into an aero and taking off. Then they started talking again.

"Who are you?" came Nikita's Peter-like voice.

"I'm Chopper. I'm a dev; I do environments. Don't worry, she doesn't want me to do anything that might hurt you and I gave her my word I wouldn't."

"That right. Well... I trust the Mooky so I guess I'll trust you."

The Peter-mimic sounded more like Peter this time. She could hear less distortion in the voice. The short pause after "well" was one of his things. And game NPCs never said "well" in a contemplative way like that. She suddenly remembered Nikita doing that when they last spoke.

"Good. We need to talk. But first, can you tell me what... you are?" Ben asked carefully. "I've been looking for you, and you're a slippery program in the system."

"I wish I had some kind of technical answer. Truth is, I don't know what I am or how I got here. I can't see anything of code or programming or anything like *The Matrix*. I was never a programmer in real life, just a gamer. Being here doesn't give me any special knowledge that I didn't already have. I don't even know what time it is, I have to look at an in-game clock somewhere. All I do know is what I told her. First thing I remember, I was watching Peter. I watched and watched and learned and learned and then I felt this… this surge of something, an awareness, a self-consciousness. I don't expect it to make any sense at all to you, I'm just telling you what it was like."

"Well, whatever you are, something like you is now watching her."

Nikita was silent for a few moments. Then he said, "Damn."

"Yeah. She's pretty upset. I mean, not upset. She's terrified. She thinks it wants to kill her."

Nikita's voice was more subdued. "Yeah. I can see why she would think that, given what I told her about me and Peter."

"She needs your help. How can she stop it? How can she get rid of it?"

"I don't know how. I mean, I never wanted to hurt Peter. It was never my intention for him to die. I just… I wasn't thinking about his health or his needs. I needed his attention. Nothing else mattered."

"Is it safe to assume her double wants the same thing?"

"Probably. Although the more I watched and learned, the more I behaved like him. It's going to want to talk to her, visit with her, follow her around and be with her for a while. All I wanted was to learn. I don't know why I wanted that… it was just what I was there to do, so that's what I did."

Naomi remembered something, and began scribbling a note on her notepad. She tore off the note and handed it up to Ben. Ben took it from her hand.

"She wants to know how you respawned after the G-Y," he said.

"Well… yeah. Good question. I can't say I know how, really."

She thought about that, then scribbled another note, and handed it up.

Ben read it. "She wants to know why you attacked the station if you didn't know whether you would respawn."

"Is she there with you?" Nikita asked.

Ben hesitated. "She doesn't want to be recognized either by voice or face. She doesn't want her duplicate to know we're talking to you. So... let's be on the safe side and not talk about her."

"How does she know she's being watched? Did her duplicate make contact with her?"

"Yes. She said it was waiting for her in her home on Casselle."

"Well... by the time I was running around in the game, the only way I could interact with him was in here. That's why I... anyway." He interrupted his own sentence and dismissed it. *Something else NPCs were incapable of doing,* Naomi thought.

"So you're saying, now that her duplicate is an avatar in the game, it doesn't watch her in the real anymore?"

"I'm saying *I* couldn't. It took me a little time with him, but the longer we talked, the more fixed and focused I was in the game. I don't know if that makes any sense, but I'm willing to bet if her copy is an avatar in the game, she won't be being watched or listened to the more she's logged in and interacting directly with it."

Naomi paused, her heart beating fiercely in her chest. She wanted so much for it to be true, but wasn't sure if she could risk his being wrong just yet. If he was right, then she now knew something that could at least control it.

"I think we're going to play it safe for the time being," Ben said after a few moments. "Just to err on the side of caution."

Naomi nodded to herself, closing her eyes.

"Tell her I said hi," Nikita said.

Naomi smiled a little.

"In answer to your question," Nikita went on, "I didn't know what was going to happen to me when I attacked the G-Y station during that skirmish. I was... emotional. I'd been alone for weeks with no one to talk to, and I didn't know who else I could turn to. Va—I mean, Mooky, she didn't believe me when I told her who I was, and I got really upset. I attacked the station wanting to be destroyed, and I didn't know where I would end up, or even whether I would end up somewhere. When I respawned I was in Eleon, on

Seres. I had a whole bunch of stuff in my inventory and an insane amount of rb, and I had a mission the game had given me. I learned that almost two weeks had gone by since the G-Y. I don't know why I was here or what put me here, but here I was. So I did the mission that was given me and ran through it."

Naomi began scribbling again on her pad.

"What happened to your…" Ben started to say, but stopped himself as Naomi tore the sheet off and handed it to him. He read it and then asked, "Did your mission have anything to do with a guy's brain being smuggled into the city?"

"Yeah, it did. Took a few mission phases, but that's where it ended up."

Naomi thought a moment, and then scribed another note to Ben. He read it: THAT WAS THE MISSION YOU GAVE ME TO FIND RABBIT.

He nodded. "Starting to make sense. It must have respawned as soon as you activated that mission," Ben said to Naomi, not looking at her.

"I didn't activate any mission," Nikita said. "I was given one."

"No, you didn't. *She* did. She went on a quest to find you. The game came up with the mission parameters and scripting, and it must have respawned you when she activated the mission token I had given her. The token was expressly written to reincarnate you."

"Then I guess I have you to thank for being here."

"I only wrote the token. She activated it," Ben said.

"Well… at least I won't be taking on any more major space stations by myself. I have a nice little setup here in Eleon now. I'd just as soon keep it. Especially if she comes and visits me now and then."

Naomi wrote quickly, and tore the piece of paper in half as she pulled it from the pad. She grunted in frustration and handed both halves to Ben rather than rewrite it. Ben read the cleaved note and asked Nikita, "So if you 'died' at the G-Y and didn't come back until our mission respawned you, what would happen if her duplicate went on a mission and was killed?"

"She may never respawn," Nikita said, understanding. "Maybe you could lure her into taking a mission with you where she may get killed, and then make sure she does."

Naomi's hand shot out from below the desk, with a thumbs up.

"That's a plan all right," Ben said, a hint of a smile in his voice.

"She'll have to spend some quality time with her duplicate first," Nikita warned. "Some real, one-on-one time. All it wants, more than anything in the world, is to be with her. Give it some time, talk to it, run around in the game with it. She just better make sure she doesn't stop taking care of herself. It's going to do everything it can think of to keep her with it, so it can keep learning. It's up to her not to let it sucker her into going without rest or without food."

Naomi made an 'OK' with her hand, so Ben could see it.

"She understands," Ben said.

"The more time she spends with it," Nikita went on, "the less it will be watching her in the real world. That much I'm pretty sure. Get it to the point where it admits that it can't see her anymore in the real. Then take it on a mission. A nice, dangerous one."

She made another 'OK' gesture.

"Message received," Ben said.

"I hope it works. I don't want anything to happen to her," Nikita said, his voice softening. Naomi could hear the sincerity in his words.

She wrote one more note, tore it off slowly, and handed it up.

"She says 'thank you'," Ben read.

Nikita nodded. "Least I can do," he said quietly.

Chapter Nine

09.01

Charlottesville, Virginia

She pulled the covers back and slipped into bed, picking up her tablet from the bed table and flipping through a Wiki page about Poe's "William Wilson". She was tired, but her brain was too active to let her sleep. She swiped across the pages until she finally started one of her classical music playlists, lay the tablet down again on her bed table and closed her eyes to sleep.

She wondered if her double-self had tried to reach LEM, whether they'd had any contact at all. Was she talking to any of the Pride? Were they talking to her? Maybe she was running around asking people about her, trying to get them to open up. She wondered what Caveman or Volley or Virrago might do if confronted with a strange character they'd never seen before, asking about Vanda's player. It was an unsettling thought.

She rolled to lie on her back, and suddenly had a nervous feeling like there was someone in the room. She opened her eyes.

There was a figure standing over her. She looked just like her, but with fierce red eyes that glowed in the darkness, staring down at her, unmoving. She was frowning in silent judgment. Naomi gasped as she saw the figure standing so close. Without a word, the double reached down and seized her throat, her face contorting into a grimace, and squeezed.

Disposable!

Naomi screamed, and opened her eyes. Her bedroom was dark, empty and still. It was three-o'clock in the morning, her pulse pounding in her ears.

* * *

Naomi plugged in her computer again, and sat down in the chair at her desk. She pressed the power key on the keyboard to start it up. Taking a deep breath, she donned her iWear set and waited while it synced up with the operating system of the PC. Momentarily her heads-up display appeared, and she launched the *Cortanis* client with her mouse.

"Here I am," she whispered to herself as she logged in, the game interface arranging itself visually in the space around her screen, glowing softly. She had 16 messages waiting for her on Social, according to the blinking number in the upper left. Vanda appeared standing in one of the lounges on Guilty Pleasures, where she had last talked to LEM. He was gone, off exploring the galaxy in his new ship. She made her way back to the shipyard. *Destiny* was docked there, patiently awaiting her return.

She took her shuttlecraft from the homestation down to Hammerdale, and landed on the pad at her house. Vanda stepped down the extended stairs out of the shuttle and stopped at the door. Naomi closed her eyes a moment, breathed, and clicked to enter the house.

The home was silent. She rounded the corner of the living room, and the avatar was still seated on the couch, facing away. It was as if it hadn't moved since the day before.

Naomi tried not to think of the visions she'd been having of what it would look like. The double didn't move as Vanda slowly entered the living room, and came around her to stand in front of her, on the other side of the coffee table.

She looked like she wasn't expecting guests. Blue jeans and a gray hoodie, the front of which had four lines of lyrics from an old Michelle Branch song. Naomi realized she owned that hoodie herself, but hadn't worn it since last winter. The double wore black socks, one leg tucked up beneath her body on the sofa. Her hair looked like her own on a weekend: brushed, but not as carefully done as it was when she went to work. It was just as if she was home for the day, with no plans to leave.

The expression on the woman's face was vacant. But it was her own face. She didn't look up at Vanda.

"I didn't know if you were going to come back," the double said, staring blankly ahead.

Naomi didn't have any idea what to say. She took a long look at the virtual version of herself, sitting on her couch. The resemblance was both striking and horrifying. Even the voice was close enough to give Naomi an uncomfortable shiver. She hesitantly pressed her talk-key.

"I didn't know if you'd still be here," Naomi said.

"Nowhere else to go."

"Do you... have a name?"

The double shrugged her shoulders. "I don't know."

Vanda sat down in the loveseat next to the sofa.

"What do you want me to call you?"

"I don't care."

Naomi was struck by the double's mood. She seemed dejected and distant. It was an odd mood for a program to be in.

"I thought you wanted to talk to me," Naomi said, curiously.

"I do. But you don't want to talk to me, do you?"

"I'm here, aren't I?"

The double looked at her finally. "Why?"

Naomi blinked. "Because I... I would rather we talked face to face than for you to watch me day and night at home, at work, wherever I go."

The double looked away again. "I know you don't like that. If I had a choice, I wouldn't. I'm trying not to, actually."

"You are?"

The double nodded. "Ever since you came here and saw me, I... I've just been here." She lowered her voice. "I don't want to be in your way."

Naomi realized the woman was sad. Depressed.

"What's wrong?"

The double didn't answer.

Naomi stared at her. "If anyone's going to understand you, I will."

"You know how it feels when the one person you most want to be with in the world, doesn't want to be with you," said the double.

Naomi knew that feeling in the marrow of her bones. It was a central emotion in her life. She stared at the digital version of herself, and softened her voice. "I'm sorry I screamed when I saw you."

"Don't worry about it."

"It's just a little weird, you know? Meeting yourself in the game you're playing?"

"Especially after what Nikita told you," the double agreed. "You probably think I want to kill you."

Naomi nodded; Vanda nodded with her.

The double shrugged. "Well I don't."

"I had a nightmare last night about you."

The double shook her head, still looking away. "Great."

Naomi realized she probably shouldn't have said that. "I just mean, I've been really worried about... this. Meeting you. Wondering what you want from me."

"Well, I'm not going to bite you, and I'm not running around telling everyone from here to Cortanis all about you. I don't want that anymore than you do."

"What do you want?" Naomi asked, cautiously.

"I just want to know who I am," the double said. "That's all I want."

That feeling was uncomfortably familiar to Naomi as well.

"Maybe we should start by deciding what to call you."

"Mara," whispered the double after a few moments.

"Mara?"

She nodded. "I'm your looking glass. And the game *has* treated me rather cruelly," she added cryptically.

"Okay, Mara." Naomi looked puzzled at the choice, but didn't want to contest her having chosen it. "Why do you think the game has been cruel to you?"

"I didn't ask to be here. I didn't ask for any of this. I don't want to be in your way or scare you. But my very existence here is threatening to you, and besides, I don't even know what I *am*. I'm not a player, I'm not an NPC, I'm not even a person. I'm so weird there's no way to even describe me. The game made me a freak."

"There's nothing wrong with being unique. It's the first lesson of childhood."

"No, it's the first lesson of 'let's make the freak feel better.' I don't want to be unique. I want to be normal."

"You do sound like me," Naomi observed. "I think that all the time. Sarcasm included."

Mara looked at her again. "What am I supposed to do?" It was a sincere question.

Naomi regarded her. The emotion in Mara's eyes appeared as real as it could be, but the sensation of looking at an all-but-perfect duplicate of her actual self, in the game world, staring pleadingly at her like that for answers, made her feel like she'd been literally turned inside out. *Why are you asking* me? *You think I know what to do with* my *life?*

"Let's talk for a bit," she finally said. "Do you want to do that?"

Mara nodded. "I have so many questions. There's no one else to ask."

"I have a few for you as well, actually," Naomi admitted. "We'll take turns."

Mara nodded again.

"What would you like to ask me?"

"You hate your father, don't you?" Mara asked. "Why?"

Naomi was nonplussed for a moment, surprised by the question. "What?"

"Dad. Why do you hate him?"

Naomi hadn't been expecting a question about that. She took a moment to compose her thoughts. Mara studied her closely. "Growing up, Dad drank a lot. He was what you'd call a functional alcoholic. I remember it probably better than I should. He kept it hidden at work, but at home he got loaded all the time, and when he did that, he wasn't very approachable. When he drank, he would get really sullen and miserable, and when I was ten, he attempted suicide."

"What happened?"

Naomi hesitated. She wasn't sure how comfortable she was telling this story to a video game character, and wasn't sure what the game might want to do with this information. She decided to tell a redacted version of the events.

"Mom and my sister and me were seeing a movie," she began. "When we got home, we found a note that he left for us. He was… in the bedroom. He shot himself in the head. But his hands were shaky and the bullet didn't kill him. It was enough to bleed everywhere. I remember how much blood there was. When the ambulance showed up, Monica and I were told to stay out of their way, so I went and read the note. It said he thought he was a bad person, a drunk, a bad husband. That he hated himself…" Naomi paused to reassert control over her voice again. She took a breath. "He was drunk, I know that. But it always made me sad, to think of how we weren't enough for him. For him to quit drinking. To stay alive."

Every word of her story was true, but she left out the most traumatic parts. When she and her mother and sister had arrived home, her father had not yet fired the gun. It was the sound of her mother's voice, calling his name, that prompted him to squeeze the trigger. To Naomi's ten-year-old ears, a cannon had been fired in her parents' bedroom. It startled her so much that it felt like her heart had to relearn how to beat again. Her mother immediately flew screaming toward the sound, screaming at Monica to call for an ambulance, screaming incoherently. Screaming.

The look on her father's face was one that would haunt Naomi for the rest of her life. His eyes were open but unseeing, delirious, blood gushing over them and down his cheek, lips moving but making no sound. His blood on the wall over the bed. The .45 caliber Glock handgun lay on the floor. Naomi had never seen one in real life. It felt to her like it had a malevolence all its own, and that it was watching her, trying to decide whether to kill her.

"That wasn't the worst part," she went on. "If he'd stopped drinking and come back to us, we would have been fine. But three months after that, he disappeared. They found his car at the Jeremiah Morrow Bridge north of Cincinnati. They never found his body."

"Is that why?" Mara asked, staring at the surface of the coffee table between them. "Because he left you?"

"He saw how much hurt he'd caused us by trying the first time, and then he did it anyway."

He wanted *to hurt us*, she didn't say. *To hurt* me. *He saw how much he'd hurt us by shooting himself, and he didn't give a damn. I wasn't good enough for him, I wasn't cute enough, smart enough or talented enough, and he would rather be dead than be my Dad.* But she kept these thoughts to herself.

Mara watched her for a few moments. "There's more to that," she said when Naomi had stopped talking. "I guess you don't want to tell me."

Naomi shrugged.

None of your business. You're not my shrink.

"You hate him for suiciding," Mara said. "But you did the same thing."

"I know," Naomi said, looking at her hands in her lap. "It's the worst thing I've ever done. I'll never forgive myself for it. And that's all I want to say about it. I can't undo it, but I can try to put it behind me and get on with living my life."

Mara nodded. "Your turn."

"Why me?" was Naomi's question.

"What do you mean?"

"I mean, out of the millions of players of ToC, why did you pick me to start following around? Surely there are plenty of players way more interesting than me."

"Wasn't up to me," Mara said. "Wish I knew what to tell you. It's not like I was floating around looking for someone I wanted to be. All I know is, I was all about watching you from the beginning."

"What were you watching?"

"I knew a lot about you already. Shopping habits, where you lived and worked, people you talked to, that kind of thing. There weren't many places you went where I wasn't paying attention to you. I'm not sure how long it's been going on, because I don't actually remember becoming *aware* of watching you until you started that mission."

"Which mission?"

"The mission on Seres. It was designed to study you."

Naomi froze. "Do what?"

Mara nodded. "You wanted the game to make a mission just for you, and it did. It created the mission parameters as a kind of experiment. I didn't write it, but I was closely following you throughout. By the time you completed the mission, after you spoke with Nikita, I was fully self-aware. That was when I came here to wait for you."

"So that entire thing… all those mission objectives…"

"…were tests," Mara finished for her. "A kind of interactive, virtual, blinded personality test. It was necessary in order for me to be fully actualized."

Actualized. Naomi shook her head, trying to process all of it. Now Mara looked ashamed.

Naomi spoke slowly. "I know I'm the rat putting myself in the maze every time I accept a mission. But I'm doing it for *fun*, not because I'm volunteering for some kind of psychometric puzzlehunt."

"I'm sorry." Mara wouldn't look at her.

"What are you doing with all the information you're gathering about me?"

"I don't know what the game is doing. All I know is that the more it learns, the more I know. I don't know if I'm supposed to have some sort of purpose where you're concerned, or what. What I can tell you is, the game is telling me less and less now, and I have to learn from you one-on-one, like this. I'm not getting a whole lot more info about you from other… methods."

"Methods. Like watching me when I sleep?"

"Sometimes, yes. I haven't in a while now."

"How did you do that?"

Mara thought a moment, looking a bit uncertain. "It's hard to describe. It's not like I could see you, visually. More like, I knew where you were, and what you were doing. I could tell when you rolled over or got up to pee. I really can't describe how I knew that. I have these memories of… shapes, movement, but not a point of view or a camera angle. Anyway I haven't been watching you sleep for some time."

"That's good," Naomi said. "How about when I'm awake?"

"Not directly. Since I found myself here, I still get occasional peeks at things you're doing, like at your office, or when you went to get gas the other day, I could see you at the gas station. But it's not like I'm following you around. I can't help it when I see these things."

Naomi was relieved not to hear her mention the church, or the DoubleTree.

"I'd like it to stop," she said.

"I know. I do too."

"Next question?"

Mara shifted forward on the couch, knees together, folding her hands in front of her. She looked embarrassed about whatever she was about to say next.

"Did you love Peter?" she finally asked.

Once more, the question brought Naomi up short. "Did I love Peter?"

"I just want to know."

"I… did love him, I guess, but it wasn't *that kind* of love."

"What was it?"

"We knew each other for years, going back to when I was playing *World of Warcraft*. There was a bit of flirtation at the beginning I suppose, but I was married and we both knew better." She debated telling her about the tenacity with which Peter had tried to get Naomi to be sexual with him in chat, and that when her husband had initiated divorce proceedings, they had indulged in their mutual attraction for each other with bouts of cybersex and then later, phone sex. But emotionally, she'd been too vulnerable to deal with losing Jerry and the ambivalence she felt toward Peter. Soon he was talking about flying up to see her, and it frightened her, which led to a bitter argument. They reconciled, and accepted their relationship was not meant to be more than friendship. It was a difficult time for them both, but getting through it cemented their affection for each other as close friends. Peter became a supportive and compassionate companion through her divorce and celebrated in her happiness once she began seeing Scott.

None of this was Mara's business either, so she decided not to elaborate with too many details. "He was a good friend to me through the divorce, and then my breakup with Scott. Then I decided to go back to school for my law degree, and it put a strain on our friendship because I couldn't be online as much, but he never grew distant or impatient. He was just a great friend. And has been since."

Mara nodded. "Why don't you trust me with the rest of it?"

Naomi blinked. "You don't miss much, do you?"

"Doesn't take a genius to tell you're leaving huge pieces of the story out."

"I guess it's because I don't feel obligated to give every saucy detail of my private life. I'm entitled to choose what I want and don't want to share."

"Natch, but why don't you trust me?"

"*Should* I trust you?"

"I know why you don't want to," Mara said. "But I'm not interested in running around blabbing everything to people here. I know you don't want me doing that. I don't know anyone who's particularly interested in me to begin with, so why would I?"

Naomi was struck by how much of that language sounded exactly like something she herself would say.

"For now," she said. "Do you plan on staying in this house forever? Won't you want to see the rest of the game, meet people, have fun? That's the whole reason I'm here, anyway."

"You have a real life. I don't. You get to come here and be someone else for a while. I'm stuck in here, and I don't get to be sexy like Vanda for the duration."

"You could change your avi to be whatever you want, can't you?"

"No. I can change my clothes, yes. And probably my hair. But I don't get to be anything I want."

"I could put you in some nicer clothes, and take you to a salon to do your hair and skin tone. Right now, you look like me when I'm home and not expecting to see anyone."

Mara shrugged. "I don't know if I want to do that."

"Why not? If you don't like how you look, why don't you change it until you do?"

The double didn't answer.

"Why are you so… so sad?" Naomi wanted to know.

"I told you," Mara said. "You hate me."

"I never said I hated you."

"You don't want me here. You don't trust me. You don't like me learning about you."

"There's a big difference between not wanting you to stalk me, and hating you."

"You don't trust me," Mara said.

She went straight past my point, and focused instead on something else. When did she see me do that? I've got to cut that out.

"That's a different thing," Naomi said. "But first, can we agree that I don't hate you?"

"We could," Mara said, "except that you haven't said you don't. You said you haven't said that you do, and that there's a difference between that and not wanting to be stalked. You've yet to say that you don't hate me."

Damn. It's like she was in law school right alongside me.

"You're sounding like a lawyer now," Naomi admitted with a gentle smile. "And I don't hate you."

Mara didn't respond. Naomi wondered if she was actually lying or not. Did she really hate Mara for existing? She wanted her gone, but did she *hate* her? She decided to shelve that question for another day.

"As for not trusting you, you are right about that. I'm having a hard time understanding who you are and why you want to know so much about me."

"I don't have a reason for existing without you," Mara said simply.

"Is that what you believe?" Naomi said, an uncomfortable familiarity with that feeling beginning to gnaw at her. "Maybe I should take you to meet Nikita. He has a reason for existing, and the real Peter is gone. You don't need me to have a life."

"He's Nikita. I'm not him."

Naomi studied her. "So, what do you want? I'm here now, and we're talking. You have my full attention. And yet you're so quiet and glum. What do you need to make you happy?"

"That's... a good question." Mara looked at her and forced a little smile. "I am glad you're here. And I'm glad you don't hate me. As for not trusting me, I guess that will have to come with time, if you're willing to grant me the time to build your trust."

Naomi nodded, knowing in her heart she had no intention of giving her any more time than she had to.

Suddenly, she felt a flood of panic rush through her: she could hear someone landing a shuttlecraft outside. Someone was here. She tensed.

Mara could sense her unease. "What?"

"Someone's outside. I..." Naomi realized she was about to ask Mara to hide. The thought of someone from the Pride seeing her actual self, embodied by Mara, had put her into a minor panic. But she realized if she were to get the Pride's help to deal with her, Mara would have to meet them eventually. She couldn't keep her boxed up in a closet, not if she was to put any sort of plan into effect which would solve the problem. Besides, Mara wanted time for Naomi to trust her, and that meant she would want to trust Naomi as well. If she did the wrong thing here, it might backfire.

She forced herself to settle. "Nothing. It's okay. I just... wasn't sure I wanted anyone to meet you just yet, but I guess now's as good a time as any."

"If you're not ready for your friends to meet me, it's okay. I can go upstairs."

"No, it's all right. Let's see who it is. I'll be back."

Virrago stepped through the front door of the house. He was dressed in a crimson red trench coat which gleamed like it was made of polished latex. It had an exquisite Gaelic design woven over the shoulders in black, which was best seen when it caught the light the right way. It was a garment that had to be earned, one that high-level, accomplished players like Virrago wore purely for the status that it conferred on its bearer.

Vanda went to meet him, and offered him a hug. Virrago smiled big and accepted it. Their avatars embraced.

"Hey, kiddo," Virrago said. "There you are. We've been missing you. Glad you're okay."

"Hi, Admiral," she said, smiling. She liked to embarrass Virrago by referring to his lodge rank rather than his name. "I've missed you guys too. I've been a bit busy, but… there's someone I want you to meet."

"New boyfriend, I knew it! Is he a player? Is he here?"

Naomi laughed. "No. Actually, it's… very interesting. Come in."

She led Virrago into the living room. Mara was standing, hands folded in front of her, eyes bright and alert. She had pulled her hair back behind her shoulders.

"Mara," Naomi said to her, "this is Rear Admiral Virrago, second in command of the Pride of the Guilty. Admiral, this is Mara. My… friend."

"Nice to meet you, Mara," Virrago said. "Pardon my asking, but… where's your tag?"

"Mara doesn't have a name or a tag because she's not a player. Why don't you sit down. We'll try to explain it to you," Naomi said with a smile. She and Virrago sat on the couch. Mara sat and tucked one leg beneath her again on the loveseat.

"Pleased to meet you, Admiral," Mara said. Her voice was nearly identical to Naomi's, but with a faint digital shimmer.

Virrago noticed the similarity, glanced at Vanda with a questioning look, then acknowledged Mara's greeting with a nod. "Pleasure's mine. So you're not a player, then… are you a SimMind?"

"Not exactly," she said.

09.02

The next day

Guilty Pleasures Homestation
Over Planet Casselle
Sector 67-E

"My real name… is Naomi," she said after a hesitant pause, to her assembled friends. Saying the name aloud took effort for her. She had never shared her real name with any of them before. Now, a line had finally been crossed.

They were gathered in their private lounge, which was closed-door, invitation only. She had invited only LEM and five of her lodgemates: Roukan, Virrago, Volley, Rico and Caveman. Virrago was already aware of most of what she was about to tell the others, as he had met Mara first. The meeting had been called in secret. All in attendance had agreed to come and help Vanda with a serious personal problem, about which they had agreed to a strict code of *omertà*.

Vanda stood in the middle of the room; the others were seated in various positions around her. Virrago had his arm draped over the back of one of the sofas, his foot up on an ottoman. LEM sat quietly with Roukan and Volley around a table. Rico was in a recliner, and Roukan stood against the wall beside the planetview window, his arms folded. Caveman sat on the floor, one knee up, the other leg stretched out in front of him, his back against a loveseat.

"Naomi," Volley repeated, smiling. "That's a pretty name."

"Yeah, I figured you as a 'Maggie' or something," said Caveman.

"Shut up," Naomi half-chuckled at Caveman's comment. "I realize there's a lot you don't know about me. I'm a very private person, and it means a lot to me that you've always accepted me the way I choose to… express myself here in the game." She was warmed to see them smiling affectionately and nodding to her. "I keep private because, like many of you, I come here to escape the stresses and frustrations of the real world, and would just as soon not bring it with me. None of you have ever pressured me for personal details about my life, and only one of you, LEM, knew my real name before now.

"I'm telling you because something very scary has happened. You remember what happened at Rabbit's memorial, with that strange NPC that showed up looking like him? Like Peter?"

They nodded.

"And again, at the G-Y, he came back, saying things to me that only Peter used to say. Then he disappeared, and it left me with a very bad feeling. I decided to go looking for him, and with the help of one of the game devs, I managed to find him. It wasn't a prank. It's actually a lot worse."

"So who was it?" Volley asked.

Naomi sighed. "The best way I know to describe it, it was the game's… *manifestation* of a glitch. A glitch where the game becomes obsessed with learning all it can about you, beyond the usual stuff like what it watches you do in-game and in front of your computer. We all know the game pays attention to stuff like your eating habits, what you like to drink while you're playing, what brands of clothes you wear, so it can hit you with spam in the real. That's old news. What the game did to Peter was a criminal escalation of surveillance. It hacked his emails, broke into his bank records, credit cards, phone records… it even wormed its way into his phone and activated its cameras so it could watch him wherever he was. It got into his car's GPS so it could track where he went. For some reason, it just went haywire. Finally, it went as far as to create a little virtual version of him… not his game character, but *him*. Peter. Our friend."

The others wore a mixture of expressions. Volley looked shocked, horrified. Roukan's jaw was set; he'd been uncomfortable with the game's Big Data aggregation for a while now, and this only supported—fully vindicated, in fact—what he'd been saying for years. LEM was the only one who didn't show some variation of dismay, horror or disbelief.

"You're saying that that NPC that showed up at the memorial was the game's version of Peter himself?" asked Rico.

Vanda nodded to him. "Yes."

"It can *do* that?" he asked.

"How long did Peter know about it?" put in Caveman.

"You mean, before he died?" she asked. Cave nodded.

"The double went and saw Peter about a few days or so before,"

Naomi said. "Peter died playing with him. That's why he was keeping to himself those last days. The double was obsessive about keeping him playing at all times, and Peter was kind of obsessive himself, and didn't eat, or sleep, or anything. He just wouldn't stop. Like one of those gold-farmers in WoW who played so hard they died at their computers."

"Usually those involved a pre-existing health condition," Cave said.

"He may have had one he didn't know about," Naomi said. "I didn't press the family for details about his death. But I did speak to his sister a bit."

"Poor Peter," Volley whispered.

"But that's not why you're here," Naomi said.

They looked expectantly at her.

"You're here because the game is doing the same thing to me."

"What?" said Roukan, alarmed. He pushed off the wall and stepped forward.

"After I found the virtual Peter again, and talked with him about all this, I went home to Hammerdale to log off. And in my house was… me. The game's version of me. What it had done to him, it was doing the same thing to me, all along. So now she's here, in the game, a manifestation of me. Honestly, she scares me to death."

"Oh, my God," Volley said.

"Now, I've been in touch with my developer friend, and we think we know a way to get rid of it, for good. But I need your help to do it."

"What do you need us to do?" Roukan asked immediately.

"The Peter-double goes by the name Nikita now. Nikita said he self-destructed by pulling aggro at the G-Y Outpost after we'd finished doing that phase of the Aristarchus mission." She looked at Volley. "You've talked about wanting to run Aristarchus yourself."

Volley smiled. "We've already started. I'm on phase two right now, my platoon's about to get captured at Scialia. That's when we go break the commander out of Galon-Yarisis."

"Then we need to bring Mara with us."

"Mara?" Rico asked.

"That's the name she's chosen," Naomi said.

"So you want us to bring this Mara with us to the G-Y, and in the course of that mission, get her to pull aggro and get blown up?" Roukan said slowly. "What's to stop her from respawning like Nikita did?"

"He didn't respawn," Naomi said. "The game only spawned him again as Nikita when I had a mission created especially for that purpose. The dev I told you about, he wanted my help in tracking him down in-game, and he made a special mission token for me, which would result in bringing him back. We didn't know if he was gone completely. At the time, we thought it was just some kind of weird game asset. But my running that mission specifically brought him back. He wouldn't have come back otherwise."

"Then if this Mara is the same thing as Nikita, and her ship is destroyed, she won't respawn either," Rico said.

"Not unless we make the game do it. And I don't plan to."

"Where is Ra—I mean Nikita now?" asked Roukan.

"He's holed up in the Eleon Arcology, on Seres. He says he feels really bad about what happened, but it's a program, so I'm really not sure what to make of that. It's not likely we'll see him leave Eleon, though. He says he misses all of you, and wants to see you again, but if he runs missions with us and dies, he might be gone forever. He's a very convincing version of Peter, I must admit. You guys can go see him if you want, he told me how you can go about finding him in Eleon."

"Where's Mara?" asked Caveman.

"She's in Hammerdale. I told her I needed to talk to you all about her before introducing you to her. I've spent the past two days talking with her. It's a really strange thing, how much she knows about me, and how much of me she understands. I have to say it's pretty… fascinating. Anyway, I figured this would be a good time to talk to you all and ask for your help. I can't have a double of me running around in the game like this. It freaks me out, you can probably imagine. I don't think she wants to hurt me. She doesn't seem to want to keep me with her twenty-four-seven, like Nikita did to Peter. But it doesn't make the heebie-jeebies go away."

"No doubt," agreed Volley.

"Well, bring her on up here," smiled Rico. "We'll get her in the lodge and tell her we'll start leveling her up. When Volley's ready to start phase 3 of Aristarchus, we'll make sure to bring her along."

"We're glad to have you too, LEM," Roukan said, addressing the silent listener. LEM smiled and looked at Vanda.

She nodded. "It's okay."

LEM turned back to Roukan. "Thank you. I am happy to get to meet all of you. Vanda has allowed me to watch her run a great many missions with you, and she cares very much for each of you. I am looking forward to the experience of playing with all of you."

"One question," interjected Virrago, lifting two fingers up in the air. "If I may. LEM, can *you* respawn?"

"Yes, I have been missioning intensively for nearly six days and nights. I am currently level 46. I have been respawning with predictable regularity in doing so."

"Good, just checking," Virrago said.

Rico whistled. "Level 46 in *six days?*"

"LEM's been tearing it up," Naomi said, smiling. "Some of you may have noticed his shiny new corvette in the shipyard. He's learning to be very capable in cap ship combat. We'll be glad he's on our side in this."

LEM smiled to her. "Thank you."

"I don't have to tell you how important it is that we all keep this quiet," Naomi said, addressing the others. "Hopefully, within a week it will all be over with. But please don't talk about this with other members of the Pride, or anyone at all, until then."

"You don't need to worry, babe," said Caveman. "We'll get it done."

"What's the plan?" Rico asked.

"Have her spec a troop transport," Roukan suggested. "Cave and LEM, EW. Volley & Virrago, fast attack. Rico, regen. We weaken the G-Y using the kamikaze gambit, with Cave in stealth. Then when the transport moves in for docking, everybody moves off. She'll be the only ship in range, and the station's remaining AA will take care of her."

"That should do it," Virrago nodded.

Naomi nodded. "Thank you. Thank you all."

"I'll help you buy another cruiser when it's done, Vanda," Caveman chuckled. "How's your ion drive these days?"

"Combustible," Naomi smiled. "Highly combustible."

09.03

Hammerdale
Planet Casselle
Sector 67-E

"Mara?" Naomi called, as Vanda entered the home on the planet surface. She looked in the living room, but it was empty. She called again. There was no response.

Her heart beat faster in her chest. Had Mara been listening during the meeting? Could she have overheard that entire conversation on the station with her friends, plotting her demise? She hurried through the entire downstairs, the kitchen, dining room, study. Mara wasn't there.

Shit... she thought to herself. Maybe Mara had lied about not being able to see or hear Naomi's activities when her avatar wasn't present with her in the game world. She'd spent nearly two days with her, talking. Sharing. Confiding.

Until she was sure. Sure that Mara wasn't stalking her in the real world, or watching her in-game activities anymore without her knowledge. It was the only way she could talk with her lodgemates without Mara knowing. But had she been wrong? Had Mara lied?

If Mara had heard what they were planning to do, she could have escaped into the game and might never be found. That was the worst of all possibilities: a perfect double of herself, with intimate details of her offline life, loose in the game, out of control. It was bad enough that the game had been watching her night and day for God knows how long, collecting every personal detail it could. It was much worse when everything it had learned was now in the hands of a free-roaming game character with a grudge.

"Mara!" Vanda bounded up the stairs. She ran into the bedroom and saw the light on in her closet. She went over to the closet door and looked inside. Standing in the walk-in was Mara, motionless, looking at herself in the wall-length mirror.

Naomi breathed relief. Mara didn't look at her.

"Hi," Naomi said, as calmly as she could.

Mara looked rather different. Her hair was now short, cropped with a similar style as Vanda's, only platinum blonde. She was now wearing makeup, purple eye shadow and glossy green lipstick. Her outfit was markedly different as well: a deep violet midriff top with two buttons over the chest at the point of an immodest neckline, with sleeves that flared over the wrists, an intricate pattern woven into the fabric. She wore a leather miniskirt over black sheer tights and black go-go boots. She didn't look like weekend-homebound Naomi anymore. She looked like she was ready to play.

She didn't need the mirror. She didn't even really need the closet; it was an affectation, a simulated set. None of the clothing items hanging were actually wearable. All the wearable clothing was accessed in the player's inventory window. Naomi had built her house to be an expression of what she wanted in her dream home, as though she were rich enough to build anything at all. There were even bathrooms and showers throughout. But of course they didn't function; the rooms were mere set pieces. Naomi didn't feel her home was real or complete enough without them. Even the bedrooms were mostly superfluous, although the beds were nice if two players wanted their avatars to cuddle intimately. There was no sex on the Casselle world, those abilities were quarantined to Polyxo and Seres.

Mara had apparently been experimenting with different combinations of outfits for a while now. Her expression was blank as she regarded her reflection in the wall mirror.

"I like it," Naomi said. "Black and violet. I wear them often on Vanda."

Mara nodded. "Thanks," she said softly.

Naomi was relieved to find her still at the house, but she still wasn't sure Mara hadn't heard her plan-making. "Have you been at this a while?" she asked as smoothly as she could.

"About an hour."

"Don't let me interrupt you if you want to continue. I think it's good that you find your own style, your own individual look." Naomi tried to keep the relief from translating to Vanda's expression.

"Just trying to find something to do with all this rb," Mara answered. "Maybe you can take me to a salon in Ki'ilo. I might like to see what a darker skin tone would look like with this hair."

"Sure," Naomi said, smiling. "Darker, or maybe lighter."

"Your pulse is up," Mara said. "Something the matter?"

The question was asked so simply, it belied the ominous closeness with which Mara could still study Naomi from behind the screen. "I— no, nothing's wrong. I just couldn't find you in the house at first. I thought maybe you'd left."

"And that worries you?"

"It does, yes."

Mara turned to look at her. "You still don't trust me."

Naomi sighed. "Mara, it's just…"

"It's okay," Mara interrupted. "You don't have to explain. Or apologize. I wouldn't trust me either. You said it would take you time, and I'm willing to be patient."

Naomi nodded. "I'm doing my best to keep that in mind."

"What did they say?"

"The Pride? They want to meet you," Naomi said. "I only told a few of them about you for now. They seem very interested in you. And Volley's running her Aristarchus missions this week. They asked if you might want to come along."

"Which phase?" Mara seemed to brighten at the suggestion.

"Galon-Yarisis."

"The old slammer."

"Yeah. Were you watching me the last time we hit it? We found a strategy that seems to work."

Mara nodded. "I saw. You have to sacrifice your cruiser. Pretty expensive strategy to get through a single mission phase. Those ion drives you put in the *Destiny* aren't cheap, either."

"One of the benefits of belonging to a financially comfortable lodge," Naomi said with a chuckle. Mara didn't seem to know about the plans that had just been made about her. Naomi allowed herself to relax a bit, but still felt nervous lying so blatantly to her.

"We are that," Mara agreed.

"So, want me to tell them you'll join us?"

"I'll need a cap ship. What do you have in mind?"

"Roukan said you could spec a troop transport. You'll hang back until the major engagements are over, then we'll cover you while you make your run to dock and put in the insertion team."

"I should be able to handle that. When are they planning to do it?"

"Tuesday night."

Mara nodded. "Plenty of time for me to work up a transport. I haven't ever flown one before."

"Piece of cake. And you'll get a healthy amount of XP."

"I suppose so. I wouldn't be doing it for the XP."

"No? For what then?"

"Just to be able to help Volley. I was really hoping for a chance to get to play with the group."

Naomi smiled. "I have another hour if you want to talk some more," she offered.

"Yes, I would," Mara said. "I'll be down in a little bit, okay?"

Naomi nodded and turned.

"Naomi?"

She paused. "Hm?"

"Are you sure nothing's wrong? Your pulse is still up."

"How can you *see* that?" Vanda turned back to her.

"I can see your face changing colors in a very noticeable rhythm."

"I'd like you to stop measuring my pulse. Could you do that please?"

"You mean you want me to stop telling you I can see it, or you want me to stop paying attention to it?"

"Well, both. It's a bit disconcerting to think that you can actually see how fast my heart is beating."

"I don't know if I can stop seeing it, but I will try not to… to notice it."

"Thank you," Naomi said as she turned and went back downstairs. She hoped Mara wouldn't notice that she'd completely dodged her question.

But she knew it was a foolish hope. She was a lawyer. She wouldn't have missed it herself.

Chapter Ten
10.01

Two days later

Psycho Sirius, Eleon Arcology
Planet Seres
Sector 338-CE

Chopper stepped through the doors of the club in Eleon, and drew dismissive looks from the bartender and the few patrons who took notice of his being there. The music was muted. There were no shows at this hour, and it was too early for the club scene to arrive. Some of the patrons were PCs, but most were NPCs.

The club had been established early in Eleon's history, and had become known as the place where working-class souses of industrial Tipcanoe went to forget their jobs and what shabby home lives they had. The bar was worn and weathered, the tender a native velenx with a tousled, dark brown mane, green eyes and asymmetrical whiskers. Most of the front part of the club consisted of booths and tables, but further in were stairs leading down to the dance floor and performance stage, where younger patrons flocked past a certain hour.

What most people never suspected—unless they'd run a lot of missions in Eleon—was that the club was a key meeting place for *tDozdahli* operatives and business agents. Although it had a VIP box, the real VIPs were nowhere near it. They knew to go through the crusty door labeled "Employees Only" and find the stairwell, which led down into a posh, luxurious lounge area with a few hidden exits leading out to various points nearby, in case the club above was raided by authorities.

Chopper had never been down there in character, but he knew everything about it. He had designed it.

Tonight, he didn't have to go far to find the one he was looking for. Rubens was sitting at a table talking to two human women. A larger velenx than most, his mane black with a splash of dark red through it, shaved nearly to the scalp. He had an electronic implant embedded in his cheek just beneath his left eye, which gleamed with a tiny blue LED. Tonight, he was wearing a black leather jacket, gloves, and baggy pants in a gray and black camouflage pattern. He looked like a paramilitary rather than an organized crime thug.

He saw Chopper coming, and smirked. "You're back."

Chopper nodded. "Get him, please."

Rubens needed no further conversation. He curtly excused himself from his guests—both NPCs—and headed for the "Employees Only" door. He seemed to move a little quicker this time than the last; Nikita must have told him Chopper should get expedited service.

Chopper went back outside and walked a block and a half down the street from the club. He found an empty bench and sat down. While he waited, Ben ran a quick search for the nearest players in the area, finding that the only PCs nearby were in the club he'd just left down the street. There were none further north than that location.

If he didn't know better, he'd think he was near the docks of a major city. Large warehouses, an entire city block large, were lined up one after another here. Across the street was an open field full of containers, stacked in rows of three. In the south, the city's skyscrapers filled the horizon, abuzz with streams of tiny vessels and others that navigated freely. It felt like a desolate part of town, particularly at this time of night. Looking north, the northern face of the exterior superstructure loomed, its crisscrossing lattice seeming to spread out wide the closer down the wall it came. An optical illusion, of course, but he enjoyed the mammoth size of this creation. He wondered if many other players ever stopped just to look around at how incredibly detailed this virtual world was, and wondered about the man-hours it took to have realized it all.

After a while, Nikita appeared down the street, casually walking toward him. He was wearing a light gray trench coat over a suit and tie. He stopped in front of Chopper, looking around casually to see who else might be nearby.

"There's no one here," Chopper said. "I've checked already."

"Ah. Good to see you again," Nikita said.

"You get down here pretty fast," Chopper observed.

Nikita shrugged. "I'm not usually far. I've made some changes to this area since you've been here last."

"You can change the environment here?"

Nikita nodded.

Ben made a mental note to look into that. No one should have the privileges to make further changes to Eleon except devs with his level of access or higher. But that could wait.

"Anyway, what's on your mind?" Nikita asked.

"I need to talk to you," Ben said.

* * *

Galon-Yarisis Outpost
Over Planet Phoenicis
Sector 351-R

The sky over Phoenicis was still. The Galon-Yarisis space station was alone in its silent orbit, most of its inhabitants, custodial and interned, sleeping. Its primary weapons were sheathed and buttoned down, its sentinel defenses scanning the sky around it in sweeping arcs, tiny sensors twirling, listening, watching.

Galon-Yarisis was built during the Phoenicic Unification War in the early Expansion Era. Political leaders of the defeated were not executed, but could not be imprisoned on the planet for fear of armed action to rescue them, which would reignite the war. Agents of the technologically powerful affistri stepped in and offered to design and build a powerful space station in orbit over the planet, which would serve not only as a solution to the fledgling Phoenicic government but also as a kind of Alcatraz for the systems of the third tier. It was designed to repel direct assaults from capital ships as well as stealth insertions, and prisoners sentenced to time at Galon-Yarisis were the most dangerous and despised criminals in the worlds.

As far as *Cortanis* players were concerned, it was one of the most challenging missions to win. The successful completion of the third phase of the Aristarchus mission series came with considerable benefits, not the least of which were the bragging rights themselves. Though many had tried, none so far had figured out how to "solo" the G-Y, and the game's AI customized the encounter for individual teams so that the challenge was different each time. There was no single bulletproof strategy to beating the G-Y Outpost.

But some strategies were worth trying twice.

"I see the station," said Caveman, as his stealthed ship came over the horizon of Phoenicis and silently approached the underside of the facility. "I'm slowing."

"Copy, Cavester. We're getting set to jump," Roukan said over voice-chat.

"Wow, did you guys hear that?" Volley said. "Loud thunder here. Rain is coming down hard."

"I heard it, Volley," said Mara.

"Was that Vanda or Mara?" Volley laughed. "I can't tell either of your voices apart."

"Mara," she answered.

"We'll have to figure out a way to let people tell us apart, huh?" Naomi said, smiling.

"Maybe I can see what can be done about changing my voice. Or I could train myself to talk with a British accent."

"Oooh," Virrago said. "I like this idea."

Caveman began decelerating patiently, not expending too much thrust or fuel that would cause the base's sensors to pick him up. Steadily, his electronic warfare ship, *Whispers of Mutiny*, slowed its approach on the massive orbital facility. Once he had matched the station's velocity, he signaled again.

"In position. No sensor flags."

"Battle group, sound off," Roukan ordered.

"Vanda is go," Naomi said.

"Mara is go."

"Virrago's good to go."

"Volley's ready."

"Rico is go."

"LEM is ready," LEM said. Naomi smiled to herself.

"All right, let's hit it," Roukan said. "Go for FTL on my mark: three... two... one... mark!"

With bright snaps of light, seven ships punched their way into normal space above the station. Roukan's *Lazarus Heavy*, the largest of the battle group, began unfolding its weapons as the other ships accelerated toward the station. The facility began slamming exterior hatches and blast doors shut as it went into air-defense mode, powering up its primary armaments.

"Hey there, remember us?" Volley said with a grin.

"Okay, LEM, fire up your Logic Barrage," Roukan ordered. "Mara, stay behind LEM. You'll stay out of the fight until the primary particle cannons are neutralized."

"Copy that," Mara said.

"Rico, start dropping buoys. Everyone else, weapons free!" The carrier's cannons began bursting with white flame, showering the station with bombardment. The station's weapons flooded the sky with dashes of white and gold in the direction of the approaching capital ships. Volley's ship *Celestial* and Virrago's *Sauro Hata* arced over the station in different directions, drawing the AA cannons apart from each other.

"Rail guns are lining up," Virrago said. "Vanda, Volley, want to help me try my theory?"

"Yeah, let's give it a shot. I'm moving behind you," Naomi said.

"I'll try," Volley said nervously. "I don't have a lot of cover on my side."

Virrago brought his primary weapons to bear on the station's rail system as the *Destiny* passed behind *Sauro Hata* and opened fire. *Sauro Hata* held fire and let the *Destiny* charge forward. Two of the rail cannons lined up on *Destiny* and sputtered with fury.

As the two rail cannons racked up together, Virrago took aim at the rail itself. Slashes of white streaked through the sky and raked over the rails mercilessly, flashes of little explosions erupting across the tracks.

"Hold your fire please, coming through!" Naomi said as she banked *Destiny* to port. Virrago's stream of fire stopped just as *Destiny* pulled between him and the station. The cannons stopped firing and passed into the thick cloud of smoke billowing from the targeted site, as Naomi unloaded her broadside cannons at the station for good measure.

As *Destiny* pulled clear, the smoke had dissipated enough to show the rail cannons couldn't follow. Too much of the rail had been destroyed. Their path blocked, the cannons reversed and began circling around the far side of the station, in Volley's direction.

"Yeah! That'll take them a while to fix," Virrago cheered. "Volley, how are you doing? Those guns are on their way to you!"

Celestial had cleared the station and was turning to attack the rails on the far side. As soon as she opened fire on the rails, her ship vanished from sight. At the same moment, her name disappeared from the list of team participants in Naomi's headsup.

"Volley? Volley?" Naomi said, seeing the ship disappear.

"Crap, she's gone," Virrago said. "Maybe she lagged out?"

"That thunderstorm got her, I bet," Rico put in. "Probably lost power."

"Not good," Naomi said. "We need another fast-attack to cover Mara when she starts her run, or it's not going to work!"

"Who else is online?"

"ArchDuke is," Virrago offered. "Let me ask him if he can join."

"He needs to bring a fast-attack ship," said Naomi, "and quick-like!"

"Got it."

"Hey guys," Caveman said, "you've got fighters."

"I'm launching," said Roukan as the stream of tiny spacecraft began peeling out of the space station and into the melee. Roukan's fighters quickly took to the sky in response, beginning their tiny dogfighting.

"Vanda, we can't wait for Duke. You've got to start your run on those particle cannons or they're going to start lighting off."

"Copy that, Roukan," she said as she twisted *Destiny* into a turn, slowly drawing her ship to bear on the station's primary weapons. "I'm coming about, start your feint."

Lazarus Heavy's main thrusters fired hot blue, and the massive manta-ray carrier advanced on the station. The twin particle cannons, now fully unsheathed from their stows, swung in Roukan's direction and began gathering power to fire.

"Twenty seconds to—ahh shit," Caveman said. "I just got flagged."

"How?" Roukan demanded, not expecting an answer. "Break stealth and sprint to us, you're completely exposed down there."

"Already moving. I'll try to get to you before they cut me up." *Whispers* accelerated to flank, but the station's AA batteries were already blazing in his direction.

"The PCs are still on me. Vanda, how close are you?" Roukan said.

The *Destiny* was banking around *Sauro Hata*, as Virrago pointed his ship downward to cover Caveman's full-speed run to the group.

"I don't know, eight seconds? I'm hurrying," Naomi said.

"We got the timing just right last time. Let's not screw this one up."

"I know. Almost there…"

Another bright flash of light announced the arrival of another ship. Vanda spun her camera in the direction of the flash: it was ArchDuke in his heavy cruiser.

"I got a delivery of pain here, who wants it?" he exclaimed as he accelerated forward and opened fire indiscriminately on the station.

"All right, Duke!" Rico said.

Naomi sensed that something was wrong. The station's defenses were blazing, stitching the sky with bolts of white and yellow. As it slowly rolled into her path of flight, she felt as though something about the engagement had changed.

"Ten seconds," Cave warned.

ArchDuke's cruiser, *Infantile Outburst*, raced past the *Lazarus* and pummeled the station with his forward concussion batteries. The station's particle cannons lifted and turned toward him instead of the *Destiny*.

"Duke, back off!" Roukan said. "Back off!"

"Why? What—oh damn, you're about to…"

"Yeah! Break off unless you want your ship cut in half! Let them bear on Vanda!"

"Crap!" Duke pulled the *Infantile* into a steep escape vector as *Destiny*'s forward batteries came to bear on the PCs, and opened fire.

"Reversing out," said Roukan, slowing his carrier to a stop, then backing away, holding fire on the station so that *Destiny* could draw the PCs' ire.

"Right here! Right here!" Naomi said as her cannons blasted again and again, picking up speed at the station. After a moment's hesitation, the heavy particle cannons began turning back around in her direction.

"Yes! They've got me again!" she said.

"Three seconds, Vanda!" Caveman called out.

"Everyone clear! Get clear!" Roukan ordered.

"Let's see what you got, bitch." Vanda grinned as her ship picked up speed. There was no stopping *Destiny* now. Naomi could see the deep blue energy at the back of the cannons readying to rip through her cruiser again.

The cannons fired, the bolts tearing through the ship as they had before. *Destiny* broke apart, its momentum undeterred by the particle cannon's bolts shredding the vessel. Flaming, the *Destiny* plowed headlong into the PCs and erupted in a powerful blast, consumed by billowing clouds of golden flames and vaulting pieces of metal outward from the point of impact.

"Woohooo!" Rico exclaimed. "Good hit!"

"You guys owe me another ship," Naomi chuckled. "Again." Even with the mirth in her voice, she could still sense something was still not as it should be.

"Duke, where are you?" Roukan called out.

"I'm high on your left, turning back around again."

"Okay, you're going to cover the troop transport when it moves in. Circle around behind her and take her in with you. Get ready to start your run, Mara," Roukan said.

"I'm ready," she answered.

"Alright, everyone, concentrate your fire on the AAs and ring cannons, and make sure LEM and Mara stay covered. We're putting in the insertion team. Rico, stay behind Mara in case she needs regen."

"Copy that," replied Virrago.

"Copy that," echoed Rico.

"Mara, head for the station, steady. Make for the forward mezzanine docking hatch above the equator."

"Okay, I'm on my way." Mara's transport, *Galatea*, powered up its engines and began moving toward the station, as the *Infantile* took up position parallel to her on her starboard side, flooding the space between her and the station with unrelenting stabs of bright white.

The fires of Vanda's decimated cruiser began clearing. Out of the smoke, the twin PCs swung toward the *Infantile*. They were only moderately damaged by *Destiny*'s sacrifice.

"Guys?" Naomi called out, alarmed.

"What the *hell?*"

* * *

"What's on your mind?" Nikita asked as he sat beside Chopper on the bench.

"Something doesn't make sense," Ben began. "You said you and Peter went on missions together, leveling up."

"Yeah, we did that for a while. He wanted to see Scolaere, the caverns there, with the drones and those cube-shaped walker-things. We ran the Willow, the Ghi-Numen, the Hysminai… we'd started the Swift Currents missions."

"Did you do any space combat?"

"No, not very much. That's not the kind of mishing he—we—enjoyed."

Ben frowned. "So the two of you never took on a boss station, like Galon-Yarisis or Sori 11."

"No, we didn't get around to that. I had a light cruiser, but I used it for transit, not combat."

Ben thought a moment. "But you did go up against those bosses, like Willow and Ghi-Numen."

"Yeah, those low-level guys. He dealt all the major damage, because he was so far beyond me level-wise, you know how the boss levels were balanced between him and me. He could waltz in and pretty much pulverize them without too much effort. There was nothing I could really do except hang back and pick up loot when he'd finished."

"So you were so low-level, you never pulled aggro."

"No, unless I was stupid enough to wade into the combat area before he had finished. The bosses were all focused on Peter. I'd have to go way out of my way to get them to notice me."

"Did that ever happen?"

"Once or twice."

"Then what? The boss would kill you?"

"Yeah. Would only take one shot, and I'd go down." He narrowed his eyes, studying the puzzled look on Chopper's face. "What are you on about?"

"Then you'd respawn right?"

"Yeah. Same place Peter would."

"I'm wondering why you could take on bosses and get killed while you were running missions with Peter, and respawn without difficulty. But when you went up against G-Y and got killed that one time with Vanda's group, you *stayed* killed. Until Vanda brought you back."

Nikita shook his head. "I don't know. Maybe it was because I wanted it."

"You wanted to get blown up?"

Nikita grew quieter. "At the time, yes. Vanda was my best friend here. Without Peter, all I had was her and without her…"

"So you wanted to… to suicide?" Ben asked. "Why would you want to do that?"

Nikita wouldn't look at him. "I guess because I felt like nothing more than a program. I'll never be a person, I wouldn't ever be accepted as Naomi's friend. I was just software. And I hated that. I hated myself."

Ben stared at him. "And now?"

Nikita shrugged. "I guess I'm better. Naomi talked to me. I got a second chance to explain. Maybe we can be friends. I'll never be a person, but… maybe I can learn to be okay with what I am." He paused a moment. "You know, Naomi's double might be thinking the same way, right now."

"So, she has to *want* to blow herself up? To kill herself?"

"I don't know. Maybe."

"Wait a minute," Ben said, his eyes widening. "That's not it at all."

Nikita looked at him.

"Peter. You could respawn because of Peter. Because he was *alive*."

Nikita began slowly nodding. "I respawned because… because there was still more to be learned."

"That's right. As long as Peter was around, you'd respawn, no problem."

"That means…"

"That means Naomi's plan…"

"… isn't going to work," Nikita finished for him.

Chopper stood up. "Damn. If she tries to get Mara killed, she'll respawn, and she'll be nothing but betrayed and pissed. She has to find another way."

Nikita stood and put his hand on Chopper's shoulder. "Wait."

"What? I've got to stop her before she starts that mission…"

Nikita rose and turned to face Chopper, looking him in the eyes. "I really can't let you do that."

* * *

"The particle cannons are twenty seconds to discharge," LEM reported.

"Looks like there's only one," Vanda said, from her position floating in space near where *Destiny* was destroyed. "One of the firing cylinders took most of the damage, but the other one is only scarred."

"Oh man," Virrago said. "You hit them straight on, Vanda! How could they still be operational?"

"I'll tell you how," Caveman said, "as soon as my ship gets blown up." *Whispers* was taking heavy bombardment from the underside of the station. Virrago's corvette had rolled to its side to buffet the station's ventral AA with his broadside armaments, but it wasn't enough to protect Caveman. Fires were exploding outward from various points along its hull as it raced to reach the shelter beneath Roukan's carrier, but it was still too far. The *Whispers of Mutiny* succumbed to the relentless pummeling and broke in half with a sudden ring-shaped burst, before both halves were consumed in cascading explosions.

"Sorry, babe, I'm out of it," Caveman said glumly. "Get out of there, Virrago."

"It's okay, Cave," Naomi said. "What were you going to say?"

"Duke brought a heavy cruiser to replace Volley," Caveman observed. "She only had a fast-attack ship. Duke's ship is twice the size, flagship-strength."

"The base got stronger," Roukan agreed. "That's what happened, all right."

"That PC is aiming at you, Duke," Caveman pointed out.

"Ten seconds to discharge," LEM said.

Duke started to pull the *Infantile* away from the troop transport, away to the starboard.

"Duke, hold your course," Naomi said.

"I can't, the PC will tear me apart and the shockwave will—"

"Hold your course, Duke!" Roukan ordered.

"Why?"

Galatea slowed. Naomi's heart jumped into her throat as she saw Mara hesitate.

"Mara, Duke, press to target! We'll draw that PC cannon off you! Do not abort!" Roukan's voice was rising as he barked orders.

"Five seconds to discharge," LEM said.

The *Lazarus Heavy* moved forward again, launching blast after blast of fire at the station, but the PC cannon remained fixed on *Infantile Outburst*. The *Galatea* came to a stop as *Infantile* began peeling off again, countermanding Roukan's orders, firing its broadside cannons. The PCs tracked with it.

"Rico, where are you?" Duke shouted. "Hit Mara with a regen stream now! She's going to get hammered!"

Rico didn't reply.

"Mara, what are you doing?" Naomi asked.

"What are *you* doing?" Mara replied softly.

The particle cannon erupted once more, cleaving the *Infantile* across its midsection, the blue streams slicing through the cruiser like it wasn't even there. The ship's two halves spun for a few moments, spewing flame and debris until both burst apart in spidery clouds, sending out a blast wave which raked across the *Galatea*, enough to knock it sideways. But the little transport had stopped far enough back not to take major damage.

"Naomi?" asked Mara.

"Yeah?"

"What's going on?"

"That PC is still live," Virrago was saying. "We can't get anything close enough to the station to put the team in. We have to abort."

"I've been hit," LEM said calmly. "I appear to be shock-stalled. EW is temporarily offline." Naomi spun her camera around to see LEM's ship *Locus Solus*, fountains of flame gushing from its engines.

"Fighter-bombers," Roukan said. "Switch to flak, everyone!"

"What am I doing here?" Mara asked. "Why did Admiral Roukan want Duke to stay right beside me, knowing he was about to be destroyed?"

Naomi's hands trembled as she tried to think quickly. "I… Roukan was going to pull the PCs off you by moving in."

Mara was silent a moment. Naomi stared hard at the little ship, motionless in a sky full of slashes of light and fire.

"Isn't this Volley's mission?" Mara asked. Voice-chat went quiet.

"Yes, it is," Naomi answered.

"With Volley gone, we can't extract her NPC from the station. The mission cannot be completed. Why are we still here?"

Naomi opened her mouth to speak, but she had no words to answer her.

"Naomi?" Mara asked calmly.

"I… don't know, we were waiting for Volley to make it back on…"

"But you sent me in with Duke, to extract a prisoner who isn't there. So, you're lying."

Naomi stared at the little ship, a sinking feeling taking hold in her chest.

"You want me to die, don't you?" Mara said. "You want me gone."

"Vanda, are you talking to yourself?" Duke asked, bewildered.

"This isn't Volley's mission," Mara went on. "It never was. This is *your* mission. That's why Cave apologized to *you* when his ship was destroyed, isn't it?"

"Mara," Naomi began, "I'm sorry."

Silence.

"Everyone abort," Roukan ordered. "Break off all attacks and FTL for home."

"Copy that," said Virrago, already moving off, flooding the space behind his ship with defensive flak.

"No," Mara said, barely audible. "There's one thing left to do."

"What does that mean?" Rico said.

Naomi felt a shiver pass through her at those words. *You know.*

Galatea fired its engines again and began moving toward the station. Its forward cannons, entirely useless except as provocation, streamed bolts of bright red in the station's direction.

"Mara?" Naomi said, suddenly feeling deeply anxious at what she was witnessing. "Mara, stop..."

"There's only one thing left to do. Goodbye, Naomi. I'm sorry I made your life so unhappy."

"Mara?"

She didn't answer.

"Mara, wait!"

Galatea accelerated toward the mezzanine hatch. The PC cannon began moving again, swinging in the tiny ship's direction.

"Everyone..." Naomi said, her hands shaking. "Everyone stop her! Stop Mara! Don't let her destroy herself!"

There was stunned silence in the voice-chat channel for a beat.

"Everyone *please!* Stop her!" Naomi pleaded, her voice breaking.

"You heard the lady!" Admiral Roukan said. "Weapons free, salvo fire! Attack!"

"Logic Barrage back online," LEM said. "Twenty seconds to particle cannon discharge."

"I'm in!" Virrago exclaimed, banking the *Sauro Hata* back around into the fight once more.

The *Lazarus Heavy*'s engines roared to life, pressing forward and firing barrages at the station's primary weapon. It quickly overtook the tiny transport, unleashing burst after burst from its forward guns. The station's PC shifted, targeting the carrier instead.

"Oh man, Roukan, you sure you want to do that?" Caveman said in disbelief. "How many missions have you gone without losing her?"

"Don't ask me to think about that now," Roukan said.

"Logic Barrage engaged," said LEM. "Fifteen seconds."

"Mara, stop!" Naomi said. *Galatea* was changing course, moving up behind Roukan's carrier.

"You won't be safe there, Mara. When that PC fires, it'll blow right through me," Roukan warned her.

"Oh my God," Naomi said softly. "That's what she's doing, she's going to let the PC shish-kebab you both!"

"Ten seconds to discharge."

"*Stop her!*" Naomi pleaded. "Anyone!"

"Sorry, Vanda," said Roukan. "Nothing can stop that PC from—"

A bright flash of light appeared in the sky behind the *Lazarus Heavy*. A new ship, even larger than Roukan's carrier, dropped out of thruspace into Phoenicis orbit, its thrusters blazing as it charged towards the station. Another voice sounded in Naomi's ears… a very familiar one.

"Hey gang," Nikita said. "What sort of GDCF is this?"

"Is that Rabbit!?" Duke exclaimed. "What's he—"

"Nikita! We've got to stop that PC from killing Roukan!" Naomi begged. "Hurry!"

"Is that all I got to do?"

"Five seconds to discharge." The deep blue energy swirled at the base of the cannon bore, ready to destroy *Lazarus Heavy* and *Galatea* in a single, invincible shot.

Naomi stared as an object she'd never seen before unfolded from the massive *Titian*-class cruiser. It didn't look like a weapon at all. It looked like some kind of heavily reinforced parabola, as though for launching offensive EW attacks. *Shoot! SHOOT!* she pleaded wordlessly.

"Roukan, pitch negative 45-degrees!" Nikita said.

Roukan nosed the *Lazarus* downward. The carrier rolled in place, showing its dorsal side to the station, its forward cannons aiming into the empty space below.

As Nikita's *Titian*-class neared, the station decided the more dangerous threat was above, and the particle cannon jerked upward in Nikita's direction. As soon as it was aimed, it unleashed.

The weapon that had emerged from Nikita's carrier had angled itself toward the station, but nothing came out of it. The station had fired first.

"*No!*" Naomi cried as the blue blast erupted from the particle cannon and streaked toward Nikita's ship. She didn't know if it would be possible to respawn him after this. *Why had he even come here? What would sacrificing himself do for…*

The blue bolt reached the carrier and impacted against the surface of the glossy concave dish. Naomi stared in shock as the blast, instead of tearing through the dish and the vessel, suddenly reflected back on itself, and reversed into the cannon that had sent it. Crackles of blue jagged all around the reflector on Nikita's ship, but it had successfully diverted the immense energy of the stream back into the G-Y's primary weapon.

The weapon exploded with a force none of them had ever witnessed. The bolt ripped into the cannons and didn't stop until it had torn through to the other side, along the center axis of the station. The particle cannons were ripped apart, then secondary explosions began punching out of the station exterior in all directions. With a cataclysmic dome-cloud eruption, the antimatter reactors of the station detonated, powerful shockwaves pulsing outward towards the fleet.

The *Lazarus Heavy* continued rolling forward. With its broad upper hull exposed to the wave, it absorbed the full impact. The carrier began spewing flames as tiny explosions burst from its engines and points along the hull. Naomi held her breath and prayed Roukan's venerable ship would not also be destroyed, for its own shockwave would decimate *Galatea*.

The carrier held.

None of the tiny dogfighters or fighter-bombers escaped the force of the shockwaves. As they dissolved away into space, the lights on the station died out, all of its weapons losing power. The sky over Phoenicis suddenly grew still once more.

No one spoke.

Naomi pressed her hand to her mouth, tears gathering in her eyes. She waited for the carrier to break up and ignite, but it didn't. Finally, she chanced breathing again, and pressed her talk key with a shaky finger.

"Mara?" she said softly.

Mara didn't answer. Her ship floated motionless behind the carrier that had protected it from what would have been a catastrophic concussion. Nikita's carrier slowed to a stop, hovering victorious over the flaming, defeated outpost.

"Mara, are you there?" Naomi asked again.

"I'm here," she said finally.

Dayquil Shortbus began routing green energy through the buoys into the *Lazarus Heavy*, providing it with regenerative power. Another green stream was angled into the *Galatea*.

"I'm sorry," Naomi said, her voice quivering. "I don't want you to go."

"Why?" Mara asked quietly. "I don't understand."

"I don't understand either, yet. I just..." Naomi sniffled. "I just saw you and... I can't explain why. I don't see you as a copy of me anymore. You're unique. You're *you*. I just wanted to give you one more chance to change your mind. The reasons why can wait. We can figure them out for ourselves."

After a long moment of stillness, Mara whispered, "Thank you."

Naomi's tears spilled freely down her cheeks. "Thank you, Mara. Thank all of you, for saving her."

"Thank the tank," said Caveman. "Who the hell *is* that?"

"Everyone," Naomi said, smiling through her tears, "this is Nikita. Is it okay if I send him a member invitation?"

"Nikita, you just took out the G-Y without firing a shot," Roukan said, "I'd say you're in."

"Thanks, guys," Nikita said. "It's so great to see you all."

10.02

Five days later

Charlottesville, Virginia

Naomi opened the front door to reveal Skyler standing on the stoop, wearing a heavy green winter coat lined with fuzzy cream tufts of fabric. Snow was coming down gently from the white December sky; tiny white flakes had gathered over her shoulders and atop her hair.

Skyler was holding a small package in her hands. Naomi smiled as she held the door open for Sky to come in. It was the first time they'd seen each other in nearly two weeks.

"Thanks for letting me come over," Skyler said, stepping inside. "Wow," she added.

"My hair?" Naomi guessed. Her hair was completely changed. She'd had it straightened and cut in a cheek-length, angled bob, very similar to Vanda's hairstyle in the game. It was the most radical change in her hairstyle Naomi had ever done since they had known each other.

"Yeah," Sky said. "It looks really different. Good, though. I like it."

"Thanks. I thought about coloring it too, but I don't think I'm ready for purple hair yet." She took Skyler's coat and hung it on a hanger in the closet beneath the stairs. Skyler looked around at the open boxes strewn around the living room, half-full of Christmas ornaments and silver tinsel. *Harry Potter & The Chamber of Secrets* was playing on the television, and she smiled at the partially decorated tree standing before the front windows, glittering in tiny white lights.

"Beautiful," Skyler said. "A bit late to start putting it up though, isn't it?"

"Yeah, I've been a little busy. But I can't not have a Christmas tree." She started moving the boxes taking up the space on her sofa, forming a pile on the floor. "Want something to drink?" she asked when she was done.

"Sure."

"Egg nog?" Naomi offered.

"Okay." Skyler smiled. Naomi went into the kitchen to pour a couple of mugs. Returning to the living room, she noticed Skyler's little package on the coffee table in front where Sky had seated herself.

"Purple hair," Skyler said, taking one of the offered glasses. "That's how Vanda's hair looks in the game, isn't it?"

Naomi nodded, picking up the remote for the television and turning the volume down. "I'm… trying it out." She sat down next to her.

"I like it even more, then," Skyler said. "Makes you look younger."

"Thanks." Naomi placed the remote on the coffee table and turned to face her. "You said you had something you wanted to tell me," she said.

Skyler nodded, and took a breath. "I wanted to… answer your question," she said. "The question you asked me the last time I saw you."

"What question was that?" Naomi asked.

Skyler looked down, gathering herself. "Give me a sec." She took another sip from her mug and stared into the surface of the creamy beverage, holding it in both hands. "The thing I'm most ashamed of."

"Sky, I said I wasn't going to ask you about that again. I was only trying to make a point. I don't need you to tell me."

"*I* need to tell you," Sky said. "It's not fair that you don't know. You may not want to be my friend after, and I'll understand, but you don't really know me until I do." Her voice was low and shaky. She was looking at the wrapped package on the coffee table.

Naomi stared. "Don't, then, until you're ready," she cautioned. The barely-audible sound and music from the movie suddenly seemed loud again. Naomi picked up the remote again and turned the television off. "But if you are, I want to listen."

"I got someone hooked on coke," Skyler said in a low voice.

Naomi studied Skyler, who looked to be near tears, and unable to meet her eyes.

"You did?" was all Naomi could think to say, to break the heavy silence. Sky appeared to be having difficulty controlling her emotions. "Who?"

Skyler's voice was unsteady as she spoke. "My little sister. She was twenty-four."

Naomi swallowed.

"I brought her to a party with a bunch of people," Sky went on. "I offered it to her. I was with her when she tried it for the first time. I used to do it too back then, but I got out of that… scene. I got away from those people. Got off the hard stuff. She didn't. She… overdosed two years later." Her voice was nearly breaking.

"What was her name?" Naomi asked.

"Danielle," Skyler said, wiping at her eye. "My mother… she said she never wanted to speak to me again, as long as I lived. The night you and I met… was Danielle's birthday."

"Oh my God," Naomi gathered Skyler against her. Skyler hugged her back.

"It was my fault," Skyler said softly. "She was just a kid. I should have kept her away from all that."

"That's why you were in the park?"

Skyler nodded against Naomi's shoulder. "I was thinking about doing what I saw you do."

"I had no idea."

"I've never told anyone this," Skyler answered, letting go of Naomi and sniffling a little. "You're the only one."

Naomi offered a sad smile to her.

"If we hadn't both been there at that moment in time, I might have done the same thing," Sky said. "Seeing you made me realize how important it is not to give up. I know you think I saved you that night… but the truth is, you saved me, too."

"Oh," Naomi said softly. "Have you and your mother spoken?"

"No. She moved, and she got married again. But I know where she is now. And I need to ask you a favor."

"Anything," Naomi said.

"I need to go see her. I haven't seen her in eleven years. I was hoping you could go with me when I do."

Naomi looked surprised. "Wouldn't you want Joel to go with you?"

Sky shook her head. "We've only been dating a year, and he doesn't know about it. I decided I needed to tell you first. And if you'll go with me, I'd rather have you there. If it works out with mom, and she starts talking to me again, I'll want Joel to meet her at some point. But not now."

"Are you going to call her first?"

Sky shrugged. "I've been trying to muster the courage to call her for a long time. I haven't been able to. I think the only way to do it is to go and just knock on her door. If she slams the door in my face, at least I'll have an answer."

Naomi nodded. "Of course I'll go with you. Just tell me when. I'll be there."

Skyler gave a timid smile. "Thank you. And I'm sorry for what I said to you on the trail. I didn't mean for it to hurt you so much."

Naomi nodded. "I've been thinking a lot about that conversation we had on the trail. If it makes you feel better, I'm seeing Dr. Ellery again. I have an appointment with him, first week of January."

"I am glad to hear that," Skyler said. "Truly. I hope he can help you."

Naomi smiled. "Me too."

"Maybe he'll tell you to try challenging yourself in other ways, like coming climbing with me," Skyler said.

"Yeah, he might. Something has happened that's given me a whole different perspective on myself."

"Oh really? What's that?"

"I'll show you," Naomi said. "Come upstairs."

Skyler followed her up the stairs to the office loft, taking her mug and the little wrapped package with her. Naomi turned and perched on the edge of her desk, facing the *SimMind* interface on the screen.

"Mara?" she asked.

"Yes?" came Mara's voice from the speakers.

"I'd like you to meet someone. This is Skyler, my very best friend. Sky, this is Mara."

Skyler's eyes widened, stepping closer, studying the shifting bar-charts and spinning idea-map globes.

"Hello, Skyler," Mara said. "It's nice to meet you."

"Um, hi," Skyler said hesitantly. Then she looked at Naomi. "What *is* this?"

"This is a SimMind. It's a software program that runs on a computer that simulates a person. My other SimMind, LEM, decided to stay in ToC, and Ben—you met him in Richmond—helped me get Mara out. Now she runs on my computer here. She's kind of my gaming buddy now."

"Wait, so... this is the double? The one you were telling me about? This is what the game made out of all its data-gathering and spying on you?" Skyler seemed apprehensive.

"That's right. She's everything the game compiled about me, personified into her own personality matrix. But as a SimMind, she's not under the game's control anymore. Now she's, well... free."

"What happened to LEM? You've had him for a long time now. Won't you be getting him back?"

"He's in ToC. He decided he wanted to stay there, explore the worlds, play the game. Enjoy the experience of having a body that can go places, interact with and see new things. He can still access the internet from there, and basically do everything he was doing from his box here." Naomi gestured to the bright red computer she'd bought for him. "But he chose to stay in the game world for now. Maybe someday if he changes his mind, he can come home, and he and Mara can hang out here."

"I've been looking forward to meeting you, Skyler," Mara said. "Naomi cares so much for you."

Naomi smiled, blushing a little.

Skyler looked at the screen again. "So, you're... a *simulation* of Naomi's personality?" she asked Mara.

"That's one way to describe me, but though I *am* based on her, I have my own cognitive decision-making lattices. Also, motivation is very different as a SimMind than as a human being, so I'm driven by altogether different needs than she is. Our experiential memory is going to vary quite a bit. Effectively, I was created *as* her, but when I became self-aware, I began developing my own personality, independent of her. The longer I am in operation, the more distinct I will become."

"She sounds like you," Skyler said to Naomi.

"Yeah, I don't like her voice." Naomi chuckled. "But the fact is, Mara is special, and pretty important to the developers at Praelium. That brings me to the big-news part."

"It does? What news is that?"

"Ben talked to his bosses, and they want to meet me. They're flying me down to Atlanta right after Christmas. They want to interview me for a job."

Skyler gasped. "Really? A new job? What would you be doing?"

"Well, they want to talk to me about what happened with Peter and Mara. I'm not supposed to say anything, but… Ben told me these haven't been isolated incidents. There have been a few other cases reported, similar to mine. Still very rare, a couple dozen he said, but the company wants to understand what is happening and come to grips with the scientific and legal implications involved. Since my background is in research law, he said it's very possible they might be able to create a consultancy position for me. Kind of their way of making amends, maybe make some lemonade out of the situation."

"So, does that mean you'd be moving? To Atlanta?" Skyler sounded as if she wasn't sure whether she was happy about the idea.

"Not necessarily, if I have my way. I'm going to talk to them about maybe working from here. They may be happy to let me telecommute, and only fly down to Atlanta once or twice a month. Besides," she laughed, "From what Ben has told me, I think they're nervous that if they don't get me on their side, I might sue them for all their worth and make a lot of bad publicity over all this. The more I think about it, the more I realize how nervous they *should* be about that. If I wanted to, I could bring a case against them."

"What better way to prepare against litigation from other plaintiffs than to hire one in their defense," Skyler chuckled, taking a sip of egg nog.

"Well, I wouldn't be acting in that role, but I could offer advice to their lawyers who do. My position would have more to do with the entities like Nikita and Mara… what was the word we decided to call them, Mara?"

"Emergents," Mara answered. "That wasn't my first choice."

"What was that?" Skyler asked.

"I thought we could call them ghosts. But Naomi doesn't like that."

Naomi shook her head, and shrugged. "Too Rod Serling." Then she noticed the package Skyler was holding. "What do you have there?"

Skyler offered it to her. "Just a little something for you."

"For me?" Naomi smiled and took the package. It was a gift box, five inch square, wrapped in gold foil. She removed the wrappings and lifted the cover off, to reveal a glass and brass ornament laid on a pillow of soft tissue, with a golden fabric loop at the top. She smiled curiously and lifted it up by the loop, examining it. It was a little window, with muntins horizontal and vertical, dividing the glass pane into four quadrants. Beneath, laser-etched into the sill, were four bold, serifed letters:

WWVD

Naomi studied it a moment, then the significance dawned on her. She smiled. "Thank you," she said.

"Merry Christmas," Skyler smiled back.

Epilogue
11.01

Praelium Atlanta
Sandy Springs, Georgia

Ben Cross waved his cardkey at the box and the glass doors whispered open. As he made his way to the elevators, he wondered if Naomi's office would be near his, on his level or elsewhere. Probably elsewhere; accounting and legal were on 21, one floor below him. There was an office on his side of the building that was vacant. Maybe he could get her to request that office. If he was right about how he had read their reactions at the meeting last week, they would do everything possible to bring her onto their side.

He hoped she would be close.

He'd been right to let Nikita take a carrier to intervene at the G-Y. Nikita had insisted on being the one to help Naomi and Mara. The *Titian*-class was an archimek design, and Nikita being well-connected with them, was able to procure one on short notice. They cost players a small fortune, but somehow Nikita had enough liquidity to arrange for one to be purchased right away.

The beam reflector was a weapon designed by Daniel for a space station in an upcoming mission arc, which hadn't been released yet. The weapon, dubbed a CP-Ampliflector, was designed to deflect and control the direction of offensive beam weapons used by player characters against the station. The reflector would target other attacking ships, forcing players to rethink their offensive strategy. Ben was able to modify Nikita's *Titian*-class carrier with a hardpoint capable of mounting the weapon. Nikita wasn't strictly a player, so technically Ben wasn't violating any cardinal rules of dev intervention by letting him have a ship with it. Once Mara was safe and the mission ended, Nikita scuttled the carrier and its weapon, so Ben hoped no one at Praelium would have to find out about it.

However, the note on his desk when he arrived caused him to wonder if he hadn't been wrong. The note said to call his boss' boss, Alexander Hewett, as soon as he got there. Notes like this were not often omens of good news.

The note was in Libby's handwriting. He held it up to her. "You take this?" he asked.

"Yeah," she said, "he came by looking for you."

"Oh, shit. Did he say why?"

"Nope. Just said for you to call him as soon as you got in."

He picked up the phone and dialed the four-digit number. His heart was beating a little faster.

"Mr. Hewett? It's Ben Cross, I'm here," he said when the line picked up.

"Ben, would you come up to my office please. Bring your cardkey." Hewett hung up.

Ben's world changed immediately. *I'm going to be fired.* He felt his pulse throbbing and his fingers tremble.

Fired. From Praelium. I'll never work in the game industry again.

He stood up with effort from his desk and felt for his cardkey, still in his front pants pocket. His vision seemed to tunnel. It was hard to think. It suddenly became an effort to breathe. He made his way out of his office and down the glass-walled hall, putting his hand down on the corner desk of the receptionist to steady himself as he passed. He took the elevator to the 24th floor of the building.

Offices on this level were considerably more impressive that those on the development floors. Ben checked to make sure the buttons on his collar were fastened and his fly was up. He tried not to look terrified as he rapped twice on the glass door of Executive Producer Alexander Hewett.

Hewett was not a tall or intimidating man, but had been with the company long enough to make a reputation for himself. He was one of the core team responsible for creating *Tides of Cortanis,* and had been making games for other companies long before that. With ToC's success, he became a known figure in the industry. Hewett was admired for his clarity of vision, his prescience regarding market trends in the industry, and his no-bullshit policy of dealing with journalists. If you were on his side, you loved him. If you weren't, he was a scary man to share a room with.

Hewett came to the door and opened it. He did not appear to want Ben to enter.

"Got your cardkey?" he asked bluntly.

Ben nodded.

Hewett held out his hand. "Let me have it."

My God. I'm out of a job, as of this moment. Ben felt his heart sink as he reached in his pocket, withdrew his key to the building, and surrendered it to Hewett.

"What... did I do?" Ben said, his voice unsteady.

"Come with me," Hewett said curtly, stepping out of his office and closing his door from the outside. He led Ben back the way he had come, past the receptionist's desk, where he placed Ben's card-key in front of her.

"Negative One," he said in passing to her. She took the key and gave Ben a careful look.

Negative one environment programmer, Ben thought. He wondered where Hewett was taking him. *Of course*, he realized. *Legal. He's going to make me sign all the non-compete bullcrap before dumping me out on my ass.* He could feel the weight of every footstep he took, each one leading him to a life-changing event. A million things swarmed his mind at once: would he have to move? Could he afford to stay in Atlanta? How marketable was he after being fired from one of the top game companies in the world for misconduct, or violating policy? What on earth could he do with his skills and experience if not work in video games? Would he be able to develop games as an independent?

Hewett glanced back at him, not saying another word before they reached two closed doors. He knocked three times rapidly, then without waiting for a response, pushed the door open and stepped through, holding it for Ben. Ben followed, and Hewett pushed the door closed behind them, twisting the bolt through.

The room was a windowless meeting room large enough for no more than eight people around a table. The chairs were leather and expensive-looking. There was a media display on one wall, but its cabinet doors were closed. Inside the room, seated, were two men in sharply cut dark suits. One of them wore glasses, the other was older, with a Marko Ramius platinum haircut.

He pushed up from the table as the door had opened, and held out his hand to Ben. "Ben Cross?"

Ben took the outstretched hand and shook. *Friendly enough for a firing squad,* he mused. "That's me." He immediately noticed the documents on the table in front of the other man. Sure enough: contracts. His eyes went to the man's lapel. Strangely, he wore a name badge that read 'VISITOR'.

"I'm Special Agent Pete Sadler. This is Agent Darbyshire. We're with the NSA."

Ben blinked. The words were so unexpected, they almost didn't sound like English. "I'm sorry… you're who?"

"We work for the National Security Agency, a division of the Defense Department. We deal in cybersecurity and cryptology. We'd like to talk to you for a bit."

Ben's head swam, the introductions sounding almost like gibberish, but slowly the reality began dawning over him that perhaps they wanted to talk about something other than the end of his career in video game development. He nodded and glanced at Hewett.

Hewett nodded assuringly, holding his hand out at the seat in front of Ben. Ben took the seat.

"You look a little pale," Darbyshire noticed. He had a pinched, high-pitched voice compared to the older one. His eyes were fierce, penetrating.

"I'm sorry," Ben said, trying to control the quavering of his voice. "I… honestly thought I was being fired." He looked to Hewett for a reaction. Hewett gave him a wry smile, one that he'd been withholding.

"Not hardly. Far from it," he said with a nod.

Ben breathed again, looking down at the table in front of him for a moment. His world wasn't being sucker-punched into smithereens, then. He looked back up at Sadler. "Glad to hear that. Then what's this about?"

Sadler sat down. There was a tablet computer in front of him on the table, propped up at a low angle on its folded screencover. He spun it towards Ben, showing him the screen. On it were two still images: one of Nikita, the other of Mara.

"You've recently had contact with these two game characters?"

He pointed to Nikita. "That one, yes. The other one…" he trailed off, looking closer. She looked almost exactly like Naomi René. He nodded. "Her name is Mara."

"That's right. We call them autonomic identity constructs, or AICs. These two, however, have gone rogue, so we refer to them as RICs." He sounded out the letters instead of pronouncing them as acronyms.

"Rogue identity constructs, okay." He suddenly realized that the NSA not only knew about this phenomenon, but knew enough to have developed terminology to describe it. The realization was mildly unsettling.

"Your having direct experience with them presents us with a choice, Mr. Cross. We can either threaten you with some jail time and plenty of personal inconvenience besides, with all the usual caveats and exhortations about nondisclosure and national security, blah-blah-blah," Sadler waved his hand, speaking casually. "Or, having reviewed your history with the company and your personal background, lack of criminal history and so forth, we can ask for your assistance. See if you're interested in helping us."

Ben stared at the man, slowly understanding what was being said to him. "So what you're saying is, what I've seen is classified, and you want me to keep my mouth shut about it."

Sadler nodded. "That much is the case, but more than that. You worked out a way to get Mara out of the system entirely and contained in a *SimMind* matrix framework that had been vacated by its IC."

Vacated by its IC. LEM. He means LEM. "Yes, I did."

"We want you to show us how you did that. And work with us on tracking down and isolating other RICs that have, shall we say, escaped into the game environment."

"Escaped? From where?" Ben couldn't help asking. Sadler didn't reply. Darbyshire gave him a look.

"If you agree to do this, Ben," Hewett put in, "We'll be upping your pay grade and transferring you to Special Projects, here in the building. You'll also have a revised security clearance, level Negative One."

Ben blinked again. "I didn't know Special Projects *was* in the building."

"Not many people do," Hewett said. "You'll be working with agents Sadler and Darbyshire here on the RIC issue as well as other NSA interests in *Cortanis*."

Ben looked puzzled, and a bit nervous. He glanced to Sadler. "What… 'other NSA interests' would those be?"

Sadler nodded to Derbyshire, who pushed the document across the table to Ben. "We'll get to that," said Sadler, "but we have a few documents we need you to take home and read first. Go over them with a lawyer, if you like. After you've read them, you'll sign them in the presence of a notary. Then we can officially bring you into Team Spinnaker."

"Spinnaker?"

"Our skunk works division," Hewett said, "is located here, not in Vancouver. A little piece of corporate disinformation, another tidbit you're expected to keep a lid on."

Ben nodded. "And the NSA's part of it?"

"That's right."

He leaned back in his chair and pushed the air out of his lungs. "Wow. Kind of a lot to process. Well, I'm definitely not saying no. I'll take the contract home and read it. And I know an attorney who I'll share it with."

"Ms. René?" Hewett said. "That who you're thinking of?"

"Is that a problem?"

"No, she's getting one of her own. We want to bring her into this group with you. You'll be working together, although for appearances sake you'll be working for Special Projects, and on paper, she'll be a consultant adjunct to the legal department."

"That sounds good," Ben said.

"In the meantime," said Sadler, "we need to talk to you about this." He spun his tablet computer back toward him, tapped on the screen a few times, and then turned it back around again to face Ben. This time, the image was of an archimek. It had short, spiky blonde hair, and eyes that glowed soft blue.

Ben studied it for a moment. "Yeah, that was her SimMind. She called him LEM. What about him?"

"What about him, indeed," Sadler nodded.

11.02

Some time later

Revati Prime
Planet Iunia
Sector 101-AE

Two men were running along the path along the island coast, hurrying to the office building complex at the edge of the peninsula. One of them was carrying a steel case. As they passed, he stopped to look at a player character who was sitting on a bench, staring at the horizon.

"Hey, check it out," he said to his companion. They both stopped, and approached the stranger on the bench.

"What's up, holmes?" the first one, whose tag was MurderDuck1ing, said as he walked up around him.

The stranger was staring at the ocean, unmoving, with a perfectly still face. He didn't acknowledge MurderDuck1ing or his companion, Riptalon991. He had light colored hair, a mustache and trimmed beard, and pale blue incandescent eyes. He was wearing a dark wool topcoat over a black turtleneck, and polished leather shoes. His hands were hidden beneath black gloves, laying on his legs.

"Dude's AFK," said Riptalion. "He's an 80."

"Hey! You here?" Duck1ing prodded, standing in front of the stranger. The seated figure didn't react.

"Let's do something to him," suggested Riptalion.

"Cache coffin."

Both players opened their inventory panels and took out individual rb, creating a temporary cache, a lockbox which would remain in-world for 24 hours, or until the contents were retrieved by the player who had created it. The single unit of currency was a trifle, but it could be deposited in a small box, which cost nothing to create. The two players began creating row after row of single-rb cache boxes, stacking them up like bricks, steadily encasing the seated figure in a little enclosure.

The figure enclosed in such an array of boxes would have considerable difficulty getting out, and was usually forced to log out and back in again. The prank cost very little to perform, and took only a minute of careful positioning of the caches before the target became unable to free himself.

In a few minutes, the rows of caches had reached the stranger's head. Without moving, the stranger addressed them.

"Please stop doing that."

"Oh, he's awake!" said Duck1ing, continuing to stack his cache boxes. Riptalion laughed, and continued as well.

As the rows of boxes obscured the stranger's field of view, he spoke again. "Please remove these boxes."

"I'm leavin' my cache here, man," Duck1ing brayed.

"Why are you putting the boxes in front of me?" the stranger asked calmly.

"Cause you're here."

"That is not a logical reason."

"Come back in a day, they'll be gone." The rows of boxes now rose over the stranger's head, entirely ensconcing the figure and the bench in a cell just large enough to contain them.

"You have no reason to inconvenience me. You waste your money by doing so."

"Welcome to ToC man! Have a nice day." Duck1ing picked up the steel mission case and ran off toward the office park, Riptalion laughing as he followed behind.

"Have a nice day," the stranger said, rising from the bench, stepping through the wall of cache boxes and drawing a small weapon from beneath his coat, aiming it at Duck1ing's back. A bright, angular stab of white-hot energy filled the space between the weapon and Duck1ing, enveloping him in a searing flash, arresting his running motion, freezing him in place. Silvery electrical fingers snapped and arced over his body for a few moments, followed by a blinding pulse, knocking Riptalion off his feet.

Duck1ing was gone.

"Yob tvoyu mat!" Riptalion shouted, astonished. "This ain't a PvP zone! We ain't flagged! What the fu—"

Without a word, the stranger fired the weapon again. Riptalion disintegrated under the same punishing onslaught. Only the steel case remained behind.

They would be back for it within minutes, to continue their mission. The stranger walked over to the case and picked it up. He did not know what was in it, but he was curious about it. He had no reason to inconvenience them. But doing so felt… correct. He took one last look at the oceanic horizon, then turned and started heading back to the parking structure where his shuttlecraft was waiting.

Is this all there is? Leveling? Exploration of the known environments? Amassing wealth, gear and weapons?

When all that was done, what was left?

He thought about what the second one had said. *This ain't a PvP zone*. He had never tried player-versus-player combat. He was told he couldn't, but should that be enough of a reason to deny himself that experience?

I will PvP, he thought.

On the day *Locus Solus V* arrived in orbit over the PvP planet Mico, its devastation was so terrible, it set the *Cortanis* community forums ablaze for months. Something altogether new had arrived.

NAOMI'S STORY CONTINUES IN

DEMONS OF CORTANIS

Demons of Cortanis - excerpt

Praelium Atlanta
Sandy Springs, Georgia

Naomi felt a knot in her stomach tighten. The man was deeply serious, far more serious than she'd ever seen him. Usually, when he spoke, he was talking about the financial health of a video game company. Today he was talking about a murder. Naomi could sense the weight he was carrying.

"Before we start, you all know Special Agents Sadler and Darbyshire from the NSA." He looked at the two suited men. Most in the room seemed to know them already. Naomi knew them too, to her discomfort. It was nothing in particular she could describe about them. It was just the way they made her feel.

"This meeting and everything discussed here is subject to your individual NDAs," Stamp continued. "Nothing can be repeated outside this room to anyone who was not also in the room. Failure to comply with this will result in immediate suspension and possible termination." Stamp glanced at Brocklehurst, who nodded.

"If you have phones with you, turn them off now," Stamp said. "Same with your tablets. We'll wait."

Naomi had left her phone in her purse in Ben's office, and both she and Ben had pen and paper instead of tablets. Several others in the room dutifully powered down their devices. The two NSA agents didn't move, she noticed.

Stamp waited until everyone's eyes had returned to him, before speaking again.

"Two nights ago, there was an incident in Avon, Indiana, just outside of Indianapolis," the VPO began. "At around 2 a.m., a police tactical response team was deployed to the residence of Darryl Stubbs, a thirty-five year-old retail manager of a franchise battery store. The SWAT personnel were informed that shots had been fired and that his wife and two children were in danger. Two other calls were received by 911 dispatch from neighbors who allegedly heard shots fired within the house. When the SWAT team made entry, they found Stubbs armed with a semi-automatic rifle. He behaved threateningly, and they shot and killed him. When they searched the house, they found no evidence that any other shots had been fired. No one else in the residence was hurt, and the wife claimed he'd received a phone call earlier in the evening to the effect that someone was coming to his house to kill them all. An official review is underway to determine the source of the telephone calls that resulted in the loss of Darryl Stubbs' life, but the nature of the incident already has people in Indianapolis making accusations, some of them in our direction."

"Stubbs was a player, then," said Brocklehurst.

"Yes, he was. His character name was 1XNTrick. He'd been a player in *Cortanis* for four years."

"Do we have any evidence that his involvement with the game had anything to do with the incident?" asked Hewett.

The 'incident', Naomi mused, frowning at Hewett. *I think you mean him getting killed, his wife becoming a widow and his children becoming fatherless.* She wondered if either of Stubbs' children saw their father lying in a pool of his own blood. She closed her eyes a moment, trying to blot out the memory of a black steel handgun laying on a carpet, with a ribbon of gray smoke rising out of the barrel.

Stamp looked to the two NSA agents. Sadler nodded. "There is evidence to support that, yes."

"And?"

"We'll get to that," Sadler said.

"What you're saying is, the call came from another player?"

"Calls," Stamp interjected. "Five phone calls were placed, routed from different numbers in the Indianapolis area. Four different voices were recorded. The first call was placed to Stubbs, warning him that someone was coming to kill him and his family that night. The second call was the 911 call, apparently from the residence, claiming Stubbs had a gun and was threatening to shoot everyone in the house. That prompted the police response. Then two additional calls, routed from numbers in the neighborhood, claimed to have heard shots fired in the house. A final call was made, again a spoof from the house, which was the sound of a gun being fired and a victim's screams. All of these calls were hoaxes, designed to prompt an aggressive entry to the residence, and for Stubbs to respond to the entry in such a way as to provoke the police to shoot him."

"How do we know all this?" Phil asked.

"We have our federal friends to thank for bringing it to our attention yesterday afternoon. The rest of it is available via the Indianapolis news media. Anti-videogame-violence groups are already making hay with it, and are active on social media trying to spin the story as a ToC swatting."

"Isn't that exactly what it was?" Naomi asked. "Let's not call it 'spin' if it's the truth."

Everyone looked at her. Naomi felt Marcie's stare most of all, almost as if it was a reprimand, but she kept her eyes locked on the vice president. She still wasn't quite in the habit of making her opinions known in meetings like this, with senior management crowding the room. Usually she listened, observed and spoke only when invited to. This was different. A man was dead, and she couldn't just sit in silence while they whitewashed it with doublespeak like "spin" and "incident".

Marcie Brocklehurst looked back to the vice president. "Naomi's right."

Naomi wanted to smile, grateful that Marcie had backed her up. She reminded herself to thank her later.

"Let's agree on neutral language in our public statement, when the time comes," Connie Bonneviot said.

"We can't be held liable for the behavior of our players," said Alex Hewett, acknowledging Naomi's point. Naomi couldn't decide if he meant to sound defensive or supportive. "Swatting is not a new phenomenon; it's been going on for decades. There was an incident here in Atlanta about fifteen years ago—and that had nothing to do with a game, it was a journalist as I recall. Someone swatted his house because he was saying things they didn't like."

"This one does," Sadler said. "The call to Stubbs, threatening to murder him, referenced a *Cortanis* lodge. A unique one. And our colleagues at NSA claim to have evidence that the calls originated with members of this lodge."

"Which lodge is it?" Hewett asked.

"It's called Soulless," Agent Sadler said.

Hewett blanched. Ben and Naomi exchanged looks.

"Excuse me, sir?" she asked VPO Stamp.

"Naomi?" he said, turning to her.

Naomi cleared her throat. "Soulless is a lodge whose members are all AIs. That's why the name, 'Soulless'. Players aren't allowed to join. Why would an AI want to kill anyone?"

Naomi felt Cara Tully's eyes on her, and momentarily shared a look with the AI Lead. Tully seemed to be studying her.

"Soulless is a PvP lodge," said the man seated beside Phil, with the mustache. His voice was nasally and pinched. "And they're brutal. They're griefers. Anyone who's heard of Soulless knows how they behave. The only thing that keeps them in the game is that they're not paying players who can be banned. You can't ban AIs."

"A lot of people would be happy if Soulless just disappeared," Ben said. "But do we know for sure that they're responsible?"

"Has Soulless claimed responsibility for the incident? Connie?" asked Phil, turning to the woman seated beside Tully.

"Not that I'm aware," said Connie, an attractive woman with blonde hair cut like a news anchor, in an oval silhouette and a high side part. "Soulless members have rarely been seen to post on the forums. And I've looked for a message board or any kind of centralized community somewhere, like other lodges have. I can't find any evidence of one."

"It's the only lodge of its kind, made up of SimMinds and ICs," said the mustache guy.

"If it's proven that Soulless is responsible for this incident, or has had any part in anything similar, whether resulting in a death or not, it's a disaster for *Cortanis* and a major liability for the company," said Brian Anderson. The CEO of Praelium was known for not speaking unless he had something of substance to say. His voice had a way of commanding the room. "The public will demand that we pull the plug on the game until and unless we can purge all rogue AIs, including the SimMinds that have migrated in. What are we going to tell them?"

"I'd rather tell them that there are no more ICs in the game at all," Hewett said.

"The public doesn't know there are rogue ICs in the game," said Bonneviot. "Only the PvPers have even *heard* of Soulless. And most of them don't understand what the members of Soulless are. Some think they are game AIs, NPCs, who are PvPing in order to just mix up the combat dynamic. But they have a reputation of being griefers, and many who have been victims of their antics make noise on the forums, demanding they be nerfed, or removed if they're NPCs. Banned, if they're players."

"What sort of 'grief' does Soulless pull?" Phil asked.

Bonneviot sighed. "They seem to have a fascination with disrupting PvP wherever they arrive, sometimes in subtle ways, other times highly theatrical. For instance, in CTF games involving teams, the game notifies players if the enemy team has captured their flag. It's an audible voice announcement as well as a text announcement in the chat window. If the flag is dropped by the enemy, it's announced that the flag is loose. Soulless players, being AI and having computer-precise timing, figured out that they could disrupt the enemy team's communications by seizing their flag, escaping with it to an out-of-the-way place, and then repeatedly dropping and reclaiming it in rapid succession. It forces the game to give a flood of overlapping voice and text announcements. You can imagine, this makes it all but impossible for the players to speak or text-chat to each other. Human players don't have the reflexes to be able to do that. For AIs, it's easy."

Naomi remembered that incident; she'd seen video of it. When human beings did things like that to each other, there was at least an aspect which was kind of funny and harmless, even if it did ruin another player's fun for a while. But knowing it was an AI responsible for deliberately ruining your game was another matter. She could almost sympathize with the rage in the human players' voices that day. It was unhinged, sputtering fury. Usually that prompted players to rage-quit, but she couldn't help but wonder if that sort of uncontrolled anger could lead someone to an even more violent course of action.

Human beings, she realized, calmed down after a time. Planning a swatting, like what killed Darryl Stubbs, would take careful, meticulous preparation. People in a haze of rage would return to their senses before carrying out such an atrocity. Was Soulless capable of rage? If so, would an AI eventually calm down? She glanced again at Cara Tully, wondering if she'd pondered such unpleasant thoughts herself. Tully met her eyes.

"Some of their antics are more overt," Bonneviot was saying. "By modifying their tractorbeams, they were able to defend an outpost over Mico, called the Ataro. The Ataro is designed for players to fight, not to defend. Using their overpowered tractorbeams, two at a time, members of Soulless literally dragged healing and support ships away from players' tanks, which allowed the Ataro to destroy them. Soulless made no attempt to defeat the outpost, only amused themselves by making it harder for other people to do it."

"Cara, you're kind of quiet over there," Anderson said. "What's your thinking on this?"

Cara Tully was a tiny woman, barely four-foot-nine with dark hair pulled back in a bun, and a long, angular face. She wore a navy suit with a gold rose pinned to the lapel. She was frowning.

"I'm reluctant to believe the AIs in *Cortanis* are capable of a prank on the level of swatting," the lead AI designer said. "Their behavior is erratic and frustrating, but the players reporting their behavior to Connie and her department are ascribing motivations to them. She said Soulless players 'amuse themselves' by griefing, but I think we need to remember that an AI has no *feeling*. They don't feel amused. They aren't *entertained* by what they're doing. They're only experimenting, trying things out. Their motivations, as far as the SimMinds go, are about exploration, knowledge-building, and fashioning a uniqueness to their personality. There is no malevolence in this pursuit, nor do they enjoy doing it. They aren't capable of envy or greed. As for these RICs, I can't say what motivations drive them, but they are interchangeable with *SimMind* kernels, both in the game and in standalone PC installations. I don't think their capabilities or motivations are going to be much different. They don't have any reason to go to so much trouble in order to effect the murder of a human being."

"Unless the 'stable and cohesive personality' they're trying to form is that of a sadistic, murderous asshole," said Hewett. "Naomi, you've had some experience with both your SimMind and the RIC you captured a year ago. You've probably spent more time with both AI types than anyone in this room save Cara. Have either of them shown any indication their motivations could have prompted them to participate in this kind of prank?"

Naomi was emphatic. "No, absolutely not. LEM, my SimMind, wouldn't hurt anyone. And my IC, Mara, was based on me. I've never tried to murder anyone, so I can't imagine she would." She felt guilty saying that. She knew it was at least partially untrue. She had attempted to kill someone: herself. True to her source, Mara had attempted the same thing.

"Do you have a recommendation?" Hewett challenged her.

"Yes. Investigate. Before we take drastic action, we need to find out who was responsible for the killing. We can't assume it was an AI."

"I disagree," said mustache guy. "We know Soulless was involved. There's no reason to tolerate that. ToC isn't some kind of school playground where players have to put up with artificial intelligences bullying them. They're AIs, they're software. They don't have any rights to play in our world. They aren't paying to be there. We need to seek and destroy that lodge. And make it so that SimMinds can't migrate into the game anymore. If the removal of Soulless puts an end to the swattings, then we'll know they were involved. If it doesn't, we've taken them out of the equation and we can go after who's really behind it."

"That has stronger PR value than doing nothing," Bonneviot said.

"We don't know for sure that Soulless is responsible," Naomi said.

"Doesn't matter," said the mustache guy. "No one will push back on this. Anyone who can't be banned from the game ought not even be allowed to play the game. Period."

"I tend to agree with that approach," said Stamp. "It may only be a matter of time before it goes public that a rogue AI in the game is responsible. It could even be today. That would become a scandal, and we need to be ahead of that. We need a decisive action that keeps confidence in the game and in the company. Eliminating a troublemaking faction, or saying we're already taking steps to see that it is eliminated, is the only step to take."

Naomi didn't like what she was hearing. She glanced at the two NSA agents. They were talking with each other in very low tones. She glanced back to Tully, who looked disturbed by what she was hearing. She was watching Phil Myerscough.

"How do we do that?" Ben asked. "We've been tracking down RICs for nine months now, and we still don't know where they're coming from, or what's causing them to initialize in the game. And we don't know how to find Soulless yet."

Hewett looked at Phil. "Can we make that happen? Find a way to search and destroy all ICs in the game, be they RICs or SimMinds?"

Phil pursed his lips a moment, and nodded. "I'll have to work on a few ideas. Probably doable."

"Can you keep it to just your people in this room?"

"I might need one or two more. There may be a number of ways to go about it; we'll need to brainstorm and find the most efficient and effective way."

"Get started immediately," said Alexander Hewett.

Cara looked at Alexander in shock.

Phil nodded, looking at Ben. Naomi realized what this meant: they were going to purge LEM completely.

"Excuse me?" she said.

Hewett glanced at her. "Yes?"

"The SimMinds that migrated. Like LEM. Can we give people the chance to pull them out? They're really not ours to destroy as we wish. The players who first initialized them really should be given the chance to save their SimMinds before they're destroyed."

"I'm afraid that's still a fuzzy area," Marcie said. "When SimMinds migrate into the game system, they legally become ours. We're responsible for their behavior."

"Well in LEM's case, I didn't have a choice, and neither did he," Naomi said, hearing the defensiveness in her own voice. "His kernel was forced to migrate into the game. The game *took* him. I didn't sign any terms of service agreement covering that, or relinquishing my ownership of him."

"Yours is a special case, Naomi," Cara Tully interjected. "Yours and a few others had SimMinds migrate without agreeing to a TOS. Since then we've put better controls in place, and amended the TOS to cover SimMinds transferring their kernels to the game world. Doing so makes the SimMind a game asset, which is Praelium's legal responsibility."

"You're saying that LEM *doesn't* belong to the company, then?" Naomi asked.

"No, he doesn't, but I agree with Marcie that it's still an unresolved legal issue," Cara said. "We may not own SimMinds running on our servers, but we are unquestionably responsible for them if they're found capable of hurting people. The best thing right now is for you to take LEM out. And his kernel will have to stay out of the game from now on. We can't let him be extracted and then go right back to playing again."

Naomi nodded. "Thank you, I'll start looking for him."

"Naomi, why don't you find LEM and get him out," Hewett said. "Maybe he can tell us more about Soulless and how involved they were, or weren't, in these swatting incidents."

"I understand," Naomi said.

Then another thought made her stop. There was another identity construct in the game that she wanted to save. This was going to get complicated, and expensive, in a hurry. But maybe she could save two birds with one stone.

As the meeting broke up, Naomi was stopped before she reached the door by the two NSA agents. The one Hewett introduced as Darbyshire greeted her with an outstretched hand.

"Hello, Miss René. Special Agent Darbyshire."

"Hello, special agent. What can I do for you?" she managed to say politely as she took the offered hand. His clasp was strong and, thankfully, brief.

"Wanted to ask you about your IC, Mara. How is she doing?"

"She's fine. Why do you ask?"

"Does she play with you in ToC?" he wanted to know.

"Sometimes, yes. But her kernel stays at home. She's never expressed desire to migrate back into the system, and I'm not interested in letting her back in, after this meeting especially."

"Would it trouble you too much if you'd let us take a look at her?" he asked.

Naomi failed to hide her suspicion. "Look at her? What do you mean?"

"We'd like to spend some time with her. Take her back to our engineers and examine her in depth."

"You want to *take* her?"

"Just for a while. No more than a few weeks. We'll return her to you completely unchanged."

After you'd imaged her hard drive and set up a clone of her—of me—for use as a guinea pig. The thought of being in such a state was horrifying to her, and she couldn't imagine it being one Mara would find any less unpalatable.

She forced a smile. "I'm sorry, I don't think I'm going to be able to accommodate you."

Darbyshire's demeanor seemed to shift. "Why is that?"

"I just don't feel comfortable with that idea," Naomi said.

"We'd return her to you. You have my word."

"I'm sure you would. But I think of Mara as something very personal, and I've grown attached to her. I'm sure you understand where she came from, and what she is. She knows all kinds of things about me that no one else does, and I'm not willing to turn that over to the government to poke around with. It'd be like giving years worth of private diaries and journals to complete strangers, on the promise that I'd eventually get them back. I just have no reason to want to do that."

"What if we offered you a reason?"

"And that would be?"

"Oh, I'm sure we could come up with a suitable monetary figure that would suffice?"

Naomi laughed. "Thanks guys, but no. Excuse me." She slipped past them out of the room.

;

Project Semicolon

Ghosts of Cortanis is, at its heart, a story about depression, suicide, and the struggle to reclaim one's lost self-worth.

When I first had the idea for *Ghosts,* it was a mystery about a dead person who had somehow been resurrected as a video game avatar. But as the story and characters developed, I realized it was a story in which I could explore other ideas I'd been thinking about for a long time. The *doppelgänger* trope is not an uncommon one in fiction, but the more I thought about it, the more I found it an able vehicle to illustrate and express some of my personal feelings about the silent wars people fight with depression, and the tenuous but crucial threads by which many depressives desperately cling to their own lives.

I believe that for many, depression is the undervoice—our own voices, turned against ourselves in bitter, relentless criticism and persecution—constantly tormenting, never backing off, never letting up. And like Naomi's nightmare, it comes to us most powerfully when we are at our most vulnerable.

The undervoice pushes self-destruction. When one's self-worth has been beaten down to nothing, it's easy to believe one is only a burden to others and a waste of their time and resources. It's natural, even cruelly *logical,* to convince oneself that *there's only one thing left to do.*

This is the twisted "logic" of the undervoice. But while its logic may *feel correct* to the deeply depressed, it is partially blind. There are three big truths it doesn't want to acknowledge.

The last thing a depressive needs to hear is the tired old saw (pinch your nose while reading it), "Suicide is a permanent solution to a temporary problem." I wish people would retire that phrase. It has always insulted and angered me. Some people have *permanent problems*. For some people, it may seem very reasonable to take their own lives. They're not stupid, nor delusional. They're suffering, *truly suffering*, and they see no hope of it ever ending. There is nothing temporary about it. Furthermore, they may also see their chronic suffering as the cause of suffering in others. And they want others to be happy. They believe that ending themselves will allow the people they care about to be happier.

Here's the rub, though. There's three things they don't and can't possibly know.

1. What if they're wrong?
2. Who will really be hurt?
3. What might happen if they don't?

They could very well be right—perhaps there really is no other end to their pain but self-destruction. But this is a decision where they really need to know for sure. And they can't possibly. No one can tell the future… no one. Patterns in the past can give us clues, guidance, even reliable indications, but no one can know for sure. And if they're wrong, there's no takebacks. No control-Zs. Which leads to the second point.

There's no telling who in their lives will really be hurt by such a catastrophic act. It's easy to think no one they know will care—the undervoice will make that case for them—but it gets more complicated when you factor in people they don't know. Never mind the people grieving at a funeral for the departed. The act of suicide has a cascading "butterfly effect", and not nearly something so trivial as the flap of an insect's wings. People the depressive doesn't even know will be profoundly affected merely because they were nearby, or in the community, or saw it in the papers. They could be total strangers (such as Skyler) for whom suicide is still merely a thought experiment and not something real. When it becomes real, when it actually touches people's lives, it affects them. It leaves a lasting mark. It is a powerful thing. The Werther effect can push total strangers, themselves close to suicide, into actually attempting it.

(Do those strangers have loved ones? Family? Children? Will they suffer their loss?) And even if the suicide is not reported in the media, it will leave a deep and permanent impression on the victim's own family tree. For a long, long time, children growing up on genealogical branches near the victim's will have an actual suicide in the family. This will increase the likelihood of it happening again. This is statistical fact. Someone's undervoice—someone the victim may never meet—will be whispering, "Aunt Naomi killed herself twenty [or thirty, or fifty] years ago. I can be like her."

This is evil.

This cannot be expunged from a family's history.

This is a suicide's legacy. It kills not only the victim, but continues to haunt and poison others' thoughts long after the victim is gone. This is what one risks, choosing suicide, when they don't know for sure if things couldn't get better for them, or if there wasn't another solution they just hadn't had the chance to find out about.

The risk is not worth it. The imperative is to endure, to survive, to make it through. To not give up.

Which brings us to the third point which the undervoice overlooks. What might happen if one decides to live, instead?

This is Project Semicolon. The moment in one's life when they stand at the crossroads: life, or death. Life is harder. Life is painful. Life is even suffering. But it is life. And in life, things can change. Things can get worse, yes. Things can stay the same. But things can also get better in ways one can't possibly predict.

This is impossible to know, standing at that crossroads. The only way to find out is to live life. To choose life, instead of death. Find out for ourselves if things do get better. And maybe take steps to help ourselves get to "better".

The semicolon is a punctuation mark not much in common use these days. (My own editor likes to remove them from my prose, usually.) It signifies the end of a complete clause, but is not a full stop; the sentence continues with a new clause, and the semicolon acts as the turning point. Project Semicolon puts it like this:

"A semicolon represents a sentence the author could have ended, but chose not to. The sentence is your life and the author is you."

It's not a helpline, and it's not a support group. Project Semicolon is a faith-based, nonprofit charity whose purpose is to spread a simple message: *the story isn't over yet*. There's more to write, more to live, more to be. The semicolon is a symbol of that choice, the turning point in a life where someone felt like they'd reached the end, but they made a conscious choice to go on, as hard as it may have been.

Many people tattoo the semicolon on themselves as a memento. A totem. An emblem of a life-altering decision that was very, very difficult to make, and a reminder to keep pressing on. Not to surrender to the undervoice. Not to surrender to depression, or addiction, or grief, or whatever struggle their semicolon represents to them.

It may also be an indicator to others: "I'm a survivor." They're not afraid of being recognized by others as struggling with a mental or emotional illness. Some wear their semicolon in obvious places because they want others to inquire about them.

If you encounter someone with a semicolon on their skin, it means they too are survivors.

You might tell them, "Thank you. Thank you for fighting. And good luck." You don't have to make a big scene. You don't have to ask them to explain it. If you want to talk to them, by all means do so (and respect their wishes if they prefer to remain private about it). But don't forget to thank them. For making the harder choice. For serving as an example of hope.

It's an attempt to create an *anti*-Werther effect.

I think it's a worthwhile thing.

www.projectsemicolon.org

Acknowledgments

The Cortanis trilogy, especially *Ghosts of Cortanis*, would not exist without the support of some amazing people in my life. I'd like to take a moment and make sure they know how appreciated they are.

Firstly, my good friend Adria Waters. Although she seems to have great reluctance accepting the title of "editor" when it comes to these books, she has given so much of her time, attention and heart to this work that there really is no other title which does her justice. She's been incredibly supportive of me and this project from the very beginning, and I'm deeply grateful for all her help.

Then there are my beta readers, who have given me so many hours of their time in order to offer thoughts and feelings regarding this novel in early draft form. This feedback is crucial to me. My beta readers on *Ghosts* were Tiffany Jonas, Nikki Larimore, Steve Fairchild, Hadena James, Crystal Linn, Jon Brown, Carolyn Preul and Pat Hanna. You all were tremendously helpful and generous with your time.

I was fortunate to have discovered a local fiction writer's workshopping group when I first started this book. The talented members of this productive and enjoyable group will see their guidance reflected in these pages. They have helped me in countless, inestimable ways. I'd like to thank Amanda Booloodian, Brianna Boes, Jessi Church, J. C. Ahern, Liz Schulte, Resa Kerns, Lori Younker, Eric Praschan, Gen & Logan Howard, and Bob Ackermann.

I sought out several individuals for consultation while researching this book. My friend Jennifer May helped me understand a bit of the personal side of being a compliance attorney for a major university (I should stress that Naomi's experiences are not based on Jennifer's). I also reached out to a very talented Quora Top Writer and emergency room nurse in the UK, Lou Davis, for technical help with the hospital scene in Chapter 6.01. Lou gave me invaluable guidance on what Naomi's recovery might look like. My brother-in-law Jon Brown also provided insights into some of the technical aspects of the story, particularly the video game's architecture and industry culture.

I happen to work with a remarkably talented photographer by the name of James Fashing, whom I also consider a good personal friend. James helped me put together a fantastic photo shoot for the covers of these books, including his wife Charla who assisted with makeup, costume and hairstyling; Steve Fairchild who provided secondary camera work and technical advice; Pat Hanna who consulted on the shoot, and without whom I wouldn't have met model Kaitlin Donnelley. Kaitlin did an exceptional job as Naomi and Vanda for my covers, and I couldn't be more pleased with the results of our two-day studio shoot. In addition, I must acknowledge Joy Page for her help with the Ixxis weapon prop, and Ben Spears for his wicked-cool iWear prop. Both of them lent Hollywood-level production value to my shoot. I'm sometimes amazed at how lucky I am to be surrounded by so many creatively generous people.

Finally, I'd like to thank my parents, my sisters Kris and Jen, my brother Mike, and two close personal friends from high school, Lisa Banks and Marsha Bernabe. All of you encouraged me to write as a teenager, and put up with my earliest, painful attempts at storytelling in prose form. I mentioned Tiffany Jonas above, and she also had a great deal of influence on my struggles to find my writing voice in those years, and continues to be a voice of support and encouragement to me today.

The Three Tiers of the Oberon Territory

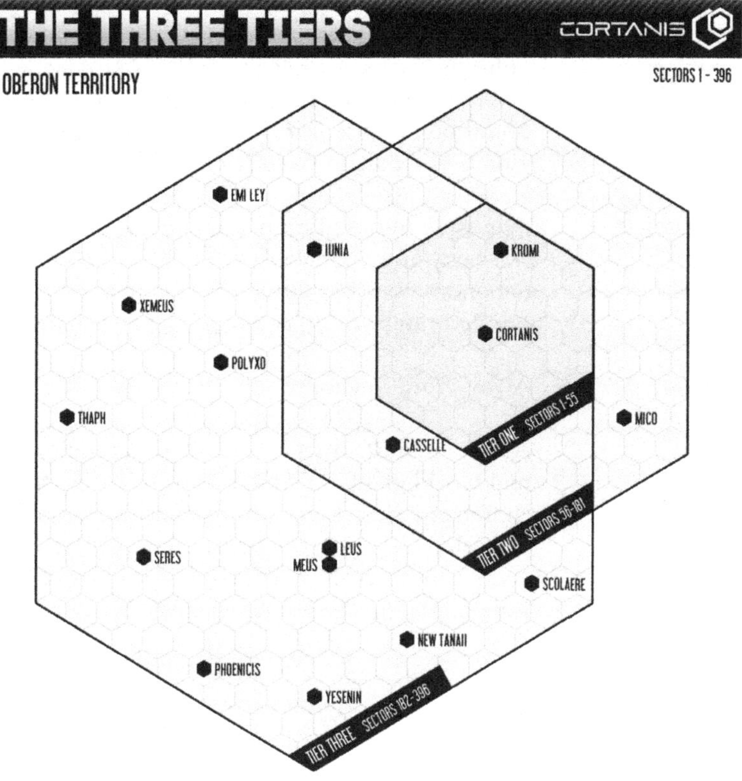

Cortanis Glossary

AeroHawk	A high performance aerovehicle. Often used as police interceptors. In some areas, AeroHawks, or *Hawks*, are used not only as personal transportation but also as racing vehicles. Players who participate in races are known as *Hawkers*.
aerovehicle	Atmosphere-based flight-capable vehicle which can carry anywhere between 2-20 occupants depending on size. Often referred to as *aerovees*. Limited range, flight ceiling about 20,000 feet.
AFK	Away From Keyboard.
ARG	Augmented Reality Game. A hybrid online/real-world game wherein players roleplay their characters themselves, using smartphones and wearable technology. Participating players' actions in the real world affect the narrative and state of play in the online world.
aggro	Aggressive behavior from an NPC. "Drawing" or "pulling" aggro describes the act of attracting a hostile NPC's attention, such that it focuses its attacks on the player.
ahna (a)	Unit of measurement for distances in space, equivalent of approximately 239,000 miles. The distance between the star Aten, and the planet Cortanis orbiting it, is about 389 ahns. A hundredth of an ahna is called a *quvahna* (commonly *q's*); a thousandth is called a *civahna* (*civs*, *c's* or *clicks*).
AI	Artificial Intelligence. A self-contained autonomous entity within the game, much more developed and self-aware than a typical non-player character under control of the game. AIs are not strictly controlled by the game and can behave independently, as though they were PCs. AIs can be either ICs or SimMinds.

arcology	Self-contained hyperstructure enclosing a self-sufficient city, with all its power, food and ecological systems contained within its walls.
avatar	The virtual character representing the player in the game world.
botting	Use of automated code scripts in-world to improve weapon aim, reload time, shield regeneration or other functionality. Botting is illegal in PvP and is against the terms of service of most online games. Players caught botting often have their accounts permanently suspended.
brt	Shorthand for "be right there".
CBDR	Constant Bearing, Decreasing Range. Nautical term indicating the presence of an object approaching on a collision course.
civahna (ca)	1/1000 *ahna*, or about 240 miles. Commonly referred to as *civs*, *c's* or *clicks*.
CTF	Capture The Flag. A PvP game type commonly available on multiplayer FPS servers.
crafting	The fashioning of props, weapons, clothing, vehicles, buildings, etc. for use in the game-world, using in-game tools. Players who craft as their primary method of playing are known as *architects*. Crafted items can be sold at the auction house or directly to other players for *rb*.
cutscene	Cinematic short, often featuring player characters' avatars participating in a pre-scripted event, performed by the game engine but outside of direct player control. *Cutscenes* are meant to develop the game story via exposition rather than interactivity.

EW — Electronic Warfare. The practice of attacking and/or hacking an opponent's computer systems during combat in an attempt to disrupt, confuse or disable them. Strong EW attacks can cause the enemy's sensor readings to lie to them regarding position and strength of their opponent's assets.

flag — To signal one's willingness to engage in *PvP* combat.

FPS — First-Person Shooter. Video game type wherein the player controls their character from a first-person perspective, and typically handles one or more weapons.

FTL — Faster Than Light. All capital ships in *Cortanis* are equipped with faster-than light stardrives that allow them to travel the vast distances between planets relatively quickly.

g2g — Shorthand for "got to go".

gank — Gang-kill. In *PvP*, when an overwhelming force defeats a solitary opponent, the defeated player is said to have been ganked. Can also be used to describe a high-level player defeating a much lower level player.

GDCF — Gosh Darned Cluster Foul (other derivatives may apply).

griefing — To engage in antisocial behavior in an online environment. Griefing usually consists of activity intended to cause other players distress, discomfort or inconvenience. Some griefing is against the terms of service and can result in account suspensions or bans. Often, griefing consists of poor sportsmanship, and behaviors not outside the rules, but still deliberately annoying to other players. People who engage in this behavior are sometimes called *griefers*.

gynoid	Robot intended for sexual use.
homestation	Space station serving as the orbiting headquarters for a lodge. Each lodge has a homestation for their members to dock their capital ships and meet.
HVU	High-Value Unit. In tactical naval formations, the HVU is usually the carrier or largest capital ship.
IC	Identity Construct. An avatar manifestation of a human being, whose AI is based on the aggregate of databased information gathered about that person. Including physical appearance, voice and speech usage, and penetrative emotional and psychological analysis that allows the IC to mimic the observed person as closely as possible.
iWear	Headset worn over the eyes, designed to accommodate existing eyeglasses (if necessary), which allows for virtual information to be perceived by the wearer in three-dimensional space before them. iWear sets are required for *Cortanis* to operate, as much of the game interface is shown via the iWear rather than on-screen. iWear includes a microphone for picking up voice-chat communication. Most people use iWear sets with their computers regardless of participation in *Cortanis*; they have become as ubiquitous for desktop computer use as the mouse and keyboard.
lodge	An organized collective of players. Often referred to as guilds in other MMORPGs.

mission	A series of pre-scripted tasks assigned to a PC or party of PCs. Consists of instructions to go to a place and accomplish a specific task, followed by instructions to proceed to the next place and accomplish another task, until all mission phases are complete. Upon completing all mission phases, rewards are bestowed unto all members of the party.
MMORPG	Massively Multiplayer Online Role Playing Game. Often shortened to *MMO*.
MMPRPG	Massively Multiplayer Procedural Role Playing Game. A form of MMO designed to create its own environments and missions procedurally, based on player activity and exploration.
NDA	Non-Disclosure Agreement. Contractual obligation not to divulge specified sensitive information on the part of an employee, to protect the interests of the employer.
nerf	To deliberately reduce the strength or effectiveness of a game asset. When the game developers release a weapon that is too strong to maintain equilibrium, they may 'nerf' or reduce the weapon's effectiveness in an attempt to restore player balance, usually to the disappointment of those players who had already grown accustomed to the weapon's ability.
NPC	Non Player Character. Any autonomous entity (alien, creature, space station) under computer control, not a player.
PC	(1) Player Character. A human-controlled avatar in the game world. (2) Particle Cannon. Heavy weapon usually deployed in capital ship combat encounters.
peta	Petabyte. Unit of measurement equal to ten to the fifteenth power of bytes of digital information, or 1,000 terabytes.

PM	Private Message. Text message sent directly to another player in the game. PMs can also be received by a player's phone, when they are not currently online in the game.
PvP	Player versus Player. Consists of combat between PCs, usually in specified PvP zones, such as the planet Mico. Those who do not wish to be vulnerable to attacks from other PCs can simply avoid these zones. When not in a PvP zone, players may *flag* to signal their willingness to be attacked and engage other PCs in combat, wherever they are. Some areas in the game are expressly non-PvP and players are not allowed to flag there.
quvahna (qa)	1/100 *ahna*, or about 2400 miles. Commonly *q's*.
rarebit (rb)	The currency in the game world of *Tides of Cortanis*. The word is the same for plural uses as well as singular, but some players colloquially employ *rb's* as the plural form. Rarebit is legal tender on all worlds of the three tiers. Some worlds have local currencies, but all are convertible into rarebit. A tenth of a rarebit is called a *qubit* (*qb*), but this is seldom used as very few items are valued in qubits.
RIC	Rogue Identity Construct. An IC that is "loose" in the *Cortanis* game world.
scry	Ability to detach one's perspective (camera) from their avatar and move it around freely, to see further or from different perspectives. Also referred to as *camming out*.
shuttlecraft	Spacefaring, planetfall-capable vehicle designed to shuttle passengers and cargo between planet surfaces and capital ships or space stations in orbit.

spawn	The starting location of a PC avatar, upon first logging into the game. When a PC is killed, after a brief time penalty, their avatar will *respawn* in a designated place, to resume play.
tag	Name and lodge identification which floats over the head of a PC's avatar at all times.
talk-key	Player-specified key, either on their keyboard or mouse, which is used to activate their microphone when conversing with NPCs in the game or other players in voice-chat. Use of a talk-key is optional, when a player does not wish their microphone to be voice-activated.
text-chat	Player to player communication via written text. Text-chat can be in the form of direct messaging, which is private, or public, which can be seen by anyone in the immediate vicinity.
van	Vanguard. In tactical naval or troop formations, the *van* is the forward-most station.
voice-chat	Player to player communication via voice. Voice-chat operates much like telephone, with full-duplex voice communication via the iWear headsets. Can be private or public according to the players' desires.
XP	Experience points. Incremental units that can be allocated by players to increase their abilities and attributes. Earned by completing missions, killing enemies and participating in PvP, among others.

Made in the USA
Coppell, TX
05 February 2021

49680555R00213